PROPHECY

THE PROPHECY

the watchers chronicles

DAWN MILLER

ZONDERVAN®

ZONDERVAN.com/
AUTHORTRACKER
follow your favorite authors

ZONDERVAN

The Prophecy
Copyright © 2010 by Dawn Miller

This title is also available as a Zondervan ebook.
Visit www.zondervan.com/ebooks.

Requests for information should be addressed to:

Zondervan, *Grand Rapids, Michigan* 49530

ISBN 978-0-310-71433-0

Editor: Jacque Alberta
Cover design: Rule 29
Cover photography: iStockphoto; © biffspandex 2008; © Todd McQueen DPI
Interior design: Carlos Eluterio Estrada

Printed in the United States of America

10 11 12 13 14 15 16 /DCI/ 21 20 19 18 17 16 15 14 13 12 11 10 9 8 7 6 5 4 3 2 1

For my son, Mitch:

"βλεπομεν γαρ αρτι δι εσοπτρου εν αινιγματι"

Reality is merely an illusion ...

– Albert Einstein

Prologue

I still don't know how it happened, but I do remember when it all started.

Sometimes I wish I didn't remember — seventeen years old, and my hands shake like some old man's as I write this — but I can feel them nearby, smell their stench spreading across the city, and I know it's time. If we don't survive today, someone out there needs to know the truth about what happened to us. I owe Sam that much. It's his story as much as ours — maybe even more so.

He knew about them before we did.

Was that his fate? His destiny? I don't know. Maybe those words are too easy — used too much to explain away the unexplainable. What I do know is that my brother would be twenty today if he'd lived ... and those are the hardest words I've ever had to write.

The real kick in the gut is that if you asked anyone who knew us, they would've bet that I would be the one to die first.

I know I would've laid money on that bet.

You name it, I've done it — and went back and did it again: drugs, booze, playing another gig, maybe some more drugs to ignore the stranger staring at me in the mirror.

I called it coasting. Like I knew I wanted something different but I wasn't sure how to get there or if it would even be worth the effort.

Sam called it dodging life.

Guess I thought I could dodge hell too …

Sometimes I watch these people walking past my window, safe in the little cocoons they call life, and I wonder: What would they do if they could see what we see? What would they say?

My theory is, two words. Same two we've all whispered once in our lives. If we're honest, a lot more than once:

I wish.

I wish I would've known. I wish I would've done things differently …

A good friend of mine says that history repeats itself until we learn from it. Well, here is what I've learned so far: Things aren't always what they seem. And truth is stranger than fiction.

So what's the truth and what's a lie?

Jonah Becker pushed away from his journal and stood as a cold, tingling sensation hit the back of his neck, causing his senses to fuse together into that rare synesthesia, or sixth sense, that kept him from anything that remotely resembled a normal life. He stepped around the desk, then ran a shaky hand through his hair as he peered out the window.

From the second floor of the old warehouse, the St. Louis Arch shimmered as a flash of lightning lit the gray morning sky. Jonah's reflection appeared in the window: messy dark hair and a haggard expression that made him look a lot older than he was.

His eyes narrowed as he scanned the street below, and then they paused on a stray dog sniffing around a trash can. The dog froze and raised its nose in the air.

Jonah grimaced. The odor was getting stronger; like burnt electrical wiring and something he couldn't quite put his finger on. Outside the window, the air began to ripple almost imperceptibly, as if a tiny pebble had been thrown into water. The dog backed up, tucking its tail between its skinny legs just as a burst of wind hit, pressing its ears back flat against its head. It yelped, spun around, and ran off down the street.

"Smart dog," Jonah murmured. He glanced at the symbols etched around all of the windows and doors, then over his shoulder to the living room, where two figures lay sprawled out from exhaustion — one on the couch, the other on the floor. A glimpse of tousled red hair peeking out from under a blanket caused his heart to squeeze painfully in his chest. He didn't want to care about her so much. Caring was dangerous — but then, so was living. At least they were safe for the moment.

Well ... *part* of their group was safe.

When will this finally be done? he wondered wearily. *When none of us are left?*

Jonah reached for the Red Bull on his desk and, realizing it was empty, tossed it into a wastebasket already overflowing with cans. The can ricocheted, hitting the guitar gathering dust in the corner, and Jonah's eyes rose to the wall plastered with posters — Dylan, Pink Floyd, Alice Cooper, Lynyrd Skynyrd ... His small corner of the universe when he was younger. In the center of the wall was a framed poster bearing the X-ray skeletal image of Ozzy Osbourne from his Down to Earth tour. Across the glowing ribcage was an Ozzy quote from *Rolling Stone* that Sam had written in black marker: Don't bite off more than you can chew. It's a dangerous world!

Jonah lit a cigarette, stared hard at the words, then crushed out his smoke and began to pace the room.

Three months was all it had taken to change their lives forever. *Three months.* If anyone would have told him back then that he would be where he was — *who* he was — he would've laughed.

Or maybe asked them to share whatever pharmaceuticals they were taking.

A low rumble, followed by a shift in the atmosphere around him, forced his eyes back to the window. Two fat crows were perched in the tree across the street from him, cawing their heads off. Their caws sounded strange, almost mechanical, like they hadn't quite gotten the sound down right.

"Freaks," Jonah hissed between gritted teeth. He watched a ripple in the air bulge and spread out as the outline of two nearly transparent figures moved stealthily beneath the current until they had positioned themselves across the street from the warehouse. He felt them searching for him as they scanned the windows of the old building ... felt their *hate.*

Stepping back from the window, he hurried to his desk and began to write.

The truth: Ignorance isn't bliss. It's just another word for jail ... with amenities. Their way of keeping the herd calm – their way of keeping us quiet until they destroy everything about us that makes us human.

Jonah paused, raising his eyes to the spot where his brother's old journal lay on top of the others. He swallowed past the painful lump in his throat and shifted his gaze to a picture on the wall. It was the five of them as kids, goofy grins, arms slung around each other's shoulders as they held up the fish they had caught.

Sam, Jenna, J, and Carly ...

Their names ran over and over through his mind, like a continuous loop of music. He had only been ten – two years younger than the rest of them – when the picture was taken, but even then they had all begun to realize how different they were. How they could feel things other people couldn't, see things other people couldn't ...

It wasn't long after that day that all hell had broken loose, scattering them across the country, blinding them from who they were meant to be.

Heirs to a war we didn't understand ...

His shoulders hunched forward under the burden he was still learning to carry. He understood now. Maybe not everything, but he had been through enough – seen enough – to know that his brother had been right about a lot of things.

"I miss you, Sam – we all do," Jonah whispered hoarsely. Another crack of lightning lit up the windows of the warehouse, and his eyes searched the darkening sky as the clouds continued to churn and swell, pregnant with what was to come.

How am I supposed to fight this? he questioned for what felt like the millionth time. *How am I supposed to fight them?*

"Show me what to do," he said to the sky, a little kid again, afraid to hope ... and too afraid not to. "Show me."

The tingling sensation swept over him again, stronger this time, and he grabbed the edges of the desk, bracing himself.

"Don't wait for them to wake up," a voice spoke into his mind, trying to duplicate his voice – his thoughts. *"You can do this without dragging them into it!"*

Then another voice, this one more frantic, like a methed-out version of himself: *"Hurry – before it's too late! Hurry! Leave now!"*

Jonah grabbed his iPod and shoved the earpieces into his ears, turning the volume up as loud as it would go. He would be facing them soon enough. He reached for his brother's journal and opened it to the date that had started it all.

Sam, Jenna, J, and Carly ...

There were really two beginnings for them, but it was the second one that broke his heart and changed all of their lives forever. The second one also gave him hope that things could change – and made him get up every day since then to keep fighting.

Jonah placed Sam's journal back on the stack, and once again began writing in his own.

The lie: There is no one else out there ...

We have never been alone. They've been here from the beginning and have moved in and out of our world pretty much unseen since then ... until we came along.

Which is how all the trouble began, how we ended up in the middle of this war.

Thieves work best in the dark, as J likes to say, and the five of us just happened to be picked to flip the lights on while they were looting the world.

1

February 12 | St. Louis, Missouri

Wanna see …?" Sam Becker jerked back at the sound of the voice, barely blocking the boot that whipped by his face. He caught a movement from the corner of his eye – someone in an old army jacket passing through the lamplight outside the window of the dojo – just as the next blow knocked all two hundred pounds of him off his feet. He landed on the mat with a startled grunt.

No *way* did the kid just sweep him like that.

He rose on one arm and shook his head, trying to clear his thoughts. Not so easy to do when you haven't slept in days, he thought as he scrubbed his face with his hand. He felt so old lately. Nursing home old. More like ninety instead of nineteen, and the nightmares were getting worse.

But it wasn't just nightmares anymore, was it?

"Wanna see how far it goes?" The voice whispered again, and Sam glanced sharply to the face that hovered over him.

"What did you just say?"

"I can't believe I just did that?" An amazed grin flashed across his student's face.

Sam grimaced; it made sense in a messed-up kind of way, because he could've sworn it was *Jonah's* voice he'd heard – not Matty's.

He glanced toward the window to the street outside. A few cars passed, their lights bouncing over the cobblestones that still paved most of the roads along the river. Then the dark swallowed up the street again, leaving only small pools of light from the ancient lampposts that flanked the old warehouse.

No guy in an army jacket anywhere.

13

Sam frowned. Maybe he'd just imagined seeing someone, like he'd imagined the voice. Jonah had been on his mind a lot lately. All of them had, and he hadn't thought of the five of them together in over seven years.

Not since ... that night.

An unexpected shiver crawled up his spine.

We were just kids, he argued with himself. *Just a bunch of kids playing a stupid game ...*

So why couldn't he remember anything other than that? Why was it that every time he woke up lately, drenched in sweat and struggling to remember, he found himself staring slack-jawed into a black wall of nothingness? What was it that made him so terrified of what was on the other side of that wall?

"Sam?" Matty's large brown eyes stared down at him, tinged with worry. "Did I do good?"

"You did good," he said, forcing a grin. It wasn't the kid's fault that he was so messed up lately. He accepted the scrawny hand and pulled himself to his feet.

"I can still stay for a while, right?"

"Have I ever made you leave?"

"No." Matty's smile broadened like it was the craziest thing he'd ever heard. He dropped to the floor and began to pull off his sparring boots.

Sam felt a tug of pity as he watched him. How the kid had managed a roundhouse and a sweep on him was a mystery. Matty was small for his age, both physically and mentally – or *challenged*, as his parents had explained when they talked Sam into the private lessons six months ago.

Challenged enough that Sam had almost told them no, until he saw the faded bruises on Matty's face – and then he knew he couldn't turn him away. Troubled kids, as Jonah liked to say, were his kryptonite.

How did you do it, Matty?

Matty stood and handed him the boots, blinking up at him in wide-eyed innocence. "Can we get pizza like last time?"

"First things first – you stink," Sam said, brushing the thoughts off as he grabbed Matty's shoulder and gave him a playful shove toward the back of the room. "You hit the shower and I'll order the pizza, deal?"

"Deal," Matty called out, his voice cracking a little as he hurried off to the shower in his crazy sideways lope.

Sam shook his head and glanced down at the boots in his hand. His smile evaporated as he spotted a glint of steel sticking out from one of the soles. He carefully pried it loose and, fingers trembling a little, turned it over in his hand. A *razor*? What the heck was a razor doing in the kid's boot? He glanced up as the shower came on, heard Matty's off-key voice rising over the sound of the water in song, and then looked back down at the small blade in his hand.

Matty couldn't have known it was there...

His mind quickly rewound over the sparring session, and he saw the boot whipping by him again – but this time he saw the razor too, saw it slicing in an arc toward his *neck*, and a cold chill washed over his body. If he hadn't heard that voice – if he hadn't jerked back just in time ... He swallowed hard.

No. He shook his head. *It was crazy – had to be some kind of mistake...*

He took a step toward the shower and then stopped, letting the boots fall to the floor as he turned and scanned the room, his skin tingling. Someone was there ... he could feel them watching him. His eyes moved slowly over the rows of chest protectors and gear along the wall, past the weights and mirrors to the entrance, where a dim light shined over the trophy cases standing on both sides of the door, and found ... nothing.

He caught a glimpse of his reflection in one of the mirrors and was jarred by the drastic change in his appearance: dark circles under his eyes; wavy brown hair that was so long it almost touched his shoulders; at least a week's growth of stubble on his face. His instructor's uniform hung so loose on his body that he had to wonder how long it had been since he'd had a real meal. He looked like he had lost at least fifteen pounds, maybe twenty.

How had he missed *that*? It was as if he were losing chunks of time, and he had no idea why or how to get the time back.

Sam turned away from the mirror, and directed his focus on the old warehouse that he and Jonah had inherited after their parents were killed.

He had started renovations the day he was released from foster care – the same day Jonah decided to run away and join a band – and was left to purge his demons alone by tearing down walls and painting the place clean. Then on his nineteenth birthday four things had happened: he opened the doors for business, he enrolled in art classes at SLU, and he met his girlfriend, Lila. Number four was that he actually dared to believe things could get better.

Until the nightmares started.

Sam crossed the room to his office and was stopped short by the mess that greeted him as he opened the door. It looked as if a small bomb had gone off on his desk: drawers pulled out, papers and old pictures scattered over every inch of available space. His journal topped the pile and was wide open for the whole world to read.

He took a step closer, feeling his stomach muscles draw up as he peered down at his latest entry. Five words – words he had no memory of writing – had been scrawled across the page, all in capital letters with thick black marker:

THIS IS NOT A DREAM

He slammed the book shut, almost afraid to look around the rest of the office. He felt his body go cold as he spotted the canvas propped against the wall in the far corner of the room.

It wasn't just the nightmares that worried him.

He was sleepwalking too. He'd googled it after finding the first painting – which he didn't remember painting – memorizing the parts that stood out like a line taken from his life: *"Sleepwalkers usually remember little to nothing, though some may have a vague memory of trying to escape a dangerous situation ..."*

Sam walked over to the corner and turned the painting to face the wall. He didn't need to look to know what was on there. Didn't *want* to look. It was the sixth painting of his that he had found in the last month – the third in less than a week. Whatever was happening to him was picking up its pace.

But why? Life seemed to make so much more sense before his parents died. It was as if all that was good and right went away with them, and he couldn't seem to find his way back to who he was before.

He frowned. Lila dragging him to the psychic and all the other craziness she could come up with hadn't helped – hadn't helped him to remember either. All he had to go on when he woke up was a nagging sense of being watched – and paintings that screamed that whatever was watching wasn't good.

Everything else was a blank slate.

"Amnesia is another hazard that usually follows a sleep-walking episode..."

Sam's hands shook a little as he scooped up the brushes and tubes of paint and stuffed them into one of his desk drawers – along with the journal. He'd have to stash the painting away upstairs with the others after Matty went home.

He took a deep, steadying breath and picked up the phone, praying that the guys he'd trained with earlier hadn't been in his office. There was no way he'd be able to explain what was happening to him – not when he couldn't even get his own head wrapped around it all.

"Hey, Sammy, this straightjacket is JUST YOUR SIZE!"

"Shut up," Sam muttered just as the pizza guy from next door answered the phone.

"I haven't said anything yet," Ryan laughed. "Is that *you*, Sam?"

"Yeah," Sam answered distractedly as he picked up a photo from the pile on his desk. They had all been so young, so happy, as they held their scrawny fish up for the camera. "Matty's here. We'll take the usual."

Ryan might have said something else, but Sam wasn't aware of it as he hung up and continued to stare at the picture in his hand: Jenna, so tiny with those huge grandma glasses ... J, looking slightly stunned, like he'd just won the lottery ... and Carly, with her long red hair, green eyes, and smile like the sun ... He couldn't help wondering if they had been hit with the same strange night-mares lately – or the feeling that something bad was coming.

Once upon a time they had been tight like that, able to sense things about each other before they even picked up the phone ...

Sam sat down hard in the chair and brushed a hand over his face. He was so tired, so overwhelmed by everything that was happening that he couldn't seem to think straight.

He looked at the photo again — at Jonah's crooked grin as he flashed a peace sign behind Sam's head, and he almost smiled. He wished Jonah hadn't taken off to New Orleans. He needed to talk to him bad, needed to show him the paintings ... tell him about the nightmares ... tell him *everything.* So why did he keep putting it off? Couldn't be that he was afraid his brother would think he was crazy. Jonah was *famous* for crazy, a guy who summed up his entire life's existence with a line from an old Ozzy Osbourne song.

He shook his head, actually smiling a little as he reached for the phone again, but just as his hand touched the receiver, he froze. The tingling sensation was back, stronger this time, rolling up the base of his neck.

Someone or something *was* watching him. He swiveled his chair around and came face-to-face with the huge Bruce Lee poster on the wall behind him, Jonah's forged autograph glaring back at him in bold black script:

Sammy! Let's do lunch.

— Love, Bruce

"Idiot," Sam said, laughing with relief.

"Can I tell *Lila* I sweeped you?" Matty asked, startling him almost out of his chair, and he turned to find his student in the doorway, still dripping from the shower. Sam shook his head. Matty's hero worship of him had been overshadowed by the recent crush he'd developed on Lila.

"Tell you what," Sam offered as he stood and walked around the desk, ushered Matty back, and locked the door to the office. He ruffled the boy's wet hair. "Next time she comes by, you can give her all the gory details. Right now I need to ask you some questions."

"I'd love to hear the gory details," Lila said with a laugh, and Sam leaned left to see her standing behind Matty, long blonde hair pulled back in a ponytail, her cheeks flushed as she balanced a couple bottles of orange Gatorade on the pizza box. His heart skipped a beat, happy to see her. "Ryan said you sounded ... hungry." She smiled. "I thought maybe after we finish the pizza, we could hook up with Nick downtown?"

"I'm not showing your cousin my paintings," Sam said with a laugh as he accepted the Gatorade she offered.

"Why not?" she demanded. "His new gallery is going to be huge – it's practically a crime to hide a gift like yours!"

"Wanna arrest me?" Sam teased, holding his hands out to be cuffed.

"Very funny." Lila pouted. "I can't believe you're turning this down."

"Oh come on, Li. He's a numbers man, and those paintings aren't for sale – *especially* those paintings. Not to anyone."

Lila searched his face and then gave him her "eureka" look. "You found another one, didn't you?" Her gaze shifted eagerly to the door behind him. She took a step forward, but he blocked her way. She sidestepped him to the left, and he easily blocked her again. Matty laughed, enjoying their little dance, and Sam grinned.

"Wanna see?" the voice suddenly whispered through his mind.

Sam's smile froze on his face as he turned his head slightly, catching a glimpse of the figure retreating from the front door of the school. The old army jacket again.

"Sam – what's wrong?"

"Why don't you and Matty start on the pizza. I need to take a walk," he said, surprising himself as much as Lila as he hastily slipped on his street shoes, grabbed a jacket, and headed for the door.

He saw them watching him – saw Lila's frown deepen – and knew how crazy it looked, but he had to get to the bottom of what was going on. He shut the door behind him and quickly made his way down the sidewalk without looking back, slipping around a group of clubbers making a beeline for the bars along the Landing as he headed in the direction he'd seen the stranger go, toward the heart of the city.

What is happening to me?

He took a deep lungful of cold air as he walked, forcing himself to weed through the chaos that had become his life. The nightmares ... paintings he had no memory of painting ... the feeling of looming danger that had crept into his waking hours ... some vague line from his childhood that kept surfacing out of the blue ... *Matty* ... and this stranger ...

He had never backed down from a fight in his life, had trained a good part of his life for some eminent battle he'd always sensed was coming, but how was he supposed to fight all this?

Sam stopped dead in his tracks at the corner, only half hearing the steady rush of traffic as he looked across the street to the man staring back at him, his tattered old army jacket flapping in the wind.

It was him – had to be.

At first glance he looked normal enough; the dark hair was a little long and windblown. The old jacket appeared to be masking some pretty huge muscles, and his stance was poised and alert like that of a seasoned fighter, but he didn't look like any of the guys Sam had fought in the ring. Sam frowned. There was something off about him ... something that felt too *new.* Like he didn't fit ...

A group of rowdy drunks appeared behind the man and then split apart, streaming around him – but acting as if he weren't there at all.

The stranger met Sam's gaze again, and his eyes flashed with a strange amber color that took Sam's breath away, scared him too. Eyes that were almost lionlike ... that seemed to say a million things that Sam knew he would never understand.

He had seen those eyes before.

Sam felt a strange tug at his mind, like someone trying to gently shake him awake, and his legs went weak, threatening to buckle underneath him.

Cars streamed by, blocking his view. He swore under his breath, waited until it was clear again, and then dashed across the street, but the man was already gone.

"I'm scared."

The words hit Sam so abruptly that he turned around to see if there was someone behind him – even though he knew there wasn't. Not this time. It was *his* voice, seven years younger, but definitely his voice.

He spied the army jacket again and took off in a jog in the stranger's direction, passing under the I-70 overpass into the dark, trash-strewn intersection that even the cops tried to avoid.

"Wanna see how far that rabbit hole really goes?"

Jonah's voice again, sounding just as young and just as scared, and Sam picked up his pace as he passed the Edward

Jones Dome, trying to keep his eyes fixed on the stranger. *That line*, he thought while he ran. *It had been the beginning ...*

His breath was coming in short gasps now as he glanced up at the night sky. A dark, smoky-looking cloud drifted over, blocking his view of the stars, and he was hit with another piece of memory.

It was dark like this, dark and —

"I remember the wind," Sam blurted out loud, momentarily breaking the spell of the past. He glanced around, startled to find himself standing in the middle of the old playground where they used to play. It was at least five miles from the Dome ... and yet he had no memory of *getting* there.

Sam shivered, pulling his coat tighter to his body. He spotted a bench and went to it, sitting down to catch his breath as he cautiously looked around. The stranger was nowhere to be found. Why had he been led here, of all places? Sam shook his head as a small burst of wind hit, blowing the swings back and forth on their rusty hinges. He turned and glanced toward the entrance.

In his mind's eye he saw the five of them as they had once been, arm in arm, laughing like they had just heard the best joke in the world. Misfits who had bonded together the way kids do when they recognize something similar in each other but are too young to put it into words.

Observed, Sam thought suddenly. *Like we were always being observed by something we felt but could never see, until ...*

He shook his head again, trying to jog his memory, and was surprised when he felt something give. His mind filled with a rush of sound and colors, of young faces that were so sharp and clear, he almost reached out to touch them.

They had weathered Barney and the Power Rangers. (Jenna and Carly had fought like dogs over who was going to be the Pink Ranger.) Jonah was the one who had declared that Pokémon was for suckers, and they all wholeheartedly agreed that Creed was the best band ever (even Jonah, who thought of most musicians after the eighties as sellouts). Sam couldn't remember who first admitted they had a journal — *maybe J?* — but pretty soon they'd realized that they had all kept journals since they were able to write. That was kind of weird. Village-of-the-Damned weird, Jonah had called it. But it was cool too.

Like being a part of something that no one else was.

A sad smile touched Sam's lips ... and then another memory bubbled to the surface: Jenna was standing in the middle of that street again, Mardi Gras beads slung around her neck, crying as the five of them were battered by wind like the hard gusts from the tail end of a storm. She's was so scared—they were *all* scared.

His heart began to race.

"Don't cry, Jenna," Carly's young voice whispered. *"It's just—"*

Sam jerked around, startled by the jolt of anxiety that rushed through him. Someone was there. His eyes struggled through the dark, searching the playground for a glimpse of the stranger, and then he felt it: the cold, a horrible, mind-numbing cold that flooded his entire being. He began to shake, his breath coming out in tiny white puffs, and he sensed something foreign slide around the edges of his mind, probing him with what felt like thin, icy fingers, searching for a way in.

"Sam."

Sam gasped and, closing his eyes, grabbed both sides of his head as the painful probing intensified. In the distance he could hear a voice, deep and filled with alarm, telling him something, telling him to *do* something, but he couldn't focus on the words. The sound of a horrible, rough wind filled his ears as a foul odor began to permeate the air, and he sensed something trying to take shape near him.

"Sam!"

He felt a shift in the atmosphere and then a heavy sensation, almost like a wave of water rolling through the air, and he opened his eyes just in time to see a massive pulse of iridescent blue light wash over the dilapidated little park.

The probing stopped.

Sam jumped up and vaulted over the back of the park bench, stumbling backward as he scanned the area around him.

"Run!" a deep voice roared, cracking through his mind like thunder, and he bolted, running for all he was worth out of the park and down the dark street as a bone-chilling current pressed in on him, brushing across his back.

He was too terrified to look over his shoulder.

Something *alive* was just beneath the cold, something that
... *hated* him. *What is that?* his mind screamed as he ran, but
he kept running, hoping he wouldn't stop, for fear he would
pass out – or worse. The horrible stench stayed with him, like he
couldn't run fast enough to escape it. He gasped for air, forced to
take the putrid odor into his lungs, and bile rose in his throat.

"Help me," he choked out between breaths. "Somebody ..."

Laughter swirled around him.

Sam groaned, gripped by another rush of nausea. He forced
himself to keep going, weaving down the dimly lit backstreets
until he just couldn't go anymore. His legs shook as he leaned
against the crumbling brick retaining wall next to an old brown-
stone. He heard a dog in the distance begin to bark, and then its
bark turned to a low, mournful howl. He leaned over and threw
up, shakily wiping his mouth with the back of his hand.

"They see you," the deep voice said, softer this time. *"But
remember:* YOU SEE THEM TOO.*"*

Sam glanced up, and the world turned silent around him, as
if it were holding its breath. Waiting.

He slowly turned to his left and saw what appeared to
be two figures expanding up out of the dark, becoming
light – changing and shifting forms that seemed to be made
up of some kind of shimmery, membranous substance that
disappeared and reappeared as they moved toward him. One of
the beings held its hand out to Sam, and he saw that the hand
was large and humanlike, except for the extra finger.

This isn't so bad, he thought, mesmerized, as he raised his
own hand. *This is –*

"Look again, Sam. You're seeing only what they want you to see!"

Sam dropped his arm, lifting his gaze just in time to see the
brilliant blue light appear above him, arcing high into the air
before viciously slicing downward through the night. He jerked
back, his jaw dropping open, as the ethereal glow illuminated the
figures, creating a pulsating wall between him and the beings.

"LOOK."

Like bulbs dimming as they burned out, the shimmering
beings before him began to rapidly fade away, revealing brief
flashes of something darker, scalelike.

Those eyes, those empty black sockets where eyes should be!

A low, rattling growl emanated from them, turning into a high-pitched chittering, and somewhere in the deep recesses of his mind — the part that had yet to be fried — he could have sworn that he felt the foreign, snakelike thing attempting to enter his brain again.

If this is another dream, let me wake up, he thought desperately, feeling his mind begin to unhinge. *Let me wake up!*

The beings snarled, and he saw drool dripping from two rows of razor-sharp teeth in each mouth.

"Run, Sam! Now, while there's still time!" the deep voice commanded.

Sam startled, slid sideways across a patch of wet grass, then turned and ran — and kept running as rapid images from his childhood began to flash through his mind.

"They see you ... but you see them too," the voice had said. Sam saw the image of their eyes again — or lack thereof — and with the sudden, sharp clarity that usually comes too late, he knew he had seen them before.

He heard his friend's screams again, mingled with his own screams of fear and disbelief ... and pain. A terrified sob bubbled up out of him, but he kept running.

He didn't stop until he reached the Landing again. Slipping into the first bar he came to, he made straight for the men's room and locked the door. He turned the water on full blast, splashing his face over and over again before daring to look at himself in the mirror. But by that time, he had begun to remember what happened to them that night when they were kids.

He remembered it all.

2

Las Vegas, Nevada

There were a lot of things worse than being scared, but Jenna Maldonado couldn't think of any as she ran toward the north end of the Strip, her ridiculous showgirl-like waitress uniform with its frilly apron flapping in the chilly night air, and crazy-high stilettos digging into the blisters on her heels as digital billboards loomed and faded. The faces and lights streamed by in a kaleidoscope of skin and neon. But she refused to slow down.

Jenna glanced over her shoulder, then let out a gasp of surprise as she turned back and saw the watery image of a scared little boy rise before her eyes again, a face from her past. "Sam?" she whispered incredulously. *That doesn't make any sense. Why would I see —*

Cold dread surrounded her like a living thing, pushing at her from all sides, pushing her through the crowds, faster and faster, until she couldn't think of anything but escape.

Her heartbeat pounded in her ears, labored breaths echoing through her head. Lights, blinding lights. The sound of fountains spouting water high into the air. She knew where she was ... and she didn't. She was ...

Confused.

Lost.

Jenna skidded to a stop as a voice ripped through the fog of her fear. A gust of wind battered her, whipping loose strands of hair around her face, and her vision cleared just as the front end of a semi brushed by — so close that it would have hit her if she hadn't stopped.

"Catch of the day!" was written across the semi's trailer. Beneath the logo, a lone fish flopped happily in a net.

She took an abrupt step back from the curb, her legs shaking uncontrollably as cars and trucks barreled by. *That voice.* Her heart pounded in her ears as she tried to catch her breath. She turned and looked behind her.

The sidewalk had pretty much emptied out, except for a guy stopping to drop his Starbucks cup into a trash bin on the corner. He glanced at her curiously as he walked by – handsome African face, sunglasses on top of a shaved head bearing tribal-looking tattoos, decent clothes, and an expensive camera around his neck.

Tourist. Her cheeks burning, she imagined how crazy she must look.

"Man, that was *close*," a little voice announced breathlessly.

Jenna looked down at the angelic face framed by a mop of unruly dark curls and felt a tidal wave of guilt wash over her. She had run at least a mile, had ducked and weaved down side streets, through a trash-filled alley, and back onto the main drag, and never once had she given her own child a second thought. His hand felt hot, sweaty in her grip – like he'd been holding on for dear life. But how in the world had he kept up with her? He didn't *look* any worse for wear.

He looked . . . *excited.*

"How old *are* you?" she asked, still trying to catch her breath.

He grinned up at her, revealing two missing front teeth. "Five."

"Is that all?" She ruffled his curls. "I was thinking more like fifty."

"Age is just a number," he said with a dismissive shrug. "In the future I'm old just like you."

"Old?" Any other time she might have laughed at Mikey, thinking nineteen was old, but this wasn't any other time. She took a shaky breath, firm grip on his little hand, and headed across the street into the seedier side of town.

What's wrong with me?

If she'd felt like being rational, she might have guessed that lack of sleep was her problem, but she didn't really feel like being rational. She felt like putting as much distance as she could between her and . . . whatever it was that was going on.

It wasn't until their feet struck the other side of the street that she recalled being at the grocery store. The guy behind her in line had said something to her, and when she turned around, it was Sam's young face looking back at her. She had jumped like she'd been Tasered, grabbed her meager little sack of groceries, and gone running out of Save-A-Lot like a crazy person. How she'd hung on to the groceries and Mikey, she didn't have a clue. After Save-A-Lot, everything was mostly a blur.

Until, on the street, she'd heard Jonah's voice.

Jenna spotted their apartment building and picked up the pace again, quickly steering Mikey past the stench from the overflowing garbage bins and down the crumbling, weed-infested walkway. *Home away from home,* she thought shakily. *Latest stop on my magic bus ride of bad choices...*

"You need to chill," Mikey noted solemnly as they reached the main entrance.

"Yeah?" A small grin curved her lips as she slid the key into the door, and they stepped inside a dimly lit hall decorated with layers of graffiti. "Do you know something I don't?"

"I'm working it all out," Mikey answered, his voice echoing in the dirty stairwell.

"Working what out?" Jenna asked distractedly as she opened the door to the apartment. Mikey dumped his backpack in the middle of the living room floor and then looked up at her, his gray eyes seeming to see into her very soul.

"Our escape."

They both glanced around the rundown little studio apartment, from the Goodwill-issue card table and plastic chairs they ate their meals on to the threadbare sofa sleeper, and then faced each other again. Jenna held her hand up for a high five, and he slapped it without hesitation.

"That guy with the tattoos was *huge,*" Mikey exclaimed.

"You are *never* getting a tattoo, so don't even think it."

"He was cool-looking — like an ultimate fighter! What's for dinner?"

"It's a surprise."

"Macaroni and cheese and hot dogs?"

"Maybe." Jenna grinned in spite of herself.

"My favorites!"

"Good answer."

She kept the smile up until he had turned his attention to the TV, and then she headed into the tiny kitchen and set the grocery bag down on the counter. She turned on the faucet and washed her hands, almost feverishly, before drying them off with the dish towel, the germaphobe in her kicking in like it always did when she was scared.

She was home now. Safe. So why were her hands still shaking so badly?

She closed her eyes for a moment, then opened the ancient fridge and glanced inside. Half package of hot dogs left. If she stretched it with the mac and cheese, he would be okay for dinner tomorrow night too.

Your hands are shaking because you're not safe. You think what happened back there was normal – that hearing Jonah's voice was normal?

She poured the macaroni into the pot and turned the burner on, her cheeks hot as she tried to blink away the tears. He had meant it as a joke! Just one of those crazy Jonah-isms made up on the spur of the moment to make them laugh.

She hated being scared. Hated it. She had lived the last five years of her life in fear: scared every time she stood at a register, waiting for the total to be more than she had; scared of the rent, the electric bill, and the phone bill; scared every time Mikey had a fever; worried that white kids would tease her son for being half black and that black kids would tease him for being half white. She jabbed the noodles with her fork. And if that wasn't enough, now she had to deal with nightmares she couldn't remember and an insane episode that had nearly driven both of them into the middle of rush-hour traffic.

How many nineteen-year-olds lived like that?

Sometimes, when things got real bad, she liked to imagine that she'd wake up and be back in her parents' home, with her bed and cable TV ... *car* ... and no worries. But how do you wake up to a different life when you don't sleep anymore?

Mikey laughed from the other room, one of those hearty, little-boy belly laughs that always made her smile. He was such a tough little guy, rolling with whatever punches came their way. As much as she hated being afraid, she wouldn't trade him for anything. He was the one bright light in her world of regrets.

Jenna peeked around the corner and watched as he scooted himself closer to the TV. She was glad that she'd been able to scrounge up enough to buy the old VCR she'd spotted in the pawnshop a couple of months ago. The owner had been in the mood to flirt and had even thrown in a free video for Mikey. She thought it was funny that out of all the videos he could have given Mikey, he had chosen *Ultimate Fighter*.

Mikey reminded her lot of how she used to be, back when it was the five of them, when she had been so sure of who she was, so ... *brave.*

Jenna frowned. Maybe that was what this was all about. Maybe she was just wishing she could be that person again.

She *had* been thinking about all of them lately, wondering if their lives had been as much of a struggle as hers.

Wondering but too afraid to call and find out. Instead she would lie in bed at night, hoping to grab on to some memory that would give her that feeling of belonging again. Yet all she came up with night after night was a grainy gray wall of ... nothing. Like a TV that had lost its reception.

Jenna reached for the wallet in her purse and opened it to the faded picture of the five of them she had tucked inside. She carried it everywhere she went, treating it more like her driver's license than she did the real thing. Like it was the only thing she had left that identified her.

"Wanna see?"

Jenna's head snapped up at the sound of the voice, and she wasn't in her living room anymore ...

... but instead in Sam and Jonah's basement, a scrawny, glasses-wearing twelve-year-old scrunched in between the two brothers on the couch while Carly and J sat across from them on the coveted beanbag chairs. She could literally *smell* the Doritos and the fizz from the Cokes as they all grinned and pulled their tabs at the exact same time ... and then she heard herself say, "Oh, I just got the most awesome idea!"

"Well, kiss my grits, Flo, let's do it!" Jonah jumped up, not bothering to ask what it was, and they all laughed. Is there anything better than that sound?

"Well, since Jonah put it like that, I guess I'm in too," J said with a reckless grin.

"Me too," Sam and Carly said at the same time and then yelled, "Jinx!"

"No!"

The cry jolted her out of the memory, and she felt a small rush of relief as she looked around. She was back in her own living room — but something still felt out of place, *wrong.* The TV screen was blue, signaling that the video ended some time ago. A half-eaten plate of mac and cheese was on the table ... She turned around; Mikey's dark curls were the only thing visible from underneath the pile of covers on the sofa sleeper. She had to have finished dinner and put him to bed –

What happened that night? Why don't I want to remember, when that's exactly what I've been trying to do for the past month?

Shaken, she rushed down the hall to the narrow bathroom, peeling her waitress uniform off as she went. She studied herself in the mirror as she loosed her thick, dark hair from its ponytail. Her olive skin looked strange, sickly *pale.* Her hands shook as she slipped into the T-shirt and boxers she had waiting for her on the vanity. She glanced in the mirror again, looking into her own eyes for answers. Eyes like Mikey's.

Almost beautiful, Mikey's dad used to say. She grimaced, turned away from the mirror, and headed back down the hallway. *I was almost a lot of things, Tony. Almost a high school graduate, almost a girlfriend, almost a daughter – until my mom and dad decided they didn't want me and, as they put it, the "extra mouth" to feed ...*

Guess I should add almost crazy to the list now too.

Jenna sighed and sat down on her side of the sleeper and glanced at the little boy burrowed under the pile of covers. *Her little boy.* A smile trembled on her lips, remembering his toothless grin ... then her smile faltered.

Why hadn't he asked her what they were running from?

She bit her lip, staring at him for a moment longer, and then reached for the journal that she kept tucked away next to the sleeper. She opened it, slowly turning the pages. When she was a kid, she had written all of her entries to God. A little girl yearning for a dad who would listen, she supposed ... She wasn't a kid anymore.

Gotta get it together, Jenna. There's no one else –

She glanced toward the window, only half listening to the neighbors fighting in the apartment below. Music from a car stereo swelled and then faded off into the distance. Across the street, a half-torn-down old Amoco station gleamed in the moonlight, its sign and windows pockmarked by bullets from local gangs. Her eyes roamed over the sandy, weed-choked lot, unconsciously searching for something she sensed but didn't know how to name. Something that was watching her … The trunk of an old palm tree blurred and shifted before her eyes, and she blinked a couple of times until it came back into focus.

Vegas wasn't far enough away, she thought, shivering a little. Far enough away from what, she didn't know, but deep down she had always felt that there was *something* she was running from.

"This is so crazy," she whispered.

"Remember …," a deep voice whispered to her, prodding her almost urgently. She squeezed her eyes shut, shaking her head back and forth. She didn't want to remember. Not anymore …

But just as she opened her eyes, she *did* remember. Not everything, but tiny flashes, snapping through her mind as the five of them stood in the middle of that dark street again. Someone was crying. She saw Jonah look up at the sky first, then Sam and Carly, but J, he looked right at *her*, his face etched with fear – and something else too.

Her eyes shot open.

"It was nothing … just the wind," she whispered firmly, attempting to force the wall of forgetfulness back up. It might have worked too, if she hadn't glanced down at the journal in her lap. It had fallen open to her last entry – or at least *a* last entry, because she had no memory of writing the two words that splashed across the page in bold black marker:

IT'S REAL

Jenna swept the book off her lap like it had burned her, watching it fall to the floor as she hugged her knees to her chest. *"Oh, I just got the most awesome idea!"* she heard her twelve-year-old voice declare excitedly, and tears sprang to her eyes.

She closed her eyes against the pain, wishing with all of her heart that when she opened them again, she would be somewhere other than this dump that Tony had ditched her in. Someplace where she wasn't alone.

"I want to go *home*," Jenna whispered, her voice catching a little as a powerful longing swept over her. She hadn't always been alone. She shivered again and pulled the blanket up over her. Once upon a time she'd had four best friends.

3

Chicago, Illinois

To say the shakedown was going slightly badly was like saying Charles Manson was only *slightly* crazy. Big J — aka J Harvey — ran a his hand over his dreadlocks, then glanced at his partner, Tiny, pulled the gun out from under his coat, and quickly scanned the shabby little restaurant. He looked over his shoulder to the dark lot outside, every one of his senses on high alert. The old woman hiding behind the counter began to cry. A bead of sweat trickled down the side of his face.

"How long have we been doing business?" J hissed as he turned back to face the short restaurant owner. "And you decide to *disrespect* us like this?"

Joey Chu remained mute, standing frozen to one spot as if he wasn't sure what to do with his arms or legs. The slight shift of his eyes said something else, though; he was waiting, killing time until someone showed up. J knew better than to wait and see who it was. Nineteen was *old* in his line of business, and he hadn't gotten to where he was by playing nice.

The old woman's cries grew louder.

J shoved the barrel of his gun between Chu's eyes and glanced at Tiny again.

"Shut her up, will you?"

Tiny nodded and headed toward the counter.

"Wanna see how far that rabbit hole really goes?"

"What the — " J whipped around at the sound of the voice, and for a split second he felt like a kid again — the kid before what he had become — and hoped against hope that he would find his old friend standing behind him with that crooked grin of his. But it wasn't

Jonah. Just some hoodie-wearing drunk staggering down the sidewalk. The drunk raised a bottle of whiskey to his lips as he came to a stop across the street from the restaurant.

Big dude, J thought as the man moved under a streetlight. The bottle slipped from the drunk's hand, and as he leaned over to pick it up, J noticed the strong set of the man's jaw. J's eyes traveled upward and caught a glimpse of red hair peeking out from the hood. The drunk suddenly stiffened, rising slowly before he turned and glanced to his left. J followed his gaze just as a black Land Rover slowly cruised into the picture. Warning bells ripped through him as he caught the back windows beginning to slide down.

"Drop, Tiny!" J bellowed, diving to the floor of the restaurant. The next moments of his life seemed to flow in slow motion. He felt himself falling through the air, and as he did, he heard something that didn't make sense, like someone whispering in his ear, *"Remember ..."*; then the sound of his heart beating hard in his ears drowned it out as the side of his face connected with the dirty tiled floor; then – bam! – glass sprayed across his back.

More shots.

More glass. It flew up into the air, and he watched with a kind of detached interest as the shards turned into tiny prisms of light before raining back down on the floor.

The old woman was crying again. J closed his eyes, trying to will the sound away as he felt the damp cold of the tiles seep into his skin. *I can't take that crying,* he thought, gritting his teeth. *Somebody make her stop crying. Where the heck is Tiny?*

The old woman's cries escalated to a horrible keening, and J looked up.

A cold wind blew through the gaping hole where the window had been, and he glanced over to see the old woman rocking back and forth over her son's lifeless body. Joey Chu's dull eyes stared back at J as blood pooled out from his body across the tiles. *Gone,* J thought, unable to drag his eyes away. *But gone where?*

He used to believe there was somewhere else – somewhere better, as his grandma put it – but that had been sucked out of him along with his dreams. Deep, empty blackness was all he saw ahead of him now.

The crying continued, scraping his nerves raw, reminding him of ... He saw a flash of *her* tear-streaked face then, gray eyes staring out from those huge old-lady glasses ...

J started to tremble but fought it, waiting a moment longer before he shook the glass off and stood and looked around. Evidently, Chu hadn't known *everything* they had planned. He glanced out the window – or what was left of it.

If he hadn't heard that voice, he would've never turned around ...

Keeping his gun ready, he quickly searched up and down both sides of the street. Then he frowned and finally lowered his weapon. Didn't seem possible that the drunk dude had escaped the drive-by, but there was no sign of him anywhere.

And who ordered the hit?

"Tiny?"

"Yeah, I'm here," was the muffled reply.

J glanced over and shook his head, seeing Tiny's head and shoulders appear as he struggled to free himself from underneath one of the booths.

"Nice place to hide, little man."

"You should talk," Tiny grunted as he stood up to his full height of six foot four, just a hair shorter than J.

Salt-and-pepper shakers, people called them, Tiny as white as J was black. And they did a *lot* of shaking – which was why what just happened made no sense to him. The little restaurant was small-time, something he didn't even handle himself anymore ... J's eyes narrowed as he shoved the door open to the street.

"Let's get out of here," he said, trying to keep the fear out of his voice.

"Don't have to tell me twice," Tiny said breathlessly as they quickly made their way across the lot to J's Escalade. "That was messed up."

"Yeah ...," J said grimly as he slid into the front seat of the SUV.

"How'd they even know we were there?"

"No idea," J said with a shrug, even though he had a theory. Right now it was the least of his worries. "Just gotta think things through."

Tiny got the hint and popped in a CD as J leaned his head back against the seat and stared at the dark scenery that slid by: alleys, back doors and side streets, empty lots littered with rubble and trash, condemned buildings that reeked of death. He rubbed at the scar on his chest. Four cities in two years, and all that had really changed was his address. If anything, things had gotten a lot worse lately.

"No honor among thieves, just goin' through the motions 'til I die," the song played on. *"Another day, another dollar, give me another sucker to buy into the lie..."*

Like this drive-by. He had been through things like it before, but something about this time had shaken him up. The urge to break down crying welled up in him, but he fought it off with everything he had.

He felt like he was going insane again — but not on his own. It was more like he was being *driven* there.

J shifted his eyes sideways. No way was he going to let Tiny know what was up — no matter how tight he claimed they were.

No sir, J thought grimly. *Ain't no one getting that on me.*

Getting shoved back into Elgin's mental ward would be better than his boys knowing he was scared. Fear was like a perfume to the South Side. One whiff and they'd have him for lunch. And there'd be no mercy either — not after all he'd done.

"Have you had any thoughts of suicide today, Mr. Harvey?"

"You want me to hit the lights?"

J frowned at Tiny, unable to comprehend what he had said. For a split second he thought he was back in that psych ward at Elgin... Rubbing the scar on his chest, he looked around and realized that they had somehow gotten inside his apartment. Light blazed from every lamp and overhead fixture in his living room. In the kitchen too — like he had lit a pathway from the moment they came through the front door.

"You want me to hit the lights?" Tiny asked again.

"No, leave 'em on."

Tiny gave him a curious look. "You buy stock in the electric company or something?"

"Or something," J said with a sigh, trying to keep it short. If he didn't, Tiny would be there all night, talking his head off.

"Long as I've known you, you've always kept it dark as a vampire's pad," Tiny said, as if physically unable to keep himself from talking.

"Maybe you don't know me like you thought." J's voice had just enough of an edge for his partner to get his meaning. Tiny gave him a worried look and then shrugged and left without another word.

As soon as the door clicked shut, J hurried around the rest of the apartment to make sure it was secure. Finally satisfied that no one could get in, he lit a cigarette and looked around. The apartment was nice, as far as things went, but not really a home. After years of being shuffled from one foster home to another, nothing really felt like home anymore. Except maybe the streets, and now even that was becoming a problem.

Maybe it's the nightmares making everything seem worse than what it is. Nightmares can do messed-up things to your head, maybe make you hear things too ...

He felt sweat lining his forehead. He couldn't remember a lot of things, but he remembered those words – remembered the night Jonah had spoken them too. Or at least part of it.

He headed across the room to the balcony, but instead of stepping outside, he hit the floodlights and peered through the glass at the city below, prisoner to his crazy fears. A hard wind battered the sliding glass door. Always the wind. Why in the world did he pick Chicago?

He missed St. Louis, the old days. When he had been a part of something so ... *righteous* ... like the time they rescued Jonah from Bud Winters. He sighed and smoothed his hand over his hair. Times like that could make you almost feel like a hero.

He didn't have times like that anymore – and even the good memories were sketchy. Like someone had taken an X-Acto knife and carefully sliced away parts he wished he had and left him with things he'd like to forget.

Like how bad things got right after that night: his grandma getting hit by that drunk driver and ending up in a wheelchair ... him getting put in the first of a long line of foster homes ... and finding that gun on the way home from school.

He remembered *that* like it was yesterday: how he'd spotted the gun on the sidewalk and picked it up without thinking twice, looking up to see the guy running in the opposite direction down the street. The guy kept looking over his shoulder, and that's when J had seen a cop car slowly cruising toward him. So he'd calmly headed to the back of one of the houses and tossed the gun in a dumpster – thinking he might come back for it later, of course.

Until its owner reappeared as soon as the cops were gone, asking for his gun.

J told the truth, too scared not to. The guy had just laughed and called him a quick thinker. And he was; he'd thought his way all the way to the top and stayed there, daring anyone to try to move him down.

Maybe he could think his way out of this mess too. He needed to do something before whoever it was got the jump on him while he was taking a walk down memory lane. Kill or be killed was his motto. He had done the first more times than he could count. Had done the second one too, if he counted his own attempt. Life just wasn't black and white, good and evil, anymore – least not the way his grandma liked to think.

"Old Devil likes you to think in grays, boy," her voice whispered to him from his childhood. *"Gray keeps you trapped in the in-between. Keeps you from looking for the one true Light that will lead you out, that'll show you who you really are ..."*

"So, who am I?" J whispered under his breath.

"Remember ..."

J startled at the sound of the deep voice, looking around in confusion, but before he could form another thought, the flood-light on his balcony exploded without warning. He stumbled back, arms windmilling as he tried to keep his balance, and fell hard on the floor ...

... and suddenly he was standing in the middle of a dark city street. He felt so *cold* as he looked around, trying to see something, *anything*, but the wind was hitting his face so hard that he could barely breathe.

"What *is* that?" he heard Jonah say from a distance – and he was *young*.

Then Sam's voice: "Guys?"

J heard the shuffling of their feet ... and the tinkling sound of beads hitting together. *Mardi Gras beads.* A shot of terror hit J, and he knew he was back in that night – even before he heard Jenna begin to cry.

Oh, that crying!

Something cold and leathery brushed against his face. He tried to run but was unable to move.

"Don't cry, Jenna," Carly said, crying herself. "It's …"

"Just the wind!" J yelled the words as if they would shield him from what might happen next …

And then the past dropped away, revealing his living room again.

He jumped up and ran to his bedroom, then slammed the door and locked it behind him. His heart was pounding so hard, he was sure it would explode at any moment. He was terrified – *really* terrified, for the first time since he was twelve years old.

He pulled his cell phone out of his pocket and flipped it open with one hand and began to pace. He needed to talk to somebody, but he didn't know *who*. No way could he call Jonah – not after being accused like that … But maybe he could call Sam. They still talked every once in a blue moon.

He scrolled through his contacts to Sam's number, thought a minute, and then hit speed dial on his cell. Tiny picked up on the first ring.

"Yeah?"

"That guy who offered us a job in St. Louis – is it still on the table?"

"Yeah. Corsa, right? The dude just left me a message." Tiny sounded slightly bewildered by J's timing. "Says if we want it, he needs us on board ASAP."

"Tell him we'll take it."

J flipped the phone closed and glanced around the room.

His eyes were drawn to the top of his dresser, where his journal lay instead of in the top drawer, where he *knew* he had hidden it away. It was open. The two lamps he had flipped on earlier shined like beacons on the page, illuminating the four words that had been written in bold black letters:

BUT YOU CAN'T SEE

What's that supposed to mean? J looked behind him, almost wishing there was someone else with him to explain what was going on.

"Ain't nothing gonna send me back to Elgin," J muttered between gritted teeth. "You hear me? Nothing!"

He told himself that everything was going to be okay, that every choice he'd made in his life was for a reason, and that whatever was going on would pass, just like every other trouble had.

He took a deep breath and turned away from the dresser without looking in the mirror. If he had, he would've been shocked by the way his eyes looked, wide and filled with anxiety.

Like two prisoners screaming for help.

The entities studied their prey with cunning interest as they moved like long shadows across the ceiling, following the human from room to room.

They raised their noses briefly to the air and, satisfied they were alone, turned back, their X-ray-like vision moving swiftly through flesh and bone to the network of arteries and capillaries that shot from his heart in saturated beats of orange and yellow.

The colors of terror.

They quivered, their restless bodies producing a dry crackle like burning paper. Though they were unable to read thoughts, reading the emotions of this species was most beneficial.

"This one you are to cease tormenting – follow but do not hinder," their leader instructed, his voice snaking through the collective, still far off, but closer than before. Much closer.

"Go."

They abruptly split apart, half of their number drawing backward through the walls before shooting forth with blinding speed through the night, minds and objectives far beyond the scope of the human imagination.

The herding continued . . .

4

Miami, Florida

Carly Hagan froze in the middle of putting away the green-glass-beaded flapper necklace she'd just finished for a woman in South Beach, and slowly raised her eyes to the front door of the shop. She'd been thinking of J Harvey for some crazy reason, thinking— She shook it off and cocked her head to one side, listening as she scanned the little waiting area bathed in shadows. She couldn't see anything, but she could hear it: a faint ... *rattling*.

A low growl sent a chill up her spine, and she glanced to her feet, where her black Lab had been lounging. He was up on all fours now, hair raised at the scruff of his neck as his eyes fixed on the front door.

Someone was trying to jimmy the lock.

The Lab's growls grew louder.

"Quiet, Doc," she whispered, hitting the panic button behind the glass counter before she switched the jeweler's lamp off at her workstation. Her legs shook as she eased off the stool and reached for her cell phone. At five foot two and weighing a whopping one hundred and eighteen pounds—at least on her driver's license—she knew she wouldn't be a match for whoever was trying to break in. Her mind raced, weighing her options.

There was a moment of silence—long enough that she had the fleeting hope that whoever it was had given up—but then the rattling grew louder, and she sensed an overwhelming anger as they impatiently shoved at the door, trying to force their way inside.

The police had to have received the alarm signal by now—so why didn't she hear sirens? It was downtown Miami, for crying out loud! Why hadn't her boss called to verify the alarm?

"Oh, God, *please* ..." A feeble prayer. Doc tilted his head to one side and looked at her almost questioningly. She grimaced just as another rattle came from the door and adrenaline surged through her body, causing her legs to buckle a little. Stepping out from behind the counter, she headed toward the back of the shop. Doc's nails clicked on the tiled floor, matching the ticks of her racing heart as he followed close behind.

I shouldn't have stayed so late – why did I stay so late? Another rattle and another rush of adrenaline. Carly hesitated, then took a shaky step forward. *Because you didn't want to sleep, remember?*

She took a couple more steps. The silence was almost as bad as the rattling; she felt something swell and enlarge within the quiet, getting ready to burst forth. Her pulse fluttered wildly in her throat as she glanced over her shoulder, hoping against hope that she wouldn't see anything.

"They're out there, Carly ..." The voice popped into her head so fast that it startled her, as if someone, a very real someone, had spoken the words into her ear. *They?* Carly flipped her cell phone open, and the rattling began again. But louder this time and a lot more furious, followed by a sharp metallic click of the door opening. Terror slid through her bloodstream like ice.

"Run! Hurry! Take the back exit!" another deep voice shouted into her mind.

She bolted, running through the tiny shop for the back door, with Doc close at her heels. Grabbing the door handle, she began to pull down.

"Wanna see how far that rabbit hole really goes?"

Carly yelped, startled by the voice that seemed to come out of nowhere, and she dove into the bathroom instead, the big Lab skidding in next to her as she slammed the door and locked it.

That voice ... it couldn't be Jonah. She scooted back into a corner, hands trembling as she flipped her cell phone open and dialed 911.

"Metro-Dade, what is your emergency?"

"Someone has broken into the shop where I work," Carly whispered, her voice shaking as she gave the female operator the address. Doc whined, and her chest tightened with fear. "Please tell them to hurry!"

Doc whined again and glanced up above her head. Carly followed his gaze to the tiny window high on the wall of the bathroom. She slipped off her heels, grabbed the bucket from underneath the sink, tipped it over, and slid it against the wall.

"No, I'm still here," she whispered as she stepped up onto the bucket and slowly cranked the window open. "Carly Hagan. Are they really on their way?" She looked out the window and almost lost her footing when she spotted the Hummer parked sideways in the alley, blocking her exit.

"Someone is parked out back too," she whispered, voice shaking. "A bright orange Hummer ... No ... I can't see the plates from here ..." She peeked out again and saw all four doors of the hummer open, and then surprisingly they snapped shut again.

Doc stopped whining.

A distant squeaking sound filtered up through the window, like a rusty toy wheel rolling over and over, coming closer, and she craned her neck, straining to see, until she spotted the figure of a man in an ancient-looking wheelchair passing under the streetlight.

"There's a—"

"Remember ...," the deep voice whispered to her through the phone, and Carly pulled her cell away from her ear and looked at it.

A loud crackling sound issued from the phone. Then the operator's voice was there again, and Carly put the phone back to her ear. "I'm still here," she said as she peered out the window. "There's someone else in the alley now ..."

The stranger calmly rolled toward the Hummer, like he might peck on the window and say hello. His silver hair was long, pulled back, with two braids on each side. That, along with the old button-covered vest he wore, made her think of those war veteran friends of her dad's. He glanced toward the window and she ducked down.

"Why aren't the police here yet?" Carly glanced at Doc, who was looking at the window expectantly, his tail now thumping against the tiled floor. She frowned, listening to the 911 operator. "No, I don't think he's with them. He's in a wheelchair ..."

The police sirens wailing in the distance gave her the courage to look out the window again. The Hummer was gone—and so was the stranger.

Carly began to shiver uncontrollably, teeth chattering, as she slid to the floor, and in spite of her best efforts not to she burst into tears. *"Don't cry,"* she heard herself whisper from the past, *"Don't cry..."*

Everything after that seemed to run together.

She vaguely remembered the police pounding on the bathroom door... the warmth of Doc's body plastered against her leg, comforting her as she answered their questions... techs dusting the damaged front door... red lights strobing over the faces of people gawking at her from the sidewalk of the corner bar across the street. Then an older policeman was helping her load her jewelry cases into the back of her Jeep, a worried look on his face.

"You remind me of my daughter—same pretty red hair," he said.

She ran her hand over her newly cropped do. She had decided to cut it after noticing the attention her long hair was getting from the guys in the jewelry district. Attention led to things like invitations to lunch and *chatting*, which led to *questions*, and she didn't want to have to explain her last couple years of wandering from city to city. Being alone was just easier.

Ask me no questions and I'll tell you no lies...

Carly glanced up. The officer was watching her, but there was nothing but kindness in his eyes. "My mom used to call it the red flag," she offered, smiling a little. "Great for spotting me in a crowd."

"Red flag, huh?" He chuckled. "I'll have to remember that one. He opened the door of the Jeep for her. Doc scrambled in first, and she gave the officer a "whattaya gonna do?" shrug before sliding behind the steering wheel. The officer shut the door for her, and she rolled her window down.

"You know, you must have an angel watching over you, kid," the officer said, leaning in. "I have an idea of who that Hummer belongs to, and... let's just say they don't like witnesses."

Carly's eyes widened.

"Don't worry; we're going to put one of our guys in front of your place." He gave her arm a reassuring pat. "I'll call you as soon as I know something. You call me if you think of anything else." He handed her his card. "You sure you're okay?"

"Oh, yeah." She smiled, her best cheerleader kind of smile, as she petted Doc's head. "I'm fine."

But she wasn't fine.

She was scared – and had been for weeks.

Smiling in spite of what you feel is just family tradition, she thought.

When she reached her apartment building, which had been converted from an old art deco hotel, she climbed out of the Jeep with Doc, grabbed the jewelry cases out of the back, and went inside. They quickly crossed the brightly colored terrazzo floors of the lobby to the carpeted hallway.

She balanced the jewelry cases on one arm as she slid the key in and opened the door to the furnished apartment. Doc gave her a worried glance before trotting inside – almost as if he could sense her fear – then made a beeline for his chow. She set the cases down on the coffee table with a weary sigh and looked around.

She had blamed the nightmares for putting her on edge over the past several weeks, keeping her waiting for some unseen stalker to walk around the corner or climb through a window. Whatever she held in her hands lately had become a possible weapon. She couldn't count the times she had pictured herself winging the remote, the phone, or her curling iron – *anything* to give her enough time to escape.

Now she couldn't help wondering if it had all been some sort of warning.

But why in the world did she think she heard *Jonah* during the robbery attempt?

She went to the door, locked it, and slipped the bolt firmly in place, and then pressed her forehead against the door. Jonah ... What had it been, something like seven years since she had last seen him, or J ... or any of them?

Carly turned and headed down the hallway to her bedroom and knelt down next to the bed, searching underneath. Finally she pulled a large suitcase out and opened it. She reached for the framed picture of the five of them, tracing her fingers over their faces.

When they were together, it had been a lot like having a huge cloak that surrounded their little group, keeping all that was bad in the world from ever coming near ... until the last time. Carly frowned. She didn't know why, but everything had seemed to fall apart after that, until one day she woke up and realized there was no more "five of us." So she packed it all up – the good with the bad in a nice big suitcase – and stored it away. It gave her a feeling of control.

There was something calming about being able to control things – especially if you couldn't control people.

She glanced at the contents of the suitcase again and stood. Then she hurried back down the hallway, scanning the living room and kitchen.

Everything was in its designated place as usual. *Everything*, from the position of the candles on the coffee table, to her small collection of books with perfectly level spines arranged in alphabetical order, to the towels that hung in the exact same length on the handle of the oven door. Even Doc's dog dishes were lined up, snug against the wall –

She felt her heart skip a beat as she glanced to the spot where Doc rested on the kitchen floor, head between his paws ... and saw her journal lying there next to him. She distinctly remembered putting it away in the suitcase before she left for work.

"I *know* I put it away," she murmured, feeling the old helpless feeling rising up in her again – that out-of-control sensation she had fought since she was a kid.

"*Remember ...,*" the deep voice whispered again.

She shook her head and quickly conjured up a big brick wall in her mind – a trick she used since childhood whenever she started to feel overwhelmed – but for the first time in seven years it wasn't working. Tiny fragments ripped through the carefully constructed wall, and she felt a cold rush of fear like ...

The wind?

Carly started to tremble. *It had felt like the wind ... at first.* She saw the eyes again, those dark, soulless eyes staring at her, taunting her: "*Who is going to help you? Where is your father's God now?*"

She inhaled sharply, and with every bit of strength she had, she pushed herself out of the memory.

And into another ...

"Come on, give us a smile, Carly!"

45

Two months after that Mardi Gras, on the night of her thirteenth birthday, her mom had taken her picture as she blew out the candles on her cake. "Got a quick errand to run, a *surprise*," her mom had said, smiling that trademark sunny smile of hers as she kissed Carly on the forehead before she waved good-bye and quickly breezed out the door.

It was the last time Carly or her dad saw her.

Kind of like the joke about the guy who said he was going out for a pack of cigarettes and never came home. *Only it wasn't a joke,* Carly thought as she stepped into the kitchen and picked her journal up off the floor. Doc glanced at her, thumping his tail as he waited to be petted, but she couldn't take her eyes off the journal in her hands.

She had glimpsed black marker before the book snapped shut, and opened it back up to see if she had only imagined it.

She hadn't.

And it was in her writing too — although she had no memory whatsoever of writing the entry or of the two words that splashed across the page in bold black marker:

THE TRUTH

For some reason the words scared her. No, they *terrified* her. Her body went weak, rubbery, and she quickly sat down on the floor next to Doc. The Lab sensed her distress and maneuvered his head into her lap as she turned and looked toward the tiny kitchen window. It was so dark. Where were the streetlights? She shivered, feeling colder than she had ever felt in her life — as if a window had suddenly been raised. Her arm felt heavy as she reached for the phone.

Carly took a deep breath and forced herself to focus on the cell phone as she flipped it open, trying her dad's number first. He had told her he would be out of the country for a few days, but she had hoped ... She frowned, terminated the call, and then punched in the number for information.

"City and state, please?" the mechanical voice asked, and Carly exhaled.

"St. Louis, Missouri."

5

New Orleans, Louisiana

Darkness comes and I can't see,
The face staring back at me …

Jonah watched them through the smoky haze that permeated the club as he sang: hands raised in the air … faces, so *many* faces … people smiling, drinking, laughing … lighters and cell phones glowing from the balcony as they swayed along with the song. A heady rush of emotion washed over him. That they were playing on the same old, wood-planked stage that had held music greats like James Brown and Stevie Ray Vaughn was like a dream come true — the first dream in a long time that he *didn't* want to wake up from.

Memories burn in my mind,
Scars and regrets from another time …

A cloud of stage smoke briefly blocked his view and then slowly evaporated to reveal a guy and girl with their arms around each other, staring up at him from the front row. The girl was checking him out big-time. Her boyfriend caught it and flipped him the bird.

Jonah winked at the girl and pressed his lips against the mic.

"Wanna see how far — ?"

The question cracked through his mind, like loud feedback — *his* voice, but different … somehow. He faltered on the chorus, staring dumbly at his mic before looking up to see a little red-haired girl walking past the stage before disappearing into the crowd. He frowned and glanced over to see his bass player looking at him like he'd lost his mind.

He opened his mouth but nothing came out. Kino scowled and hurried to pick up the song where he had left off:
Where is the road that leads me outta here?

Jonah scanned the crowd, only half listening to Kino sing as he felt his gaze unconsciously drawn to a huge guy who stood at the edge of the dance floor. He was at least a head taller than everyone else, with long black hair and a build that said he'd have no problem taking care of himself — but that wasn't what made him appear out of place. Jonah's eyes roamed over the crowd, then back to the man. He was too *still*, for one thing ... like he was waiting for something.

> *Where is the place I can lay my head?*
> *Where is the road that leads me outta here?*

The stranger looked right at Jonah and then raised his eyes to the ceiling. Jonah followed his gaze to the monstrous stage light swinging directly above him in the rafters.

All sound dropped to a crawl, and he heard Kino's voice drag out on the next line ...
Feel ... like ... I'm ... the ... walking ... dead ...

... and everything around him slowed down except for the light, which now swayed back and forth with a frantic pace, each swing gaining momentum. Jonah stood perfectly still, feeling like he was in some kind of weird trance, and calmly watched as the light made another wild arc in the air before snapping from its cords and beginning its rapid descent toward him. The club turned deathly quiet.

Falling, falling ...

"Wanna see how far that rabbit hole really goes?"

Jonah stumbled back at the sound of the voice, hands pressed against his ears as the light crashed down in the exact spot where he had stood, shooting sparks and shards of glass across the stage. Screams erupted from the crowd as cell phone cameras flashed to capture the moment for posterity — or YouTube.

"What the –" Bobby stood up from behind the drums with a wide-eyed, hysterical look on his face, one of his "I'm gonna die before we make it big" looks. For a moment Jonah had the insane urge to laugh. Then he spotted the huge stranger heading for the exit.

He knew that light was going to fall, Jonah thought, his heart pounding wildly. *He knew!* "Hey!" he yelled – or tried to – over the chaos. "Hey, someone get that guy before he gets away!"

Everyone turned and looked at him like he was suddenly speaking in a foreign language. Kino frowned from the other side of the stage, still clutching his bass guitar to his chest like a shield.

Jonah jerked his strap off, deposited his guitar on the stage, and hopped down into the crowd, ready for a fight. *Always ready for a fight,* he thought as he shoved his way through the crowd toward the bouncer at the door.

"Lindsay went to see if you're okay," the bouncer said, referring to the general manager. He jerked a thumb back at the stage. "Man, if that light would've hit you –"

"Which way did he go?" Jonah interrupted, fists clenched at his sides. The bouncer frowned as he finished putting wristbands on a couple who had just walked in.

"Which way did who go?"

"The huge dude who just came by here. Really tall, black hair …"

The couple pushed past Jonah, rubbing the bald-headed bust of Tipitina's famous mascot, Professor Longhair, for luck before disappearing into the crowd.

"Nah." The bouncer shook his head. "No one like that came by me."

"I *watched* him head this way from the stage."

"I'm telling you, no one has left the club since you started your set."

Jonah brushed past the bouncer, shoving the door open and stepping outside to the corner of Tchoupitoulas and Napoleon. Cars whizzed by as he first checked the sidewalk that ran along Tchoupitoulas Street, then glanced back to the darker, tree-lined side of Napoleon. Dark shadows, painted by the streetlights shining through the ancient oak trees, seemed to creep their way toward him. He pivoted back around and caught a movement to his right—same height and buffalo shoulders, same long black hair whipping in the wind as he moved quickly down the sidewalk, away from the club.

Jonah dove across the street, dodging cars as he tried to keep his eye on the stranger.

"Hey, you can't leave," the bouncer called out from the door. "Lindsay'll want you to get checked out, man. Make sure you're okay—for the insurance company!"

But Jonah was already on the other side of the street, trying to catch his breath as he looked around, dumbfounded. The guy had disappeared. Somehow, some way, the stranger had dodged him, and that ticked him off more than the stage light nearly crushing his skull.

"Wanna see how far that rabbit hole really goes?"

A dim kind of terror swept over him at the memory of the words. He pulled a cigarette out and lit it, trying to ignore his shaking hands. He remembered the line. He ought to—it was his line. Funny thing was, he couldn't remember what came after it.

Let it go, it's nothing, he thought. *Just a crazy fluke.* He studied the cigarette between his fingers and frowned. *But what about that stranger? How did he know the light was going to fall—unless someone had rigged it?*

Jonah sighed out a stream of smoke, glanced back at the club, and quickly headed for Rouses' parking lot, where his Bronco was parked. No way was he going back in there to face his band and their questions—not until he had some answers that sounded believable.

But then, what part of his life had ever been believable for most people? Not before ... and not after either.

That was how he thought of his life—in blocks of time he called before and after. He didn't like to think about before too much. After started when he'd rented his apartment, got the band together, and actually started playing some gigs.

But after isn't all it's cracked up to be either, Jonah thought grimly as he slid into the front seat of his truck and hit the auto lock. As a matter of fact, it was starting to look and sound a lot like before. Why was it that every time things looked like they were finally getting better, he ended up sliding back into the black pool of sludge that was his life?

He forced himself to look in the mirror. His pale blue eyes stared back at him fearfully, like ... he was some kind of *stranger.*

Freaking nightmares, and now this ...

A cold chill washed over him, and he looked around the dark parking lot, beginning to hum the old Ozzy song he always hummed when he felt a panic attack coming on.

He thought about calling Sam but decided against it. Sam had spent a good part of his life bailing him out of one thing or another. What he needed to do was learn how to suck it up.

His hands shook a little as he leaned sideways and flipped the glove compartment open, continuing to hum as he searched. His heart began to speed up, slamming against his chest so hard that he wondered how much more of a beating it could take. *Never gonna be as strong as you, Sam,* he thought, finally locating the little plastic bag. *Just don't have what it takes ...* He took a deep breath and leaned back against the seat. He had to try to relax, get his heart to slow down before he ended up in another emergency room, begging them to knock him out with something.

How was that for sucking it up?

He continued humming as he lit the joint, and then inhaled.

His cell phone rang and he jumped, coughing out the stream of smoke as he glanced down at the caller ID. A wave of guilt coursed through him, and he stubbed the joint out and flipped the phone open. He grimaced. *Stupid.* Sam couldn't see what he was doing over the phone.

"Bro?" For a moment there was nothing on the line but silence, and Jonah felt odd, like something was really off. "Sam?"

"It's me," Sam's voice crackled over the line. He sounded breathless, maybe a little ... scared? "How's everything going?"

"Been one weird night here," Jonah breathed out. "How about you?"

"Way past weird. Sorry the reception isn't so great – don't know what the deal is with this phone."

"So what are you up to?"

"I actually just got back from the park."

"*Park?* What were you doing at a park at two in the morning?" He would have pushed it, would've asked Sam if that's where Ken and Barbie went on date night … but he sensed something in his brother's voice that sounded troubled.

"Actually, it was *the* park," Sam said quietly. "Remember where we used to hang out as kids?"

"How could I forget," Jonah said cautiously; it was the one thing he did remember about that night. And neither one of them had been back to that place in seven years. He felt his stomach muscles draw up. What was Sam doing?

"So, what's your schedule like the rest of the month?"

"Clear — no solid gigs lined up until the middle of March. Why?"

"Well," Sam said, clearing his throat, "I just was thinking that maybe it's time we get the old gang back together in St. Louis. Like a reunion or something. Mardi Gras is coming up. You and I could hit Fast Eddie's for some shrimp and then meet them downtown."

Meet up at Mardi Gras? Now Jonah knew for sure there was something really wrong. He also knew his brother well enough to know that Sam wouldn't spell it out for him, so he played along.

"Sure, that might be cool."

"Good," Sam said, sounding relieved. "I'll give them all a call in the morning."

Jonah frowned. "Everyone but J, right?"

Sam was quiet for a moment. "All right."

Jonah felt a little better with that out of the way. He would put up with a lot for Sam's sake — his brother was the one decent thing that he clung to — but he just didn't have it in him when it came to J. Sam could believe J didn't have anything to do with their parents' deaths all he wanted, but he wasn't buying it.

A thought hit him. "You know what's weird about this? I've been thinking about them lately."

"Yeah … me too."

"Well, maybe you're right. Maybe it's time we got together and jawed about the good old days," Jonah said with a grin. He was feeling calmer now.

"The good old days," Sam said with a shaky laugh. "I kind of thought I'd be looking back on the good old days when I was maybe like … ninety." They both laughed, and then Jonah heard Sam take a deep breath.

"Don't get mad, but I gotta say this, okay?"

Jonah opened his mouth and then shut it. Whenever his brother started with "Don't get mad, *but . . . ,*" it usually meant he was going to get mad.

"I know it's going to be a big party," Sam began, "but if you could just lay off the stuff for one night … Is that cool? I mean, we haven't been there since – "

"Yeah, yeah," Jonah muttered as he reached for his lighter.

He had almost told Sam about the nightmares – about the dude at the club and everything that had happened, until Sam ticked him off.

Instead he lit his joint, listening as Sam told him what time they should meet up at the warehouse, and he exhaled instead of arguing, letting the moment pass like those kinds of moments do between brothers.

And then he was alone again.

Jonah flipped the phone closed and tossed it on the seat next to him. He turned and stared out the windshield of his truck. He *had* been thinking about them – he just hadn't told Sam the part about not being able to remember things. Like why the five of them had busted up. He seemed to recall everything going crazy for them at the same time, as though some dark storm had rolled through their lives and scattered them in all directions … Except for him and Sam, and they had just barely managed to stick together. Their parents' murder had been the icing on the cake.

Big, thick icing. The kind that made you want to puke after you swallowed it.

He sighed. Was it any wonder that he smoked a little dope to get through it all – or that he preferred watching reruns on TV Land to reality? He'd had enough reality to last him a lifetime. The fact that he still wanted to write songs and play a few gigs here and there was a pure miracle … if there really was such a thing.

With every tragedy that hit his life, he found it harder to believe that there were miracles, a God – or anything else, for that matter. Maybe he had believed something when he was younger … when hope shined its sunny face on him for one brilliant nanosecond.

Jonah leaned his head back against the seat again and closed his eyes. A reunion ... after all this time. He hoped Sam knew what he was doing, because there was a part of him – a big part – that was pretty sure it wasn't such a good idea.

A hard gust of wind rocked the old Bronco, rattling the windows in their sleeves, and his eyes flew open. Bits of trash and debris skittered across the lot as he sat up and looked around uneasily. That *sound*. He cocked his head to one side and listened to it swirl around him once more. He knew the sound but couldn't name it, like a song he had once known by heart.

Like soft wind chimes or tiny pieces of glass. No, it was *beads* ...

"*Remember* ..."

Jonah turned slowly to the right – where he thought the voice had come from – but before he could raise his hands to shield his eyes from the light, he was back in that night ...

... young again and *scared*, standing in the middle of that dark street as the wind pummeled the five of them so hard that they needed to huddle together for protection.

Jenna was crying like her heart was going to break, and something about the sound made him feel like his heart was going to break too. Only moments before he had been so mad, shouting at the top of his lungs. If only they had left, walked away when things were still good and right ...

Now they couldn't; it was like all five of them were frozen to one spot. He glanced up to the sky, and that's when he saw the eyes – staring right at him, *inches* from his face.

"*Don't worry, you won't be first,*" they mocked. "*We want you to watch* ..."

Jonah let out a groan, covering his eyes like a little kid, and he sensed the past retreating. *What happened to us – what the heck were those things?*

Terror began to rise in him, and he grabbed his cell phone and chucked it so hard against the passenger's side window that it splintered into several pieces before falling onto the seat ... next to his journal.

The same journal he remembered stuffing under his mattress before he headed to his gig at Tipitina's.

His hands were shaking so badly, he could barely pick up the journal off the seat. He located the dome light and flipped it on, startled to find that there was a new entry – one that appeared to have been made in his handwriting, even though he had no memory of writing it.

But that didn't surprise him as much as five words written in black marker that covered the entire page:

UNTIL YOU OPEN YOUR EYES

They followed the restored 1970 Ford Bronco effortlessly as it sped through the streets of the Big Easy, their dark, ever-changing bodies rapidly brushing by and through tourists, through the giant live oaks that had somehow survived Katrina, past the partially renovated buildings and narrow, car-lined streets, until the human abruptly pulled into the lot of a dilapidated old apartment building and killed the truck's lights.

The entities quickly spread across the lot, sharp eyes watching as the human lugged his guitar case inside. Soon lights appeared in one of the upper apartments, and the flashing glow of a TV. Not much later he exited the building, carrying two bags of trash to the dumpster.

They pressed forward, whispering, voices upon voices that pushed at the subject's mind with all of their combined strength, just as they had done with the other four – manipulating emotions, feeding fears that would keep him immobile, *contained.* The human stopped in his tracks and slowly raised his head. A bead of sweat glistened as it ran down the side of his jaw; then he turned and looked directly at them.

They drew back, stunned.

One of the beings rushed him, making a wild dive to enter the human, but only a faint breeze rippled over him, briefly illuminating the dark hair that fluttered back – eyes widening, blindly searching the dark as an invisible barrier sent the creature careening backward.

His eyes, they thought in unison.

The collective shot forward, just inches from the human's face, studying the pale blue eyes that still bore the layers of

half-moon-shaped scales they had implanted seven years ago ...
except for one tiny, hairline slit.

A ripple of fear moved through their ranks as the implications of what was happening settled in. Another memory block
had been compromised.

But if they could keep the five in the dark for one more week,
the world would be theirs.

6

St. Louis, Missouri

TJ Levine frowned as he scrolled through the satellite imagery of the strange weather patterns developing across the country. He had never seen activity like it before: jet-stream-like winds pouring into parts of the West, South, and Southeast in long cloud formations that snaked and curved along until stopping to hang suspended over a particular city ... almost like they had a mind of their own.

He clicked on the next screen, leaning in to study the fourth system moving from Chicago toward St. Louis, and then jumped as the phone rang, displaying "PRIVATE" on his modified cell phone's caller ID. By the second ring, his de-scrambler had stripped away the block, replacing it with "US GOVT", and his eyes widened in surprise.

"You gotta be *kidding* me," he whispered, quickly terminating the satellite connection. There was only one reason why the feds would be calling him: the access given by the Resistance's contact at the National Geospatial Intelligence Agency had been discovered.

He was busted.

The phone stopped ringing, bypassed his voicemail, and started ringing again.

TJ pushed his glasses to the top of this head and threw an uneasy glance around the mobile headquarters he'd hidden away inside his old VW Bus. At twenty-seven, he already held a PhD in theoretical physics from MIT, had a master's in archeology and ancient languages, and knew enough about computers and electrical engineering to make him dangerous, but he evidently hadn't yet mastered the fine art of avoiding trouble.

His eyes dropped to the panic button hidden beneath his desk. Once the button was hit, there would be no turning back. The thermite charges he had installed would crank up to two and a half thousand degrees Celsius, turning his hard drives into a pool of molten metal within seconds, destroying all data – *everything* he had been compiling over the past year.

"A little help here?" he said, glancing to the ceiling. He took a deep breath and flipped on the voice changer, answering the call with a mechanical "Hello?"

"TJ?" There was a faint electrical crackle over the line, a pause, then, "Come on, Toshi; I've got something you're going to want to hear."

TJ exhaled; there was only one person besides his mother who called him that, and that was only because they had been best friends since junior high. He grinned and switched off the voice changer.

"You know, you almost gave me a heart attack, calling me on that line."

Chris Chambers laughed. "I only called you on this line because their sat phones are the only ones working around here. Our equipment has been malfunctioning all day long."

"And you didn't leave a message because ...?" TJ interjected as he flipped his glasses back down. He logged back into the NGIA's GEOINT site again, directing the satellite on a sweep of the Arch grounds, where Chris was working with the Corps of Engineers.

"*Because* I knew if I called back enough, you'd answer. What's with the drama?"

"I'm Japanese and Jewish; my DNA is permanently wired for drama." He glanced back to the screen. "Man, a lot of GI Joes hanging around," he murmured, zooming in. "Please tell me that is not your truck with the 'I heart Yorkies' sticker on it – new girlfriend?"

"I *hate* when you do that! Aren't you hippie types supposed to be against invasion of privacy?"

"Who said I was a hippie?"

"Ponytail, John Lennon glasses, VW Bus. It all screams hippie."

TJ grinned and picked up the sub sandwich on his desk. "So tell me what you've done that has the feds sniffing around a bunch of engineers testing the flood protection system."

"It's not what we were doing – it's what we found."

"Yeah?" TJ took a bite out of his sub.

"We were doing a stress test this morning at one of the reflecting pools near the Arch when we hit this sinkhole. I thought at first maybe a sewage pipe had burst … but then we sent lights down to inspect the damage, and the hole just kept going …"

"What do you mean, kept going?" TJ asked around a mouthful of sandwich.

"I mean over thirty-two feet of sloping incline – with *carved* steps in it."

TJ dropped the sub on his desk. "You're joking, right?"

"Dead serious! We lit it up the rest of the way and found what they say is some kind of ancient structure buried underneath the Arch …"

TJ's heart began to pick up speed. He glanced at the monitor and saw three men in dark camouflage setting up a huge white tent next to one of the legs of the Arch. Two more men appeared and attached a long white tube at the entrance of the tent. *No way is this a coincidence,* he thought uneasily, *not with all of the activity going on …*

"I don't even know how to describe half the stuff I saw," Chris said, "but it *felt* ancient."

TJ's eyes shifted to the file on his desk. The fact that they found something didn't shock him – the entire area had been on the radar of the archeological community since the discovery of the star observatory under an ancient mound in East St. Louis. It was how fast the site had been had been seized that had him worried. And *why …*

"What they called a ceremonial platform had to cover at least a half acre, and there were two huge stone pillars, one on either side of the staircase," Chris continued in an odd, breathless kind of voice.

"Chris."

"I don't know if it was a gas pocket that made us all sick or what –"

"*Chris!* Did any of the Corps' archeologists check it out?"

"Never had the chance. Their archeologist was down there before they had yanked us all out. "

Their archeologist...

An eighteen-wheeler appeared on screen, slowly backing up to the front of the tube, followed by a sleek-looking black sedan that parked next to the cab of the semi. *The Alliance...* It had their mark all over it, and that meant that whatever was down there would soon be loaded into the back of the semi and off to destinations unknown.

"I guess there's no way you can sneak me down there tonight?"

"Are you kidding? *I* can't even get in there – they've got it guarded tighter than the Pentagon. *But...* I did get a picture for you."

"What?" TJ barked out a surprised laugh. "How did you pull that off?"

"I was only able to get one shot off when I heard the engineer they pulled out ahead of me yelling that he wanted his wallet and cell phone back," Chris said, clearing his throat. "Thought it might be a good time to tuck my memory card into my shoe."

"Where's the card now?

"In this sat phone." Chris laughed softly. "Better tell me where to send this picture before they realize I borrowed it."

"You are one crazy brother, has anyone told you that lately?" TJ said, typing. "Okay, go to File Den and login with IM, password Toshi2009. As soon as the download's complete, I'll erase the account."

"Picture is on its way. You know what's weird?"

"There's more?"

"I think whoever is running this already knew what was down there. I think they already had plans to get it out too – no way could they put an operation like this together in less than an hour after getting the news."

It was the Alliance, all right ... TJ glanced to the monitor again just as two plainclothes men exited the semi and were met around the back by two more men in suits. Alarm swirled in the pit of his stomach. "Chris, I want you to wipe the phone clean and dump it ASAP. Can you get out of there without anyone noticing you?"

"They're holding us in the Arch museum, but I don't think we're in any danger right now. They want us to do seismic testing on the grounds in the morning." Chris cleared his throat again. "One more thing before I toss this phone: Those stone pillars I mentioned? The one I wasn't able to take a picture of has writing on it that supposedly predicts an event that will take place on the twenty-fourth of this month ..."

TJ's eyes dropped to his desk pad calendar. The twenty-fourth fell during Mardi Gras in St. Louis – but what did that have to do with what was going on? *"Fat Tuesday?"*

"I mean, to hear *that* date being read off some kind of ancient – fat what?"

"You know, Fat Tuesday ... *Mardi Gras.*"

"That's strange ..." Chris fell silent, and in the silence TJ heard the sound of muffled voices. He thought he heard someone say Chris's name. "Hey, someone's here, so I better run," Chris whispered in a rush. "I'll be back in touch as soon as I can – try to get some more pics for you too."

"Be care – "

The phone went dead.

TJ hit the desk with his fist and flipped the speaker off. On the monitor, a flatbed truck carrying a large hoist rolled into view. A group of men streamed forth out of nowhere, one directing the truck to the front of the tent while the others began to scurry into the tube like worker ants hurrying before winter set in. But why the rush if they already had full control of the site?

Unless they were actually following that date ...

Keeping the live feed of the Arch grounds going, he pulled the file Chris had sent up on the monitor to his right. A cold rush of adrenaline shot through him as the image took shape. It wasn't just one of the largest stone stelae he had ever seen – it was the *proof* he had been searching for. He grabbed his voice-activated recorder and clicked it on to document observations he planned to attach to the picture and forward to members of the Resistance.

"February eighteenth: Subject picture attached. The good news is that I guess I'm not nearly as crazy as I look after all. The bad: the Alliance is already all over this, so this picture may be our only window into why they've been in a rush to get into St. Louis. According to my source, they believe that these stelae predict a future event – future as in the *twenty-fourth* of this month – so we need to hold a powwow ... like yesterday."

He leaned forward. "Okay … judging by what little I can see of the structure behind it, this freestanding stone stela is approximately twenty-six feet high by eight-and-a-half feet wide, one of a pair that was found beneath the grounds of the St. Louis Arch. Composition appears to be limestone, style very similar to those produced by Mesoamerican or Mayan artisans that recorded their ruler's victory over an enemy …"

TJ frowned, enlarged the picture on his screen, and continued.

"These glyphs are definitely not the norm." He shook his head as he scanned the top of the stone. "Instead of the image you usually find of a man in a plumed, birdlike mask to represent the sky world or heavens, we have a *blank* band at the top … almost as if it's purposely been left out." His mouth went dry. "A single bolt of lightning slashes downward to a crescent moon, tipped over on its side and suspended over what appears to be an eight-spoke wheel. The wheel symbol is widely recognized in ancient glyphs as a star gate – *or doorway* – in which gods traveled between dimensions …"

Could this be it? he wondered incredulously. *The leaders of the Resistance suspected that something big was getting ready to go down … but could it be …*

His hands shook a little as he dragged the image slightly to the left.

"To the right, a large grouping of people stand with their backs to the star gate, facing us. Under their feet, we see the image of a crouched, snakelike man that greatly resembles the Vision Serpent, symbolizing the passage of their gods of the underworld into our world. The tail of the serpent is different – greatly exaggerated in size and wrapped … around the ankles of the people …"

TJ hesitated.

His eyes moved slowly over the star gate and then stopped. He enlarged the picture again and saw for the first time the faint markings of a river that ran in front of the star gate. His gaze moved from the position of the river to the star gate and back again. If he didn't know better, it looked to be in the exact position of the –

He glanced at the strange crescent moon shape over the star gate. It wasn't a crescent moon – it was an *arch*. A chill slid down his spine as the full name of the monument rose in his mind.

"The *Gateway* Arch," TJ said softly. "I think we found our point of entry, gentlemen – and this one is on *public* land."

Rising 630 feet above the skyline of St. Louis, taller than the Statue of Liberty or the Washington Monument, second to only the Eiffel Tower in size, the architectural anomaly had taken only a little over two years to build ... and all without a single loss of life. He remembered seeing the old film clips of the construction workers confidently walking the stainless steel girders like circus performers without a net. As though they somehow sensed something was keeping them safe, making sure that the construction would go uninterrupted.

A hidden gateway between dimensions ...

It had been his love of theology and physics that started him on this journey that opened his mind to the possibility that the supernatural realm in the Scriptures and the eleventh dimension that had the scientific community buzzing could be one and the same. When he uncovered the interlocking grid matrix that connected the ancient mound sites across the U.S., his gut feeling from the beginning was that they were entry points. Much like the pyramid temple systems across the world. But the Alliance had always been one step ahead of them, buying up the land where the sites were located and posting their quasi-military forces to guard against intruders ...

Until St. Louis.

He opened the file on his desk and began to lay out in front of him the documents he had compiled: an old tintype photo taken in the early 1800s of a crowd dressed in their Sunday best, standing on top of a huge mound near the river, one of over a hundred and twenty such mounds located in the area, all of which would be leveled to make way for the city of St. Louis (or *Mound City*, as it was called by the first settlers); a brittle newspaper clipping boasting the archeological sketch of the earthen pyramid discovered beneath that mound, estimated to span five football fields; and finally, present-day photos of the mass grave recently discovered beneath a newly demolished parking lot just north of the Arch, filled with bodies covered by conch shells decorated with weeping eyes and flying, winged human figures. Conch shells from the Gulf of Mexico.

The ancient culture that once dominated the region hadn't mysteriously disappeared – they were exterminated once they were no longer of use.

Mayan travelers, he theorized, had been visited by what they called *star gods*, who taught them feats of astronomy and archeology beyond their wildest imagination, and then sent them forth to locate and establish star gates for the return of these beings. When that was accomplished, their final mission – one that would supposedly make them like gods themselves – was the mass sacrifice of their own people.

How many times had these beings used humans to do their dirty work, the destruction of their own race? He looked up in time to see the trucks pulling away from the Arch grounds and scowled. *Too many times to count.*

The Alliance was just the new kids chosen to help finish an old plan.

"So what is it about the twenty-fourth?" TJ wondered out loud, causing his recorder to begin rolling again. He tapped his pen against the calendar on his desk, his mind racing through what little he knew about Mardi Gras: pagan in origin, the circus-like celebration had evolved into a kind of letting-off-steam party before the forty days of fasting and prayer of Lent … and St. Louisians loved to let off steam. He stared hard at the dates for what felt like forever. Then it hit him.

"Wait: Fat Tuesday is the *final* day … the last call on a three-day party that's … attended by *thousands* of people."

TJ lifted his gaze to the picture of the stela, to the group who stood with their backs to the star gate, and a heavy feeling of foreboding settled in around him. *They're positioned that way for a reason,* he thought. *Like someone was saying that they wouldn't see what was coming …*

"Classic battle strategy, ripped right out of Jeremiah fifty-one," he said with a sick, sinking feeling in the pit of his stomach. "Attack the city while the enemy is gathered in one place for a celebration. That way they'll be distracted, too wasted to think straight … or fight back."

TJ slid his chair in and began typing, pulling up the screen captures he had saved of the strange weather patterns in other parts of the country.

There was no doubt in his mind that they were connected to what was going on in St. Louis. He just wished he knew how. His gut told him that once that was figured out, they would be a step ahead of the game — *if* they could find the answers in time. He quickly copied the screens, attached them and the electronic recording of his observations to the file made for the Resistance, then typed in the coded sequence and hit send.

It's really happening, he thought, leaning back in his chair heavily. *Just as the prophecy said it would...*

A burst of wind rocked the bus, and he glanced nervously at the old Hebrew script he had painstakingly printed above every window and door.

TJ picked up his phone and quickly punched the number in for two men who, unfortunately, were halfway around the world at the moment. His text was short:

Review file ASAP. We have to find the five before they do. The fate of the world is in their hands. It's beginning.

He flipped the phone shut and closed his eyes. By all accounts, they would soon be confronted by a race of beings that would use any means necessary to see their agenda accomplished.

God help anyone who stood in their way...

7

February 22 | Las Vegas

The fog had rolled in during the night, a rarity in Vegas, but even rarer was that it lingered on into the next day, at one point shifting from the north end of town to the south with such speed that it caused an eight-car pileup on the Strip. It took thirty minutes to clear – *thirty minutes* – and every talk radio DJ in town launched into yet another gripe session on driving in Vegas.

Jenna slapped her license down on the counter in front of the clerk, dropped her carry-on at her feet, and bent over to catch her breath. Sweat trickled down her back as the voice on the loudspeaker welcomed them for what felt like the fiftieth time to McCarran International Airport. She raised her head and watched the Southwest Airlines logo swim out of focus behind the clerk. *Just hang on a little longer,* she thought, squeezing her eyes shut. *As soon as you get on the plane, you'll be able to sleep – just get on that plane!*

"Wow, you cut it close," the clerk noted cheerfully. She tapped a few keys on the computer. "The good news is, the fog moved out about ten minutes ago, so they just started boarding."

"I think you can let go of my hand now, Delores."

Jenna glanced sideways as Mikey spoke. Her boss's pretty face was slightly flushed, her short dark hair all askew, as she held his hand in the death grip that had started when Delores's car broke down in the middle of the gridlock on the Strip and had lasted through the wild cab ride, the out-of-service tram, and on to their mad dash through the terminal. If it hadn't been for Delores, they would have never made it. That she had been brought in only two short weeks ago to run the diner where Jenna worked made it even more amazing. They shared an exhausted smile and looked down at Mikey.

"What?" Mikey said with a shrug as he glanced between the two of them. "I got it covered now."

"Your lips to God's ears, handsome," Delores said, making a sign of the cross before smoothing over the wrinkles in her purple jumpsuit. Mikey smiled shyly. At fifty-three, the ex-showgirl was still tongue-tying men, and he was no exception.

"Flight 1252, nonstop to St. Louis." The clerk smiled and handed Jenna their boarding passes. "You'll have to make your good-byes quick."

Jenna sent a quick text to Carly, picked up her carry-on, handed Mikey his backpack, and then hesitated right before they reached the gate. She suddenly felt scared and overwhelmed, like she was standing at the edge of some unknown ... *thing* ... that was bigger than she could handle. She glanced at Delores. The older woman seemed to sense what she was feeling and leaned over and hugged her tight.

"You're going to be fine."

"Thank you so much," Jenna whispered, tearing up a little as she returned the hug. "For everything. I just wish we'd met sooner — "

"Me too, honey. But you *have* to do this. I can feel it all the way down to my frosted-pink toenails."

Jenna nodded. "I feel it too."

"You guys are kind of squishing me."

Delores grinned and hugged Mikey against her leg. "And where am I going to find a sidekick as handsome as you to ride in my car?"

"I don't know," Mikey said earnestly. "Maybe I can come back for a visit, if you really need me."

"Another admirer?" Jenna shook her head as Mikey grabbed her by the hand and tugged her along. He was looking at the gate like he was worried it might disappear at any moment.

"It's just smoke and mirrors," Delores said wryly. "You'll never take the show out of this pony, though; I'll be nipping and tucking all the way to the glue factory."

In spite of the grin, Jenna saw a sadness in Delores's eyes as she watched the last of the passengers trickle through the gate ahead of them.

"Find out who you are," Delores said, impulsively hugging her one last time. She dropped her voice down to a whisper. "But be careful. What's going on isn't ... natural. I have never seen the odds stacked against someone like they were for you today – almost like something is trying to keep you from going home. Must be something real important for you on the other side of all the trouble ..."

Jenna and Mikey watched their lift-off from McCarran with a mixture of relief and apprehension, like two prisoners afraid that their get-out-of-jail-free card might be taken away at any moment. Jenna unconsciously squeezed the armrests of her seat as the plane rose above the Strip and over the black Luxor Pyramid, its high-powered laser beam shooting up through the overcast sky with such intensity that it created a strange, misty gray shroud that hung over the city. A loud thump resounded as the landing gear retracted back into the plane, and she relaxed her grip a little.

"Spence Jacobi says the guys on the ISS can see the Luxor beam from space," Mikey said as he leaned against her. His warmth felt good.

"ISS?" Her eyes climbed with the light through the sky, and she saw more fog slide in. An odd fluttering noise filled her ears, and she yawned a couple of times, trying to relieve the pressure. The sound only got louder.

"International Space Station," Mikey said in a strange, muffled little voice.

The fluttering sound stopped.

Jenna started to turn back to Mikey but saw something dark and startlingly fast cutting through the Luxor's beam before darting into the bank of fog. She scanned the sky uneasily, hoping to catch another glimpse, but the plane was already banking away from Vegas, the dull glitter of supersized hotels and casinos fading off into the distance.

They both uttered a loud sigh of relief.

"Pretty good escape, huh?" Mikey said, sounding more like his old self.

"*Amazing* escape," she said, turning to see him grinning up at her like he had just rescued her from a fire-breathing dragon. She felt her heart skip a beat. The dark circles under his eyes seemed to stand out even more with the overhead light shining on him, and she wanted to kick herself for not noticing it before.

The night before, she had caught him faking sleep — while she was faking sleep — and both of them had opened their eyes to see each other at the same time. They had laughed when it happened, and she'd chalked it up to the excitement over their trip to St. Louis. But now she wondered if it was more than that ...

A tone sounded, and the Unfasten Seat Belt sign flashed above their heads.

Mikey pulled his coloring pad and crayons out of his backpack, gave her a small smile, and then turned his attention to his next drawing.

He had been the one to convince her to call her old friends, shaking her awake one morning with a look of rabid determination on his little face as he held out the photo of the five of them in his hand: *"I think you should call these guys, Mom."* She had only listened out of an amused kind of politeness at first, but the more she stared at the picture in his hand, the more she realized she wanted — no, *needed* — to talk to them. After living through another week of never-ending nightmares, she had run out of ideas on how to survive on her own.

That Jonah, Sam, Carly, and J were all experiencing the exact same things was crazy enough. That they had been trying to reach her — had *tickets* waiting for her and Mikey at the airport — was way more than she had ever hoped for. Almost like a miracle ... and it scared her and awed her at the same time.

St. Louis wasn't just her last hope; it was the last hope for all of them now, it seemed. There was something important about their past, something that happened during the Mardi Gras seven years ago that was drawing them all home. Like a great hand arranging the pieces of a puzzle together again. But what? What could have possibly happened to make them all forget so much of their childhood?

"Find out who you are ..."

She pulled their old picture out of her purse and stared hard at it, just as she had done over the past couple of days, and got the same results. She sighed. If she could just remember *something*, it might help her get rid of her guilt. It had been her idea to sneak off to the Mardi Gras celebration that night—that much she knew for sure now.

Jenna glanced up, sensing someone's eyes on her, and turned to see the businessman on the other side of Mikey staring at her. Her cheeks flushed under his scrutiny. His gaze moved from her to Mikey, taking in the clean but slightly frayed jacket she had picked for him to wear on the trip. Mikey continued to draw, oblivious. The man met her gaze again and smiled sympathetically.

She leaned back against her seat and closed her eyes, trying to allow the dull roar of the plane's engines to lull her. She had never been great with the pity deal. It made her feel even more aware of the fact that she didn't fit in, didn't quite measure up in people's eyes. Tony had given her the pity look when he left, and that had killed her worse than his leaving. Jenna sighed.

Maybe things would change when she got back to St. Louis.

"Come on home," Sam had told her over the phone, his voice sounding tired but so good. "You shouldn't be by yourself with all of this going on—none of us should."

"That's right, Shades," Jonah added on the three-way. "We were always stronger together, remember?" Jenna smiled a little. She hadn't even remembered the nickname until he said it. But as soon as he did, the memory of her looking at herself in the mirror with those awful, oversized glasses her parents made her wear—the kind that turned dark in the sun—came rushing back. The kids at school had made fun of her, calling her granny, but Jonah had turned it around in no time.

Shades had made her sound almost cool.

Boys like Sam and Jonah were rare. Men like them were pretty much *extinct.*

A low rumble shook the plane, and her eyes startled open to find Mikey staring up at her with a look of dread. He was clutching his black crayon so hard, it looked like it was ready to snap in two.

"It's just a little turbulence," Jenna told him, ruffling his hair. A crackle of feedback came over the plane's intercom, and they both glanced up.

"Nothing to worry about, folks; we're just experiencing some mountain wave turbulence generated by the jet stream winds this time of year," the pilot reassured them. "We'll be landing in St. Louis as scheduled."

"See?" Jenna smiled.

Mikey studied her for a moment with an odd, troubled look in his eyes and then lowered his head and began to draw in his tablet again. His silence made her nervous.

"Mikey?" Another roll of turbulence hit, and she frowned and turned to look out the window. *What is with* — Her blood turned to ice as she saw something large and dark flash by her. She froze, unable to take her eyes off the window, unable to *move.* Whatever it was looked like it went right through the side of the plane!

Jenna started shivering and felt herself being drawn back to that night at Mardi Gras, standing in the street with her best friends, feeling the dark getting even darker. *They're coming for us ...*

"Mom?"

More turbulence. Why couldn't she move? The sound of the plane's engine slowed down, almost as if it were losing power, and she felt herself being lifted off her seat. A few passengers gasped. Rows up, a baby started to cry. A strange odor filled the cabin, causing her eyes to tear up a little.

"Mom!"

Jenna jerked around, forced out of her frozen state by the fear in Mikey's voice, but his back was turned to her. He appeared to be whispering something urgent to the businessman. She leaned forward and was shocked to see that the man was leaning sideways, clutching his chest. His eyes were glassy, only half open.

A bolt of panic had her on her feet and punching the button above her head before she had time to think. "Hey, somebody! This man needs help!"

Turbulence rocked the plane once more, and she saw the man's face turn a horrible shade of gray. She hit the button again even as two flight attendants rushed down the aisle toward them, both blonde, their tanned faces drained pale by this new development.

She glanced back; the businessman's eyes were closed now. Mikey was holding his hand, and as she stared down at them, an odd sensation came over her. Something more was happening—more than what she was seeing. She didn't understand it, but she felt it, like a swelling darkness getting ready to burst free.

A third attendant, a young redheaded man who looked like he just came from a pep squad meeting, cleared his throat nervously before he picked up the mic: "If there is a doctor or nurse on board, we need your immediate assistance ... uh, *immediately.*" His eyes skimmed hopefully over the rows of seats. A few people stood and looked around.

"If you aren't in the medical field, please remain seated. The captain will have us through this turbulence shortly, but you must remain seated—for your safety as well as that of the gentleman who needs our immediate attention."

More passengers craned their necks like motorists looking at an accident; faces already tight with tension became grim masks of morbid curiosity as people watched the businessman being lowered to the floor in the aisle. *No, this is all wrong!* Jenna thought, watching an attendant with short bobbed hair loosen the man's tie. *This shouldn't be happening!* She inhaled and exhaled slowly, trying to calm herself ... and wrinkled her nose.

That smell; something is burning!

"Honey, are you okay?" The attendant who had been loosening the man's tie was studying her with a look of concern. Mikey looked over his shoulder, and she saw panic spring up in his eyes.

Didn't anyone else smell it?

Jenna took another deep breath. "I'm okay, really," she said, forcing a smile. A young guy, maybe fourteen or fifteen years old, stood up across the aisle, popped the top off his can of Mountain Dew, and guzzled it as he watched them.

"Everything's under control," a second attendant, with long hair and even longer nails, explained in a voice meant to calm her. "The captain is getting in touch with dispatch now. They'll patch them through to a doctor. If we can't get him stable here, we'll have to—"

Please don't say we're going back to Vegas, Jenna thought, hating herself for being selfish, but unable to stop the overwhelming desperation that rose in her. *Please don't ...*

" – turn back for Vegas."

Jenna felt the floor drop out from under her. Mikey's bottom lip trembled. He climbed over the armrest and into her lap.

"Excuse me," a voice announced abruptly.

All heads turned to see a well-dressed African-American man walking briskly down the aisle. He was tall with short hair and … Jenna frowned as one of the attendants stood, blocking her view. There was something familiar about him, commanding almost. She suddenly realized why he seemed familiar; it was the way her dad acted when he was in the military.

With his back to them, the man knelt and checked the businessman's pulse. He lifted an eyelid back and shined a penlight in it, then pulled his wallet from the inside of his sports jacket and handed it to one of the flight attendants. "My physician's identification. Med Link will be able to vouch for me – if you could inform your captain." To the other attendant he said, "If you have a defibrillator on board, please bring it to me as quickly as possible." They both hurried off toward the front of the plane.

The doctor leaned over the businessman once more and gently placed his hand against the man's chest.

What is he –

Jenna's heart skipped as the businessman's eyes started to flutter open. She stared at the doctor in disbelief, then shifted her gaze back to the man as he raised his arms slightly, trying to sit up.

"The defibrillator," the short-haired attendant announced breathlessly, appearing next to the doctor. "This crazy turbulence … Pam twisted her ankle."

As if on cue, turbulence shook the plane once more. The doctor stood.

"He has a heart condition, but it appears to have stabilized for now. If you could keep an eye on him, I will return shortly."

"Sure …" The flight attendant quickly took the doctor's place, kneeling next to the businessman.

Nodding, the doctor headed toward the cockpit of the plane just as another roll of turbulence hit, so hard this time that it popped some of the overhead bins open. More passengers raised their voices in alarm. An older woman cried out somewhere behind them, something that sounded like a cross between a bark and a scream, and Mikey hid his face in Jenna's shirt. The doctor continued down the aisle, unfazed by the turbulence, glancing toward the windows on his left as he walked. He calmly closed the bins, turned to his right, and made his way toward the lavatory. Jenna's vision blurred, and for a crazy second his image distorted, becoming longer, almost gigantic in proportion.

What's happening to me? she thought, terrified. She blinked and rubbed her eyes hard. Blinked again. Her sight cleared just as he shut the door behind him.

The plane wobbled in the air, and she wrapped her arms around Mikey, wondering dejectedly how so many things could go so wrong in one day.

A hard jolt hit the plane, almost as if it had been struck by something, and she cried out along with the other passengers. She hurriedly deposited Mikey back into his seat and belted him in just as the cabin began to shake violently, rattling the oxygen masks out of their hiding places. More cries of alarm, lights flashing erratically for passengers to return to their seats. Jenna pulled Mikey against her side as she peered fearfully out the window. She hadn't been to church in years, but all of a sudden she got religion, praying fervently, a jumbled mix of *Our Father* and *Yea, though I walk through the valley of the shadow of death...*

"Please remain calm," the flight attendant called out shakily as she remained crouched next to the businessman. "Please remain calm!"

The plane shook and tipped to the left, and Jenna and Mikey both let out a terrified scream as two dark masses burst by her window. Another much larger form exploded by and then... silence.

The silence was so deep that Jenna wondered if the other passengers had passed out — or worse, *died* — but as she looked around, she noticed they were just in a kind of zombie-like state of shock.

Something changed in the air. It felt cleaner maybe — definitely lighter — as though a heavy weight had been lifted, and she turned and hugged Mikey tight. They felt the plane right itself again, flying smoothly through the sky as if nothing had ever happened.

"Looks like the worst of the turbulence is over, folks," the captain announced over the intercom. "We are a little behind on our arrival, but it shouldn't run over ten, maybe fifteen minutes at most."

"So we're not turning back?" Jenna said, turning to the flight attendant, who was covering the businessman with another blanket. The attendant's top lip glistened with sweat as she glanced up and gave Jenna a bewildered smile.

"Doesn't look that way," she said, positioning the business-man's arms on the outside of the blanket. He gave her a confused smile, and she patted his hand.

"Everything is going to be okay, Mom," Mikey said softly.

"I'm telling you, man, he went in but he never came out!" a petulant voice insisted loudly, and they all turned to see the kid with the Mountain Dew standing in front of the lavatory, shifting from foot to foot with the pained expression on his face as the redheaded — *red-faced* — flight attendant slid a screwdriver into the Occupied sign. He flipped it to Vacant and cautiously opened the door to reveal an empty stall.

That's crazy, Jenna thought. She had seen the doctor go in the lavatory with her own eyes.

"What's going on isn't ... natural," Delores's voice whispered through her mind, and she shivered again, looking bleakly around the plane as if the answers had to be there ... somewhere. Her thoughts ran in a hundred different directions, to a hundred different possibilities ... but none of them made any sense.

"Everything's okay now, Mom," Mikey said again, firmer this time. Like if he said it enough, said it strongly enough, it might actually come true.

In the tongue of the ancients they were called MazziKim, but they had other names throughout their history: half-breeds, no-bodies, tricksters ...

From inside its host, the creature listened to the multilay-ered voices of the collective with mounting worry. Things were not going well in the West — which made its mission even more crucial. It turned back and watched the monk heading toward the old St. Louis monastery.

Just a few more steps.

It worked the bird's wings once more, fluttering them noisily, and glanced down at the small cat that was creeping its way up the tree. The cat paused only inches away, eyes widening in shock as the MazziKim exited the bird. It dove inside the animal without warning, a red haze of feline muscles and internal organs momentarily blinding it as the cat howled and retracted its claws from the side of the tree.

The young monk turned and looked just as it hit the ground in its new host's body.

Perfect. It limped toward the unsuspecting monk, manipulating the cat's vocal chords into a pitiful mewl.

"I've been looking for you everywhere!" the monk declared as he squatted and scratched the cat's head.

It mewled again and held up its injured paw; eons of deceiving humans at its disposal.

"Come on, little fella, let's get you inside," the monk said.

The MazziKim smiled inwardly as it was scooped up into the monk's arms and carried through the gate. *"Do not relent this night, brothers,"* it spoke through the collective. *"Our time of wandering will be over soon."*

8

Atlanta, Georgia | En route to St. Louis

C arly shifted gears in her Jeep and peered up at the darkening
sky as she inched forward in the rush-hour traffic.

"Shoulda got away sooner, Doc," she murmured to the
Labrador as he lay sprawled across the backseat. She would've been
way ahead of the rush hour *and* the storm that looked to be heading
their way if she hadn't been too scared to step outside her own
stinking apartment. If Jonah hadn't called, she might still be there,
going over and over the image on the security tape the detective had
showed her. How could the steel handle of the door just twist off
and no one be on tape doing the twisting? Her eyes roamed across
the five lanes of traffic, the bare, grassless median, the huge sound
barriers between the houses and the road, and then she felt her gaze
being drawn skyward again.

The clouds *were* strange – foggy gray but thick, with a dark
underbelly that formed a kind of winding trail through midtown
Atlanta before coming to hang low over the northbound side of I-75.
Really low.

"Come on," she whispered under her breath, forcing herself to
loosen her grip on the steering wheel as she looked around. "You see
anyone else tripping?"

Ever since talking to Sam and Jonah, she had felt there was at
least some light at the end of the tunnel. Just knowing they were all
sharing the same "freak fest," as Jonah put it, was enough for her to
make the eighteen-hour drive to St. Louis.

As much as she hated to admit it, she knew she couldn't handle it
alone anymore.

"Ever feel like you've become a stranger in your own life, Carly?"

She had almost laughed at Jonah when he asked her that over the phone – and almost came back with some smart-aleck reply, but the truth of it had hit her so strongly that it had taken a minute before she could even answer him. When she finally did find her voice again, they had talked for hours. And talking to him had been so *easy*, like they had only been apart seven minutes instead of seven years. She wondered if he felt the same way ... wondered if he was curious to know what she looked like now too.

Carly glanced in the rearview mirror, noting the dark purple smudges underneath her eyes, and held her thermos of Joffrey's coffee up in a mock toast before taking a sip. A large drop of rain splashed against the windshield, then another drop, and then with no further warning came the downpour.

"Perfect," Carly muttered. Doc chuffed as if he agreed with her, and settled back on his blanket for a nap. She flipped her wipers on and tried to see the sky, but the heavy rain blocked her view.

Just like that night. Looking up and seeing nothing but that wall of ... She swallowed hard, struggling with the sudden memory. The memories were coming more often, but only in brief flashes that cut off before she could figure out what she was seeing. She peered up at the rainy sky again and shivered.

"Papa's Got a Brand-New Bag" blared from her cell phone, and she eagerly reached over and hit *speaker*.

"Hey, Dad."

"Just got your message," her dad said warmly. "Promise me you'll check the weather before you go – reports are saying there's a nasty storm moving up from the coast."

"It's already here."

"You're *driving* in it? Where are you?"

"Just north of Atlanta now," Carly said with a laugh, relaxing a little in spite of the alarm in his voice. She felt a little more human, more connected to the real world, with her dad on the phone. "Weren't you the one who said that storms were the only things that could hold my attention for more than two minutes?"

"Your mom was the one who said that, but I guess not much has changed."

Carly gripped the steering wheel a little tighter.

"Carly?"

"Why do you even give her credit?" she blurted out finally. She didn't have to look in the mirror to know her cheeks were flushed. He was so *blind* when it came to her mom, forgiving her because, after all, that's what *God* said to do. She loved her dad, felt sorry for him, but wanted to seriously choke him for forgiving her mom so easily. It was his only flaw as far as she could see, but the truth was, she was mad at herself more than anything. As soon as the words were out of her mouth, she remembered that her mom *had* said that. Why she was thinking about that woman so much lately was a mystery, not to mention a big pain in the —

"Come on, Carly."

Is it because anything and everything that could possibly go wrong lately has gone wrong, and it might be nice to have a mother who actually cared?

Doc whined, as if sensing her distress, and pushed his big head between the seats, nudging her arm with his nose.

"All right, all right," she said with a sigh. "So where are you this time?"

"Retired Chaplain's Breakfast in London. We plan to fly back tomorrow night if all goes well."

"Because ... there is always a chance that you or one of your preacher friends might do something really *wild* and end up on the BBC News?"

He laughed and then cleared his throat.

"You know ... you're going to have to forgive her one of these days, honey."

"One of these days."

"So, is there ... something else you want to talk about?"

"What do you mean?"

"This sudden trip to St. Louis. It's great that the old gang is getting back together — I'd love to see them all myself — but it just seems to have come out of the blue ..."

"We're *nineteen*," she said, sidestepping the question. "Random spur-of-the-moment decisions kind of come with the territory."

"Maybe ..."

"What? If there's a problem with Jenna and me staying at your place, we can always get a room." Carly smiled to herself, waiting.

"Don't be ridiculous!" her dad sputtered. "I left house keys under the mat. I just wondered if there was something else that you're not telling me." The rain patters on the roof of her soft top began to increase in intensity. She glanced up at the odd fluttering sound.

"What about your job?" her father asked.

Carly hesitated. She actually hated leaving her job. The little mom-and-pop store where she designed jewelry had been one of the few places where she felt like she fit in. *Because you worked by yourself,* she thought, snorting contemptuously.

"What?"

"Sorry, Dad. I — "

Something darted in front of the hood of her Jeep, and she tapped the breaks, slowing down even more. *An animal, maybe?* She turned the wipers up another notch and tried squinting through the deluge. "Hey, Dad? I gotta go — rain is really coming down now. We'll catch up when I get in town, okay?"

"Sounds good — but be *careful*. Heaven watches over you, Carly."

A small smile curved her lips; it was something he'd said every time she left the house when she was little. "I love you too, Dad. See you soon." She turned her phone off before he had the chance to ask any more questions — and instantly regretted it as she peered at the sky once again.

The storm was pushing twilight upon her sooner than she expected — a lot sooner.

A flash of lightning illuminated the highway, and for a split second she thought she saw someone standing on the shoulder just ahead of her. She leaned against the steering wheel just as lightning flashed again, and she spotted a woman with long hair standing in the rain.

Wind buffeted the soft top of the Jeep, and she saw the woman pitch forward a little as she was struck by the sudden gust. Just as she regained her balance, the car ahead of Carly sped past, splashing her with a sheet of water.

"Oh, that bites…," Carly said. She wasn't exactly in the habit of picking up total strangers off the side of the road, but something about being a recent inductee into the really-bad-month club herself made her want to help. She sensed Doc rising on all fours and sought him out in the rearview mirror. "What do you say, boy? Think we should pick her up?"

The Lab growled, and she was startled to see the hackles stand up on the scruff of his neck. It was so out of character for him that for a moment she almost drove on by, but the desire to have someone to talk to, to take her mind off everything, was stronger.

"What's up with you?" she said to Doc, pulling over before she changed her mind. She leaned over and opened the passenger door, blindly yelling her offer of a ride into the storm, and before she knew it, a waterlogged middle-aged woman was sliding into the seat next to her, long brown hair plastered to her head. She was wearing threadbare jeans and a faded yellow "Do you Yahoo?" T-shirt, and her expression was friendly.

"Thanks for the ride," the woman said in a breathless voice, shutting the door. "Thought I was going to drown out there."

"Thanks for the *company*." Carly grinned.

Doc's growl rose in a sinister way, and Carly shot him a warning look over the seat. He lay back down grudgingly but kept his eyes riveted on the woman. "Sorry about that; he's not really dangerous. I think this storm's just got him freaked out."

"Oh, storms can get to the best of us," the woman said with an understanding smile. "I had a friend – *a grown woman* – who was so scared of storms that she would hide under her bed until they passed. Didn't care if she had a whole houseful of guests."

Carly laughed as she eased back onto the highway.

"My name is Sue, by the way. Isn't that crazy? I climb in your Jeep, sit here telling you my friend's dark little secret, and I didn't even give you my name."

"Don't feel bad; I've had people confess the craziest things to me while I'm checking them out at the register, and then I never see them again."

"Like a drive-through priest," Sue said, laughing. "So where are you headed?"

"North," Carly said and then grinned. "That tells you a lot, right?"

"Covers a lot of territory," Sue agreed. "What city?"

"St. Louis."

"Sure, I know it – you have a long drive ahead of you."

Carly nodded as she maneuvered around an old, beat-up pickup doing a snail's crawl through the rain. The lights from her Jeep illuminated the truck's "It's not paranoia when they really are out to get you" bumper sticker. "So what about you? Where are you going?"

"Oh, here and there," Sue said slowly. "I never stay in one place too long. Pretty much wherever the wind takes me ..."

Carly glanced over and then did a double take. She could've sworn she saw something dark pass over the woman's face. She turned her attention back to the road. Maybe it was intuition – or maybe it was years of living with a father who had drilled her since preschool on everything from stranger danger to Jeet Kune Do (which she was terrible at). Whatever it was, it was dawning on her that it might not have been such a great idea to pick the woman up. She peeked at her again, trying to appear like she *wasn't* looking.

"Are you okay?" Sue gave her a sly sideways glance. "You don't look so good."

A strong wave of nausea swept over Carly, and she took a deep breath, trying to steady her stomach. What was wrong with her? She had felt fine only a moment ago! Another, much stronger, roll of nausea hit and her vision blurred. Doc growled somewhere behind her. She blinked a couple of times, and the rain-slicked road warbled and cleared before her eyes.

"Are you *okay*?" Sue asked again.

Carly blinked again. There was construction going on up ahead – orange cones, concrete barriers narrowing the road. She could hear Doc barking, but his bark sounded distant, muffled, and her head swam dizzily. She shook her head, trying to clear her thoughts. She *had* to get off the highway before she reached those barriers – that or crash into them.

"I - I have to pull over."

"I don't think you want to do that, Carly."

There was a moment of disbelief; confusion and then cold terror flooded Carly's veins. "I never told you my name."

Silence.

Carly couldn't bring herself to look at the woman. She looked along the road, and then in the rearview mirror, hoping she might spot a cop. But she saw Doc instead. He was frantic, barking his head off, but no *sound* was coming out. Her legs started to shake, and she eased her foot off the gas, preparing to pull the Jeep off the road, when an odd, static-electricity feeling crackled in the air around her.

Carly turned slowly to find the woman's face only inches from her own. Her eyes looked different – like they didn't belong to her. Foreign ... like nothing she had ever seen before. The pupils elongated into slits, like those of a reptile.

A scream tore out of Carly as she jerked the steering wheel to the right, and the woman's hand snaked out and grabbed the wheel, trying to force her back onto the highway. Another wave of nausea hit, forcing bile to rise in Carly's throat as they fought for the wheel.

The woman suddenly relinquished her grip.

"Who *are* you?" Carly choked, regaining control of the wheel. "What do you want?"

The woman ignored her and instead raised her nose like she was sniffing the air. A look of terror filled her eyes. *"Irinim,"* she whispered in a strange voice. She pulled back from Carly, leaning against the passenger door.

"Now!" a deep voice thundered through Carly's head.

Without thinking, she grabbed the wheel with both hands and pulled to the right again with all of her strength. The Jeep hit the shoulder in a spray of gravel and water, and she felt a jarring thud as they came to a stop and the passenger door popped wide open. The woman shrieked as she was unceremoniously sucked backward into the storm.

Doc scrambled over the console, teeth bared as he lunged for the door, but she snagged his collar just in time. She pulled him back and reached for the door handle, unconsciously taking her foot off the clutch. The Jeep lurched and stalled as she slammed the door and locked it.

"Go, now!" the voice commanded.

Carly let out a startled cry, her hands shaking as she turned the key in the ignition, trying to wrap her mind around what she had just seen. No way could that woman – *that thing* – no way could it have been human.

And what was that voice?

The Jeep fired to life on the third try, and she stomped on the gas, fishtailing back onto the highway, horns blaring, lights slanting sideways as cars swerved to get out of her way.

9

Just north of Galva, Louisiana | En route to St. Louis

He had his radio tuned to oldies, his window down, and was barreling down the road, busy adjusting his side mirror when he first heard it: a far-off thrumming like wind battering the sails of a boat. Jonah's hand paused on the mirror as he squinted through the rain-soaked fog, its soupy mix illuminated by the headlights running the length of the narrow two-lane highway. He frowned and rolled his window back up, increasing the volume as Creedence Clearwater Revival sang about good men trying to find the sun. But the sound just kept getting louder.

A loud bang suddenly reverberated through the air, and he felt the Bronco begin to vibrate, veering out of control as it pulled a hard right.

Blowout.

A horrible stench filled the vehicle as he tried turning the wheel in the opposite direction. He glanced around desperately for a way out. To his left, the fast lane was lined bumper to bumper with cars and trucks; to his right, a low concrete guardrail was the only thing that stood between him and the swampy canal connecting Lake Pontchartrain and Lake Maurepas. He tried to stay focused, tried to apply only small amounts of pressure to the brakes, but the Bronco's engine revved, lurching forward like he had hit the gas instead, and he saw the guardrail looming before him. Beyond that, the cold black waters of the canal.

Jonah's heart stuttered.

"No way," he gasped.

Everything from that moment on moved forward in terrify-ing, this-is-really-it slow motion. He closed his eyes and felt a blinding light hit his eyelids just as the Bronco made impact with the guardrail. Images and thoughts flashed through his mind with lightning speed: He thought longingly of the stash he had tucked away in his glove compartment for a rainy day, wish-ing he had just a little in his system (it *was* raining). Then he thought of his promise to Sam and was glad he didn't. Finally he thought of Carly, of how talking to her had made him feel good, almost *normal* again ... And then his body smashed against the steering wheel, jaws snapping shut, shooting a searing pain all the way into his ears. But instead of pitching forward, he felt the front end of the Bronco rise in the air, pressing him back against his seat.

Jonah's eyes shot open just as the truck came crashing back down on the highway, and he bounced in his seat, gritting his teeth against the second impact. The truck settled, and he heard a hiss of air from what was left of his right front tire. Rain drummed steadily against his rooftop.

He was still alive.

"Kiss my grits, Flo," he whispered incredulously as he slipped his seat belt off and looked behind him.

The Bronco was slanted sideways, rear end sticking out across the slow lane, where traffic had come to a standstill in the rain. Jonah grabbed his cell phone, opened the door, and stepped out onto the highway, feeling his legs buckle a little as he made his way around to the back of the truck. He opened the rear hatch, set off two flares where he stood, and then walked to the front of the vehicle, bracing himself for the worst. The tire problem could be fixed easily – he had a spare in the back – but the rest of the damage, if it was as bad as he thought, might make changing the tire pointless. The all-chrome grill had to be mangled and the radiator was most definitely gone, as hard as he'd hit. If the frame was bent –

The truck didn't have a scratch on it.

Jonah let out a bewildered laugh. It didn't make any sense. He had *felt* the impact – his entire body was still feeling it. He shook his head, starting to pace around as he flipped his cell phone open to call Sam.

If he had been looking, he might have noticed the dead opossum lying on the road in time.

Instead, Jonah tripped, hitting the blacktop on all fours, and watched in horror as his cell phone — *his brand-new cell phone* — slid across the rain-slicked highway and into the traffic in the fast lane. An old, rusted-out AMC Hornet station wagon crunched over the cell phone as it sped by. An *AMC Hornet*! He looked up at the black sky as rain pelted down on his face, and he suddenly felt like he was smothering. As if the dark sky were pressing down on top of him. *"Why isn't Jenna crying anymore, Sam?"* Jonah heard himself whisper from the past. Then J's line: *"Why can't I see you guys?"*

Jonah gagged with fear, his gaze shifting back to the road just in time to see a set of unusually bright headlights heading right for him.

10

St. Louis

The large doors of the Jesuit monastery slammed shut as TJ stepped inside, pausing long enough to wipe the rainwater from his glasses before following the monk down the narrow stone passageway.

Reaching the end of the tunnel, the monk pulled the old iron cross mounted on the wall, and the huge stone slabs separated, opening to an underground conference room filled with top members of the Resistance.

TJ nodded to the retired full-bird colonel standing off to one side, surveying the crowd, and then turned his attention to the center of the room, where Rabbi Lefkowitz, Father Parmely, and Bishop Harper stood hunched over a long table littered with old books, maps, and scrolls. Suspended above the table, four large monitors glowed with images of his recent findings. The men glanced up, a slightly shell-shocked look on their faces as they nodded to him and moved back from the table.

TJ slid into a chair and hooked his phone into the USB port of the computer system. He glanced at his watch and noticed his hand shaking—aftershocks of his mind still coming to grips with what was happening.

"It is now five a.m. Iraq time," TJ announced. "According to Chaplain Hagan, their rendezvous should take place shortly."

"It's my understanding that the activity has increased over the past twenty-four hours?" Colonel McClure asked from across the room, and TJ nodded at the older man.

"Yes ... and no. What I mean is that it isn't just increasing but also *converging* as it moves closer to St. Louis—gathering strength, so to speak."

"The speed at which this is unfolding…," Rabbi Lefkowitz murmured.

"We were warned," Father Parmely said, glancing at his old friend. "We were all warned – we just never knew *when*."

The room fell silent, and in the silence TJ shifted his gaze to the monitors, scanning the images he had been staring at for the past three days. His eyes moved from the picture of the stone stela, made even more imposing by the size of the monitor, to the strange weather patterns, and then back again.

He frowned as a fragment of conversation flitted through his mind, and without warning another piece of the puzzle fell into place. Could it be? Too much had already transpired for him to believe it was just a fluke…

"Watchers?" TJ blurted out, incredulous, as every eye in the room turned his way. "You're not going to believe this… but I think I know who they are."

"Then we'd better get to work, son," Colonel McClure said, crossing the room, his expression grim as he came to stand next to TJ. "Because I'll wager my pension that the other side knows too. According to the prophecy, if the fallen and their lackeys get to the Watchers before we do, we not only lose our greatest weapons in this war that's coming – we'll have front-row seats to the enslavement of the entire human race."

The silence in the room was suddenly pierced by the demanding cries of a small, grayish-brown cat as it pawed feverishly at the stone door, trying to get out.

11

St. Louis, Missouri

Mr. Becker?" "Yeah?" Sam continued putting groceries away in his refrigerator as he glanced down and saw "unavailable" on his caller ID. He frowned and dropped a six-pack of Red Bull on the shelf before shutting the fridge door. He didn't have time to mess with salespeople – not with Jonah and the others on their way in. He was already on edge, waiting for their calls. "Listen, I'm not inter – "

"Mr. Becker, I'm one of the ER nurses at River Parishes Hospital in Galva, Louisiana. Your brother Jonah has been in an accident and asked us to call."

"What!" A flash of fear ripped through him. "Is it bad? Is he going to be all right?"

"He has some pretty serious injuries."

"Galva, Louisiana?" Sam repeated, slipping on his jacket as he rushed for the door. *Jonah hadn't even made it out of the state?*

"That's right," the nurse replied. "And you might want to get here as soon as you can." Her voice sounded nervous, like she was worried she had said too much. He opened his mouth to ask her what Jonah's injuries were and heard the dial tone.

"What the – "

Sam slammed the door behind him, taking the back stairs two at a time, and bolted for his car. *All my fault,* he grieved as he fished for his keys in the dark. *He was on his way here because of me!* He had spent most of his life worrying about what kind of trouble Jonah was going to get into next, and he had ended up putting him in the worst danger of all.

Was I so wrong to think I could protect them if I had them all in one place?

He fumbled, dropping his keys on the ground, and leaned over to pick them up. Then he heard what sounded like a large flock of birds landing in the trees around him—but he knew it wasn't birds.

Something rough brushed his ear and he spun around, immediately going into a defensive stance as his eyes swept the area. A frigid burst of air swirled, encircling him, and his breath began to come out in white puffs.

"Their trackers are everywhere…" Words from his latest nightmare. The image of Jonah's face flashed through his head, and he felt his anger momentarily rise above his fear.

"You're not going to stop me," he said, trying to keep his voice steady as he saw the outline of their huge bodies in the dark, shifting into different shapes at will. He remembered their attack on him and the others when they were kids—knew they were only the beginning of this … *thing* … that was coming, but there was still so much he didn't remember.

Sam forced himself to turn around and slip his key into the door. As much as he feared them, he was more afraid of not getting to Jonah in time. He felt the air around him getting colder, denser, pressing down upon him, and his hands shook as he fought to open the door.

Then with no warning they were gone.

Sam glanced over his shoulder, his breath ragged in his ears. It was too easy.

He hesitated for only a moment, then jumped into his car and started it, hitting Jonah's number on his speed dial as he backed out of his space. As he turned and peeled out of the lot, Jonah's cell immediately went to voicemail. He punched Lila's number in next, glancing in his rearview mirror as he drove.

"It's Jonah," he said as soon as she answered. "He's been in some kind of accident. I'm heading to the airport right now."

A streetlight flickered and dimmed in his rearview mirror, and he frowned.

"Oh no! Is he going to be all right?"

"I don't know," Sam said, trying to keep his emotions in check. "All they said was that it was serious and that I need to get there as soon as possible ..." He gripped the steering wheel and quickly made a left, heading east on Lucas.

Another light dimmed.

"Do you want me to go with you?"

"No ..." He tried to focus on Lila's voice as he glanced in the mirror.

Two more lights dimmed, one right after the other, as he flew past the riverboat *Admiral* docked on his right. The lights around the entrance to the casino lowered and then brightened again ...

"Okay, well, promise you'll call me when you get there."

"As soon as I get to the hospital. And Lila ..." He struggled. "There's just been a lot going on that I haven't told you ..."

"I'm not going anywhere. We'll talk later," she said in a soothing tone. "You just worry about your brother now ... I love you, you know."

Sam paused, caught off guard by Lila's words – words she had never spoken before – and he felt a sliver of joy inside. "I love you too."

Flipping the phone closed, he turned the corner onto Biddle. He looked up in time to see streetlights behind him dimming in rapid succession as he sped down the narrow, tree-lined street. He floored it, willing the red light at the intersection ahead to change.

"Come on, *come on*!" Sam whispered under his breath as his eyes zeroed in on the entrance ramp to the highway on the other side of the light. If he could just get through the light without stopping ...

The light turned green.

His car flew toward the intersection. Almost there ... almost ...

Whispered voices began to pour into his mind like a raging waterfall – foreign words that were guttural, filled with malice – and he watched in horror as a shadow passed over the light and it turned red.

A man suddenly appeared on the road right in front of him.

"Move!" Sam yelled hoarsely. He slammed on his brakes and felt the car slide sideways, and the man turned and raised his hand. Sam saw a brief flash of amber eyes just before the air between them wobbled like a wall of clear, shimmering Jell-O.

"What the – "

The horrible shriek of truck brakes filled his ears as the side of his car struck the gelatinous wall. Veins of iridescent blue light shot through the shimmering substance as it absorbed the car's impact, and he looked up to see a semi roar by, missing him by only a few feet as it careened across the road.

Sam gasped, trying to catch his breath, his eyes widening with horror as the semi jackknifed, flipping over onto its side before finally coming to a thunderous, metal-crunching stop against the traffic light. The back door of the trailer had popped open, shooting large wooden crates out onto the street.

The shimmering wall disappeared from around him.

Survival mode kicked in, and Sam floored it around the wrecked semi, car tires squealing as he hit the entrance ramp and merged onto the highway.

Gotta get to Jonah…

His mind spun wildly, his body shaking with adrenaline as he moved into the fast lane, continuing to check his rearview mirror as he drove. He wasn't just being tracked. They had been *herding* him, pushing him through that light and into what they believed would be his death. And what about the stranger? The memory of the gold eyes rose in his mind – eyes of a lion, terrifying, watchful … but revealing nothing that could tell him what the man's agenda was.

His cell phone rang and he reluctantly flipped it open.

"Bro, you are *not* going to believe the night I've had!" Jonah exclaimed, causing Sam to have an abrupt standing-outside-your-body moment. "Can't talk long – I'm on someone else's phone – but I wanted you to know I probably won't get in until morning now …"

"Wait … what about the hospital – your *injuries*?" Sam blurted out, finally finding his voice. He was still weaving in and out of traffic, still heading for the airport.

"What hospital? I had a blowout. One that nearly sent me into the lake, but I'm okay now. Be even better if my phone wasn't crushed to smithereens."

"Did Jenna or Carly get in touch with you at all today?" Sam asked as he eased up on the gas pedal. A cold wind of anxiety was working its way through him. He would be insane to think it was all just a coincidence – not after what he'd seen – so it wasn't much of a stretch to think that the girls might be in trouble too. And what about J? He'd sent a text earlier saying that he was only an hour away, but nothing after that.

Trying to keep us separated, he thought.

"I talked to Carly earlier today – but haven't heard anything since then," Jonah said warily, seeming to pick up on his fear. "You think maybe you should try to reach them?"

"Yeah, I do." He moved over to the far right lane and exited off the highway.

"The freak fest continues," Jonah said with a sigh. "I had a feeling … Okay, I'm hanging up now. *Call them.*"

"Jonah – don't stop unless you have to," Sam said hurriedly as he whipped into the Waffle House parking lot and put his car in park. "And if you do, make sure there are a lot of people around."

Jonah laughed, but there was no humor in the sound. "You know something I don't?"

"No," Sam lied. "I just want you to be careful."

He flipped his phone closed and leaned back against his seat. It was killing him not to be able to tell Jonah everything he knew. But every time he started to, he was hit with the overwhelming feeling that it wasn't time – and that jumping the gun would put them all in even more danger.

"Why can't I see you guys?" J's young voice echoed from the past, causing him to wince and shy away from the memory.

Sam took a deep breath and flipped his phone open, punching in Jenna's number first. There was something in their memories of that night – what it was, he wasn't exactly sure, but he knew it was important. He sighed, listening to the phone ring. The only thing he did know for certain was that he had to get them back to St. Louis, back together again.

Back where it all started …

He just hoped with all of his heart that whatever it was they were being led into, they would be able to survive it.

12

St. Louis

J's head pounded as they hung upside down in the darkened cab, dangling by their seat belts. He braced one hand against the ceiling of the truck and fumbled with the button long enough to realize it was jammed. He fished for the knife he kept in the front pocket of his jeans. *Where are all the cops?* J wondered impatiently. *The fire trucks? Any other time they would be swarming the street.*

"Hang tight," he rasped out, sawing at the belt with his knife. "I'll have us out of here in no time."

"Well, we're off the job now," Tiny grumbled worriedly. "And lucky if that's all he does to us. That white boy doesn't mess around. I've *heard* things."

"Who are you calling white boy?" J asked as he cut through the last of the belt. "Only thing I can see in here is that pasty bald head of yours." He fell with a grunt.

He knew Tiny was just scared. He was scared too—though he had been surprisingly free of the nightmares ever since they accepted this job in St. Louis.

"I'm just saying, Corsa's gonna be trouble," Tiny said, returning to his original rant. "How did this happen, anyway?"

"I don't know," J admitted, frowning. "Saw that green light and next thing I know, it's shining so bright, I can't see anything else. Didn't notice the idiot with the car until the last minute ..." He didn't mention the queasy feeling that had gripped him when he saw the green light—or the insane laughter he'd heard. Insanity was starting to sound a lot like his great uncle Lester ... with a bad cold.

"They're here."

J backed up on his knees and glanced out the window that had been shattered by his head when they flipped. Two dark sedans were parked next to the overturned semi now. He saw the back door of one of the sedans open, and a pair of expensive dress pants walked by. A large engine rattled in the distance, getting closer.

"Are you planning to leave me like this?" Tiny hissed.

"Maybe." J grinned in spite of his aching head and crawled over to Tiny, quickly cutting him from the viselike grip of his seat belt. "Think I should get out and talk to him?"

"If you have a death wish." Tiny groaned on impact and rolled over onto his side.

"You lose something on the way to St. Louis?"

"What do you mean?" Tiny asked, raising his head. "Like what?"

"I don't know ... your *spine*?" It was downright embarrassing how Tiny had become such a quivering mass of fear since they hit town. They had dealt with a lot worse than some rich antique dealer. A lot worse.

J shook his head as he squeezed his large frame through the window. He hadn't met Nick Corsa face-to-face yet, but the only job he'd had them on so far was hauling a bunch of crates filled with ancient history that had been buried under the Arch. Not exactly their normal score, but the money was too good to turn up his nose at—even if Corsa's goons were a little on the odd side.

He brushed the glass off as he stood and looked around. Two men were busy setting flares around the upturned semi while two more scurried around the crates on the road, nailing lids back on. A man in his late twenties to early thirties with stylishly tousled dark hair and a handsome profile—the only one in what he guessed to be Armani—was kneeling down next to an open crate. It was Corsa—no doubt in his mind. J wiped his sweaty palms against his pant legs and made his way over to the man. He didn't like groveling to anyone, but if saying he was sorry for the wreck helped them keep their jobs, he'd do it. He wasn't going back to Chicago. He needed time to sort things out, and hopefully Sam could help him do that now that he was back.

"Mr. Corsa?"

The man looked up, dark eyes studying him so hard that he actually squirmed.

"Listen … I'm real sorry about the accident," J began awkwardly.

"Accidents happen," he said, smiling as he stood. "J, right?"

He offered his hand, and for a second J had the craziest feeling, like Corsa expected him to kiss his ring or something – but it wasn't until they actually shook that he knew he didn't like the man. He couldn't put his finger on it exactly, but there was something under the smile that made him uneasy. Not that his feelings would stop him from taking the guy's money. Business *was* business.

"And please call me Nick. I would prefer it if we're going to be working together."

J nodded, and the man gave him another smile. A semi bearing the Corsa International name on it pulled up behind them, air brakes hissing as it came to a stop, and three of the four men began loading the spilled crates into the back of it.

"The truth is, I need someone I can trust, someone who doesn't ask questions, and you come highly recommended. This recent find is just the beginning of my work here." Corsa motioned one of his men over, and they both reached into the crate he had been inspecting and withdrew what looked to be a startlingly long blade with strange symbols etched down the length of it. "Two-handed great sword," Corsa supplied, beaming like a proud parent. "Can you imagine the *power* it took to wield this?"

J stared at it, fascinated; weapons were kind of his thing, but he'd never seen anything like it before. It was massive – lethal-looking with serrated edges and a smaller, wing-shaped blade that jutted out from its side like an ax. Even with the handle missing, it had to be at least nine feet in length.

Who – or what – could handle something that big?

"The metal cannot be matched with anything on earth," Corsa continued in a reverent voice, sounding as if he were standing in a museum instead of the middle of a road at night. "Yet the writing has been identified as ancient Aramaic." He ran his hand down the blade and then glanced up at J with an odd gleam in his eyes. "There is no way to put a price on something like this …"

J could only nod, wheels turning in his head as he stared at the blade; if someone was willing to settle for a little less than priceless, they could make a *fortune* off the sucker. He lifted his gaze. Corsa's expression was unsuspecting, eager, like someone wanting to share a secret.

"Would you like to hold it?"

J reached out and touched the cold metal of the blade, then took a step back. His throat suddenly felt like it had dust in it. *It's ... what the heck is wrong with me?* The crazy urge to run hit, almost overpowering him, but he was unable to take his eyes off the blade.

"Interesting. I've heard that it could have that effect on people — never seen it myself, but I ...," Corsa continued pleasantly, but J could barely hear him over the sound of pummeling wind in his ears.

Watery images from that Mardi Gras filled his mind: Jenna's tear-streaked face; Carly, Sam, and Jonah looking up one by one; and then nothing but blackness pressing in. Then he heard his own voice, so young, so petrified, playing in his head: *"Why can't I see you guys? Where are we? What is that?"*

"... one of our archeologists at the site."

J's stomach rolled. His legs trembled as he took another step back. He had to get out of there before he hurled — or worse.

"Are you ... all right?" Corsa sounded oddly more curious than concerned.

"What?" J tore his gaze away from the weapon and looked up; Nick's eyes had become sharp, searching his face for ... for *what?* Signs of weakness?

"I ..." J looked toward the overturned truck and saw Tiny still leaning against the outside of it. He forced himself to relax. It helped that he wasn't looking at that thing anymore. "No, I'm cool. I think I just banged my head too hard when the semi flipped."

"You should have said something sooner," Corsa said, his eyebrows drawing together. He and his assistant carefully returned the blade to its crate. Corsa motioned for the man to close it up and turned back to J. "You need to be seen by a doctor. I'll have my driver take you."

"Oh, I don't need any of that. Think if I lay down for a while, I'll be fine."

"Then my driver will take you back to your vehicle."

They rode back to the Suburban in silence, Tiny appearing nervous but grateful to still have a job, and J staring straight ahead, unable to shake the memory of the strange feeling that had hit him when he touched the blade – or the shadow that crossed Nick Corsa's face as he turned to walk away.

The shadow that moved and shifted, almost like it had a life of its own.

February 23 | Two a.m.

Jonah will be here any minute, so I'd better get this down while I can. Just found Mom's diary – how could I have missed it before? I probably pulled those old boxes out of the living room closet a hundred times while I was restoring the place ...

Mom's last entry was written the day she died – just a couple of scattered lines, like she was jotting down thoughts. On the first line she wrote, "Sam and Jonah," then the next line down, "Their trackers are everywhere."

Yeah ... just like my dream ...

If Mom knew about these trackers, what else did she know? Was this why she and Dad were killed? My mind keeps going back to "their trackers" – that means there's someone calling the shots ...

13

February 24

St. Louis, Mardi Gras

They moved through the crowds unseen, seven of them, their long brown robes obscuring immense, ten-foot-tall frames, hoods hiding grim expressions as masked faces swirled around them, laughing, shouting, and blaring their horns, oblivious to what moved amongst them just off the grid of human awareness.

Oblivious to what they fed . . .

The Irinim leader turned his head slightly, sensing an ebbing life force as he neared a human shuffling down the sidewalk, telltale white walking stick moving slowly in front of him. The old man's spirit turned its head, spotting him as he passed by; iridescent palm prints glowing through the tired shell of skin. The Irinim held his hand up, and the spirit reluctantly settled back into its body.

He paused.

"MazziKim," the leader murmured as he lifted his nose to the air.

His second-in-command came to a stop next to him, flawless African features like stone as they glanced up to the rooftops of the city. From the Old Courthouse, with its copper dome and spire, to the bars and the bandstand erected in the middle of the plaza, the Irinim saw reptilian eyes that glittered in the dark as they studied the crowds below, waiting.

It wouldn't be long now.

"I forgot how insane this is," Sam said with a kind of disturbed awe as they made their way through the crush of people jammed along Market Street.

Jonah grinned, looking around. Insanity *ruled* the final hours of Mardi Gras — the constant roar of voices as beaded necklaces flew through the air, landing on tree branches like psychedelic icicles while huge floats rolled by, one bearing the weight of Jimmy Hendrix's head as "Purple Haze" blared from the speakers. A pretty brunette tottered through the crowd, wearing scary heels, a large floppy hat, and a bikini.

He glanced over his shoulder at Sam.

Sam's eyes trailed after the brunette, appearing a lot less disturbed, and Jonah laughed as they continued south toward Kiener Plaza. He was glad they were together again — even if he was a little scared about *why*, it still felt good. There was just something about his brother that made life a lot easier to swallow, a kind of goodness that made you believe that the world wasn't as bad as it looked after all.

A group of partiers jostled him, scrambling for beads being tossed by masked krewe members, and he glanced back, making sure Sam was still behind him.

He had been so shocked when he first saw his brother — the dark circles under his eyes, the fear, *the freaking weight loss* — that he'd acted as if the blowout was no big deal when Sam pressed him about it. Then he heard about Carly and Jenna's troubles and wanted to call off the whole crazy reunion. Sam practically begging him to go had unnerved him, though. More than nightmares, roadkill, and an AMC Hornet running over your cell phone put together.

"I *got* it," Jonah said, stopping Sam in the middle of the crowd with a feigned look of wonder. "You know who you remind me of?"

A small smile played on Sam's lips. "If you say Bruce Lee, I'm pretty sure I'll have to kill you."

"I was actually thinking more like a weird combination of Forrest Griffin and — "

"Who in the heck is Forrest Griffin — and what did you mean exactly by *weird*?"

"You're kidding me, right? Sprawl and brawl, *Ultimate Fighter*?"

Sam laughed and pushed him on through the crowd. Jonah smiled to himself; it was a game they had started as little kids, joking around to ease each other's fears.

"Okay, so *you* remind me of—"

"Do I really want to hear this?" Jonah asked without turning around, and they both laughed.

"Maybe Dane Cook … and/or a young Bob Dylan—except with better hair."

"Not bad."

"I meant *Dylan* had better hair."

"Wow. Who knew there was all that humor lurking beneath the Confucius exterior?"

Sam laughed again. "Jerk."

Jonah grinned as his eyes roamed over the sea of heads, searching for Carly and Jenna. Two drunks stumbled in front of him, looking like poster boys for the Dollar Store, their sweatshirts covered with buttons, necks ringed with stacks of beads. He sidestepped them and then did a double take. For just a second he could've sworn he saw J's troubled face turning to stare at him through the mob of people.

"So, you never said if you talked to J."

"Didn't think you'd want to know."

"I'd want to know if he's going to meet up with us," Jonah countered.

"He's *not*," Sam said, exasperated. "I got a text from him when he first got into town, but that's it."

"I'm pretty sure I just saw him."

"Were you always this annoying when we were younger? I can't remember."

"Only when I opened my mouth," Jonah admitted, shooting a sly grin over his shoulder.

"Something we actually agree on." Sam laughed, then said, "Why the heck isn't my cell phone working?" His voice suddenly sounded far off, weird.

There was stillness in the air, a heaviness that wasn't there only moments ago. Jonah almost asked Sam if he felt something weird—but then he realized he was afraid of the answer. He fished for his lighter and quickly lit a cigarette. He should've never listened to Sam about staying sober.

A low concussion, almost like a sonic boom, echoed across the dark sky.

"What's –," Sam murmured, his voice sounding cautious, even farther away.

Jonah turned around just as another group of partiers squeezed by, oblivious to the strange sound as they drunkenly jostled each other, blocking his view of Sam. A strange kind of humming sensation moved through him like an electric current. He looked up again and saw dry lightning crack across the sky, and had just enough time to think how odd that was for February when a warm rain began to fall.

Then it started to hail.

Not a little hail but huge, golf-ball-sized hail that came out of nowhere, pummeling the crowds as they ran for cover. Car alarms began to go off all along the street, lights flashing wildly as people slipped and skidded through the deluge.

"Sam!" he called out, throwing the hood to his jacket up over his head as he frantically tried to squeeze through the mass of people that surrounded him, but they blocked him in. He craned his neck, trying to see his brother, then spotted a gap in the bodies and darted into a doorway.

More people shoved in around him, nearly smothering him against the doorframe. He turned his head for a breath of fresh air and saw a hippie-looking dude with John Lennon glasses standing stock-still in the middle of the street. Just standing there, staring toward the Arch with his mouth gaping open while rain and hail pelted down over his long black ponytail.

Jonah followed the hippie's gaze to the Arch and felt his own mouth gape open, felt the soggy cigarette fall from his lips as he blinked a couple of times to make sure it wasn't some crazy trick of the eye. But it wasn't. Something was *moving* beneath the sheet of rain and hail at the center of the Arch, bulging outward like – He glanced at the outside edges of the structure, then back to the center. Like there was something big ...

I'm not really seeing this.

... just beneath the air's surface that was trying to ... *break through?*

He felt the electric charge humming through him again, growing stronger. A blast of wind screamed down Market

Street, tearing through the Purple Haze float and flipping the Egyptian "Restoration of the Gods" float on its side before slamming against the building where he hid, with such force that he couldn't breathe.

The sensation of something huge and cold streaking by hit him, and he had the crazy thought that something *was* in the wind, when it happened again ... and again ... over and over until he lost count.

"Just the wind," he heard Carly say, and he clung to the words. Tears ran from his eyes as he opened and shut his mouth, trying to catch his breath, and just when he was sure his lungs were going to explode, the wind vanished.

The rain and hail stopped.

Jonah looked up at the sky as the crowds came back to life again, cheering and surging against him. He glanced back to the spot where the hippie had been, but he was long gone, probably at a bar, downing the shot of Cuervo that would've been *his* if it weren't for —

Sam.

He dove back into the jam-packed street, barreling his way through the crowd as he scanned the sea of bobbing heads for Sam. A man moved right into his path. He turned to avoid slamming into him and almost mowed over a raggedy old black woman in the process.

"Sorry," he murmured, distracted. He reached out to help steady her, but the old woman shrank back from him.

"Don' you tech me," she rasped, clutching an old cardboard sign to her chest.

Jonah took an unconscious step back as he tried to catch his breath. She didn't *look* like much of a threat — maybe five feet tall, ninety pounds tops, with large dark eyes that stared out of a tiny, wrinkled old face. It was the look in her eyes that had unnerved him, cold and accusing ... and filled with ... *hate.*

He jerked away from her gaze and glanced to the sign, where the words *fortoon teler* were printed in large, childish scrawl. An insane urge to laugh hit him — and then evaporated.

He had seen the sign before.

Jonah looked back up at the old woman, and she smiled broadly, revealing a beautiful set of white, even teeth. Too natural to be fakes – and too young-looking to be real … He had seen that smile before too.

Can't be her, his mind warred with him. *That would mean she'd aged at least –*

Jonah stumbled backward, almost falling this time, and she laughed.

"You stumble like the blind, but *they* know that you see, *Watcher-man.*"

He backed up even more and then turned and bolted, running blindly through the mob scene in the street as her laughter trailed after him, peeling back the years. Jenna's pitiful cries ripped through his mind as he ran, and then …

… he heard his own voice, ten years old and terrified, scream, *"She's not GOD! She doesn't know anything about us!"* He felt the cold weight of the brick in his hand again just before he sailed it through the air … and heard the crash of glass echoing in the dark street … and then the wind … and a darkness that he couldn't escape settled over him, *on* him, and Jenna stopped crying because …

"Sam!" The echo of his scream brought him to a screeching halt at the entrance to Kiener Plaza, gasping for air as a soggy group of onlookers stared at him with that delicate mixture of curiosity and caution usually reserved for the truly insane.

"What?!" He shot them a wild look, zeroing in on the guy in a Rams jacket, who was at least twice as big as him. His target gave him a wary glance and then turned back to the stage as the band began to play.

Jonah ducked his head, blindly pushing his way through the crowd. Maybe he *was* nuts. But he knew what he had seen. He couldn't have just imagined it all – but he didn't want to believe it either.

He raised his eyes again and uttered something between a sob and a sigh of relief as he zeroed in on Sam, Carly, and Jenna standing just a short distance away.

He picked up his pace, determined not to let them out of his sight. People moved in and out of his line of vision, giving him only brief glimpses; he saw the three of them laugh, then a stricken look on Sam's face as he looked down at something in his hand before giving it back to Jenna. A couple moved in front of him, and he leaned to the right, trying to see around them.

He got just a quick look at Sam's startled face as he spotted something over the heads of the girls … and then a wall of bodies pressed in around him, blocking his view.

"There," the Irinim leader breathed, his eyes narrowing as he caught sight of the two large Grigori leaders appearing and moving unseen through the crowds near the bandstand. "And there …" Five more warriors followed close behind the twin Grigori, wasting little time as they split and veered off in different directions. Back to finish what they had started … His hand tightened around his weapon.

"Seven have breached the gate so far …"

"Two hundred in all, if memory serves me." Jahdiel's lips thinned into a grimace. "We'll soon be outnumbered."

"An optimistic way of looking at it," Arieh said, smiling a little as he turned to his second-in-command. "But it's not their numbers that concern me." He scanned the rooftops again, noting the MazziKim grunts that remained in concentration near the Arch. "The remaining Grigori are waiting until the threat is dealt with before they breach the gate." He nodded to Azaniah, Neriah, and Kallai, three of his most formidable fighters. "You know what to do."

With stealth, the hooded warriors slipped into the throng of humans, their cloaks morphing into casual street clothes familiar to the race, bodies sizing down.

"It's time," Arieh announced, clapping his friend's broad shoulders.

Jahdiel nodded somberly as he considered what was about to unfold. He turned back to Arieh, a grim smile suddenly appearing.

"Think they'll be happy to see us again?"

"Jonah!"

Carly grinned, the same funny grin he had fallen in love with when they met as kids, and rushed forward to hug him. Same pretty red hair and big green eyes too, he noticed, but the hip-huggers were ... new. He smiled in spite of himself, and then she pulled back and their eyes caught.

"Can you believe that hail?" she said, sounding a little nervous. "They had us packed in O'Riley's like sardines." Her grin turned wry. "I feel like I've been violated on so many levels."

"It's been one of those kinds of nights," he said dryly and their eyes met again for maybe a second or two. Long enough for his already-spinning mind to take another trip around the block. She was beautiful. A little more of a guarded look in her eyes than he remembered, but still ... beautiful.

"So where did Sam run off to?" he asked suddenly, trying to keep his mind from sliding off in a million different directions. He was way past overload.

"Sam *was* just here," Jenna said, stepping forward to give him a quick hug. "I think he must've spotted someone he knew, because he just kind of took off."

Jonah nodded, distracted; three bodybuilder-types in jeans and faded green army jackets were watching him with interest. The big redhead glanced at his friends, one with long black hair and another with silver braids, and they turned back to watch the band. Jonah turned back to Carly; her eyebrows were drawn together, lips pursed, like she was trying to figure out what was going on with him.

"So, no trail of guys following you two from O'Riley's?" he asked, trying to sound more normal than he felt.

Jenna rolled her eyes. "I'm not going *near* another guy for a very long time."

"As per the restraining order," Carly quipped, and they both laughed.

"We haven't changed much, have we?" Jenna grinned.

"Not so much," Jonah said, really looking at Jenna for the first time. With her dark hair and olive skin, she was the opposite of Carly in everything but height. Both of them were on the petite side, but Jenna seemed more fragile, uncertain ... like she wasn't sure where she fit in. He seemed to remember Sam telling him that she was raising a kid all by herself. Even more reason why they should have stayed away.

"What about *you*?" Jenna asked.

"Yeah, Sam said you're all Dylan-esque now, writing your own songs," Carly said with a mischievous glint in her eye.

"Hmm ... I don't see it," Jenna teased, squinting up at him. "Except maybe the all-black thing."

"Dark and moody *is* in this year." Carly grinned.

"Glad you approve." Jonah grinned back.

"So ... Sam said you barely made it home," Carly said, more a statement than a question, and he brushed a hand through his hair as she and Jenna looked at him expectantly.

"Yeah, I heard it wasn't a party for you two either."

"I thought our plane was going down for sure," Jenna said, exhaling. She shivered as she glanced to Carly. "And you should *see* the bolder-sized dent in Carly's door."

"I don't even know what could make a dent like that," Carly added hesitantly, her voice turning hollow. She shook her head like she was shaking the thought from her mind. "My dad *freaked* as soon as he walked in and heard our plans — didn't want us coming anywhere near Mardi Gras."

"I haven't seen your dad in forever," Jonah said, and their eyes held again. He finally pulled his gaze away, glancing between them. "None of it makes sense, does it? I guess Sam thought that if we were together again, it might help us figure it all out."

They nodded like they understood, but Carly's eyes had become so wide, they seemed to swallow up her face, and Jenna looked scared to death. He realized there would be no perfect time to tell them about the old lady.

"I ... ran into the fortune teller — *literally* ran into her during the storm."

"You mean *the* fortune teller?" Carly asked, her eyes growing even wider. "I didn't even *remember* her until right now — until you said that."

"I didn't remember her until I almost knocked her over."

"The one we went to when we were kids?" Jenna asked, sounding a little winded. "The one I ..."

Jonah nodded and felt the dam of what he had been holding in finally break. "It was her – but she looked way too old, like she'd aged forty years or more. That's what threw me off at first, but it was definitely her." He fished a cigarette out and lit it. "This whole deal is insane."

"You're right, it is insane," Carly said, her voice shaky. She exhaled loudly. "What did she say to you?"

"Not much," Jonah said, shrugging, but in his head he heard, *"You stumble like the blind, but they know that you see ..."*

"Wait, there's Sam!" Jenna said, sounding relieved, and they turned and followed her gaze past a little cluster of musicians near the bandstand. Jonah's brows pulled together as he watched his brother hurrying through the crowd, weaving his way around people – not in their direction but *away* from them.

What in the heck is he doing? Jonah's attention was drawn to two men who appeared to be shadowing Sam's steps. They looked like a tag team for the WWE – both pale blonds, both close to seven feet tall, and both wearing jeans and long jackets that looked like they had just been pulled off a store rack, giving the men a slick appearance. *Too slick.*

As if sensing his thoughts, one of the men jerked around and looked right at him, and then the other one turned. *Twins.* At least for the most part: the first appeared a little bigger; the second had done some weird half-shaved-head thing that made him look like he'd escaped from the local insane asylum. The first one stared at Jonah for a long moment, his expression dead of all emotion, and then he glanced back to Sam, as if he were trying to figure something out. *Like a gambler looking for some sign of weakness,* Jonah thought warily.

The wild-looking twin lifted his nose to the air and then turned around, forgetting Jonah for the moment. Jonah followed his gaze and saw two more impossibly large men with their backs to him, moving in Sam's direction – one with a dark mane of hair that fell past his shoulders, wearing an old camouflage jacket, the other, an African American with a shaved head, wearing jeans and a solid green jacket, much like the three men he'd seen earlier. As big as they were, they moved fast – startlingly fast – their bodies *blurring* as they cut the distance in half, then down to a third; before he could blink, they had somehow maneuvered themselves between the twins and Sam. His brother froze in mid stride as though he sensed them, but he didn't turn around.

All sounds of Mardi Gras ceased.

The larger twin raised his head to meet the men's gaze, and an agitated *tick*, *tick*, *tick* sound filled the silence. The wild-looking twin feinted to the left, like he was testing them. Neither man moved, but a deep rumbling sound filled Jonah's head – almost like the low, throaty warning of a lion. The air began to bend and waver around them.

"Jonah – what is it?" Carly asked, her voice sounding far off.

The twins pivoted at the same time and disappeared into thin air. The two in camouflage blurred before his eyes again and then appeared to shoot upward into the sky before they disappeared as well. Jonah's body went rigid with shock, his ragged breathing filling his ears as he dropped his gaze in time to see Sam dart off through the crowds again. It had all happened so *fast* ...

"Jonah?"

"Hey, Jonah!"

He spun around. "Did you *see* that?"

Carly and Jenna stared up at him. "See what?" Carly asked warily. She looked like she wasn't so sure she wanted to know.

"This is my fault. We shouldn't have met here. Not tonight," Sam said, coming up from behind. He looked bad, shaken up, as he glanced toward the Arch. "I just thought it would help us to come back, you know, start at the beginning and try to put all the pieces together ... But they – " He pressed his lips together.

"They?" Jonah glanced sharply at his brother. "You mean the guys who were following you, right?"

"What?"

"The muscle heads," Jonah said impatiently. "They had the whole professional wrestler thing going – blond hair, dark jackets. They were kind of hard to miss, bro."

"I didn't see anyone like that," Carly said, sounding almost relieved. She turned to Jenna, who shrugged and shook her head.

Sam looked away. But not before Jonah had seen the flash of terror in his eyes.

"Tell us what's going on," Jonah growled. "You can't drag us all back here and then keep us in the dark."

"No, you're right," Sam said quietly. His eyes were restless, searching. "We just can't stay here – it's not … safe," he said, almost to himself, before turning to Carly and Jenna. "Can you two meet us tomorrow? I'll call you in the morning and tell you where."

Jonah swore. Sam gave him a pained expression, and he immediately felt like a jerk for being so hard on his brother; all of his plans for the night were going down the drain.

"Why can't we just talk *now*?" Jenna pleaded.

"I agree," Carly said, hugging herself. She glanced to Jonah. "I don't want to put this off another night."

But Sam stood there like a big statue, arms folded across his chest as he looked between the three old friends, appearing troubled but refusing to give in.

"Are you scared?"

Carly glanced at Jenna before turning back to watch the brothers walk away from them. She hadn't realized how strong the connection she felt with Jonah was until he'd turned to leave – almost like a part of her was leaving with him. Sam too – although it wasn't quite as strong … *Shouldn't have let them go,* she thought. *We need to be together tonight …* "I don't think I've ever been this scared in my whole life," she answered finally. She let out the breath she had been holding in and felt Jenna reach for her hand. *Just like when we were scared as kids,* she thought, shivering a little as she watched Jonah and Sam until they faded into the distance.

"Come on, let's get out of here."

They walked in silence, Jonah trudging alongside Sam, his mind racing over and over everything that had happened. He didn't care what Sam said; there was no way he was going to wait – no way he *could* wait – until tomorrow to talk about it.

"Listen – ," was all he got out before he felt a rush of cold air sweep up his back. He and Sam looked over their shoulders at the same time.

A short distance back Jonah spotted their pursuer, his long, dark jacket fluttering open as he appeared to pick up his pace. This one had long black hair plaited with cornrows, and a pale face with a black war-paint-like swath across the bridge of his nose, reminding him a little of the eighties singer Adam Ant. But the dead look on his face was the same as that of the twins.

Jonah glanced at Sam, but he was staring straight ahead.

"Who is he?" Jonah prodded.

"Not now," Sam said between gritted teeth. "Just keep moving."

Jonah stole another glance over his shoulder and was surprised to see that the big guy had stopped at the corner for no apparent reason.

They were almost to the truck when he chanced another look, when he saw *another* huge man standing beneath a light at the edge of the lot, and he suddenly had the oddest feeling ... like he had been thrust into the middle of some live game of chess.

His eyes moved from the camouflage jacket to the broad, buffalo-like shoulders, and finally to the black mane of hair, and he couldn't help thinking how much the stranger looked like the guy back in New Orleans. The man studied them both for a long moment before he glanced up at the sky, searching for something Jonah couldn't see.

"*Sam.*"

"Just drive," Sam said, his voice sharp with anxiety as they climbed into the truck. "For once in your life, listen to me and *drive!*"

They finished the short trip home in silence: Jonah trying to figure out how so much could go so wrong in one night as the DJ on the radio rambled on about the huge jump in crime across the city — and Sam, lost in thoughts he chose not to share, just stared out the window.

As soon the truck pulled in front of the warehouse, Sam went for the door, but Jonah put his hand on his brother's arm.

"Before you get out, I'd just like to say that we've been putting up with each other too many years to stop now. I mean, I know I can be a pain, but I thought you'd be used to it."

"You got the pain part right," Sam said wryly. "Carly was looking good, wasn't she?"

"Yeah, that freaked-out look was *hot*." Jonah grinned with relief. They were in the game again, talking about everything but what it was that scared them. "You should've used your sensitive-artist bull on her when you had the chance," he added and was surprised by a stab of jealousy. She actually *did* look hot …

"I meant for you — not me." Sam grinned knowingly. "Besides, Lila is more than enough for me to try to handle." He glanced sideways, his expression turning uncomfortable. "She's got this cousin who just moved to town." He shrugged. "Owns some kind of gallery or something … Anyway, she's been badgering me to hook up with him, says he can help me. You know, show my paintings …"

"Ah … Grasshopper goes Hollywood. Are you going to do it?"

"Nah. Struggling keeps me humble…." He glanced down at his hands. "She's coming by in a while … Want to stick around?"

"I kind of need to air my apartment out — haven't set foot in there in months. Besides, I'm not exactly on Lila's list of favorite people."

"She has a short list," Sam admitted ruefully. "But that doesn't mean you can't stay over. Technically, it's your place too."

Jonah nodded, falling silent.

"I totally gutted the inside," Sam said, looking back out the window. "It doesn't even look like it did …" He shook his head. When he glanced at Jonah again, something about his brother's demeanor changed. "Did Carly mention how her dad was doing?"

Jonah stared at Sam for a moment, trying to figure out what was going on in his brother's head. He finally shrugged. "She didn't say much, just that he freaked and didn't want her anywhere near Mardi Gras."

Sam nodded, lost in thought. "Remember him taking us fishing?" He glanced toward the warehouse and brushed a shaky hand through his hair. "That was a good time, wasn't it?"

"The best."

"Ever wish you could go back to being a kid again?"

Jonah felt a sick kind of dread come over him that he couldn't explain.

"You mean like start over?"

Sam nodded.

"Nah, I kind of like the way I messed everything up," Jonah said. Not getting the response he was hoping for, he sighed. "We all wish we could do things different. But no way do I want to go back — you might decide not to bring me home with you next time."

"I think I'd go back," Sam said. He fell silent as he looked around the empty street. "I definitely think I'd go back," he said softly, as if he were talking to himself.

"You know, you're starting to freak me out, and after tonight I'm not so sure I have any nerves left. The best is yet to come, right? Isn't that what you always tell *me*?"

"Yeah." Sam attempted a smile as he opened the door and climbed out of the truck. "I'm just tired. I better go, though. Lila will be here soon."

Jonah leaned over and rolled down the passenger window. "Listen, whatever is going on — and there's a lot that *I* haven't even been able to tell *you* yet — we're in this together. I got your back, right?"

Sam leaned back through the window. His smile was genuine this time, like the thought of Jonah wanting to solve their problems tickled him. Jonah couldn't help but grin too.

"Jonah to the rescue?"

"Something like that," he answered dryly.

The streetlight behind them dimmed, and Sam's smile faded.

"You know, sometimes the snakes *are* real, bro ...," Sam said in a low voice as he peered around the dark city street. He looked worried, like he might have said too much, and Jonah held his breath, hoping he would say something more. Instead he put his fist though the open window.

"Brothers?"

Jonah hit Sam's fist with his own. "Always, man."

"I'll call you first thing in the morning, and we'll pick the girls up," Sam promised as he stepped back from the truck. "Better get your butt home and get some rest, though — I know how much you like to get up early." He smiled, as if he'd read the worry in Jonah's mind. "Everything is going to be fine now that we're all together again. You'll see."

"Five percent. That's all astrophysicists claim we can see – five measly percent of the entire energy and mass of the universe," TJ murmured as he stared at the multiple monitors in front of him. "Knowing that used to drive me crazy – until I saw that storm burst out of the center of the Arch." He tapped a few keys, and the printer began to spit out pages. "I don't know what I would've done if I had seen what came with it."

He stood, slipped off his soggy Grateful Dead T-shirt, plucked a clean one off the stack to his right, and pulled it on. He grabbed the printouts as the last one fell into the tray, and handed the pages to his boss.

"What's this?"

"What came with it," TJ answered grimly as he watched Professor Kinney rise from his chair. His coffee-colored skin had an ashy look to it, and his eyes were bloodshot. No doubt in TJ's mind, the trip to Iraq and the news Professor Kinney and Chaplain Hagan had received en route home had taken its toll. TJ hadn't even had the chance to begin translation on the second scroll ...

"I highlighted in red the areas where strange occurrences have been taking place around the city since the storm: jumps in crime, power outages, equipment malfunctions – all of them off the charts."

Professor Kinney nodded, his dark brows drawing together as he flipped through the pages.

"The black dots with the bull's-eye around them are where the unusually large concentrations are." TJ pointed to one of them. "That is where Chaplain Hagan lives ..."

The professor glanced up at him, startled. "So what we suspect is true?"

"Everything fits," TJ said with a nod, feeling as if he had just handed the five a death sentence.

"But they're just kids." The professor's hands shook a little as he flipped his cell phone open. "We have to warn Jeff. Good heavens, *Carly* ..."

"I already gave him a heads-up on it, Prof," TJ said, stopping him. "But there's something else: this other location is where Sam Becker lives."

Jonah stared out the windshield of his Bronco, reluctant to pull away. There was no way he was going to be able to sleep. Not without some answers. He felt like he'd been sucked into some weird episode of *The Twilight Zone* that kept looping around to "a word from our sponsors" before he could get to the end of the story.

He turned his radio on, and it gave off a high-pitched whine before disintegrating into a static hiss. An eerie sense of déjà vu crept over him.

He hummed a little Ozzy, looking around as he punched through station after station of static.

The streetlight above his truck began to buzz loudly, then it exploded in a shower of glass and sparks that danced across the hood. Jonah jerked back. A huge shadow spanned across the hood, followed by two more shadows that skimmed the windshield before they disappeared.

"No … freaking … *way*," he choked out, hanging on to his steering wheel like a life raft as he cautiously looked through the windshield.

The dark sky was empty, almost calm.

Jonah laughed a strangled kind of laugh that sounded crazy even for him, and reached for his second new cell phone, which had fallen to the floorboard. Then he realized he was sitting right in front of Sam's place. Why would he need to call him on his cell?

Because I'm terrified to step outside, that's why …

Jonah glanced up in his rearview mirror and felt another rush of adrenaline — *how much adrenaline can one person hold?* — at the sight of a huge man with cornrowed hair turning down the alley that led to the back of the warehouse. The same guy who had stalked them when they left Mardi Gras.

He placed the phone in his back pocket as he stepped out of the Bronco, and was struck by an overpowering wave of nausea, so overpowering that he began to retch and throw up in the street, driving him down to all fours. He struggled to lift his head.

At first glance the street was empty, but then he noticed that the shadows beneath the streetlights were *moving* toward him. Another wave of nausea hit, and he gagged and scrambled for the door of his truck. He yanked the door open, slid behind the wheel, and slammed the door, taking a couple of deep breaths to steady his heaving stomach. He grabbed his cell phone and dialed Sam's number.

"Sam, it's me." Another deep breath. "Pick up the phone!" He turned and locked the door of his Bronco as he waited. "Listen, I don't know how to explain it, but there's stuff going on out here ... That freak who was following us just stepped around the back of your place, and when I tried to go after him, I started throwing up so bad, I couldn't even get past my truck. I'm going to wait here until you call me back." He sighed into the phone. "We gotta get to the bottom of this, bro. It's been one weird freaking night ... and I'm not even *high*."

The Grigori twins turned their heads in unison, cunning smiles hovering at the corners of their lips as they regarded their prey from their perch on the roof across the street. The sound of heavy footfalls echoed across the surrounding rooftops as more warriors dropped into place and the first wave of MazziKim streamed forth, quickly fading into the side of the warehouse. Shammah lifted his nose to the air and, sensing it was clear, turned and nodded to Tola. The younger twin dropped effort-lessly to the street, withdrew his two-handed sword from the back scabbard hidden beneath his coat, and headed in the direc-tion of the warehouse.

14

Sam held his breath and allowed them full view of him standing in the window until the Bronco's taillights faded off down the street; then he exhaled shakily. *The call worked,* he thought with grim satisfaction. *You won't be able to hurt him now — not ever, if I can help it.* He was scared for Jonah. He didn't know how to explain it, but he sensed that Jonah was in even more danger than he was — if that were possible.

The giant with the half-shaved head lifted his gaze to the spot where he stood, and Sam saw the flash of a smile, then the flash of something else: a staggeringly long, lethal-looking blade that gleamed in the moonlight.

Sam spun away from the window, grabbed hold of his kitchen table, and slid it against the door in one fluid motion. He stacked every chair he had on top of the table and pushed them against the door, then looked around and grabbed the box Lila had left behind, brimming over with books, candles, and an old Ouija board, and slid it under the table. He finally stepped back, breathing heavily as he surveyed his handiwork. It wasn't much of a barricade — not for what he was up against. A little like erecting a wall of toothpicks to protect you against a hurricane.

Whispers echoed around him, and he braced himself for the onslaught. *Psychological warfare 101,* he thought, shaking. *Send in the grunts to weaken me before the big guns arrive . . .*

An image of J rose in his mind, rubbing the scar on his chest as they walked along the riverfront together at sunrise. *"Thought I was going crazy — and no way was I going to end up like my uncle, stuck in a loony bin for the rest of my life,"* J had said. *"But nothing I tried worked. Started feeling like a cartoon character. You know, like Road Runner or something . . . like no matter how hard I tried,*

I couldn't die ... But now ... now I'm thinking that just maybe there's a reason I've been kept around."

Sam's gaze fell to the journal on top of the table, which had somehow made the trip across the room without sliding off. He grabbed a chair and sat down. He had to at least try to warn them. *There was a reason they had been kept around – and Jonah, for whatever reason, was the key.* He knew this, maybe in his own way had even been preparing for it since he was a kid ... but it still didn't keep his hand from trembling as he began to write:

Jonah,

I don't have much time.

This thing that's going on with you – what you're seeing – is real. I see them too. I didn't mean to lie to you, bro; it's just that I got scared and in my own messed-up way thought I could protect you until I had more answers ... Something has happened – something so strong that it unearthed memories in the five of us that we didn't even know existed ... As crazy as this is going to sound, I think we're kind of like "sleeper cells" that have all been activated for some purpose ... and whatever that purpose is, it's ticking these things off ...

I was hoping that meeting at Mardi Gras might help us to piece it all together and maybe – just maybe – we could come up with some kind of plan. My mistake was, they were already one step ahead of me. Know your enemy, so the saying goes, and the truth is, all I have are theories right now ...

I do know that these things aren't from here ... and by that I mean earth ... and that they are more evil than anything you could ever imagine.

I have seen evil ...

Outside, Tola raised his weapon as he caught the scent of the Irinim presence. His reptilian eyes glittered as he spoke through the minds of the collective, quickly issuing his orders. Streetlights began to go out in rapid succession down the old cobblestone avenue as a wave of MazziKim materialized out of the dark.

Evil is real, Jonah — but so is good …

"Guard yourselves; their sorceries are strong here," Arieh warned his warriors as they morphed out of the side of the building across from the warehouse, weapons drawn.

They raised their gaze to the second floor of the warehouse, which was shifting before their eyes as enormous, lethal-looking talons flexed outward from each corner of the building, and mammoth sets of scaly black wings peeled away from the structure and began to beat back and forth …

Sam paused, pen raised just above the page as he shook his head, fighting the explosion of thoughts that had crowded into his mind as he wrote — random, confusing thoughts with no order, no break or pause to give him time to try to sort it all out. He gritted his teeth and continued to write, scribbling almost furiously, as though if he wrote fast enough, he might get it all out before … Sam glanced up. *Before what?*

… way down deep is the kid who reminds me of the good.

The hit came with no warning, hurling Tola forward with such velocity that his sword was knocked from his hand. He twisted his body, catching a glimpse of the massive arms that bound him — bronzed and sinewy, bearing the golden, lion-head arm-bands of the elite guard.

"Jahdiel," Tola snarled.

"And I thought you'd be happy to see me," the Irinim warrior rasped, tightening his grip as the foul wind battered them.

The sound of a car door slamming shut startled Sam out of his seat. *Lila.* How could he have forgotten about her? He knocked the chair over as he scrambled to the window, pushing the curtains back in time to see her stepping out of her car. A blur of a huge figure suddenly loomed behind her, and he felt his heart twist up in his chest. *No!* Dark, shadowy forms began to appear, moving in, and the giant figure pivoted as if sensing them. He saw another figure appear in the midst of the shadowy forms — the larger twin. Sam shoved the lock to one side and threw open the window.

"Lila, *run!*" he yelled, his voice hoarse with terror. She startled and scrambled around the front of her car, her face wreathed in fear as she ran for the back entrance of the warehouse.

He turned and lunged toward the table, winging chairs over his shoulder before sliding his flimsy barricade back from the door. He flung the door open and reached for Lila's arm just as a dark-headed man stepped out from behind her. He gave Sam a frazzled smile as he offered his hand.

"Nick Corsa — heck of a way to meet."

Sam opened his mouth and then hesitated, hearing a far-off sound ... like someone calling his name. His heart began to pound harder.

"What's going on?" Lila asked, her eyes darting around fearfully.

"Sam, listen," the voice said, louder this time. Urgent.

He jerked his head around and saw a huge man with long brown hair at the bottom of his steps, one hand grasping the railing as a hard wind blew against him — same guy he'd seen outside his place, and again in the middle of the road when the truck almost hit him. *Something's holding him back, something in the wind.* Sam's mind reeled, trying to get a grip on what was happening to him. The stranger suddenly raised his eyes, and Sam saw that flash of amber again and noticed the deep gash that ran the length of his jaw. *Fresh wound,* he thought, unable to take his eyes off the man. *So ... why isn't there any blood?*

"Sam!"

"Do not invite them in," the stranger said, speaking into his mind.

The whispers behind him grew louder, and then the laughter. *"Friend or foe?"* they taunted. *"FRIEND OR FOE?"* More laughter.

Panic seized him as his eyes shifted from Lila to the stranger again.

"What is it?" Lila followed his gaze to the bottom of the steps. She pursed her lips and shook her head as she turned back to him. "Sam – you're freaking us out! Aren't you going to invite us in?"

"SAM – DON'T!" the deep voice said, sounding alarmed.

"Honey?" Lila stared up at him, her big brown eyes so full of concern, and he felt his ping-ponging thoughts slow down a little. This was *Lila.* What was he thinking?

"Sorry ..." He turned sideways quickly, allowing them by.

"You were really starting to worry me," Lila said, stopping to give him a kiss on his lips before stepping inside.

Sam turned back to the stranger and felt a thread of something tug at him, like something he should know – *did know* – but it slipped away as quickly as it had come. Another gust of wind blew, and a horrible smell hit his nostrils.

"Sam, are you coming?" Lila called out.

He jumped a little at the sound of her voice and hurriedly pulled the door closed – but not before he saw the profound look of regret on the stranger's face.

A flood of jumbled, racing thoughts swept through his mind as he turned to face his guests. He tried to smile as Lila made the introductions, tried to act normal, but it wasn't working. Sweat trickled down the side of his face.

"Are you okay?" Lila whispered as she and Nick helped him pick the chairs up and set them back around the table.

"No – " He hesitated as he sat down, his eyes sweeping the room nervously. He'd thought he would feel better once they were all inside, but he didn't.

"Nice picture," Nick said, drawing him out of his thoughts. He and Lila were sitting across the table from him, studying a framed photo of the five friends at the lake.

Sam took a deep, steadying breath and leaned forward for a closer look at it. Something about it calmed him, and he smiled a little, remembering Jonah's face when he surfaced in the lake to find the four of them treading water around him. *"I knew you wouldn't let it get me,"* Jonah had said, teeth chattering, grinning that crazy grin of his as he turned to the others. *"You guys really are like heroes or something – the kind that goes off to save the world ... and ..."* – his teeth chattered again – *"... noble junk like that."*

"I understand you have some paintings I would be interested in seeing ..."

He glanced back up at Nick and Lila, and the smile on his lips slowly vanished. The strange hum of electric current that he had felt during Mardi Gras was back, winding through his body, drying up his spit as he watched the air around them bend and waver. He jumped to his feet. A soft ripping sound – like fabric being torn – echoed around him as a huge figure began to materialize between them.

Terror froze him in the spot where he stood. It was the larger twin ... *thing* ... that had been stalking him at Mardi Gras. The being turned to Sam and smiled, and his leather coat began to melt on his body, slowly forming over his massive chest and shaping around his shoulders into a suit of black and silver body armor. Small, shadowy creatures slid out from inside the box filled with Lila's stuff and sidewinded across the room before rising to heights only slightly smaller than that of their leader. He saw those teeth again, heard the strange rattle from their throats.

The being glanced pointedly at the box and then turned his gaze back to Sam. "I invite you in – you invite me in," he said smugly. "Funny how that works ..."

"Nick, *look*," Lila said excitedly. "He *sees* something!"

"Of course he does," Nick said, keeping his eyes on Sam. "Why do you think we're here?"

"But *I* don't see anything! I thought you said they would let us see if we got them invited in."

"Shut up, Lila, and let him talk. The Alliance isn't paying you to whine."

Sam turned to Lila, stunned. *She couldn't be a part of —* The thought evaporated as he watched her eyes dart expectantly — almost greedily — around the room. *Oh, Jonah, I told her about it all, about us — not everything, but enough …*

"Tell us what you see, Sam," Nick urged, pressing his hands down on the table as he leaned forward.

"Lila?" Sam's voice was hoarse, even to his own ears. A small curve of a smile touched her lips as she looked up at him, and he was shaken to the core by the emptiness in her eyes.

She shrugged. "They said you were too old to train."

"Tell us what you see, Sam," Nick repeated.

Their faces looked darker now — as if a shadowlike mask had dropped over them. He had seen the shadow masks before. But why hadn't he remembered?

Sam's eyes slid back to the being that now seemed to dwarf everything in the room. "Where did you come from?" he thought — then realized he had spoken it out loud when the being laughed.

"We are nowhere and everywhere," he said, sweeping his hands through the air as if to say, *The greatest showman on earth!* "We are no one and *everyone!*"

To prove his point, the being began to change, morphing into a beautiful woman, then into a feeble old man, then into a young kid down on his luck, and finally into the fortune teller. She smiled at Sam, and in a flash the being was back to his original form.

"We are a remarkable race," the being said proudly, though his tone remained polite, almost as if he were in a classroom. He inclined his head to the spirit-like creatures moving over Lila and Nick. "Unfortunately, our children cannot perform these feats — not without actually inhabiting the organism — but that's not entirely their fault."

"Why?" was all Sam could get out.

"Why? To give your world something to believe in again." The being smiled. "I am Shammah." He leaned down between Lila and Nick and studied the picture briefly. He then rose back to his

124

full height and assessed Sam with a kind of disdainful interest. "You were their leader even back then, weren't you?"

Sam remained mute.

The being took a step closer. "Always keeping them together ..." His dark eyes glittered malevolently as his voice took on a hard edge. "Always shepherding the little flock to safety."

Sam saw no point in answering him. He had a feeling where it was going and was strangely calm about it. His eyes slid to Lila and Nick, who appeared to be in a state of ecstasy as they stood and gazed blindly around the room.

"And that brings us to why I am here," Shammah continued. "Have you ever heard the term, 'cull the herd'? As in removal of problem animals?" He took another step toward Sam. "If you haven't guessed it yet, *you* are my problem – one of five, really – but I'm getting ahead of myself.

"You see, you and your friends were born with a flaw, a little defect that allows you to see things that ... you have no business seeing." He shrugged. "I cannot allow this to continue."

A wave of nausea rolled over Sam, and he reached out, trying to steady himself.

"I did try to stop it before it came to this," Shammah added, sounding almost contrite. *Almost,* Sam thought. "First when you were children ... and of course when I learned of the little glitch in the memory blocks. They would have never thought of a reunion without you."

Shammah took another step, bringing him only inches from Sam.

"Without you they will fall apart ... scatter to the wind again ... and *we* ..."

" ... will pick them off one ... by ... one," the crazy twin said, appearing next to Shammah.

"My brother, Tola," Shammah announced.

Sam's legs buckled under him. His body felt so weak ... why was he so weak?

"Feeling bad?" Tola inquired in a pleasant voice.

Sam glanced at the blade in Tola's hand, and Shammah laughed, sensing his distress.

"Our blades are for those who would try to save you. Our *weapons* against you? Well, let's just say we prefer to use your own kind. It's worked well over the years. Eons, in fact. And it makes my job so, much, more ... *interesting*."

The being was next to Lila in a flash, the motion so quick that it caused strands of her blonde hair to flutter around her face. She took a step back, her eyes wary but curious too. Shammah smiled and brushed a large finger over her lip. "The kiss ... of death." Lila's hands trembled as she touched her own lips.

"They are really here," she whispered, awestruck, as she looked around the room. Her eyes met Sam's briefly, but she barely registered that he was there. A deep sadness washed over him.

Betrayed ... The word stretched out in his mind like a rubber band, and Sam touched his own mouth, remembering her kiss. He swallowed hard, fighting off another wave of nausea. He felt bad, really bad, like something was going wrong in his body.

He dropped to his knees and grabbed a hold of the table to keep from going down altogether. The table tipped a little, and he caught the journal in his hands just as a horrible weakness overtook him. He fell sideways, clutching the journal to his chest as he lay on the floor, listening to himself pant. It was getting harder to breathe.

"It's nothing personal," Shammah offered, his tone friendly again.

"War *is* hell," Tola added casually. "Or should I say heaven? I get them confused."

They both laughed.

Sam felt the darkness pressing around him and with it, a startling clarity that came too late. He closed his eyes slowly to the beings that stood over him, so immersed in their gloating that they failed to notice him slip his journal open and tear a page free.

What was the line of that poem his mother loved to say? *"Truth ... crushed to the ground ... shall rise again ..."* He closed his fist around the page, praying with all of his heart that it would fall into the right hands – the hands of the only one who would know what it meant.

Oh, God, forgive me ..., he thought, feeling himself fading away. *I've been such a fool ...*

A strange wind beat against his ears, distant yet coming closer, and in the haze of his last ragged breaths he saw faces. Young and old. Beautiful and battered, all moving around him, greeting him, and he realized *they* were his history. They were the shining moments of love and laughter, times of dark despair, the warnings he had chosen to ignore and the chances he had thrown away. A single tear rolled down his cheek as another face loomed before him, the lionlike eyes brimming with an intense sadness, not for who he was ... but for who he could have been.

And then one last face, dirt-smudged and skinny, the smile crooked but made beautiful with hope ...

"... knew you wouldn't let it get me," his brother's ten-year-old voice echoed through his mind as if from a great distance, and Sam felt a sharp stab of regret.

"Jonah," Sam whispered.

15

February 25

He was ten years old again … skinny, all legs and arms …
shivering with excitement as he looked down into the soft
green waters of the lake. He started to shake harder – this
time out of fear – as he watched the huge, poisonous-looking snake
skimming over the water toward the dock where they stood.

"I'm not going in there," Jonah whispered as he stumbled back
into Sam with a thud.

"What's wrong now?"

"Snake," he croaked out, unable to say anything else. Sam leaned
against him as he peered over his shoulder. He felt some of his
shakiness fade with his brother's hand on his back. Sam won't let
anything bad happen.

"Come off it, Jonah," Sam said after a moment. "Whatever you're
seeing, it isn't real. There's no snake." He turned Jonah around to
face him. "Don't you trust me?"

Jonah nodded vigorously, even though he was pretty sure he
was going to pass out or puke. Maybe both. Sam must've seen him
going green too; he let out the heavy sigh of a martyr and then took
Jonah's hand.

"You're going in with me?"

"We're all going in with you!" he heard Carly say, laughing, as he
dove with Sam into the water –

– and resurfaced, seventeen years old, standing in the middle of a
dark living room. No lights, but candles burned everywhere he looked.
He saw Carly, Jenna, and J, each positioned in the remaining three corners of the room. They looked just as stunned as he was to be there.

But where's Sam?

The air vibrated around them, and he saw other people begin to slowly melt into the room. Only it's not just other people – it's the five of them, seven years younger. He watched in horror as the fortune teller came into the room, and he knew he was powerless to do anything. She slithered around the young versions of them, studying each of them like bugs under a microscope ...

He knew he was powerless, because this event had already happened.

"Prophecy you want, prophecy you have," she announced, her smile turning cold. She stopped in front of a young Sam and slowly rose her hand above his head.

She was saying something, something he didn't want to hear. Jonah glanced at the younger version of himself.

He was looking at Sam with a kind of hopeless terror – the kind that comes from years of being made to think it was pointless to stand up for yourself, to try to fight back.

He remembered this part, remembered thinking, *She's like ol' Bud Winters with a different face.* Never in the ten short years of his life had he felt rage like he did at that moment – but he'd never been faced with losing his brother before either. He took a deep breath, and before he could stop himself, the words were out of his mouth:

"Don't ... you ... touch ... him ... you ... HAG!"

Silence.

A horrible cold wind blew around him, and he turned to find himself standing with his brother and best friends in the middle of the street again. Broken shards of glass glittered around his feet. "Why isn't Jenna crying anymore?" he heard someone ask, and they all looked up at once to see the dark sky pressing down on them. Pressing down until he was sure they were all going to suffocate.

"Sam?"

"Why can't I see you guys?" J's young, terrified voice echoed around them. Silence ... a ragged breath (maybe his own), and then: "What IS that?"

Something shone in the dark. He wasn't sure what it did, but he was sure it was something bad ...

He opened his mouth to scream, but nothing came out. None of them could scream. They were paralyzed by the cold, glittering eyes that surrounded them. *Almost reptilian,* Jonah thought as he felt his legs turn to rubber. *Eyes like sn* —

"SOMETIMES THE SNAKES ARE REAL, BRO ..."

Jonah shot up in his bed, gasping for air as his eyes darted fearfully around his room. Sam's voice had broken into his dream like a radio station temporarily transmitting to the wrong channel. *Almost like he was yelling it in my ear, not in my dream* — He froze.

He grabbed his phone off his nightstand and punched in Sam's number. As soon as he heard voicemail pick up, he threw off his blankets, slipped into his clothes from the night before, and headed for his Bronco.

Outside, the bright sunshine did nothing to alleviate the cloud of worry that was fast closing in around him. Something wasn't right — he could feel it in his bones. Sam would've been waiting impatiently for his call. And there was no way he would have just taken off somewhere without his cell phone — not with their plans to meet up with Carly and Jenna.

He opened the door of his truck and slid behind the wheel. *How could I just fall asleep like that?* he thought, disgusted, as he shoved the key into the ignition. *Especially after everything that happened last night. I shouldn't have listened to Sam — I should've stayed!*

The Bronco's engine caught and then sputtered out. He felt a spark of anxiety flare up in him as he tried it a second time; it started but began to knock wildly, shaking the entire vehicle before dying out altogether.

Jonah swore and pounded the dashboard with his fist. Something flashed past the passenger's side window, and he jerked his head around. A couple walking a large dog glanced back at him curiously; both had dark crosses smudged on their foreheads. He frowned as he reached for his cell and hit Sam's number again.

"Come on, come on," he murmured as he watched the couple continue down the street, and it hit him: *Ash Wednesday ...*

Someone picked up Sam's phone, and it disconnected as soon as he started to speak. A jolt of fear shot through him.

Something's not right ..., he thought, scrambling out of the Bronco. *SOMETHING IS NOT RIGHT!* He broke into a fast jog down the street, a jog that quickly became a full-out run as soon as he turned the corner and saw the blond giant watching him, with a small smile on his face, from across the street.

He ran wildly, panic mounting in him as he crossed intersections and dodged pedestrians. *Please, God, please just let Sam be okay,* he silently pleaded as faces swam in and out of his line of vision, faces like the couple in front of his apartment building with those eerie smudges on their foreheads. Cars flashed by, one blaring its horn loudly as he darted blindly across a street, glancing over his shoulder to make sure he wasn't being followed.

Fragments of his dream rose before him; he saw the fortune teller raise her hand, saw those dark, glittering eyes again ... and he heard Sam whisper, *"Sometimes the snakes are real, bro."*

He glanced over his shoulder again. The one with the half-shaved head followed a short distance behind him now.

Jonah gasped for air, pushing himself on.

Five miles felt like twenty as he finally rounded the corner to Sam's place – and was hit by the strobe of flashing red lights from the police cruiser and ambulance parked in front of the old warehouse.

He felt all of his strength leave him. No warning, no one to step in front of him and block the sight of the paramedics as they rolled a body covered with a sheet across the sidewalk.

Oh no ... please, God ... no ... no ... No!

Everything stretched out before him like slow motion. His legs buckled a little, and he saw J appear out of the crowd, heading in his direction. The horrible look of anguish on J's face caused his chest to squeeze into a tight knot of pain, and he held his hand up, warning J not to come any closer.

Jonah glanced back to the paramedics, putting his hand over his mouth like a little kid terrified to see what was behind the door, and took another step forward.

He knew it was Sam – knew it before he fought his way past the police officers – before he saw something fall from Sam's lifeless hand. He rushed forward and tucked his brother's arm back under the sheet. Then, without thinking, he reached up and pulled the top of the sheet down just enough to uncover Sam's face. He felt his legs completely give out underneath him as his heart crashed hard in his chest, almost coming to a complete stop. *Sam, oh why ... Sam ...* He couldn't breathe.

In his mind he saw Sam alive and laughing as they walked together through the crowds of Mardi Gras, and again as he leaned through the window of the Bronco, hitting Jonah's fist with his own before telling him to go home and get some rest. Big brother. Protector of Jonah. Patron saint of the biggest lost cause the world had ever known.

"Sam, please ...," he sobbed out finally – dry, raw sobs. "*Please* don't leave me alone!"

No one moved. Jonah slowly pulled himself up. With tentative fingers, he reached forward and touched Sam's face, as if to convince himself that what was happening was real. Then, with a small sob, he leaned over and kissed his brother's forehead, whispering his name over and over again.

But Sam wasn't there anymore. He didn't know how to explain it, but his entire being sensed that everything that was his brother, everything that made him *Sam*, was gone.

Sounds came trickling back, but muffled, like he was underwater. He heard someone crying in the distance and slid his dull eyes across the street to see Carly and Jenna hugging each other as they sobbed ... He saw J again, standing behind them with a look of intense pain on his face, and somewhere in the recesses of whatever mind he had left, he knew they had dreamed of the fortune teller too.

Together again – all of us ... Just like Sam had hoped we would be. But what good did it do us? What good will it do Sam now?

Jonah glanced down at his feet to the place where he had seen something fall out of Sam's hands. He picked up the crumpled piece of paper and shoved it in his pocket, and somewhere under the rush of water that seemed to be filling his head, he heard one of the cops say, "Not sure about cause of death ..."

But he was somewhere else, younger, shivering and cold, watching Sam take his own shirt off and slip it over his head ... *"Don't leave me,"* he pleaded, looking up into Sam's face.

Sam smiled.

Jonah caught a flurry of movement and saw the paramedics loading Sam's body into the back of the coroner's van. One of the wheels caught on the edge of the back bumper, and he watched in horror as Sam's body slid a little, almost tipping over the side. The attendant jerked the gurney up and shoved it carelessly into the back of the van.

"Stop that!" he cried, something between a primal scream and a sob. He rushed forward, trying to get to the gurney, but was blocked by two uncomfortable-looking policemen. "You can't take him yet!" Jonah grunted, fighting against them with all the strength he had left in him. When that was gone, he began to cry pitifully. "He's all I have, man ... He's all I have ..."

The sound of doors closing ... of the van driving away ... echoed through Jonah's mind as the two cops finally released him.

"I'll be praying for you, son," the older cop said softly.

"Pray for yourself," Jonah muttered. The God he'd believed in as a kid turned out to be just a fairy tale, a foolish dream, and sooner or later you had to wake up and smell the coffee — that or have it tossed in your face. He didn't belong to anyone or anything anymore. Alone ... just as he'd always feared he would be.

He watched them move the barricade off the street, watched the cars begin to drive by — slowly — people craning their necks to see. When he saw Carly and Jenna head across the street toward him, he finally turned away from the scene — from them — even though he knew it might be better if he was around people who understood. What was left of the rational part of Jonah's brain told him this — and hinted to him that he may be going into shock, but he didn't see any sense in listening.

Instead he slowly shuffled down the sidewalk like an old man who had been through too much and seen too much, listlessly searching the faces of the people he passed ... searching for Sam.

A soft wind blew in the in-between, stirring multifaceted prisms of light through the membrane-like force field as Arieh and Jahdiel observed the scene. Police officers and spectators brushed by them, oblivious to their presence. They turned their eyes to the three humans huddled together in the middle of the street.

"We stand watch for now," Arieh said somberly, "ensure no more lives are taken."

"And let the Grigori have free reign," Jahdiel said with a note of impatience in his voice.

The Irinim leader understood his old friend's worry: the Grigori would soon be moving on to Jonah and his friends, testing them for signs of weakness, separating them and making them run, their way of systematically picking off their prey.

"They will destroy them — just as they did this one, if we don't intervene —"

"He was deceived," Arieh interjected, regret tingeing his voice. "The door that was opened could not be shut in time ..."

"Because the Grigori know what's at stake." Jahdiel nodded, then glanced to Arieh. "Now that they are beginning to see again ... This battle will not be easily fought."

"No," Arieh agreed. He turned back to watch the humans, who were unaware of the mission that had been laid on their shoulders. "Let's hope that they are strong enough to endure what's coming."

16

What do you think we should do?" Carly said with a sniff, snapping her phone closed before turning her tear-streaked face to Jenna and J. "He won't answer his phone." They were sitting scrunched together like scared little kids on the curb outside of Jonah's apartment building. Jenna and J stared back at her, their grief making them mute.

"I guess I should call your dad so I can check on Mikey," Jenna said finally. "How long should I tell him we'll be gone?"

"I don't know. Just tell him as long as it takes. He'll understand." Carly glanced over her shoulder at the building.

They had followed Jonah from a distance after the coroner's van pulled away, knowing instinctively not to get too close, in the same way you'd stay at arm's length from a wild animal that had been injured, waiting until it realized you were there to help.

Sam would've wanted them to watch out for Jonah — to stick together.

That had been his plan all along after all, hadn't it? For them to reunite — to stand together against this thing that seemed to be stalking them all?

She rewound over the dream that had startled her and Jenna both awake at the same time the night before — and had sent them rushing to Sam's place without saying a word to each other. She shivered, wondering if she would ever feel warm again.

Everything felt surreal, like one of her nightmares. She wished it *were* just a nightmare. She would go through a thousand nightmares to have her old friend back.

"I keep thinking of the time Sam saved up and bought me my first pair of contact lenses — we were what, twelve? 'You're too pretty to hide behind those big old glasses,' he told me. What twelve-year-old thinks of those things?" Jenna dropped her head in her hands and began to cry again, and Carly felt her own eyes well up with tears as J put his big arms around both of them.

Sam... Carly squeezed her eyes shut as a wave of pain rushed over her. How could she just assume, just take it for granted, that Sam would always be there for them. If any of them had ever doubted the connection they had as kids, their doubt was gone now. Losing Sam was like losing an arm, a piece of you that could never be replaced ... and all that was left behind was the horrible phantom pains to remind you of what you had lost.

She couldn't imagine what Jonah was going through.

Sam — how are we going to help Jonah when he won't even let us near him? Carly thought, blinking through her tears. She flipped her cell phone open again for another try, hoping with all of her might that Jonah would be able to make it through the night.

Sam, after all, had been the one who showed Jonah that there were still good people in the world ... and after their parents died, the only one who was able to keep Jonah from checking out of a world he was born to hate.

17

February 26

No one will tell me anything.

The freaking coroner just hung up on me. What did he expect? "We must perform an autopsy on the body before we can determine cause of death," he says to me. "THE BODY? His name is SAM!" I screamed into the phone. "Don't you freaking touch him! Don't you—"

Click. Dead air.

Dead, just like me. Just like—

Where is that laughter coming from?

February 28

NOtE to Jose: dEAr MR. CUervO, YOU AREN'T a FrieNd of MiNE.

I sHot YOU DOWN and I ... STILL HEAR the PHONE ringing ... STILL HEAR THE CHANT IN MY HEAD: SAM IS DEAD, SAM IS—

SAM IS DEAD!!!!

February 29

My apartment is destroyed.

Just woke up to find everything smashed to pieces except for the Gibson Les Paul Sam bought me for my birthday. My spare guitar is sticking out of the middle of the TV screen —

Guess TV Land wasn't cutting it anymore.

Neither is the tequila … the dope … or whatever else I've found to drink or smoke or swallow. WHY?

Because there isn't enough of ANYTHING that will help me forget …

Can *you* hear *me*, Sam? Who did this to you? What were you going to tell us? It's because of what happened when we were kids, isn't it?

I'm scared, bro. Carly and Jenna sound scared too — been leaving messages on my phone for days. I almost beat my door down with his fists.

He's lucky I'm too tired to care …

18

W e're all seeing this, right?" Jenna shot a nervous glance at J, who sat next to her in the front seat of his Suburban, and then shifted her gaze back to the street.

"Yeah," J said, blowing his breath out in a long, wary sigh.

"We're seeing it," Carly answered from the backseat. Her troubled gaze met Jenna's in the large side mirror before they all turned back to the huge figure of a man dressed in camouflage who stood under the streetlight in front of Jonah's place. Long black hair, strong face, exotic, almond-shaped eyes that constantly watched the coming and going of people in front of the building...

He wasn't doing anything wrong, really—just standing there. But there were things she'd noticed since he appeared that made her think there was more to him. Like the way people walked by as if he weren't there... or the baby that jerked around and reached for him over her mom's shoulders, chubby outstretched fingers struggling as the mom turned and looked right at him with a puzzled smile, seeing *nothing.*

"Mikey, you want to come up here with me?" Jenna asked with forced cheerfulness.

"No," came an exasperated little voice from the backseat. "I want to sit with Carly."

Jenna glanced at J again, gave him a tired smile, and then turned back to watch the man.

It was their third night of keeping vigil outside of Jonah's place. He still wasn't answering Carly's calls—or the door—but at least they knew for sure he was still there. *"Get away from my freaking door, J!"* he had yelled earlier, the horrible cracking despair in his voice driving them all back down the stairs. J had looked so stricken, so *haunted*, that she couldn't help wondering if he was thinking about the night Jonah and Sam's parents were killed.

She brushed her hair back with her hands and secured it with a clip. She wondered if Jonah had noticed the guy standing outside—if he had been jolted by the sight of the old army jacket as much as they had been.

"You know, it's like he's posted himself here," Jenna said slowly, "like he's waiting for something to happen."

"Please don't say that—I don't think I can take anything else happening," Carly said in a tight voice. "Especially to Jonah."

The man turned their way and stared right at them—as if he knew what they were talking about—and they all drew back into the dark recesses of the Suburban. None of them mentioned it after the first time, but Jenna knew they had all seen the weird amber light coming from his eyes.

"Who *is* he?" Carly asked with a tremor in her voice.

"I don't know," J answered quietly. "It's like he's—"

Something not human, Jenna thought, but she didn't say it out loud—not with Mikey in the vehicle with them.

Mikey was too busy to be bothered with their conversation.

They had been so caught up in watching the man that none of them had noticed him quietly flipping on his little flashlight as he labored hard on the new picture in his coloring pad. Mikey frowned as he dug through the giant box of crayons Carly had bought him. He had to find just the right shade of yellow for the big man's eyes ...

19

*J*onah."

Jonah groaned and wrapped a pillow around his head in an attempt to tune out whoever it was who was calling his name. It was the fourth day of his self-imposed exile from the world, and the first time he felt he might actually be able to sleep. He had discovered it was hard to continue to rage after nearly thirty hours of no sleep. With all of the booze and drugs in his bloodstream, it was a wonder he hadn't *died.* But he hadn't – at least not yet.

He let out a sigh as he felt his body being drawn down, down, down through a swirl of inky blackness that wrapped around him, promising him relief from the pain and grief that racked his body.

Take it off me, he pleaded silently. *Someone please take it off me…*

"*Jonah! Don't move!*"

The loud voice shot through his head, startling him so badly that he jerked and rolled off the couch, arms flailing as he tried to keep himself from falling, and just as he felt himself hit the floor … he wasn't in his living room anymore. He was …

… sitting in the middle of a dingy, gray wasteland with no sky or land to tell him where he might be. Just a flat plain of onyx that stretched out on either side of him, and a hard, gusting wind that battered him as he struggled to stand.

For just a brief instant, he sensed people around him – or at least what felt like people. Hundreds – no, more like thousands – of bodies flashing by him so fast, he couldn't see who or what they were. Almost like everything was going in rapid fast-forward but him. They made no sound, but he *felt* them … felt their torment, like a high anxiety that wouldn't quit. He sensed their coldness too. This cold was so horrible that their very beings screamed through his mind, begging for warmth. A black mist began to rise around him, rolling and thick, and the tormented cries turned to a fevered pitch of terror that caused him to shake uncontrollably.

"*DON'T MOVE,*" the voice said again, urgently – just as he was about to take a step, and he froze in his spot.

"Who are you?" he cried in a shaking voice, staring into the black mist. "What is this place?" There was no sound except the wind, and even that sounded different to his ears. No smell either – as though anything alive had left a long time ago.

"Hello?" he yelled into the wind, and after a long, excruciating moment, he saw a sliver of light piercing the dark mist as if coming from far away. The feeling of being surrounded evaporated with the mist as the light drew closer, and he squinted, shielding his eyes against the glare and the wind, until he finally spotted three large, cloaked figures walking toward him in the distance.

A wide swath of pale light passed over them, and he felt his breath catch in his throat as a narrow, silver-colored suspension bridge materialized under their feet, two long arms of metal shooting out from its sides as it propelled them over an immense, lifeless gorge with staggering walls of shiny black onyx that dropped thousands of feet down into ... nothingness.

Jonah's heart stumbled as he glanced down to his feet, planted halfway off a thin precipice that jutted out over the gorge. Just one more step and he would've been gone, history – if it hadn't been for the voice.

He glanced up again, his heart hammering hard as he watched the three men – *if that's what they were* – draw up before him, and the bridge slowly retreated back from the gorge, disappearing into a pale, misty fog.

The smallest of the three raised his head then, and Jonah felt his legs go weak as he stared in shock at the face beneath the hood.

"Sam." A ragged sob filled his throat, and he threw himself into his brother's arms, shaking like a scared little kid as he felt the strong arms wrap around him.

He felt so *real. It has to be real.* He had never felt pain and joy this vivid in any dream – hallucinogenic or otherwise. He stared up at Sam's face, mesmerized.

Let me just stay here – wherever here is – let me just stay with Sam ...

"I don't have much time," Sam said gently, pulling back to look at him. His expression was surprisingly grim. "Listen to me?" Jonah nodded. "You have got to turn off the self-destruct mode. You are opening a door to something you don't understand – something that wants to destroy you, bro ..."

Jonah nodded again, numb after years of Sam lecturing him. He was too excited to really hear much as his mind began to run through all of the crazy movies or TV shows he had ever watched, sifting through the possibilities to support what he was seeing. *Maybe they made a mistake ... maybe Sam really wasn't dead ...*

"Jonah – *listen*," Sam said, his voice rising as the wind began to pick up again, blowing hard around them. "You don't know what I had to come through to get to you!"

Jonah stopped in mid thought and looked up at Sam. Another gust of wind struck, and the front of Sam's cloak blew open to reveal the exact same shirt he had been wearing the last time Jonah had seen him ... *lying on that gurney.* Only this shirt looked like it had been ripped to pieces.

You don't know what I had to come through ...

A cold rush of fear washed over Jonah.

"Where are we, Sam?" he asked cautiously, his eyes sweeping over the two men who stood on either side of his brother. They were massive, at least ten feet tall, their faces shrouded by the hoods of their cloaks as they stared straight ahead. He looked back at Sam.

"Where *are* we?"

Sam shook his head, and Jonah was a little ticked that he didn't look sorry – just determined.

"Can you at least tell me what happened to you?"

Sam shook his head again. "You're going to have to look for the answers, Jonah. I know this doesn't make sense to you right now, but it will, I promise. You remember the place, right?"

"What are you talking about? Why can't you give me a straight answer?"

"Mom and Dad's murder – it wasn't J," Sam rushed on, like he needed to get it all out of his head at once. "It wasn't his fault."

A strange rain began to fall, thick and luminous, mixing in with the wind, and Jonah watched as the man to his brother's right bent down and whispered something urgent to Sam — something that sounded almost musical — in a language Jonah couldn't begin to describe. *"The first language,"* a soft voice whispered through him.

"First language?" he asked out loud, glancing from Sam to the men, but they didn't seem to hear him.

Maybe this is *a dream,* Jonah thought, feeling the cold tentacles of grief wrapping around his heart again. *Things like this don't happen in real life . . .* He leaned forward anyway, straining to hear what was being said.

Something inside of him clicked then, and their odd language began to change — like someone had pressed a button somewhere — and he heard the musical notes slow down to something slightly more stilted.

"Tele-im," the man said. "Telll-im . . . Tell him!"

Jonah almost laughed when he realized he was hearing his own language. Then the man on Sam's right turned his way, momentarily blinding him with a brilliant flash of gold light that obscured the spot where his face would've been.

"This isn't a dream, Jonah — it's real," Sam said, his voice growing urgent as it rose above the wind and the rain. "But you can't see the truth . . . until you open your eyes."

The man to the left of Sam turned around. A huge staff appeared in his hand, and he struck the ledge of the gorge with it. The suspension bridge materialized once more . . . and Jonah knew with sudden heartbreaking clarity that their visit was coming to an end.

"Sam — don't leave me here!" he cried, and for the first time since he had arrived in this strange place, he saw regret flicker over his brother's face.

"We *have* to go," Sam said. He glanced around expectantly, as if some kind of giant alarm clock were getting ready to go off, and then he put his hand on Jonah's shoulder. "It's not safe to stay here any longer. Just remember what I told you. The five of you have to stick together — no matter what it takes. They're going to try to split you up. There's a reason we were all drawn together, Jonah . . . never forget that."

"Five? But there aren't five of us anymore."

Sam smiled and then glanced to the men waiting for him. "All of that stuff we talked about, dreamed about, as kids? It's true ..."

"What are you *talking* about?" Jonah's eyes welled up with tears, in spite of his best efforts to keep them in. He didn't want to hear anymore; he wanted to stay with his brother – wanted desperately to keep the only bit of family he had ever known.

But Sam was already following the two men back onto the bridge.

Jonah made a mad dash to join them, running against the battering wind and rain, but just as he reached the bridge and lifted his foot to step out onto it, it withdrew from the ledge, refusing him access.

"Who's going to save the world?" Jonah choked out. He fell to his knees, shivering, as the rain pelted him. He was a little kid again ... and so afraid of being alone. "Who's going to be the hero now?"

Sam turned back and looked at him one last time.

"*You* are, little bro," Sam called out over the storm. He smiled then, a beautiful smile, like he had saved the best for last. "Don't you know? It's always been you ..."

A harsh cry ripped from Jonah as he found himself on his knees in the middle of his own living room again, looking around like a man who had just woken up to find himself on a deserted island.

Lost. Everything was gone ...

Tears streamed down his face as he slowly surveyed the chaos that had once been his apartment. *I don't want to be here! I want to go back. I want to be with Sam again!*

That rain ... He felt his clothes ... How could they be so dry when only moments ago he had stood with Sam under a torrent of wind and rain?

Because it was just a dream, he thought angrily, *just a stupid dream that was about as real as the stupid TV Land shows with their perfect families and happily-ever-after endings.*

He reached for the almost-empty bottle of tequila on the coffee table, picked it up ... and then a better idea came to him, and he set the bottle back down.

J caught the sudden movement and leaned against his steering wheel as he peered up through the windshield. The window to Jonah's apartment flew up, sucking the curtains outside, where they fluttered in the wind like pale ghosts in the night sky. J's heart began to skip wildly.

Come on, Jonah, don't do this—

He grabbed the handle, shoving the door open, and jumped out of the Suburban just in time to see a TV appear in the window, with what looked like … *a guitar* sticking out of its screen. His mouth fell open as the TV/guitar tumbled down, exploding against the pavement with such force that it startled the others awake.

The window slammed shut and J exhaled, not realizing until then that he had been holding his breath the entire time.

"There went my last nerve," he announced as he slid behind the wheel again. "I guess he wants to see me back in the loony bin." The girls didn't even flinch at the mention of his recent address. They appeared amused that someone as big as him—with a reputation like his—would admit it. J smiled in spite of himself.

Another crazy night, he thought as the chime on his cell phone went off again, and he wondered if he should check his voicemail. Tiny had left fifteen messages. The other messages were from Nick Corsa, furious that he hadn't returned his calls. J had turned the phone off after that, almost hoping pretty boy would send someone looking for him. He was itching for a confrontation.

He glanced up at Jonah's window. "What do you think he's doing?"

"No telling," Jenna said, groggy. "But at least we know he's still alive."

"And kicking," Carly added. "Wouldn't be Jonah without the kick."

They all looked at each other and laughed—a bittersweet laugh, but the first one they had been able to share in over three days.

Then the rain started in. They couldn't remember the last time it had rained so much in February. The rain was all they could talk about – *wanted* to talk about.

None of them mentioned another word about the stranger in the army jacket who continued his silent vigil in front of the apartment building.

20

Nick Corsa lifted his gaze through the rain-splattered windshield to the lights hovering above the two large cranes as they slowly inched backward along the Arch grounds, cables taut, straining under the weight of the mammoth stone tablets. Everything was moving forward just as planned, thanks to the efficiency of the Alliance and the network of influential followers they had throughout the city – not to mention the world.

But then, unimaginable power is the ultimate motivator, he thought, turning his attention to some of St. Louis's finest guarding the entrance to the grounds. Soon all evidence of the star gate would be moved to a safe location – away from the prying eyes of those who would try to thwart the return of the Grigori and the rest of their kind.

Namely, the Resistance.

Nick frowned. He was going to have to take care of the cell that had been planted in St. Louis soon – before they could make contact with those they were calling the Watchers. The Alliance was too close to removing that obstacle once and for all to have the Resistance get in their way now.

One down, he thought smugly, *four to go ...*

"I have news for you," Lila announced, drawing him from his thoughts as she snapped her cell phone closed. "The old lady believes there is another Watcher." Her smile was almost feline. "A child."

Nick glanced at her sharply. *A child? If that is true ...* His mind raced through the possibilities. To have one so young, one whom the Alliance could shape and mold, one who could converse directly with the ascended masters ... The implications were staggering.

A child ...

"Might be worth looking into," a deep voice whispered through his mind.

"Might be worth looking into," Nick said to Lila before he turned to look out the window again. He lost himself momentarily in the heady dreams of wealth and power. But mainly power.

Once you had power, everything else just kind of fell into place.

21

March 2

"You going to the funeral, Jeremiah?"

"No."

"You boys were thick as thieves once."

"Long time ago, Grandma," J said. He took a drag of his cigarette and exhaled, watching the smoke. "Things change."

"What's in the past is in the past. Sam put it away – can't you? Out of respect?"

"I don't want to talk about it, Grandma ..."

Eighty-six-year-old Willa Harvey shook her head slowly as she sat in her wheelchair on the front porch of her tiny row house, feeling troubled in spite of the warm morning sun. Her eyes moved over her grandson as he leaned over the railing, staring off across the yard. His long dreadlocks were pulled into a tam, allowing her to notice the bowed look of his shoulders – as if the weight of the world were on them.

She'd heard the rumors, heard he'd become leader of some gang in Chicago. She'd heard about the shooting too, though he wasn't the one who told her. The old woman grimaced. At least he hadn't stopped visiting every once in a while. It gave her hope that the sweet boy he'd once been was still there ... somewhere. She pursed her lips, sensing a fear on him that she had never sensed before – at least not since he was a small boy. Confusion too. Like he didn't know where to go or what to believe anymore ...

Thief has come to your door, old woman, she thought grimly. She knew all about thieves; she was a little girl during the Great Depression, a youth when the Nazi war came, and a wide-eyed teenager when folks went plain out of their heads with riots and burnings and assassinating three of the best men the world would ever know.

150

Yes sir, she knew about thieves.

"You know what your grandpa told me just before he died?" she said, watching his profile carefully. "He said, 'Why should we fear death, Willa? The Almighty allowed it the same as he did life.'" She cocked her head to one side, issuing a rueful sigh. "Course, he mostly talked crazier than a bedbug at the last. But I like to think it was one of his clear moments."

A hint of a mischievous smile peeked out on J's face as he turned and looked at her. "An Uncle Lester kind of moment?"

Willa raised her brows. "You're a piece of work, talking about your grandpa's brother like that," she said, laughing and shaking her head.

"I learned from the best," J said with a grin. She let out a startled laugh and swatted at him. His smile faded. "Don't worry about me so much, Grandma. I'm doing okay. Really."

She frowned. She had never been the preachy type, but truth was, she didn't know how many chances she had left to talk to the boy. Lollygagging around was risky at her age. Like eating too much cheese.

"The Lord will help you if you let him, Jeremiah."

"Been a long time since I thought about any of that, Grandma," J said, meeting her eyes with a haunted look, and Willa felt an alarm go off inside her.

There was a terrible war going on inside him – she could see it as clear as day. *A war within a war,* she thought and then frowned at the strange turn of phrase. He threw his cigarette to the ground and crossed the porch to give her a quick hug.

"Gotta go," he said, pecking her on the cheek.

"But you just got here!" Willa exclaimed, her frail arms falling to her lap as he took a step back. He reached out again and took her bony hand in his.

"I'll be back to visit soon," he assured her. "Just got to deliver something before it gets too late."

"Nothing wrong?"

"No ma'am," J said, shaking his head. "I'm hoping it'll do some good."

Willa felt a cold breeze stir around her as she watched her grandson pull away. A really cold breeze ... and it had been so mild only moments ago. She glanced to the only tree in her yard and frowned slightly. *Funny. Ain't a twig moving on that old tree ...*

But there *was* something there. She craned her neck and squinted her eyes against the sun.

The MazziKim stared down with hatred at the old woman from their perch at the top of the tree. She couldn't see — not like her grandson — but the strength of the spirit inside the feeble shell made her just as much of a threat. They considered tormenting her, until the sharp command came cracking through their minds. Two of them raised their eyes to the birds coming in for a landing and shot into their bodies through a blur of veins and tissue. They lifted off, manipulating the fat crow wings from inside their hosts as they took to the sky.

22

Jonah stubbed his cigarette out, slammed the door of his truck, and headed toward the huge, wrought iron gates leading to the cemetery – the last place on earth he wanted to be. Everything felt surreal. The sunny day after what felt like a lifetime of rain ... The old church with its boarded-over windows and surrounding desolation, which made him feel like he was standing in the middle of a ruined German village right out of *Call of Duty* instead of his old stomping grounds ... and Sam ...

How did everything get so crazy, bro? he wondered bleakly. *How can I really be going to your funeral?*

He unbuttoned the top of his shirt and yanked his tie loose, trying to ease the pressure in his chest. Just thinking of the words *Sam* and *funeral* in the same sentence caused a spike of anxiety through him so sharp and painful that he almost turned around and got back in his truck – and would've turned around if he hadn't spotted Carly heading toward him through the gates of the cemetery in her black dress. She looked good – better than good, and it irritated him that he would be thinking such things on the day he was burying his brother.

"You know, this isn't exactly a great neighborhood to be taking a stroll through by yourself anymore," he said.

"You're here now," Carly answered with a sad smile as she hugged him tight. He didn't realize how good it felt – or how much he needed it – until she pulled back to look at him. "I had to take a walk, anyway – started thinking too much about ... everything ..." She let the rest of the thought fade off as she reached for his tie.

"Any more nightmares?"

Carly shook her head as she fiddled with his tie nervously. "What about you?"

"No," he said with a sigh. "That's weird, isn't it? I mean, knowing where we were coming today? I hate to even say it out loud, but all that kept running through my head this morning were the words "calm before the storm.""

Carly looked at him, fear in her eyes. "Why is this happening to us? The last dream I had didn't even feel like a dream, Jonah. It felt like we were really together in that fortune teller's place again, watching our *past*. Jenna and J had the same dream."

Jonah glanced at her sharply. "That's why you were all there – in front of Sam's place ..."

She started to say something more but hesitated.

Jonah hesitated too, trying to decide if he should tell her about what happened that night outside of Sam's place or about the strange dream with Sam and those two ... *men?* ... but finally decided to keep his mouth shut. She was scared enough.

"I'm sorry I bailed on you ... and everyone," he said finally, watching her finish up with his tie. He felt a lump in his throat and tried to swallow it away. "I didn't mean for you and your dad to have to ... arrange everything. I was ... I guess I went a little crazy."

"I would be worried if you weren't crazy," Carly said quietly. She smoothed his tie down against his chest before looking up at him again. "Sam was probably the best friend any of us ever had." Her eyes shined with tears as he took her hand and they began to walk.

"You know, the hardest part about coming here was knowing how bad he wanted us all back together," he said. "Here we all are ... and he's gone. How messed up is that?"

"You want to hear something really messed up?"

Jonah glanced down at her. There was something about the tone of her voice that made him think maybe he *didn't* want to hear it. When she avoided his eyes, he *knew* he didn't want to hear it.

She cleared her throat. "My dad got a call from the coroner this morning – "

He stopped walking. "The one I threatened?"

"That would be him," Carly said, nodding. She gave him a wan smile before looking at the ground. "He told my dad that there were *fifteen* empty pill bottles found around Sam's body – but none of the drugs were found in his bloodstream."

"Wait a minute – he thought Sam *killed* himself?" Jonah asked incredulously, throwing his cigarette on the ground. He suddenly felt like he was going to be sick. "That's why he was acting like such a jerk."

"Well, it was his first theory."

"Yeah – what does he think now?"

Jonah turned away, his eyes sweeping the area around them. Something was wrong around them ... like the air had somehow changed ...

"They don't know yet," Carly said. She glanced around like she felt something off too. "That's what scares me. Sam wanted us all back together because *he* was scared. I think he had figured something out about that night when we were kids ..." She shook her head. "I think he *knew* something was about to happen to us."

A cold breeze buffeted them, blowing their hair back, and then was gone.

"Did you feel that?" Carly asked haltingly, touching her hair.

"Yeah ...," Jonah said as another gust of wind hit – this one warm – and he felt Carly reach for his hand again.

Arieh burst through the barrier between dimensions, his feet hitting the grounds at the far end of the cemetery without breaking stride as he came face-to-face with the Grigori leader, who was dressed in the decorated black body armor worn by the high chiefs of his kind. In spite of the pale, plaited hair and alabaster skin, his very presence exuded a darkness that shot out at Arieh, trying to latch on to his consciousness with a viselike grip.

"You trespass, Shammah," Arieh said, evoking a thin smile from his old adversary. "You and your lackeys are not welcome here."

"This sounds a lot like another conversation we had, *Irinim*," Shammah said with forced casualness as he stroked the backs of the two crows that perched on his finger. "Besides, they have promised to behave ... right?"

The birds bobbed their black heads up and down, then craned their necks and looked at Arieh.

"Abominations," the Irinim leader spat.

"I could say the same for your little herd," Shammah countered. Tension between the former comrades began to fill the air.

"Tell me, then, why are you so afraid of them?"

"I wouldn't exactly call it fear." Shammah glanced toward the gravesite and continued to pet the birds. "They're more of an annoyance—like cattle that have slipped through the fence."

"Then why the rush to destroy them? Because of the prophecy?"

"Our prophecy or yours?" Shammah's eyes changed from the amber color of their kind to black pools of hate—the very thing that had separated their race. He smiled finally. "Let's just go with, I destroy them ... because I *can*."

"And continue a war you have no chance of winning?" Arieh pressed, taking a step closer. The birds trembled on their perch.

"How soon you forget the score. Tell me, where is their little leader now?" Shammah's expression turned wicked. "Sam? Sam, where are you?" He called mockingly, cupping his hand over his mouth. He turned back to Arieh. "Oh, that's right. *Dust* can't speak."

Arieh took another step closer, his eyes flashing as his gaze bored into Shammah's. He circled the Grigori leader. "Do you not still feel the weight of the chains I placed on you? Does your brother?"

Their eyes locked, both gripped by the memory of a battle that happened eons ago—the harsh cries of two hundred rogue warriors as they were bound ... the echoes of the cavernous door slamming shut behind them ...

Shammah was the first to look away, distracted by movement from the corner of his eye, a flash of light near the inside portion of the stone wall that encircled the grounds of the cemetery. All at once six Irinim warriors morphed out from the ornately carved angel statues planted like concrete sentinels along the wall. A line of Grigori warriors materialized, weapons drawn, blocking their way.

Arieh reached over his shoulder to draw his weapon, but Shammah had anticipated the move.

"Now!" Shammah cried as six Grigori warriors materialized from out of the earth around Arieh in a shower of dirt and leaves. They drew their swords on him at the same time, encircling him, closing in like a pack of wolves. Tola appeared, the shaved left side of his head giving him a look that matched the insanity in his eyes. He lunged forward from the center, his sword narrowly missing Arieh's throat.

A lion's roar ripped from Arieh, and he struck Tola and the six Grigori warriors to the ground with one massive blow of his fist. Shammah took a step back.

"Did you think you could move on hallowed ground – that you can go beyond the Law?" Arieh thundered, moving until he was only inches away from Shammah's face. He lowered his voice to a whisper. "It is the Law that keeps me from cutting you down where you stand."

For a split second he saw the fear on Shammah's face; then Shammah's eyes began to suffuse with unholy power, and the old arrogance returned.

"You might hold this little piece of territory – but what about the air? Who rules the air, *Irinim*?" A ripping sound came out of nowhere as the air began to bend around them ... and he and his warriors were gone.

Jonah slowed his pace, stalling for time as they got closer to Sam's gravesite. He glanced at Carly. He felt winded all of a sudden. Weak. He loosened his tie again. Carly squeezed his hand in reassurance, and he looked up in time to see a huge black Lab bounding toward them. It hit him in the chest with both paws, nearly knocking the air out of him, and then licked his face.

"Doc! Get down!"

"Is this the *puppy* you told me about on the phone?"

Carly smiled. "Yeah – he's not usually this friendly with strangers."

Jonah gave her a small smile as he scratched the big dog behind the ears. The dog let out a soft bark, and he glanced up and saw Carly's dad quickly making his way over to them.

Chaplain Hagan hadn't changed much; the intense blue eyes now stared at him from behind glasses, but other than that, he still reminded Jonah of the shaggy-haired throwback from the sixties who dropped Carly off at school every day in a vintage VW Bug with a "Don't trust anyone over thirty" bumper sticker.

He shook Jonah's hand warmly, and a memory popped into his head: Sam standing in that makeshift gym in Carly's basement as her dad put him through Wing Chun drills—a routine Jonah would have feared almost as much as math. "You want me to teach you Jeet Kune Do, you gotta learn the basics," Chaplain Hagan had teased Sam. "Wash on, wash off, Grasshopper!"

The determined smile on Sam's face ...

"Jonah, I'm so sorry about Sam," Chaplain Hagan said, his voice dragging Jonah from the memory. He hesitated for only a second and then pulled Jonah to him in a strong embrace. "You're going to get through this, son."

Jonah looked up at the older man and sensed there was something more he wanted to say.

Carly's dad hesitated again, then pulled a small book from his coat pocket and handed it to him. "Sam's professor said this was left on his desk this morning. He thought you should have it."

Jonah stared at the book in his hands and felt a fresh stab of grief. *Sam's journal ...* He *never* went anywhere without it. So why would it be on some professor's desk? He followed Carly's dad's gaze down the row of mourners who were already seated around the grave, until it stopped at the distinguished-looking black man with a light peppering of gray in his hair and goatee. As if sensing their stares, the man glanced their way. He nodded at Jonah and then turned and said something to the man next to him.

Jonah almost did a double take as the other man leaned forward, and he saw the long black braid and glasses—the same Asian guy he had seen standing in the middle of that storm at Mardi Gras.

He suddenly had the eerie feeling that Sam's funeral wasn't a funeral at all ... but a weird gathering of some kind.

"I'm Mikey," a little voice announced, and Jonah looked down, shocked to find that he was now sitting between Carly and Jenna, next to Sam's gravesite—the voice apparently coming from the boy sitting on Jenna's lap.

The kid brushed his curly hair back from his face and stared up at him with a solemn expression. Something about the old-man look in his eyes reminded Jonah of J when he was young. Jonah glanced around him. A lot of people had come to pay their respects ... but no sign of J.

The kid was still staring at him.

"Jonah," he said, recovering. "Nice to meet you, little man." He held his hand out, and the kid slapped him a hard five without hesitation. Jenna tried to smile, but her eyes held a dazed, lost look that for reasons he couldn't explain made him uneasy.

He turned his attention to the group of mourners on the other side of the casket and saw Lila checking her face in a tiny makeup mirror as she dabbed at her eyes with a tissue. On the other side of her was her cousin, who appeared strangely ... keyed up, and next to him was one of Sam's students — Mickey or Matty or something — who just looked *tortured* before turning away from Jonah's gaze.

"I came here today not really knowing what to say ...," Chaplain Hagan began. "Truth is, in all of the years I've preached, I've never known what to say or how to explain the whys to those grieving a loved one. Especially one as young as Sam."

Jonah felt his anxiety kick into high gear as soon as he heard Sam's name. *I can't do this ...*

He looked at Sam's casket — as if in some miraculous way Sam could still come to his rescue — and immediately regretted it. First it was the pain, like thick shards of glass stabbing him through the chest ... and then it was rage.

Fifteen empty pill bottles ... nothing in his bloodstream ...

He had promised himself that he wouldn't lose control, that for once in his crazy life he would behave like other people —

But he had never been like other people.

His eyes darted desperately from Carly to Jenna, hoping one of them could talk him down before it got too bad, but they both had their heads down, crying. *Should've never come here, should've never come here! Sam would've understood —*

"What I do know is that God tells us that for *everything* there is a season, and a time for every matter under heaven ..."

Jonah caught Lila staring at his hands with a strange look on her face. He glanced down at Sam's journal and then back up to her; her eyes were flat, emotionless, as he opened the journal.

"A time to be born ... and a time to die ..."

He began to turn the pages, comforted a little by the sight of Sam's handwriting. *You were here,* he thought as he traced his fingers over the words, *you were just here* —

The writing suddenly came to an end, and he frowned, turning another page ... and then another ...

"For Sam, that time has come — but does that mean his journey has ended, or has it just begun? Do we really believe this is all there is? Or do we, like Solomon, feel that *eternity* God has placed in every heart? That while we don't understand everything right now, we know deep down that there *is* a plan —"

Plan? Jonah furiously flipped through the remaining pages, finding nothing but blank, lined paper. *What kind of stupid plan wouldn't let Sam finish his journal?*

Mikey suddenly jerked back on Jenna's lap, his foot accidentally knocking the journal from Jonah's hands. Jonah fumbled for it and caught it just before it hit the ground, then glanced sideways at the boy —

"Sorry," he heard Jenna whisper.

— but Mikey seemed oblivious to it all as he stared up at the sky. He followed the kid's gaze and saw the two fat crows lazily circling each other in the sky above them.

Jonah felt his mouth go dry as the crows dipped lower in the sky and then *hovered,* cocking their heads at him as they observed him through black, glittery eyes.

" ... for a future that goes beyond what we can see ..."

Jonah felt a cold fear growing in the pit of his stomach. He heard Mikey say, *"Mom?"* and felt Carly grab his arm — *"Do you hear that?"* — and then their voices faded under a horrible sound that was growing louder, the sound of hundreds of grasshoppers in late summer, but different ... more menacing.

He glanced from Carly to Mikey, whose eyes were glued on the crows, to Jenna, who didn't seem to notice anything was wrong, before reluctantly lifting his eyes to the sky again. The sound was coming from the birds, growing louder ... A voice added to the mayhem, deep and sinuous, snaking through his mind with its poison chant: *"Fifteen empty pill bottles, fifteen empty pill bottles and nothing in his blood. HE'S NEVER COMING BACK!"*

"Stop it!" Jonah bolted out of his chair, not caring that all eyes were on him now. The sound was driving him crazy, fanning the flames of anger and frustration that had been building up inside him. "Just stop it!"

"Jonah!" Chaplain Hagan's voice brought an abrupt end to the sound, and as Jonah glanced up to the sky, he realized the birds had vanished with it. He turned back to the shocked faces that surrounded him.

"What kind of *plan* would let my brother die?" he yelled hoarsely as he held the journal up to the crowd. "What kind of *plan* wouldn't even let him finish this? Why couldn't he finish his stupid journal?"

Before Chaplain Hagan or anyone else could answer him, he stormed off toward his truck.

"Jonah!" Carly called out as she hurried after him. "Don't go—not like this!"

Can't run away this time, bro. Gotta keep everyone together, remember? a voice that could've been Sam's whispered to him, but he ignored it. Put a big, fat Do Not Disturb sign up in his mind as he picked up his pace.

"Jonah, please!"

He whipped around and saw Carly come to a stop a short distance away.

"You're not alone in all of this. I'm with you—so are Jenna and J. Come back, and maybe my dad can help us figure out what's going on."

He held his arms out as he walked backward. "What else can he tell me that I don't already know, Carly? That I'm crazy, having some kind of weird hallucinations? That for once in my life, I shouldn't run from my problems?"

"It can't be a hallucination if I'm seeing it too!"

Jonah wasn't listening; he was on a *roll*. "Or maybe just cut to the chase and say what everyone's thinking anyway: that I should've died instead of Sam."

"Why would you even say something like that?" Carly asked, stunned. She took a couple of steps closer, and he saw the tears in her eyes.

He knew he was acting like a jerk, but he couldn't help it. Sometimes you just had to say what was on your mind. Say it or explode.

"Because *I* think I should've been the one to die. Don't you get it? Whoever planned this got their wires crossed. Throw some pill bottles around *my* body, and the world would've shrugged. I'm already damaged goods, Carly, remember? But Sam? Come on – even I know better than that."

He jerked the door of his truck open, slid inside and slammed the door, and peeled out of the lot before she had the chance to say another word.

"Mind if I join you?"

Jenna glanced sideways as Nick Corsa slid into the empty seat next to her. Trendy haircut, warm smile, sleepy brown eyes that watched her from beneath thick lashes.

"What would you do if I said no?" She swiped the tears from her face and managed to smile back, even though her heart felt like it was breaking in two. Jonah losing it like he did scared her. How were they going to fix things with Sam gone?

"Well, if you said no, I suppose I would just slide back the other way."

Jenna smiled again. Sam's girlfriend had introduced them earlier, but at the time she had chalked up his interest in her to politeness; the whole you're-here-I'm-here thing when you find yourself standing next to a stranger. She glanced around for Mikey. She wished she hadn't taken that pill Lila gave her for the panic attack. She still felt fuzzy, off ...

"Didn't Lila leave already?" she asked.

"She did." His smile faded, and he looked down at his hands. "I don't know why I stayed. I guess I was in shock. I mean, I just *met* Sam, and now he's gone." He shook his head sadly. "Seeing his brother fall apart like that ..." He shook his head again. "It was just so horrible."

"Jonah's a good guy—he's just had a really hard life," she said slowly, trying to decide how much she should tell. The understanding in his eyes prompted her to go on. "Their parents were killed a couple of years ago, so Sam was the only family he had left ..." She spotted Mikey a short distance away, staring up at a tree like it was the most interesting thing in the world. She frowned. What was he *doing*?

"No wonder he was so distraught," Nick said, sighing. "I lost my own parents when I was nine, and there is nothing worse than realizing you're all alone in the world."

Jenna turned back to him, mildly surprised that he would open up to her like that, and she saw the loneliness sweep over his face as he stared off across the cemetery. *He's just like me,* she thought. Her parents might as well have died, as much as they were in her life these days.

"I know exactly what you mean," she said as he turned to look at her. Their eyes met, and she felt a sudden connection ignite between them, a kind of understanding that was more powerful than anything she had ever felt before. She'd heard about things like this but never believed they really happened. She exhaled shakily and Nick smiled, almost like he felt it too.

Her eyes flicked over the expensive dark suit, sensing the air of success, and she felt her old doubts and insecurities well up in her. A guy as successful-looking as him wouldn't be interested in a girl who'd dropped out of high school to have a kid, after all.

Nick cocked his head sideways—like he was listening for something—then glanced to Mikey, who was heading toward them ... cautiously. "Do you and your son need a ride some-where?"

"Well, we were kind of waiting on my friend, Carly ..." Jenna glanced toward the spot where Carly and her dad stood, deep in conversation, and felt a tug of loneliness. She turned to Nick. "We flew in from Vegas, so I'm staying with Carly and her dad for now."

Nick nodded.

"I want to go with Carly, Mom," Mikey said as he plastered himself against her leg.

Jenna smiled, ruffling his curly dark hair, but he seemed oblivious. His eyes were fixed on a spot somewhere behind Nick Corsa ... with the strangest look on his face.

"I want to go with Carly," Mikey repeated. "I don't want to go with him."

"Mikey – don't be so rude!" Jenna choked out an embarrassed laugh while cringing inwardly. *Great. I'll be a first in the medical journals for actually dying of embarrassment ...* She gave Nick an apologetic smile, and when he returned it with an understanding smile of his own, she took the plunge. "If you could drop us off at Chaplain Hagan's place, I would really appreciate it. I'm not sure how long Carly is going to be, and I have to get some food in Mikey ..."

"I would be happy to," Nick said – and he actually did look happy.

But Mikey wouldn't budge. Jenna took his hand and even gave him a tug, but he held his ground.

"Come on, Mikey – cut it out!" She glanced at Nick and then did the unthinkable – at least as far as Mikey was concerned – and scooped him up in her arms. "I don't know what's gotten into him. He *never* acts like this."

"Oh, he's just being a kid," Nick said.

Jenna could have cried with relief. She had never been so mortified in her life. For Mikey to act like that was crazy enough – but did it have to be in front of a good-looking, *really* nice guy? It wasn't every day that someone like her met someone like him, after all ...

"Jonah?" The voice was deep, cultured – definitely not someone he would know. He glanced at the words *private caller* on his cell phone's screen as he weaved in and out of traffic, swiping his eyes with the back of his hand. He had no idea where he was going, but he had to get away – had to somehow escape the unbearable pain that rolled through his body in waves.

"Jonah? This is Professor Garrett Kinney. I'm – I was a friend of Sam's ... I was wondering if you had a moment to talk?"

Jonah winced, feeling a fresh stab of pain at the mention of Sam's name in past tense. He brushed his hand through his hair as he came to a stop at the traffic light. "Listen, I appreciate you bringing my brother's journal to me. It means a lot—more than I can tell you …" His mind started to race again. "I … just can't talk right now."

"No, and I'm sorry for that, sorry for your loss, Jonah, but I think maybe you should hear me out. You and your friends are in serious danger—and things will get worse in a matter of days."

Jonah hesitated. How did he know they were in trouble?

"Okay," he said slowly. "I just left my brother's funeral. What was your first clue?"

"You're seeing things, aren't you?"

Jonah clenched his jaw tight. *How in the heck did this guy even get my number?*

"Sam was seeing things too," Professor Kinney offered. "I was hoping you would allow me to help you."

"Like you helped Sam?"

Silence.

Jonah heard the older man take a deep breath and flipped his phone closed just as the professor started to reply. He didn't need anyone telling him what was wrong—or what they thought he should do to fix it.

He didn't need anybody.

Mikey froze as he watched Mr. Corsa reaching across his mom in the backseat, offering him his hand.

"Shake?" the man asked pleasantly.

He stared at the hand and then looked at his mom. *No way,* he told her with his eyes. Her smile drooped a little. He felt bad about that—but there was no way he was shaking the guy's hand.

No way …

Not with those two dark shadow-man things on either side of Mr. Corsa—the same two he had seen in the trees, acting like birds. *"Divide … ,"* Mikey heard them whisper to Mr. Corsa. *"Divide … and … conquer …"* Whatever that meant. He shrank back farther in the seat and hugged his backpack to his chest as the shadow men continued whispering in Mr. Corsa's ears.

He wanted to tell his mom, but he knew he'd better wait until they were alone. She probably wouldn't hear a word he was saying right now. She was too busy giving Mr. Corsa that googly look again. Mikey frowned and turned and looked out the window as the word DANGER kept flashing in his head like a big red neon sign.

He had started seeing words in capital letters around the same time the bad dreams started – shortly after he'd found that book in one of his mom's boxes in the closet. It kind of scared him at first, but the longer the words were around, the more he realized they were good.

Like the time DON'T GO IN THERE popped into his head when he and Spence Jacobi had found the lid off the sewer behind the apartment building. They didn't go in, but Spence told Dustin, and he had climbed down there and couldn't get out. Meeting the firemen was cool, though ...

Then there was that little thing with the baby snakes. He and Spence were going to divide them up and keep them in jars in their rooms, until DON'T TOUCH THOSE SNAKES came to him. Just to be sure, he had taken his mom for a look, and her words had sounded almost like the capital words in his head: "COPPER-HEADS, MIKEY! IF THEY HAD BITTEN YOU, YOU WOULD BE DEAD!"

"I don't bite, you know," Mr. Corsa said, startling him, and he heard him and his mom laugh like it was a funny joke. The car started up then, and in spite of all his efforts to be brave, he felt a scary feeling winding its way through his body.

He didn't want to look – didn't want to see those shadow things again. He wished they would've gone home with Carly. Wished that J guy was here – or even Jonah. He *liked* all of them. He felt safer when they were around, for some reason ... He liked the word that kept appearing in his mind lately too.

"*Watcher ...*" Mikey whispered the word, letting it roll off his tongue.

"What did you say?" Mr. Corsa asked. He leaned forward in his seat, sounding suddenly more interested in talking to him than in talking to his mom. Mikey pretended not to hear him as he watched the old buildings and houses go by.

Something flashed by, so close that if the window had been down, he could've reached out and touched it. He pressed his face against the window to get a better look ... and found himself staring directly into the face of a shadow man. It grinned at him.

Mikey sat back in his seat and stared straight ahead. He didn't need words – not even capital ones – to tell him that he and his mom were in serious trouble.

23

J watched the last of the vehicles pulling away from the cemetery and quickly unhooked his seat belt. Dark would be on them soon enough, and cemeteries at night didn't exactly appeal to him. Especially not with everything that had been happening. He quickly looked to his right.

"Staying or going?"

"I'll wait here," Tiny said, sounding nervous. "You know, in case we get a call."

"Sure." J nodded slowly. He reached for the door, and Tiny grabbed his arm.

"Wait ... Okay, I'm going," Tiny said, giving J an I-got-your-back nod that caused him to smile a little. And there wasn't much he could smile about lately, he thought as they exited the vehicle and made their way toward the grave. He glanced to the open hole where Sam's casket was and ducked his head, shoved his hands in his pockets, and forced his legs on.

"So, you guys were friends when you were kids?" Tiny asked, huffing a little as he picked up his pace alongside J to keep up.

"Yeah ... long time ago," J said and frowned, hearing his voice crack with emotion.

Tiny reached inside his coat and pulled out a crumpled bouquet. "Thought you might need these," he said, holding the flowers out to J — flowers that looked suspiciously like the ones J had seen in a vase in the hotel lobby.

"Thanks, dude," J said, nodding. "But we're going to have a talk later."

A cemetery worker glanced up, muscles straining in his arms as he pulled the large tarp off a mound of dirt next to Sam's grave. He let go of the tarp and brushed his long red hair away from his face.

"Sorry," the man said, his expression kind. "I thought everyone had left."

"I'm kind of late," J offered, and the man's eyes moved to J's hand.

"Nice flowers," he said, smiling.

"I thought so too." Tiny beamed, and J was taken aback by the look of concern that crossed the man's features as his gaze shifted from Tiny back to J. Appearing deep in thought, the man took his work gloves off and slapped them against his leg, sending puffs of dust through the air. "Stay as long as you need," he said.

"I appreciate it – this ain't exactly easy for me."

"It never is," the man said in a tone that hinted that he might know grief firsthand. "But as my father likes to say, 'There is nothing worth doing that is easy.'" He smiled again, gave them a small wave, and walked away. Tiny waved back, but J watched the man until he faded out of sight, unable to shake the feeling that he had seen the guy somewhere before.

J frowned and again glanced back into the gaping hole that held his friend's casket. For a second, he had the oddest sensation that he was standing at the edge of his own grave. *Only the good die young, though – isn't that what they say, Sammy?*

"So, how far away do you think heaven *is*?" Tiny asked, squinting up at the sky.

"Wish I knew," J answered after a long moment. He laid the flowers next to Sam's grave and then stepped back and glanced up at the sky too, saying a silent good-bye to his old friend.

"Wish I knew ..."

Arieh passed through the stone wall of the cemetery to the street outside, weapons drawn as he surveyed the area. A car pulled into the gas station across the street, and he saw a man exit the vehicle, saw the long telltale shadow trailing his steps as the man pulled a small gun from the back waistband of his pants. Eri, the Irinim warrior who had been posted there, morphed out of the side of the building, and the shadow quickly retreated. The man stopped and glanced around, an expression of confusion and fear crossing his face as he turned and hurried back to his vehicle. Eri glanced toward Arieh and nodded.

The Grigori's lackeys are getting bolder, increasing their activity throughout the city, Arieh thought somberly and then glanced to his right just as the big redheaded warrior Azaniah came through the wall to stand next to him. "I suppose the skirmish was to be expected today," the fierce fighter murmured as they scanned the street. "Their tactics have not changed."

"No – and they will use any and all means to stop the five now in order to secure their stronghold over this city. For reasons I haven't been told yet, they have chosen this site to be their beginning." His eyes roamed over the streets and buildings of St. Louis, taking in both its beauty and its starkness. *Planted in the heartland of the country,* he thought. *Yet visited by popes and presidents ...*

Arieh turned and looked at the warrior, knowing that his instructions would be no less palatable to him than they had been for the others. "You will continue to keep watch over him, prod him to remember."

"But no more?"

"For now we engage the Grigori only when absolutely necessary," the Irinim leader said, understanding Azaniah's frustration. They were *warriors*, born to defend those who would come against the Order. But he also understood the wisdom of the Law – and obeyed it. "They have to go through this – have to remember the truth on their own. It will leave no doubt in their hearts as to who they really are," Arieh said, turning to study the Arch in the distance as it shimmered in the setting sun.

"They will never survive their future otherwise ..."

24

Carly drove aimlessly, not really sure where she was going or what she was even doing anymore. She was scared — and mad at herself for being scared. Her dad had looked stressed out at the airport, but nothing like he looked when she left the cemetery — exhausted, edgy, almost as if he were ready to crawl out of his skin.

"All I'm saying is that it would be better if we got everyone in one place and talked this through instead of you running off again," he'd said, following her to the Jeep. "There are things going on that we need to talk about — things you don't understand."

She swallowed hard.

Everything was unraveling so fast that she didn't know how to control it anymore. To top it off, there was no one around for her to talk to — no one who would understand like her old friends. It was like they had all been scattered to the wind: J a no-show at the funeral ... Jenna taking off with Nick Corsa — *what was that about?* — and Jonah ...

Of all the times to be falling for someone ... She should be listed in the *Guinness Book of World Records* under bad timing.

Oh, Jonah — why would you think it should have been you who died?

She had replayed the moment when he stormed away from the cemetery at least a dozen times, and still couldn't figure out how she could have stopped him.

"Already damaged goods, Carly, remember?" he'd said.

Damaged goods ...

She had heard those words the first day she met Jonah. In a way, it made sense that she would be led back to that day; seemed like nothing really began until Jonah came along. He was like the final piece of the puzzle that something — or someone — had been waiting to put into place. Jonah was their beginning ...

"Back to where it all started," a voice whispered through her mind. *"Retrace your steps, and you'll find what you're looking for."*

She turned down a little side street, then another, feeling as if she were being reeled in by an invisible line, until she found herself idling in front of their old school, staring at the large sign that read, "Daniel Junior High: Home of the Lions!" The sign was pockmarked with bullet holes.

She glanced over at Doc, who was curled up in the passenger seat, watching her intently, then pulled into the parking lot, killed the engine, and got of the Jeep before she could change her mind. Doc scrambled out to join her, and they hurried across the lot to the front entrance.

The place had definitely seen better days. The city had closed it down only four years ago, but it looked as if it had been vacant for more than twenty years. Tall winter weeds choked out the little bit of lawn there had been, and some enterprising thieves had gouged out the decorative brick. Night security consisted of heavy chains that crisscrossed the doors, held together by an ancient, mammoth-sized padlock.

Carly stood on her toes and looked inside. The glass trophy cases and student awards that used to line the walls were long gone. So were the two benches Mrs. Flowers had painted with – big surprise – *flowers* that used to sit on either side of the principal's office. Nothing left but a dirty, dimly lit hallway in desperate need of a fresh coat of paint.

Kind of makes it hard to take the warm and fuzzy trip down memory lane, she thought sarcastically as she tugged halfheartedly on the doors.

"Try again ...," a voice whispered through her mind.

Carly stepped back from the doors and looked around uneasily. Doc whined as a warm breeze rustled around them, and then he wagged his tail.

"TRY AGAIN ...," the voice urged.

Reaching out tentatively, she grasped the door handles with both hands, but before she even pulled on them, something heavy dropped next to her feet. She looked down. The padlock!

"AGAIN."

She tugged the handles once more, and the chains burst into nothing, powdering the walkway with particles of fine gray dust as the doors opened wide before her. Doc trotted inside, turned, and sat on his haunches, waiting patiently for her to follow.

"No one's ever going to believe this," she whispered, voice shaking slightly. "*I* don't even believe this." She hesitated and then felt a pressure on the small of her back, like something was pushing her inside, urging her on.

"This is crazy," she added in the empty hallway, secretly hoping no one would answer. She took another step forward.

Echoes of laughter swirled around her. She smelled the familiar scent of stale peanut butter and glue that seemed to be permanently imbedded in the halls, and with it, the old feeling that she didn't quite fit in with the rest of the world. Or at least ninety-nine percent of the world.

There was a shift in the air, and her heart began to pound as she watched the old trophy case appear, fade out, then reappear again, along with the student awards and the massive portrait of Principal Lang. She felt someone small brush against her, and then another small person brush by, and she realized she wasn't just remembering being a sixth-grader anymore ... she was *there* ...

... in the cafeteria, shuffling through the jungle of losers (which they'd be called for at least another year) and abusers (thanks to the eighth-graders) with her three best friends as they made their way up the lunch line. She was not happy that their art teacher, Mrs. Triefenbach, had just handed her a lousy B for her painting of Rousseau's *Tiger and Buffalo in Combat*, when she gave Sam an A – *a stinking A!* – and he'd only chosen to paint *Dreams* because it had a naked lady in it.

"Hey, is that a new one?"

Carly glanced up to find Jenna's eyes, which looked even bigger behind the huge, owl-like glasses she'd lifted from the drugstore, zeroing in on her latest creation: a little beaded hippie necklace she'd been inspired to make after looking through some of her dad's old stuff.

"You can have it if you want," Carly said, taking it off.

"For real?" Jenna grinned. She whipped around, pulling her hair up.

"For real," Carly said as she secured the necklace in place and then lowered her voice. "You see BW yet?"

"No. What about you?" Jenna whispered. She turned back around, and Carly saw her eyes cloud over.

Carly shook her head no and glanced to Sam and J, who stood in front of them in line—anything to take her mind off the creepy janitor who had been haunting their nightmares over the past two weeks. "What are they arguing about *now*?"

"The never-ending debate," Jenna murmured, studying her new necklace. Carly leaned forward, straining to hear them over the dull roar of voices in the cafeteria.

" … No, it's Morpheus," J was saying. "*Morpheus* is the stronger one … he gives everything he has to Neo so he can become their leader. I don't know about you, but that doesn't happen in my neighborhood."

"We live in the same neighborhood, J," Sam said sardonically. "Besides, Neo saves Morpheus's butt *and* gets the girl. I think that kind of proves my point." He glanced over his shoulder at Carly and Jenna and grinned. Carly grinned back in spite of herself.

"Aren't you forgetting about someone?" she asked, planting her hands on her hips.

Sam laughed, seeing that he'd gotten a rise out of her. "Sure, Trinity's tough—but she's hot too, and … Well, *you know* …"

"I know what?"

"That being hot makes her not as tough as them?" Jenna asked, trying her best to look fierce as she pushed her glasses up.

"No," J said, "it makes it hard to think of her like Morpheus or Neo."

"You're just sad," Jenna said. "A sad, chauvinist pig."

J was unfazed. "All I know is, I see Trinity in a dark alley, I sure don't want to run *away*." He broke into a slow-mo version of his "mojo move" with Barry White sound effects as he closed in on Jenna and then promptly put her in a headlock.

"You're disgusting!" Jenna said, laughing, her voice muffled beneath his shirt.

"I'll tell you what's disgusting—this food," Carly said as she reached for a lunch tray out of the bin, but she got no further, because someone tapped her on the shoulder. Not just anyone either. It was *BW*, aka Bud Winters, the school janitor. He was so close to her that she could see the dark stubble on his shaved head as he bent his bulky frame down to look at her. His eyes were bloodshot, like he hadn't slept in days. His tiny nose ring glinted under the glare of the cafeteria's fluorescent lights. *What kind of janitor wears a nose ring, anyway?* she thought in her heightened panic mode.

"Hey, *Red*, you blind? The bin's empty," is all he said, but something happened to her as he touched her shoulder.

A shock wave hit her and Carly reeled back, fear and nausea crashing over her as she stared blankly at the lunch tray he was holding out to her. She felt cold. So cold that she was sure she was going to pass out. She gave her friends a scared look as their frightened faces began to swim before her eyes.

"Je –," was all she could say as she watched Jenna slowly raise her inhaler to her lips.

Evil, Carly heard Jenna thinking. *And he's going to do something evil…*

She knew it was Jenna because her thoughts sounded just like her voice. *This is crazy. How can I hear your thoughts?*

"What's that on his face?" she heard J say. His voice sounded like it was coming from far away … but it was terror stricken too, like he couldn't believe what he was seeing.

She tried to turn and look, but she was falling backward down a dark tunnel, falling as three-dimensional images zoomed into her mind with frightening speed: a tiny shack of a house with a shutter hanging sideways, trash and tires littering the yard … someone singing … then two crows sitting on the branch of a pitiful-looking tree. The crows were looking down at something in an alley, looking down like vultures. Then they turned and looked at her. She knew they saw her because she could feel …

"Carly!"

The tunnel evaporated around her. She blinked a couple of times, almost afraid to see the face above her – afraid to see Bud Winters' dead-looking eyes staring down at her – but it was only Mrs. Flowers, their school nurse.

"Honey, I'm having a hard time getting a hold of your mom," Mrs. Flowers said, perpetual worry causing her heavy-set face to sag. She held out a little plastic bottle of OJ, and Carly almost giggled, noticing her screaming-red fingernails were adorned with little white hearts. "Is there another number I could try?"

Jenna, Sam, and J were standing behind Mrs. Flowers, vigorously shaking their heads no – kid code for *Ditch Flowers; we gotta go NOW.*

"Low blood sugar," Carly croaked, struggling to sit up. She took an impressive swig of the juice and handed it back to the nurse. "I'll be okay – really."

"We got her back, Mrs. Flowers," J announced, standing a little straighter. At five foot eleven, he already dwarfed all the kids – a lot of the teachers too. Sam was slightly shorter but big for his age as well. Mrs. Flowers gave them one of her rare smiles.

"I'm glad you boys have her back, Jeremiah," she says, "but it's her head I'm worried about. She hit it pretty hard when she fell – "

The final bell rang and they all bolted, hurrying to join the stream of kids who were rushing the opened doors – hurrying before Mrs. Flowers could stop them, ask a million questions, call Carly's parents.

"I can't believe this!" Jenna said breathlessly, hanging on to Carly's arm as they followed Sam and J, who were using their bodies to clear a path through the swarm of kids.

"What *happened* to me in the cafeteria?"

"I don't know. You just kind of passed out." Jenna glanced at Carly, and she noticed that slightly blue tinge to Jenna's lips that happened when she got scared. "Something happened to us too."

"Are you okay?"

"Yeah," Jenna said as she steered them toward the bike racks in front of the school. "Just a little freaked out."

Carly's grimaced, more than a little freaked out herself. It wasn't like the other times when they felt like they were being observed or when they sensed stuff about people. This was darker, way scarier than anything she had ever felt before.

The four friends started to unlock their bikes, and Carly felt them all hurrying, as if some unseen hand was pushing them along.

"So, what do you think he's up to?"

"Something bad." Jenna pursed her lips and pushed at her glasses again. "I keep seeing these capital-letter words in my head, like *DANGER* and *EVIL*." She frowned. "But I see *GO NOW* too, if that makes any sense."

"I can't shake the feeling that it has to do with a kid," Sam said as he dragged his bike chain through the spokes. He was only twelve, but he had a thing for sensing strays that were in trouble – of the animal *and* kid kind. "Saint Samuel of the Lost Cause," they called him, but the truth was, they all had the same rescuer gene.

"Whatever he's up to isn't just bad – it's really bad," J said, shouldering his backpack as he pulled his bike out. "Bad juju, man, just like my mom used to say. I can feel it. I ain't ever seen anything like that dark shadow on ol' Bud Winters' face. Not even in a *horror* movie."

"I thought his face was just dirty at first," Sam said.

"It was like the shadow was *alive*," Jenna added as she kicked her kickstand up.

"What shadow?" Carly said, glancing between them. "And what's *bad juju*?"

"There he is!" J said.

"Bad juju means bad spirits," Jenna whispered as all four sets of eyes turned on Bud Winters, who was hurrying from the side exit of the school. There was something even weirder than usual about him. He wasn't doing his normal cockroach scurry – which was a pretty creepy thing to see, considering his size – but was actually walking with long, purposeful strides as he approached them. Like a man on a mission.

Carly spotted the dark shadow on his face, and after a brief flash of shock thought, *Jenna's right; that shadow is alive – but not just alive…*

The shadow pulsed on the janitor's face and then shifted, almost like a mask sliding to one side, and they gasped. It wasn't just a shadow; it was another face. A completely different face that seemed to stare directly at them for a moment before imbedding itself once more into the janitor's features just before he passed them.

"What was that?" Jenna asked, scared.

"They're *feeding* his rage," Sam said under his breath.

"Why? What are they?"

"Why?" Sam said, repeating her question. There was a slightly dazed expression on his face.

Because evil uses man's hands to do his dirty work… Carly thought suddenly. It was something she'd heard her dad say before, and had never thought much of it until now. She turned to see J looking at her strangely—almost like he heard her thoughts too.

"Yeah … He's going to hurt somebody—maybe even kill them," J said—then looked slightly shocked that he'd said it.

"That's why we're going to follow him," Sam said, getting on his bike.

Carly glanced at Jenna, who still appeared pale but looked determined now, then to J, who was pretty much frothing at the mouth to go, and finally back to Sam.

"So, we're really doing this?" J asked.

"Yeah, we're doing this," Carly said in her I'm-not-taking-no-for-an-answer tone.

Sam smiled at her. It was a beautiful smile. *The kind that will melt a lot of girls' hearts in a few years,* she thought. She knew it as sure as she knew the sun would rise in the same place tomorrow morning. She also knew it's the goodness, the pure *bravery,* in his smile that infected them all, and told her racing heart that there is no one else who *could* do this but them …

Carly stumbled back, nearly tripping over Doc as she tried to regain her balance. How in the world could she have forgotten the details of that day? That beautiful, crazy day when they had still been young enough to believe that people were decent and that good guys triumphed over evil. When the last thing she would ever imagine was her mother walking out the door and never coming back. Something in her broke then, and she felt a yearning she couldn't explain to be the girl she was back then—bold and alive, throwing caution to the wind and never, ever trying to control *anything.*

Well, except maybe the radio station. There were some things you just couldn't ignore, and bad music was one of them.

Carly glanced up at the sky and did something she had not done—couldn't have considered doing—since her mother abandoned her and her father holed himself up in the church; she talked to God. *Where did that girl go?* she asked the darkening sky.

If there is anyone up there, can you at least tell me that? Where did I go?

As if in answer, a warm breeze began to blow around her, and once again she felt the pressure of a hand at her back, urging her on. *Journey's not over yet, is it?* she thought as she automatically snapped Doc's leash on. She knew without having to ask where she was going.

She was following their bike route to Bud Winters' house.

"Retrace your steps, and you'll find what you're looking for," the voice whispered through her again.

Carly walked in a dazed, dreamlike state until she turned the corner onto Hickory Street. The neighborhood was bad seven years ago, and time hadn't changed it for the better. Most of the tiny houses had been torn down or condemned, making it feel more like a war zone than a neighborhood. She stopped and stared at the group of thugs who stood under the streetlight several feet away from her and Doc.

They glanced her way.

Her dad had drilled her on moments like this, but there were *six* of them, decked out in colors that ID'd them as one of the most violent gangs in the city, and although they hadn't noticed her yet, they didn't look like they wanted company. Truth was, in spite of her dad's best efforts, she couldn't fight her way out of a paper bag. Her heart picked up speed as she debated what she should do.

Doc whined, but not out of fear—he was trying to tug her along toward one of the few houses still standing at the end of the cul-de-sac.

"Some watchdog you are," she whispered. He wagged his tail.

"Okay, okay. I get it; we've come too far to stop now ..." She squared her shoulders and started to walk toward the group, and with each step she took, she felt an odd sense of purpose, of *knowing* that she was getting closer to the answers she was looking for. She finally stepped into the gang's line of vision and turned to look them in the eye, her heart thudding wildly as she forced her legs to move.

It was the strangest thing. They were looking right at her— more like right through her—as if they couldn't see her at all.

She took another hesitant step forward, keeping her eyes focused on the end of the cul-de-sac.

Someone swore loudly, and she glanced over her shoulder, ready to run – but was startled to see them backing away almost fearfully, their eyes riveted on a spot just behind her.

Carly picked up her pace, walking, walking faster, and then jogging until the creepy feeling shifted into a shaky kind of relief, like the feeling she got when she was driving away from a dangerous part of the city ... even though she was still in a dangerous part of the city.

She shook her head ruefully and glanced up just as she neared the driveway that led to Bud Winters' house.

More like shack, she thought, staring at the peeling paint and old tar roof that looked like it could collapse at any moment.

What now?

"Remember ...," the voice whispered through her head again, and the old shack began to fade in and out before her eyes, brightening to that saturated-yellowish tint of an old photo, then fading and brightening again until the shack stood before her just as it had that clear sunny day all those years ago.

There was that shifting feeling in the air again. But this time it felt electric, almost as though a summer storm were coming.

A swift burst of warm air washed over her, blowing her hair back, then another burst and another. So many that she finally lost count and instead turned around and around in the middle of the dark little cul-de-sac, her heart filling with childlike wonder as she caught brief flashes of the huge, hooded figures that surrounded her.

"Who are you?" she whispered.

"Remember ...," a deep voice answered.

Carly's breath caught in her throat as one of the figures turned to her, and as he did, the hood of his cloak dropped away and a bright flash of amber blinded her momentarily. He wasn't in a wheelchair anymore, she thought, mesmerized. Long, silver-blond hair ... and those eyes: beautiful and terrifying eyes ... eyes like a lion.

And then, from somewhere off in the distance, she heard a kid begin to sing.

25

J stood up from his perch on the stairs and glanced around the yard. He was sure he had heard something in the night ... He sighed and sat back down. Spooked was what he was. He'd tried to convince himself that it hadn't gotten to him – that seeing Sam's grave was just like seeing any of the graves of his boys who'd been wiped out on the street – but lying to yourself was like trying to run from yourself. You never got anywhere with it.

Just like the dark. How were you supposed to escape something that happened at the end of every day of your life?

He struck a match and raised an unsteady hand toward his cigarette, only to see the flame disappear, carried off by a gust of wind that came out of nowhere. He tossed the match and glanced around uneasily. He should've never agreed to meet at Sam's place. It wasn't just bad karma or the fact that the dark was creeping him out worse than it had ever done before. There was something in the air. A feeling that hung over him, like something was waiting ... *watching.*

He jerked around, searching the area behind him. Someone was singing; he could almost make out the tune.

One of those eighties bands. Aerosmith? Rush? No, it's Ozzy, and ... I remember hearing a song of his coming from the dumpster behind that shack that day ... Nearly scared the crap out of us –

"Where did *that* come from?" J whispered under his breath. Another memory ... He continued to look around. If he wasn't already certifiable, he might think he was going crazy. *Can't be going if I'm already there,* he thought and almost laughed – would've laughed, but then he spotted Jonah coming around the corner.

J stood and braced himself for the confrontation he knew was coming.

"What are *you* doing here?" Jonah said, closing the distance between them. His eyes were red, and he was swaying on his feet a little, like his anger was all that was keeping him standing.

"I'm sorry about Sam, man—"

He saw a brief flash of movement behind Jonah and leaned a little to one side, trying to see around him. Whatever it was disappeared so fast that he wondered if it had been there at all.

"I *said*, what are you doing here?" Jonah demanded, stepping into his line of vision again.

So, this is how it's going to be, J thought, shoving his hands into his pockets as he glanced back to Jonah. *No "Thanks for watching out for me," no "Maybe we should talk about all this," just "What are you doing here?"*

"Guess I needed to come and get my head wrapped around all that's happened," he said finally. He hated lying to Jonah, but he didn't see any way around it for the time being.

"Yeah? It's funny how you just seem to be around every time someone in my family dies."

"If you say so," J said, narrowing his eyes. *You and your stupid temper, Jonah—* He spotted the journal in Jonah's hand and felt his heart begin to hammer. If he didn't have bad timing . . . He glanced nervously toward the street again.

"Oh, I say so," Jonah said, taking another step toward him.

J looked down at Jonah but heard Tiny's voice in his head: *"What are you waiting for? Put that boy in his place!"* But Tiny didn't know Jonah. He had never witnessed them sparring together as kids night after night, or the look on the others' faces as they watched Jonah get back up no matter how hard he was hit—or how many times he fell.

Once he learned he could fight back . . .

Jonah wouldn't stop this time—not until one of them was dead. J could see it in his eyes. Sam's death had driven him to that place, and J knew he didn't have the time or words to talk him out of it.

So he did what he knew Sam would've wanted him to do. He gave Jonah one last look and turned and walked away.

"I know you had something to do with this too!" Jonah called after him.

J stopped in his tracks, clenching his fists, holding in his own anger and frustration, and forced himself to walk on. He *had* done a lot in his life and gotten away with it. Maybe it was just payback to be blamed for something he *hadn't* done.

Sam believed me – least I can hang on to that …

He stopped again, glancing over his left shoulder just in time to see the black Lexus pull up alongside him. He felt his insides tense up as the back passenger window slid down.

"Why don't you just pull right up to his place – then everyone can see you," J said disgustedly as he turned to his boss.

Corsa's face was expressionless.

"Did you find the journal?"

"Nah, man. It's gone," J said, lighting a cigarette in an effort to avoid Nick's gaze. Another lie – but he didn't feel bad about this one. "Looks like the cops went over the place pretty good."

"What about the paintings?"

"Nothing like that anywhere," J said, telling the truth this time.

Corsa stared at him for a long moment and then nodded.

J felt a flood of relief wash over him. If his boss found out that Jonah had that journal – or that J had been the one to leave it on the professor's desk – he and Jonah would both be joining Sam a lot sooner than they ever imagined.

If it were a one-on-one fight, he wouldn't be so worried, but he had a feeling that Corsa had never fought fair in his life.

Gotta play this smart – buy enough time to get the goods on him before he figures me out. Gotta makes things right this time …

"You know, those things will kill you," Corsa said slowly. He was looking at the cigarette burning between J's fingers, with a strange smile on his face.

"A lot of things will kill you," J said, trying to keep his temper back. He threw his cigarette down and ground it out with the toe of his shoe.

Corsa's smile remained even though he didn't say another word. He continued to smile at J until the tinted window rose between them, ending their conversation.

Goofy white man.

A smothering kind of rage rushed through his body as he watched the car drive away. What he wouldn't give to just let loose and bash those perfect pearly white veneers into pieces. *Bet you'd have an aneurism if you knew who called the cops on the little party you were having at Sam's …*

He turned around and headed down the street to where he had parked his Suburban. He'd been with Tiny when Corsa called and gave him the address for a cleanup—had been sitting right next to him when the idiot told Tiny to wait until three a.m. No doubt in his mind that Corsa had killed Sam. What he hadn't figured out yet was why.

And how had Sam's girlfriend gotten caught up in it all?

J pulled his coat tight around him as he walked, his mind so plagued by questions, by *rage* that he couldn't put anywhere, that he forgot about the dark for a moment.

I'm going to get them for what they did, Sam—for you, for Jonah, for all of us ...

He stopped in his tracks as another thought hit: if Corsa had taken Sam out, who's to say he wouldn't go after the rest of them now? But why would someone like Nick be interested in them? What was so special about all of them, other than the fact that they were friends when they were kids?

He rubbed the scar on his chest—even though he wasn't so sure that was what was causing his pain. Golf-ball-sized entry wound is what the nurse had told him when he finally opened his eyes in that hospital room. "Lucky to be alive," the doctor had added.

"Shouldn't have bothered," was all he'd said before turning his face to the wall, but the old doctor didn't take the hint and leave.

"I might agree with you," he'd said, flipping the chart closed. "Particularly after learning who you are and all the despicable things you have done. I might even go as far as to say that I've had a few sleepless nights wondering how God could spare someone like you and allow an innocent child to die. Do you want to know what conclusion I came to?"

"Not really."

"He wants you alive, son," the doctor pressed on. "You are here for a reason—and I can assure you that it isn't to be one of the most notorious gang leaders in the city."

J grimaced. There was a time when he did think he was alive for a reason, when he had been a part of something bigger than him. Something almost heroic ... He reached out to open the door of his SUV, but just as his hand touched the handle, a warm wind began to blow around him.

"Jeremiah..."

He whipped around, his hand automatically going for the gun in his waistband, but found no one standing behind him in the dark city street. The voice was real—at least he thought it was.

He quickly climbed into the SUV and slammed the door, his breath hitching a little in his throat. He tried to start the engine, but nothing happened when he turned the key—no lights, nothing. Then he watched the power locks go down one by one, and he felt a rush of fear. The radio came on next, flipping wildly through station after station until it came to a stop on the far-off sound of a kid singing. That song again. He tried to start the engine again, but it was dead.

So, how—J's eyes flicked to the radio before slowly raising to the windshield. He stared hard into the night, searching the deserted street, and then all at once the street changed... fading in and out from night to a strange yellowish day, and he wasn't in his SUV anymore. He was...

... crouched down in the side yard of that dingy little shack on Hickory Street, feeling the briars digging into his ankle from that overgrown hedge they were hiding behind as they watched Bud Winters unlock the front door and step inside. J was all pumped up, his heart still racing from their wild tail-the-janitor bike ride, but he knew that if the janitor spotted him too soon, it would be over before they had a chance to do anything.

"What now?" J said, glancing to Sam. "I don't see any kids around here."

"Just wait," Sam said and then stood up from their hiding place, ignoring J's efforts to pull him back down. He cocked his head to one side. "Do you hear that?"

Carly stood too. J glanced over at Jenna, who was now on the rise, and threw his hands up in defeat. *So much for covert operations.*

"It's a kid ... singing," Jenna said.

"It's creepy, is what it is," Carly said, searching the yard. "Where's the kid?"

J gave the yard a once-over too. There was nothing that convinced him a kid lived there—no toys, no bike, nothing. There wasn't even any *sound* until the singing started. The singing freaked him out a little, but the voice was ... almost beautiful. So clear and pure that it hit J right in the heart. A little like those kids on the Christmas specials, the Vienna Boy's Choir or something.

The screen door – minus the screen – popped open at the back of the house, and J saw Bud Winters clomping down the steps. He had a big tire iron in his hand and swung it like he was looking forward to using it. They ducked back down behind the hedge, holding their collective breath as he wove around the old tires and trash that littered the yard.

He must have heard the kid singing, J thought. He felt Jenna shaking like a leaf next to him.

"He's going to do something bad now," she said, sounding a little like a robot, and J shot a scared look to Carly and Sam.

"I was kind of hoping we were wrong about this," Carly said quietly – almost forlornly.

"Bad juju. I *told* you guys." He took a deep, unsettling breath. "Only thing we can do is take ol' BW down and get the kid."

"Wait," Sam said. "We gotta wait until we know we – "

" – can catch him off guard," Carly finished and then looked surprised that she said it. "Okay, that was weird."

The singing stopped, and they turned to see the janitor running the tire iron along the outside of the dumpster. With no warning, he reared back and gave the steel container a hard whack with the iron. The kid let out a startled cry.

"Well, there he is, alive and well in the dumpster!" Bud Winters said conversationally. He leaned over the edge and peered inside. "Get enough to eat?"

A young voice answered from the depths of the dumpster, and the janitor let out a harsh laugh.

"No? Well, I'm thinking if you'd just go ahead and *die*, we wouldn't have to worry about that no more."

"That's it, he's going down," J said, fury cracking his voice a little. He'd never been so mad in his entire life. Never been so *horrified.* Being tossed to his grandma every time his mom got tired of playing house wasn't so great, but compared to this kid's deal, it was *heaven.*

"You know what you remind me of?" Bud Winters continued, oblivious to their presence. "A cockroach. You step on it and step on it, and it just keeps getting right back up."

"What in the heck do you think you're doing!" Sam said as he took a step toward the janitor. His voice was so full of horror and reproach that the man stopped and turned around, tire iron poised above his head.

Bud glanced at Carly, his bloodshot eyes growing wide with recognition. He looked almost normal for a moment, unsure – but then a sneer appeared. "You and your buddies better clear out, Red – unless you want to be next."

Carly opened her mouth to speak but appeared unable to get her voice to work. J saw why.

The dark shadow was pulsing over the janitor in waves now, and a horrible cold seeped into J's being. He felt like he was going to puke any moment but somehow stood his ground. They all did – and he felt a swell of pride to have friends like that.

"We're not scared of you – or that thing on you," J said, and a strange pause filled the air, almost as if something had taken notice of their little group. Something bad. A sound like hundreds of grasshoppers rolled across the yard, and he felt his legs start to shake. *Grasshoppers in March?*

"*On* me? You mean my tattoo?" Bud Winters said with an amused smile. He flexed his left arm, and the dragon tattoo rippled across his skin. It was something J would have expected his crazy drunk uncle Lester to pull at a family reunion, something he might have laughed at – if not for the malevolent look in the janitor's eyes. A look that said he knew what J meant but had chosen to play with them – *taunt* them.

"Leave them alone," a small voice said, and J saw the kid for the first time as he popped his head up over the lip of the dumpster. For a split second they froze, mouths gaping open as they stared at the very reason they'd been led there.

His eyes were the palest blue J had ever seen, and *old*, staring out of a painfully skinny face smudged with dirt ... or bruises ... or maybe a little of both. His short dark hair stood up all over the place, like it had been chopped by a blender. His expression was curious as his eyes flicked over the four of them, but calm too – like he was ready for whatever might happen.

"You back-talking *me*?" Bud Winters roared, turning back to his original victim. "You're damaged goods! Nothing! You got that? *Nothing!* And nothing can't make sound!"

The kid remained speechless as the janitor – was Bud his *father?* – raised the tire iron above his head once more. A bone-chilling growl erupted from the man as he threw every ounce of his weight into the downward swing.

"*No!*" they all yelled at once. Their cry hovered in the air and then spread out like ripples in water, growing wider to cover the entire yard, and they saw Bud Winters' big arm freeze in mid swing. He appeared to strain against whatever it was held his arm back, and strained *hard.* The muscles in his arm bulged. Sweat trickled down both sides of his face.

"GO – DON'T STOP UNTIL YOU REACH THE BOY," a deep voice urged, rolling through J's mind, and from the looks on the others' faces, it appeared to have entered all of their minds. It was like a strong wind, propelling their legs, and they all hurried around the janitor as he grunted, struggling.

"We get the kid out and then we bolt, got it?" Sam said softly. He was holding his arms out a little as he stepped past the janitor to the dumpster. *Like he's walking a tightrope at a circus,* J thought, following close behind.

"Oh, man," Carly said. "I *saw* this …"

J glanced over his shoulder, knowing he shouldn't. Carly was peering up at the sky with a pained expression on her face, and he followed her gaze to the scraggly tree above them, where two fat crows were perched. They were hunched over, staring down at them through flintlike eyes.

"Reminds me of –"

" – vultures," the kid said, finishing J's thought, and they all turned back to him.

He's like us, J thought in a dazed, dreamlike way, and he felt his thought linking with Sam and the others.

J heard Jenna take a puff off her inhaler and felt the muscles in his stomach draw up tight. *Got a bad feeling about this –*

"I'm scared," Jenna said breathlessly, and all hell broke loose.

The crows spread their huge wings, flapping them, and with each beat of their wings, the grasshopper sound grew louder, more persistent, until the janitor's arm broke free from its invisible hold. He wasted no time, swinging the tire iron wildly at Sam and J.

"Leave … them … alone!" the kid screamed, trying to haul himself out of the dumpster to help his rescuers. His cry was desperate and tragic, so filled with outrage that J felt it deep in his soul, like it railed against all that was wrong in the world – a cry that J imagined smashing against the gates of heaven, begging for someone, *anyone,* to take notice.

"Oh, God, *please* help us ...," J whispered under his breath as the tire iron narrowly missed his head.

The grasshopper sound disappeared. The crows flapped their massive wings and scrambled upward through the sky, like they were clawing at the air in an effort to get away as fast as they could.

Something is happening, J thought as he watched Sam duck and weave in slow motion around the janitor.

J felt a *click* go off inside him, as if a switch had been turned on, and their minds – *all five minds* – felt like they were drawing together to become one. An electric current ran through J, and then there was this surge of *power,* a strength he'd never felt before.

Sam turned and gave him a wide-eyed look, like he felt it too.

Whatever it takes, J thought. *We're in this together. We're going to get you out of this, kid, and I don't even care if I get the snot beat out of me and end up in the ER.*

The janitor appeared to sense that something had changed. He stepped back, chest heaving, as a flicker of uncertainty crossed his eyes.

"I told you to clear out!" he yelled, taking another swing at J's head. J ducked, and Sam made a grab for the tire iron, and they all fell into a crazy fight choreography that only four kids who had never fought a day in their lives could likely manage.

"Sam!" Carly shouted as the janitor dropped the tire iron and grabbed the collar of Sam's hoodie.

Jenna dropped to the ground, inching forward on all fours, and promptly sunk her teeth into the janitor's leg. He bellowed, trying to shake her off, but she hung on like a Chihuahua with its teeth sunk into the leg of a mailman. He finally shook her off, and she rolled across the yard, losing her glasses in the process.

The kid almost made it over the edge of the dumpster before he lost his footing and slipped, then fell. J heard him cry out in frustration and made a dive toward the dumpster when he felt a hand grab his dreads, yanking him back with such force that tears sprung to his eyes.

"Get your hands off them!" Carly snarled in a voice J had never heard before. He turned his head to watch her deliver a perfectly executed front snap kick squarely to the middle of the janitor's groin. He doubled over in pain.

"Oh ...," the janitor groaned miserably. "Oh, you dirty ..." He made a weak grab for Carly, and she seized his hand, grabbed his index finger, and shoved it back with such force that he dropped to his knees.

"I'm going to kill you, Red," he said, somewhere between a growl and a groan. "I'm going to *kill* – "

"No, you're not."

Carly shoved his finger back even farther, and the janitor began to gag like he was going to puke. J was unbelievably impressed – Carly wasn't much bigger than Jenna and seeing her in control of the steroid-freak janitor was something else. Like learning your friend has superhuman strength. She walked backward with the man, pulling him along on his knees until he was no longer within striking distance of the others.

"... kill you," the janitor blubbered.

"You're *not* going to kill anyone," Carly said grimly as she applied more pressure, until he finally did puke. He then did a weird sideways lean before surprising them all by passing out. They stared down at him for a moment.

"That was *awesome*," Jenna said, standing and dusting herself off. "You went full *Matrix* on the creep!"

"How much time do you think we have?" Sam asked, trying to catch his breath as he nudged the janitor with his foot.

"How should I know?" Carly shrugged. She gave him a shaky smile. "It's the first time I ever tried it."

"It'll probably be awhile," said the young voice from the dumpster. "He shot up before he came outside."

"You mean steroids?" J said.

"I mean drugs," the voice answered.

"Come on out of there, kid," J said, reaching his hand into the dumpster to help the kid out. "Don't be scared."

"I'm not scared," the kid said, with a peace that seemed to go against everything that was happening to him. "I already knew about you guys."

As he hopped down, J noticed that the bruises weren't just on his face but also on his arms – and that was just what he could see. *He's so skinny*, J thought. He could see the boy's ribs protruding through the rips in his shirt. The kid shivered a little but managed a crooked smile. The smile nearly broke J's heart.

"Here, take my shirt," Sam said, pulling his Cardinals hoodie over his head. The kid slipped it on happily, apparently not caring that it fell past his knees.

"I'm Sam and that's J – well, his real name is Jeremiah, but he froths at the mouth when you call him that. Jenna is the biter."

"A little improvisation never hurt anyone," Jenna said with a shrug. "Except maybe the person you're biting."

The kid nodded and flicked a nervous glance toward the janitor. He was still out, one side of his head smeared with the dirt and debris he'd gathered in the fall.

J swallowed thickly, trying not to blubber as he stared at the kid. J was tough – they all were, born and raised in the heart of the city – but he'd never witnessed anything like this. And his family ranked right up there in America's Top Five Loony Families of All Time.

"I'm Carly." She gave the kid one of her killer smiles, and J saw the kid turn to mush. *Another one bites the dust ...*

"Where did you learn how to do that?" the kid asked, unable to take his eyes off Carly.

"My dad – but that was the first time it worked."

"I *gotta* meet your dad," the kid said.

Jenna grinned, sliding her glasses back on, and turned to J with a triumphant smile. "Who do you want to meet in a dark alley *now*, lover boy?"

They all burst out laughing – a heady combination of relief, jangled nerves, and wonder over all they had witnessed. Maybe a little fear too – but J didn't want to concentrate on that. For now, things were looking up. The kid smiled his crooked little smile again as he looked around at them all.

"You guys are almost like ... *heroes* or something."

J leaned back in his seat, surprised to find tears on his face – and not so surprised. It was a sad deal to look back and realize he was a better human being as a kid than he was as an adult. *What happened to us, man? We were so righteous that day,* he thought, wiping the tears away with the sleeve of his jacket. *So sure nothing could stop us.*

But something had stopped them.

He glanced around the dark street from the safe confines of his SUV. What was it that had stopped them? Why hadn't he been able to remember the details of the day with Bud Winters until now? And what about the other memories – the night they went to see that fortune teller? Why could he only remember pieces of that night but not the whole thing?

It was like their memories had been erased – no, not erased, *blocked.* He struggled to draw up another memory, anything that might help him understand, but there was a strange tug-of-war feeling in his head.

Maybe if I could get some sleep, some nice dreamless *sleep,* he thought wearily. *Maybe I could figure this out …* But no sooner had he closed his eyes than he felt the old fears return. If he slept, the nightmares might come back, and he didn't think he could hack another nightmare. Not with everything else that was going on. Might just send him straight into the loony bin again, and then who would watch out for Jonah?

In spite of these thoughts, J felt himself being sucked down into the welcoming sea of sleep. As if from a great distance, he heard Sam's young voice again, sounding so happy that they had actually defeated the evil janitor, but tinged with caution too. They still had to get the kid away before …

"Better hurry before he wakes up."

26

J enna startled awake in the dark, blinked a couple of times so
that her eyes could adjust, and then listened. She could've sworn
she had heard Sam. He'd sounded so *young* too ... like back when
they were kids –

She jolted up on the dark leather couch and glanced around the
large room uneasily – vaulted ceilings, expensive furniture, fancy-
looking vases, *huge* paintings on the walls ... Definitely not Chaplain
Hagan's house. Where was she?

Where was *Mikey*?

She swung her legs around and stood, scanning the deeply shadowed room, then breathed out a sigh of relief as she spotted Mikey
wrapped in his usual blanket cocoon on a love seat that had been
turned to face the big-screen TV. One little hand dangled off the side
of the couch, still clutching a game controller.

Nick's place. She remembered now – remembered him inviting
them back to his home for dinner. She just didn't remember much
after getting into his car. *That stupid pill!* she thought. Why had she
let Lila talk her into taking it? She glanced at Mikey's sleeping figure again and felt a sharp stab of guilt. What kind of mom was she?

"You are too weak to handle it," her own mother had warned the
last time they had seen each other. *"You're never going to make it,"*
her dad added furiously as he shoved the last of their suitcases into
the trunk of their Camry. *"You're going to fail, and you're going to
drag that child through your failure ..."* Moving in with Tony had
been the last straw for her parents, the straw that had sent them
running to Florida, where there was only sunshine and golf and
maybe a Tangueray and tonic or two if the thought of her came to
mind ... She remembered watching them getting in the car, remembered acting like it didn't matter. But in her head she'd thought

dully, *Why are you so mad if you never wanted me around anyway?*

Tony had been mad when he left her too …

Jenna shook her head, shaking off the thoughts that always came back to haunt her when she was scared, and made her way around the large coffee table to the love seat. She felt like she was on the hamster wheel again – always running and never getting anywhere. Only this time was much worse, because her hopes of Sam showing her the way off would never be realized now. She reached out to pick Mikey up, heard a snapping sound, and yelped in surprise as light splashed across the room.

Nick stood under the arched entranceway, holding a large cup and saucer in his hand. His dark eyebrows were raised slightly as he took in what she imagined to be her really bad deer-in-the-headlights look.

"I thought you might like something to drink," he said, sounding slightly amused.

"Oh … yeah. Thanks," she said, straightening. She brushed a hand through her hair, trying to appear casual. "I was just checking on Mikey."

They stared at each other for a long moment and then grinned at each other.

"Okay, so I almost jumped out of my skin – *literally.*"

"You really *do* need to relax." Nick chuckled. He handed her the cup and saucer.

"What's this?" she asked, looking up at him as he led her back to the couch. "Not another one of your cousin's cure-alls? I still feel like I have cotton stuffed in my brain after taking that pill she gave me."

"Lila means well." Nick laughed. "But no – that's just a little chamomile tea. It's supposed to be good for stress – I picked it up while you were … napping."

"You didn't have to go to all of that trouble!" Jenna groaned, even though she was secretly pleased that he did go to all of that trouble. "And I am *so* sorry for passing out like that!" They sat next to each other, and she looked up at him, chagrined. "I wasn't the greatest company, was I?"

"The little guy kept me busy," Nick said, inclining his head toward the TV.

"I guess I should be grateful that I don't *snore*."

"True ..." Nick nodded, and she noticed a teasing look in his eyes. "You just talk in your sleep."

"I *what?* I don't talk in my sleep! What did I say?"

He laughed again, and a small part of her – the part that still hoped every once in a while that her life could be different – couldn't help thinking how good it felt sitting next to him. *Really* good, actually. She took a polite sip of tea.

"Well ... I'm not sure." His soft smile caused her heart to skip a beat.

"What do you mean?" she demanded, laughing. "What did I say?"

"'Damaged goods.'" He shrugged. "Does that ... mean anything to you?"

The cup and saucer rattled slightly in her hands, and she set them down on the coffee table. *Jonah ...* Bits and pieces of the dream-memory were coming back to her now. Why hadn't she remembered it before? They had been so brave that day. She smiled a little.

"Jenna?" Nick pressed.

She looked up at him, uncomfortable even though she wasn't quite sure why. "Just something I heard when I was a kid," she said quietly.

"Something good, I hope?"

"Nothing bad ever happens to you when you're a kid," she answered with a wry grin. Not exactly the truth, but she didn't want to make him mad by avoiding the question altogether – not when he seemed so interested in knowing more about her. She reached for her cup, took another sip of tea, and glanced toward Mikey, listening to his soft snores. *Someday I'm going to tell you all about it, kiddo,* she thought wistfully. *Someday you're gonna know that your mom wasn't always so scared ...*

"Lila said you were all pretty close as kids."

She nodded. "Best friends I ever had."

"So what happened?"

"Oh, I don't know ..." Jenna stared into the cup, feeling tongue-tied. No, it was more than that. She *couldn't* share it with him; it was as if a wall had risen up from somewhere deep inside her, refusing to give him access. She looked up at him again. "I guess we just drifted apart."

"That's a shame," Nick said as his smile slowly faded. He studied her close and then shook his head sadly. "Maybe Sam wouldn't have taken those pills if he'd had someone to talk to."

Jenna glanced at him sharply. "Wait a minute – you're saying that Sam *killed* himself?" She felt like she had been slapped. "Who told you that?" she demanded.

"Jenna –"

"That's the craziest thing I have ever heard!" Her mind reeled as she glanced blindly around the room. It didn't make any sense. *Sam did have someone to talk to; he had Jonah – he had us! We were all planning to meet the next day!*

It's a lie, she thought, her mind racing. *Sam was always a fighter ... he would've never done something like that!* She leaned forward as her breathing grew shallow. *Why didn't anyone say anything to me?*

"I think I need to leave now," she whispered hoarsely.

"Jenna – please don't go. I am so sorry for blurting it out like that," Nick said softly. He pushed a lock of her hair back to see her face. "I'm sorry."

She nodded in spite of the turmoil rolling inside her. She felt so ... *lost.* A lone tear slid down her cheek, and Nick slid closer. She felt his arm go around her shoulder as he reached for her hand and held it. She barely knew him, but there was something so touching about the way he held her hand. Like he wanted to take care of her.

She couldn't remember the last time she'd felt that feeling ...

"It's going to be okay," he said gently. "Take another drink of your tea and just try to relax. I really didn't mean to hurt you – I just assumed someone had told you ..."

She obediently swallowed some more tea. *Why* didn't *they tell me?* she thought, feeling like the wounded little kid she had been all those years ago. She was so sure they had been brought back together for a reason.

"This is so crazy ...," she whispered as she tried to will her breathing back to normal. If what Nick was saying was true, why didn't they tell her? Her mind flashed to an image of Jonah in the cemetery, the *look* he had given her ... like there was something wrong with her. She had thought at the time that it was his grief and nothing more. But now she wasn't so sure.

Maybe they didn't tell her because they didn't want her around anymore. A wave of exhaustion swept over her.

"I really should go," she said. She set her cup down and glanced at Mikey. "It's getting late and – "

"Just rest here a little longer," Nick coaxed. "I'm not going anywhere. I'll keep an eye on Mikey, and when you wake up, I'll take you two anywhere you want to go. I just think you'll feel better about it all if you get a little more rest."

She doubted she would feel better about any of it. But it did feel good to have someone with her. Someone who seemed to care. She had been alone for so long – *scared* for so long. She didn't feel so scared now.

"*He's the perfect guy for you,*" a deep, reassuring voice whispered through her, "*the kind of guy who would take care of you, the kind of guy who never leaves ...*"

"I'm not going anywhere," Nick whispered again.

She doubted that too. People left all the time – her parents, Tony ...

"Trust me," Nick added softly, and in spite of her doubts, she allowed herself to be lulled by the soothing sound of his voice and closed her eyes, letting her mind drift. She thought about J being a no-show, about Jonah and Carly keeping the truth about Sam from her, about how they had never even bothered to talk to her after the funeral, about how Nick had been the only one to even offer her a ride ... and like seeds planted in fertile soil, her thoughts began to grow.

How could Jonah and Carly have just shut me out like that? she wondered painfully as she began to nod off. *How could they just slam the door on our friendship – after everything we've been through? How could they do that, when there's so much we haven't figured out about our past yet?*

But maybe that's why Nick has come into my life. Maybe God really did hear my prayers but was just waiting for the perfect time to answer them. When I needed someone the most ...

In spite of this new, comforting revelation, her mind continued its journey as if it weren't quite finished with her yet, and she saw a burst of soft yellow that faded off and then grew brighter until

she was able to make out the tire-strewn backyard of Bud Winters'
old place.

"*Remember ...,*" another deep voice whispered, breaking her
body's grip, and she felt herself being drawn back to that day
again, back when she had been a part of something so good ...

"*Heroes?* I don't know if I'd go that far." Jenna grinned at the
kid and on impulse took his grimy hand in hers. The thought
of germs didn't even faze her like it normally would. She felt
good — better than she'd ever felt, like she could chuck her
inhaler and run nonstop to the top of a mountain and yell,
"Tawanda!" — even though she had just been through the craziest ordeal in her whole life. "Come on, let's get out of here before
Dr. Demented rises."

The kid grinned, allowing her to lead, and then stopped in
his tracks. "Wait. I gotta get something out of the house first."

Jenna glanced to the others. Sam nodded. "Better hurry
before he wakes up."

The kid led her to the back of the house — *shack, really* — up
a few steps, and through the door to a rundown old sun porch.
Once inside, Jenna's germaphobe nature tried to kick back in.
The place was beyond dirty, and it made her *feel* dirty.

The kid broke free from her grip and hurried to a corner of
the porch — the only spot clean of trash and debris — and she saw
him rustling under a thin old blanket for something, and it hit
her. *This is where he sleeps?*

"*Hurry,*" she said, even more determined to get the kid away
from this place. She turned to watch him as he scooped up a
few meager belongings and stacked them together to stuff
into a pillowcase: a grimy-looking children's book, an old Ozzy
Osborne record, a spiral notebook ... And there was something
else that he hurried to stuff into his pocket before she could
catch a glimpse.

"I'm done," the kid announced. He held up the old pillowcase
for her to see.

Through the door that led into the main part of the
house, Jenna heard a commercial for TV Land playing in the

background and glanced inside. It was even dirtier than the sun porch.

"I forgot to turn it off," the kid said, and she realized he was talking about the TV. "That's probably why he got mad. I only watch it when he's at the school. He doesn't let me inside when he's home."

"Sounds like a real prince," Jenna said as they clambered back down the steps together. "What's TV Land?"

"You're kidding, right? *The Addams Family, Leave It to Beaver, Good Times*?"

Jenna shook her head.

"Well, it's got all the good shows – most of them, anyway. I only flip the channel for *Alice.* Flo the waitress is pretty funny, does this whole 'kiss my grits' line. Oh, and *Fresh Prince* – that's pretty good too."

The kid was a *talker.* "I've never heard of any of those shows," Jenna said, laughing.

"Well, you should check them out sometime."

"You get your stash?" J asked as they rejoined the group, and Jenna watched the kid open up his pillowcase for the rest of the group to get a look. He seemed almost proud of his tiny haul, and she bit her lip, willing herself not to cry. She gave J a look daring him to say something stupid, but he only appeared intrigued as he stared into the pillowcase.

"Hey, can I have a look at that book?" J asked, and Jenna was a little surprised by the excitement in his voice.

The kid pulled the book out and reluctantly handed it over.

"*Alice in Wonderland*?" J glanced sharply at Jenna. "*Alice in Wonderland*? How crazy is *that*?"

"At least I read." The kid scowled as he snatched the book back from J. *It's an imperious kind of scowl,* Jenna thought. Like a king looking down upon peasants – a pretty impressive performance when you've just crawled out of a dumpster.

J laughed. "No, it's cool, kid. Follow the white rabbit and all that."

"Do you wanna see how far that rabbit hole *really* goes?" the kid said with a small smile, and they all laughed.

"You ever see *The Matrix*?" J asked.

"What's that?"

"You got some catching up to do if you want to hang with us," J said, slapping him on the back. It was an affectionate slap, but the force of it nearly pitched the kid forward. Jenna frowned at J as the boy righted himself. The kid studied their faces cautiously, like he was trying to figure out if they were making fun of him or not. Satisfied, he smiled again.

"So what was that song you were singing earlier?" Sam asked as they headed for the hedge, where their bikes were hidden.

"Ozzy," the kid replied.

Sam dragged his bike out and graciously offered it to the kid. He looked at Sam with something like wonder.

"Ozzy, huh? You're a really good singer," Sam said, sounding genuine, and the kid gave him another look of wonder.

Almost like nobody has ever been kind to him before, Jenna thought. She felt something profound pass between the two of them as they stood together ... like two long-lost brothers who'd finally found each other again.

She watched Sam help him up on the bike. No one said a word as the kid struggled to reach the pedals, his mouth set in a grim line of determination. *I'm getting out of here,* she could just hear him thinking, and she knew without looking around that each of them would gladly stand up against Bud Winters all over again to make it happen.

"By the way, my name's not 'kid,'" the boy said, turning back to them as they grabbed their bikes and climbed on. "It's Jonah."

Something was wrong. Very, very wrong.

A wave of frenetic anxiety moved through the contingency of MazziKim as they darted around the human lying on the couch. They paused, hovering over her, studying the rapid eye movement beneath her lids, listening intently to the soft murmurs whispered in sleep. She was remembering.

They suddenly froze as their leader seized their consciousness, directing a wave of unimaginable pain through their ranks.

"The Irinim are using something to trigger memory, something we haven't been able to identify," the first sentry provided, speaking through the collective.

"They – ," the second one began.

"Silence!" Shammah snapped through their minds, and they obliged, accepting whatever was to come.

He spoke only one word to them: *"Go."*

They spread out through the night, minds fusing into a massive commune of shared hate. If the Irinim were successful in bringing down the mind blocks, they could lose most of the ground they had gained. Not to mention their chance to live in the hosts of their choice.

They had lost their bodies once.

They could not – would not – allow it to happen again.

27

Someone had messed with the police tape on the door. That was the first thing Jonah noticed. The second thing he noticed was that he would rather face a firing squad than go inside Sam's place. His heart felt like lead, heavy with the burden of grief ... and haunted by memories of another time.

The echoes of two boys laughing rose around him as he stared at the door.

And why wouldn't they be laughing? Jonah thought, fighting the tears. Bud Winters had disappeared by then – *thank God and Greyhound for that* – and they had been granted their wish, the biggest wish two kids had ever dared to hope for: he was the brother Sam had always wanted, and Sam and his parents were the family he had always dreamed of having.

Seven years, Sammy. That's all we were given. But they were good years, weren't they? Until the end, they were the best ...

He started to turn away but then thought better of it. A slight breeze blew around him, warm and maybe a little comforting in spite of the surrounding darkness ... like a gentle but firm hand.

Jonah sighed heavily, pulled his keys from his pocket, opened the door, and stepped inside.

He wished he hadn't.

There was a dark pall in the room, a feeling that immediately weighed on his shoulders, and he sensed the residue of something evil that had transpired there, a horrible feeling he couldn't shake off – like a bad taste in your mouth that you're unable to get rid of no matter how many times you brush or gargle.

The answering machine blinked full ... a bottle of Gatorade and a paper plate with a half-eaten piece of pepperoni pizza sat on the kitchen table ... a laundry basket, overflowing with clothes, sat in the hallway ... He tried to ignore it, brushing by as he hurried down the hallway to escape the evidence of a life that had been cut off in the middle of living.

The bedroom they had shared as kids was even worse.

As soon as he opened the door, he spotted the trash can, on top of which were the pasty heart monitors that the paramedics must have used while trying to revive Sam. He had the brief thought that maybe he should try to clean the mess up, that Sam wouldn't want anyone to see this – His legs started to give out. He stumbled to the bed, sat down, and after a long moment of staring off into nothing, he opened Sam's journal to the last entry he would ever write. He swallowed thickly as he saw his name at the top of the page, realizing the entry had been written directly to him. The next five words hit him with a sharp blow to his midsection:

I don't have much time.

Jonah's heart began to race as he stared at the words; did Sam *know* something was about to happen to him? He hurried on through the rest of the entry, swallowing thickly as he read.

This thing that's going on with you – what you're seeing – is real. I see them too. I didn't mean to lie to you, bro; it's just that I got scared and in my own messed-up way thought I could protect you until I had more answers ... As crazy as this is going to sound, I think we're kind of like "sleeper cells" that have all been activated for some purpose ... and whatever that purpose is, it's ticking these things off ...

"Who are they, Sam?" Jonah whispered tersely.

... Evil is real, Jonah – but so is good ...

... way down deep is the kid who reminds me of the good.

He grimaced and continued to skim downward, desperate to find out what happened – who *they* were. He turned the page: blank. *No, no, NO!* Infuriated, he almost threw the journal across the room – until he spotted a page that had writing on it. Sam must have been in such a rush that he didn't realize he had flipped the new page over and written on its back side. Just two words – two important words – that had been overlooked as the journal made its way to Professor Kinney's desk:

Lila's here –

"I bet you never told the cops *that* little detail, did you, Lila?" Jonah said between gritted teeth, and then another thought struck: *What about that piece of paper – when they were taking Sam's body away?*

He frantically grabbed his jacket off the bed, searching through his pockets like a madman until he felt the lump in his right breast pocket. It was still in the crumpled ball he had picked up off the sidewalk. He opened it slowly, feeling his hands shake as he caught sight of the words written in thick black marker … all in caps:

THIS IS NOT A DREAM

Jonah dropped back down on the bed. The entry was dated a week before Mardi Gras. He knew without having to check his own journal that the date would be the same. But what did it mean? "This is not a dream"? It made about as much sense as "until you open your eyes."

Oh man, Sam … how am I supposed to figure this out without you here to help me?

"Remember …," a deep voice whispered through his head, and he jumped and looked around the room. Nothing … except Sam's old windup alarm clock ticking loudly in the silence. But then why did he feel like something was getting ready to happen? His heart began to pound hard and fast.

He squeezed his eyes shut.

"Stay right here, okay?"

Jonah's eyes flew open, and he jerked around on the bed to find a twelve-year-old Sam standing at the bedroom door. He looked kind of ghostlike at first, fading in and out with a pale yellow light surrounding him, but then his image grew clear and sharp ... and so *real* that Jonah had to resist the urge to reach out and touch him ...

"Okay?" Sam asked pointedly.

Jonah nodded and leaned back against the bed, just as he had done all those years ago when Sam first brought him home – the best day of his life. His mind raced through the images of his rescue, of him and Sam finally splitting off from the rest of the group, and felt the wonder and hope again of the scared, messed-up kid whose life had changed in a moment.

If he were going crazy, he couldn't think of a better way to go ...

He heard the voices of Sam's mom and dad, and then Sam's voice telling them, like a parent tells a child, to call that cop friend of theirs ... telling them Jonah's going to stay ...

"Biggest mistake you ever – ," Jonah started to whisper, but before he could go on with that line of thinking, another memory hit. The day the Beckers signed his adoption papers. He knew it was the day, because Sam ...

... was sitting next to him on the bed, dividing up his toys, books, and comics, giving half of everything he owned to Jonah. And he was *happy* about it.

Sam glanced up at Jonah.

"Got something else to show you," he said. "It's my secret place, but we're brothers now, so I'm going to share it with you ..."

"Gee whiz, Wally!" Jonah said, giving him a huge grin. It was a nearly perfect imitation of the Beaver, and he got the response he'd hoped for.

"Dork." Sam laughed as he made his way over to the –

Jonah's eyes snapped open. He scrambled off the bed, crossed the room, and threw open the closet door, shoving hangers and clothes out of his way as his hands ran down the back wall, feeling for the latch.

His hands began to tremble as soon as he located it. He flipped it up and stuck his finger inside the hole where the knob had once been and tugged. The small hidden door swung open, and he reached inside, hands swimming blindly in the dark until he struck what felt like some suitcases. It wasn't until he dragged them into the light of the room that he realized they were Sam's art valises – six of them, to be exact.

Jonah carried them over to the bed and unzipped the first valise, and then stared dumfounded at the perfect likeness of Jenna's little boy, Mikey.

His eyes darted to the bottom right corner of the painting, to the date just under Sam's signature. His brother had painted it over a week before they all met at Mardi Gras.

His mind flashed back to the image of Sam's stricken face at Mardi Gras as he'd handed the photo back to Jenna, and he realized what had bothered Sam so badly.

He had never seen Mikey before Jenna handed him that photo – and yet he had painted him with stunning accuracy. But it wasn't just the likeness –

Jonah's skin began to crawl as his eyes roamed over the painting. Sam had always been gifted, but this was so real – like a still frame of terror from a nightmare.

The image was that of a kid's bedroom. It was the kind of room most kids would give their right arm for, but Mikey was scrunched into a corner on his bed, stark terror on his face as he stared at the partially opened door.

Jonah bent down closer. On the other side of the door was a hand covered in dark scales, its long claws glinting in the light as it gripped the knob – almost like it was about to push its way in.

"... the heck?"

"Keep looking. You're seeing only what they want you to see ..."

Jonah's gaze shifted to the left side of the painting. His eyes widened as he spotted the mirror on the dresser directly across from the doorway, and in it the reflection of a huge, powerfully built man who stood gripping the door. His looks were striking. A lot like the guys he'd seen at Mardi Gras, except this one had long, chestnut hair that partially concealed one side of his face.

Jonah's cell phone went off, Ozzy laughing like a maniac at the beginning of "Crazy Train," and he jumped, dropping the painting on the bed. He glanced at the caller ID and flipped the phone open. "Carly?"

"Hey, Jonah," she said, her voice sounding a little hesitant. "I just wanted to see how you are doing ..."

"I'll live," he said quietly. He brushed a weary hand over his face and looked bleakly around Sam's room. "I'm sorry about the way I acted at the funeral …"

"Nothing to be sorry about," Carly said, and then he heard her exhale. "Listen, we need to get together and … talk about all of this. That stuff that happened at the funeral — it's not over …"

"I know …" Jonah's eyes shifted back to the painting again. "Is Jenna with you?"

"What? No — she got a ride home with Lila's cousin, Nick."

"Huh."

"Why?"

"Just a gut feeling. If this guy is related to Lila … I don't know, maybe call and at least check on her." He sat down on the bed again, trying to get his thoughts together. *Too many thoughts.* But one rose above the rest. "Carly, did you find a weird entry in your journal — dated just before we met at Mardi Gras?"

"How did you know?" Her voice was strained. "I didn't even tell Sam about that."

"Can you look it up — tell me what it says?"

"I don't have to look it up," she said softly. She cleared her throat. "It was two words, all in capital letters: 'THE TRUTH.' Don't ask me what it means, because I don't have a clue. All I know is that it terrified me."

"Will you ask Jenna if she has an entry like yours?"

"Sure. You want me to ask J too?"

"Might as well — but be careful. He was coming out of Sam's place when I got here."

"You don't think *J* is involved … do you?" Carly asked, incredulous.

"Would that be such a stretch?"

"Oh, Jonah … Didn't they clear him on the other charges?"

"*Sam* dropped it — that doesn't mean he's innocent." Jonah frowned, remembering the strange dream with Sam and the two men. He reached for another valise and heard a large thud below him. Pulling his ear off the phone, he cocked his head to one side. It sounded like someone was rustling around in Sam's studio below him.

"Jonah?"

"Someone is here," he said, dropping his voice to a whisper. "I can hear them downstairs."

"Do you want me to come over?"

"I think I better handle this by myself."

"We're better together," Carly said tersely. "We've always been better together—I think that's what Sam was trying to get us to remember. Don't you—"

"I gotta go. I'll call you back when I find out what it is."

"At least call the police before you go down there!"

"Sure, okay." He flipped his phone closed and shoved it into his pocket as he stood. He had no intention of calling the police—but he *did* have every intention of making whoever it was down in Sam's school pay. It actually made him feel a little better, like he was *doing* something instead of just sitting around, spinning his wheels.

He started for the door, adrenaline pumping, fists clenched.

"Don't do it," a deep voice shot through his mind, stopping him in mid stride, and he slowly turned around and looked behind him. His heart pounded like a sledgehammer as he searched every corner of the room. He couldn't see anything out of the ordinary, but he felt the change ... almost as if the remaining traces of evil he had sensed when he walked in had returned to reclaim their ground ...

Do you really want to be the dork in the horror movie who goes to check out the noise in the basement?

The sound of laughter, soft but menacing, pricked his ears, and he shivered, turning his head in the direction of Sam's kitchen.

"Move quick now," the voice said. But this time it was almost like it was talking to someone other than him. *"They must live— he must live to fight!"*

He wanted to ask the voice who he was going to fight, but he was too scared to ask. Hearing himself talk to someone who wasn't there might send him over the edge. Of course, there was a good chance he was already over the edge and just didn't know it.

"Hurry. Don't stop until you get to your truck."

Jonah gathered Sam's valises together and bolted for the front door, taking the steps two at a time until he was on firm ground again. He sucked in deep gulps of air as he stared up at the building that had once been his home. His only real home. Now it felt ... infested by something he couldn't explain.

"Freaks!" he shouted at the building. It was a childish thing to do, but it made him feel a little better about being chased out. He tightened his grip on the valises and headed around the corner toward his truck, which was parked along the street.

He stopped and looked around.

It was a strange sensation. As if something dirty had settled over him. He glanced up at the night sky.

The two huge crows were back, circling each other just above the streetlight.

He felt a horrible panic seize him, and then with no warning they were dive-bombing, heading right for him. He scrambled backward, but they were too quick, banking easily to match his position.

No way, his mind rebelled. It was just some fluke, some crazy coincidence ...

Jonah watched in terrified disbelief as two dark shadows burst free from the crow's bodies, flipping backward in perfect unison before dropping on either side of him. He saw them rise to their full height and felt the air rush out of them. They were *huge* – almost as large as the strangers at Mardi Gras. A dry, crackling sound filled the air, and he saw their wings unfurl – huge, monstrous wings that disappeared and reappeared as they moved closer.

He froze, bracing himself for their touch, but all he felt was their eyes. A wave of nausea swept through him as the sound of a thousand whispering voices flooded his being.

Jonah didn't look at them – couldn't look at them. He was worse than the dude in the horror movie. He had become the little kid who refused to look under the bed: *If I don't see them, they're not there ...*

A dry rattle of grasshoppers began to beat close to his ears as a mind-numbing cold ripped through his body, working its way from his feet up to his chest. His teeth started to chatter uncontrollably, and somewhere deep inside of him, beyond the shock, he knew he was going down.

Oh, God, help me, he thought weakly. *I remember that sound now ... They were in the tree ... back when I was a kid, trying to get at us even back then ...*

The creatures moved in closer, almost as if they could smell his defeat. The grasshopper sound rose in his ears. The horrible image of Sam's lifeless body lying on the stretcher popped into his mind, followed by mocking laughter, and he knew that they had played a part in Sam's death.

They were taunting him with it.

Rage boiled up within him, temporarily wiping out his fear, and all that was left was the single thought to fight, to turn and face his attackers – *Sam's* attackers.

"Not yet ..." The voice whipped around him, carried on a burst of wind that battered him.

Jonah felt a shift in the air around him, and for reasons he couldn't explain – and in spite of everything in his body screaming not to – he looked.

The huge stranger was back – the same one he'd seen at the club, at Mardi Gras too – same long black hair, same eyes. Jonah watched, awestruck, as his heavy cloak melted into his body, running rivulets of red and gold that spread across his chest and over his shoulders to form body armor.

Jonah opened his mouth to speak, then spotted the ancient-looking weapons in the guy's hands, saw the massive steel blades glinting above him as they descended in his direction.

"MazziKim!" the stranger roared.

Hot wind blasted Jonah's face as the first blade sliced down, striking the dark entity's head. Blue light shot through its body like luminescent dye, lighting up its insides as it fell to the ground just as the second blade sang through the air, severing the hold of the entity on his right. The grasshopper chatter rose, high-pitched, almost like a scream, as a powerful hand gripped the sleeve of his jacket and yanked him backward with such force, he was sure his arm was going to be ripped off, and –

He found himself kneeling on all fours, still in the middle of the street – but not exactly the street. He could see the street-lights, the buildings, and the cars that lined each side of the street, but it was as if he were seeing it all through beveled glass ... almost like looking through a fishbowl.

Jonah glanced down at the black cinders digging into his hands and knees and shuddered. *Why don't I feel any pain?* He inhaled, and the air he sucked into his lungs was so pure, it shocked his system into a strange awareness, making everything around him crystal clear. Everything he thought he knew about the world, everything he counted on always being normal – even when he wasn't – had disappeared.

The hem of a cloak brushed by, and then another, and three-dimensional images began to flash through his mind: a massive figure falling through the sky as lightning cracked across a field of storm clouds that seemed to stretch on forever. "*And I saw him fall…,*" a soft voice whispered. Next he saw an immense white horse, lying on its side, start to take shape out of the clouds. His breath caught in his throat as the horse stood and its coat was suffused with a brilliant red that swept from its head to its tail.

The horse turned its mighty head and stared at him.

"*Watcher…*" The word whispered through him, and the images unexpectedly evaporated to reveal huge, cloaked figures that surrounded him in the middle of the street.

They were an impressive sight – staggering in height, at least ten feet tall, sinewy, and battle hardened. Even though they were cloaked, he sensed their power, elite fighters whose bodies had been shaped and honed into perfection for war.

"What *are* you?" Jonah asked in a hoarse whisper. He struggled to stand in spite of the rubbery sensation in his legs. He was determined to get some answers, even if it killed him. But the three figures remained silent, faces shrouded by hoods as they kept their attention trained on the street, where the dark spirits still lurked. The air around him was thick with tension, like being in the middle of a military battalion on high alert. The one who seemed to be the leader turned toward the warehouse.

Jonah turned his head too, and his heart lurched as he spotted Carly in the middle of the street, looking around uneasily.

He stepped forward, maneuvering himself in front of the cloaked figures that surrounded him, and felt a shiver of apprehension. He scanned the street for the shadowy creatures. He didn't see anything but sensed they were there, waiting for the right time to attack. He tried to take another step toward Carly but felt a powerful hand on his shoulder, holding him back.

"Jonah?" Carly glanced around again. Her voice sounded muffled, weird, like he was hearing it from underwater.

In a flash, the dark shadow being was at Carly's side. Jonah felt his insides melt as he watched her eyes widen in fear. A horrible terror seized him—worse than anything he had ever felt for himself—as Carly began to shake uncontrollably.

"No!" he growled, as though he were declaring war, and he made a dive for her through the fishbowl barrier that surrounded him.

Carly gasped, and Jonah knew he must've seemed to suddenly appear out of nowhere. He reached out and grabbed her, and an unbearable cold washed over him.

The being pounced, swirling around them, piercing their ears and minds with their high-pitched grasshopper sound, and just as Jonah felt his will to fight seeping away, another huge silver-haired stranger appeared. He lifted his huge broad ax and with a sideways slice, sent the creature flying backward through the air.

With lightning speed, the stranger wrapped his free arm around Jonah and Carly and pulled them back into … wherever it was … and they dropped to their knees just as a black Lexus barreled down the center of the street right for them, with an SUV on its tail.

Carly screamed, and Jonah shoved her out of the way just as the Lexus was about to strike.

A powerful wave of air rushed over him, and then another. He gasped for breath as he turned his head to see the brief flash of taillights on both vehicles before they rounded the corner at the end of the street.

Both vehicles had passed through him as if he hadn't been there at all.

A heavy silence descended as Jonah stood, his chest heaving. He looked around the dark, deserted street. They were alone again.

"What do you want from us!" he screamed in frustration, fists clenched as he pivoted, searching for signs of life, for even the barest flicker of movement in the air.

"That was J," Carly said hollowly, standing to her feet.

"What?"

She opened her mouth to say something else and swayed a little as if she might pass out, and Jonah cut the distance between them and held her in his arms.

"Carly, come on, stay with me," he said, patting her cheek. "What did you say?"

She blinked up at him, like she couldn't believe – *didn't want to believe* – what she was about to say. Her eyes filled with tears.

"That was J driving the Suburban."

Twenty miles away, Willa Harvey, propped up with pillows in her bed, glanced up from reading, a worried expression, crossing her wrinkled old features.

"Things gonna get real bad before they get good again, ain't they, Lord?" she whispered.

28

The Grigori leader rolled beneath the current as he made his way down the street in front of the warehouse, brushing by two unsuspecting humans as they exited their vehicle. The couple broke into an argument, blind to what had just passed them by.

Blind to reality, Shammah thought contemptuously.

Every once in a while there might be a feeling of something different or wrong in their little world of constant *want* and *need*, something off that they couldn't quite put their finger on. An over-whelming feeling of gloom, or a sense of being lost when they knew perfectly well where they were, or maybe a flicker of movement out of the corner of their eye when no one else was around. Rare were those who detected a hint of an odor, so foul to their senses that their insides drew up in defense to it.

He'd had eons to study them.

And even rarer were those who were able to see.

He watched the taillights of the Bronco disappear as it turned the corner, and he boiled with rage. He turned his eyes on the wounded MazziKim still lying in the middle of the street and drew his weapon. The creature screamed in terror, and he felt the wave of fear shudder through the collective in the distance as he drove his sword through the MazziKim's body.

An electrical charge split the air, and a second Grigori appeared. Shammah turned and inclined his head slightly. "They must learn the consequence of failure."

"I agree," Tola said slowly. "We cannot afford any more missteps if we are to keep the gate open for the others to join us."

Shammah glanced at Tola curiously; it was probably the sanest statement he had ever heard his brother utter.

"Tiria," Tola announced. A dark-headed warrior sporting a Mohawk appeared. "Follow him. Attack as soon as you find an opening."

The Grigori fighter disappeared.

"There is always more than one way to skin a cat," Tola said, his eyes glittering malevolently. "A whole litter, for that matter ..."

Shammah smiled as his twin began to lay out his strategy in his mind.

29

March 4

"J, it's Tiny. You said to call when I knew something, so I'm calling. Corsa doesn't know it was you—he wants *us* to find out who it was that tried to run him off the road. Come on back. The coast is clear and all that."

J deleted the voicemail and took a sip of lukewarm coffee as he stared out the window of his Suburban. Six in the morning, and his old buddy Mike was just now locking up the bar and heading across the parking lot to his car. Another day on the East Side. He rolled his window down.

"Hey, thanks for letting me take up space."

"You going?" Mike smiled. They had been in foster care together and tried to keep in touch as much as they could.

"Yeah, I'm going. Two nights of sleeping in this truck seems to be my limit."

"You're lucky someone didn't try to break in on your crazy butt," Mike said, laughing, as he climbed into his car. "They crawl out of the woodwork around here at night."

If only you knew, J thought, his body pumping pure caffeine through his veins as he started his Suburban and pulled out of the lot.

The party going on in his hotel suite was in high gear by the time J arrived, strangers all of them, kicking it like no tomorrow. They slapped him on the back as he walked through, told him how great his party was. He smiled and nodded, pounded a few outstretched fists even though he was so tired that he could drop. Any other time he would've cleared the place. But this wasn't any other time, he thought, glancing around. Most of the guys he recognized as the Arch crew who worked for Corsa.

J kept his eye on them as he made his way through the crowd to the living room. Dope was rolling heavy in the air in some places, but he steered clear of it. He couldn't afford to have anything else messing with his head – not after all he had seen.

He wished he had never seen any of it – not Nick going after Jonah and Carly like that, and especially not those creatures ...

He'd been trying to start his SUV for the twentieth time when it roared to life and he glanced up just in time to see Nick's Lexus streaking by. Then he saw Jonah and Carly standing in the middle of the street like sitting ducks as two giant ... *things* ... swirled around them. Despair had hit less than a second later when he realized there was no way he could get to them in time, and he'd stomped on the gas, determined to take Nick out. He remembered bracing himself as he gunned his SUV down the street, prepared to see his old friend's bodies flying up in the air when Nick's vehicle hit, but they seemed to just disappear into thin air the moment the Lexus reached them.

The real mindblower was looking in the rearview mirror to find them standing in the middle of the street again. How had they just disappeared and reappeared like that?

There were some things you could wrap your mind around – and some you couldn't. The only conclusions he had allowed himself so far were that Nick Corsa definitely wanted them all dead and that he was somehow involved in what was happening around them.

Couldn't be a coincidence that Nick appeared in town around the same time they all started getting those weird nightmares.

J maneuvered around a group of tight-looking dancers and slumped down on the couch next to Tiny, who greeted him with a wary grin.

"Whose idea was this?" J asked.

Tiny gave him a who-do-you-think look. "Been thinkin'," he said in a low voice. "Any of these dudes here can drive a truck, so why bring us all the way from Chicago? Then your buddy ends up dead like that?"

"Been thinkin' the same thing," J said, glancing sideways. He thought again of the huge freaking blade that Corsa had held in his hands, and he shuddered.

All at once J went still.

Something felt off, like a feeling of cold anxiety washing through him. He glanced around the rest of the room, then back, and spotted the dark shadows creeping up toward the ceiling above him before breaking away and darting around the room, slithering in and out of the crowd ... in and out of *bodies.*

"What the —" J squinted his eyes, trying to convince himself it was the smoke, but deep down he knew better. He had seen those things on the street, even if he didn't want to accept it.

Nah ... this is too much, man. This can't be real. J rubbed his hand over his face and then opened his eyes again. In a flash, he saw something else begin to take shape, growing upward from the floor at lightning speed until it morphed into a huge being with a dark Mohawk, wearing what looked to be black body armor.

J started to stand, then thought better of it and sat back down.

The being moved toward him and their eyes met; it narrowed its eyes, and then with a snarl it lunged at him, causing him to jerk back on the couch — just as it smacked up against something he couldn't see.

"What's up with you?" Tiny asked, looking at him curiously.

But J's attention was on the being as it narrowed its eyes at him again. He felt his temperature plummet, and a cold, lead feeling filled his legs. Unable to move, he watched as the giant slowly strutted around the room, studying him.

"What makes you?" a sinister voice sang through his mind. *"What makes you tick?"* Its eyes slid over him. *"What makes you care?"* The being suddenly smiled at J. Then it disappeared into thin air as if it had never been there at all.

"You see that?" J said, his voice cracking a little as he turned back to Tiny. He was still shivering, even though the cold had evaporated along with the thing.

"See what?" Tiny said, casually dragging on a joint as he checked out a chick gyrating to some wordless beat in the center of the room.

"Nothin'." J stood up unsteadily. "I need some air."

"Want me to go?" Tiny offered, and J shook his head.

"I'm cool."

But he wasn't cool. He pushed his way through the crowd as he headed for his room. Nowhere near cool ...

Harsh laughter pulled him from his thoughts, and he glanced over to see two of Nick's guys holding up a young girl, so stoned that she couldn't walk on her own. For a split second their faces changed, and he saw garish, shadowlike faces leering at him before they shifted back into place.

He hurried into his room and shut the door. It was just like when they were kids. Except he had a feeling that whatever it was that found them as kids wasn't going to be content to just scatter them again. It wanted to destroy them once and for all.

A horrible fear rose in him, and he felt himself slipping back into crazy land, the place he hated ... and yet ran to whenever things got too much to bear.

"I can't take this," he mumbled, out of breath. "I can't."

The image of the giant being lunging at him and then striking some kind of invisible barrier flashed through his head, and he grew still, feeling an unexpected peace wash over him.

Something had stopped it — but what?

"Remember ...," a deep voice whispered, and then ... he heard the sound of kids laughing.

J jerked around and saw the bedroom door begin to ripple before his eyes. A bright golden light filled his vision, and when it faded, his four old friends were standing on the other side of a glass door, dressed in bathing suits and trunks, looking so young ... so *excited* to see him.

"Come on, *J*," Jonah said with his crooked I-dare-you smile.

The glass door melted away, and J was with them, stepping out into the hot August morning. They took off for their run, falling into single file as they hit the dusty little trail that went down to the lake. Sam was in the lead, followed by Jonah, then Carly and J. "Pick up the pace, J!" Jenna called out from behind him. Turning, he saw her bringing up the rear, taking a quick puff from her inhaler as she ran.

J grinned; her new tough act since Jonah's rescue never failed to amuse him.

"We're still going fishing, right?" J asked as he navigated around a clump of roots in the middle of the trail. He'd never been fishing in his whole life, and hearing Carly's dad talk about it had made him feel like he'd been missing out.

"We're going fishing," Jenna said dourly. Fishing was definitely not her thing.

J smiled and turned his face up to the sky, relishing the feeling of the warm sun beaming down over him. The summer camp that Carly's dad oversaw was like a small version of what J imagined heaven to be—full of laughter and dreams that whisper that you are a part of something big and wonderful and that no one can ever take it away. He didn't want to miss out on *anything* if he could help it.

"We're fishing—*after* we finish our laps," Sam added in his no-goofing-off tone. He took everything Carly's dad said was good for them as gospel—including the gospel.

"How many laps does Mr. Miyagi want us to do today, Samson?' Jonah asked, trotting so close behind Sam that he was literally breathing down his brother's back. Sam threw his towel back without looking, and it landed on Jonah's head.

"I am *so* telling my dad you called him Mr. Miyagi." Carly snorted. "He'll probably make you spar with Sam."

Jonah growled, his voice muffled beneath the towel, and they all laughed.

In spite of his shaky beginnings, Jonah fit right in, as if he had been with them all along. He had a mind like a steel trap too and enjoyed quoting lines from every movie, TV show, or song while they ate, swam ... or tried to sleep. It drove them all crazy—and they loved every minute of it.

Well, most of the time, J thought, and glanced up just in time to see Jonah skid to a stop ahead of them as they reached the docks. He'd already maneuvered himself in front of Sam—something he somehow accomplished every morning—but instead of diving in and swimming out to the buoy, he stared into the water like it was filled with sharks.

"I'm not going in there," Jonah whispered, backing up against Sam.

"What's wrong now?" Sam says as he glanced around Jonah into the water.

"Snake," was all Jonah could seem to manage.

"Whatever you're seeing isn't real," Sam said, sighing heavily.

J saw Sam put his hand on Jonah's back, almost protectively, and J felt a hum of warning sing through his body ...

Something's up, J thought, and he felt Sam, Carly, and Jenna linking to his thoughts. Their new gift came and went sporadically, the last time being when they found Jonah ... which told them whatever was up was big. They moved together to form a tight huddle around the brothers, and glanced down into the water.

J's heart leapt into his throat as his eyes fixed on the huge, poisonous-looking snake moving through the water toward them.

"Oh, man, oh, MAN!" J heard in his mind as Jenna took another quick puff off the inhaler.

"I hate snakes!" Carly shouted through their minds. *"I've always hated snakes, and this one looks like some kind of freaked-out python."*

"Don't say anything – not out loud," Sam warned them. *"I see it."*

"Why can't Jonah hear us?" Carly asked.

"You have to go into the water with him," another voice ordered, a deep voice, rolling through their terrified ramble. *"You have to do this together. The prophecy cannot be fulfilled without Jonah; he holds the key."*

"Who the heck is that?" J glanced around. *"Who are you – "*

"Well, whoever you are, I'm not going anywhere near that – "

"You have to go into the water if you want to live," the voice said urgently. *"Tell Jonah it's not real. Hurry! The water is life! Choose life, and the snake will go!"*

"Come off it, Jonah," Sam blurted out. His voice was shaky but firm, and J realized that he believed the voice with all of his heart ... that he somehow *knew* this voice. "Whatever you're seeing, it isn't real."

He's going for it!

"There is no snake." He turned Jonah around to face him. "Carly's dad said he'd take us fishing after we finish our laps – and I'm *going* fishing. Don't you trust me?"

Jonah nodded, even though he looked like he might pass out.

"I think whoever that was talking to us is telling us the truth," Carly whispered through their minds. J felt something else too ... something new, like their spirits were connecting somehow, agreeing with each other. *"I'm going ..."*

"Me too," J and Jenna thought at the same time. They looked at each other and smiled.

Sam grabbed Jonah's hand and squeezed it reassuringly. "Let's go," Sam said grimly.

"You're going in with me?" Jonah asked. All the bravado from earlier had left his voice, and they heard the childlike wonder as he looked up at Sam.

"We're *all* going," Carly said, and they all joined hands as they ran down the dock and jumped into the water ... just as the snake rose its massive head, preparing to strike.

30

C arly dropped the knife in the middle of the pile of lettuce she had been chopping and held her finger up to inspect it. It was only a small cut, but it hurt like crazy. She had been listening to Jenna when the memory of that snake they had seen at summer camp came out of nowhere. She remembered summer camp ... just not *that* memory. How did just certain memories get wiped out of her mind?

"You okay?"

Carly glanced at Jenna as she wrapped the Band-Aid around her finger.

"I'm not sure," she answered slowly. "Hey, do you remember – "

"So, what do you think about my news?"

Carly frowned and played with the Band-Aid as she tried to come up with a polite way to tell her old friend that she had lost her mind.

"I think you've lost your mind," she said finally, but Jenna just grinned – which frustrated her even more. It had taken forever to get a hold of Jenna, and there had been a long, drawn-out conversation with Nick Corsa before her old friend agreed to stay at her dad's place for dinner instead of running off with him again. Carly wasn't normally so pushy, but after what Jonah had told her, she was afraid that Jenna was being used.

"I just don't have a good feeling about him, Jenna," Carly said slowly, searching for the right way to ease into what she had to say without scaring Jenna off. She forced a smile. "What's that old saying about fools rushing in?"

"You're not going to go all fortune cookie on me now, are you?" Jenna laughed as she leaned on the island where Carly had been working on the salad. She avoided Carly's eyes as she reached for a carrot.

"So he just decided that he wants you to move in with him?"

Jenna took a bite of the carrot and smiled shyly. "Yeah ... Can you believe it?"

"Jenna! No, I can't believe it," Carly said, flabbergasted. She glanced toward the front room to make sure her dad hadn't come in without her hearing. "You don't even know him," she continued, lowering her voice. "Did you forget what Jonah told you about Lila? That's his *cousin*, and they are thick as thieves, if you haven't noticed."

"Lila's really upset that Jonah said that," Jenna said with a frown.

Carly stared at her, stunned — and more than a little frightened — that Jenna had actually told Lila what Jonah said. This wasn't the Jenna she knew at all. What in the world had happened to change her so much in such a short time?

"Will you listen to yourself? Lila was probably there when Sam died — why would you care what she's upset about? Sam was your *friend*. Jonah and I are your friends. Why do you think I called you a million times? There are things going on that we need to figure out together. Please just wait until Jonah gets here, okay?"

"If we're such great friends, why didn't you tell me that Sam overdosed on a bunch of pills?"

"This thing with Nick ... it's insane! Way too soon," Carly said as she reached for their plates, in a rush to push her point. "You just met him. How can you think you know someone you just—" She stumbled in mid sentence and went into rewind. "Wait a minute — who told you that Sam OD'd?"

"Nick told me, okay? To tell you the truth, he was shocked that you and Jonah had kept it from me. Do you know how embarrassed I was, going on and on about how tight we were, and I didn't even know how Sam died?"

"Nick told me ..." Carly reached out to Jenna, her arm accidentally sweeping the silverware off the counter, and just as she made a grab for it, something changed in the air. She watched the forks drop in slow motion, and as the last one hit the floor, the clatter echoed strangely in her ears.

Something's here ...

"And as far as me not knowing Nick for long, well, I knew Mikey's dad for *years*, and look where that got me!" Jenna continued as if nothing had happened.

Carly rose and cautiously looked around the room. It was so cold. "Do you feel that?"

"Feel what?" Jenna frowned. She glanced around the kitchen and looked at Carly again.

There's something wrong with her eyes, Carly thought. "What –"

She caught sight of something scurrying by. Doc growled low in his throat from the corner of the room, sending a chill up her back. When she turned to look at him, his eyes were fixed on Jenna.

"Doc!"

He scrambled up and trotted out of the room.

"You know what? I don't think this was such a great idea," Jenna said as two red splotches bloomed on her cheeks. "I think I better go – Nick wanted Mikey and me to have dinner at his place anyway. He rented some movies for Mikey and everything."

"Wait," Carly pleaded, putting her hand on Jenna's arm. "You're lonely, I get that, but what *about* Mikey? What does he think about all of this?"

They both glanced toward the living room, where strains of *SpongeBob SquarePants* could be heard from the TV. Mikey was oblivious to them as he lay on his belly, coloring in the tablet he carried with him everywhere. Doc lay curled up next to him.

Jenna turned back to Carly. "Mikey's a kid. He'll get used to it. Besides, Nick says he can give us a better life."

"Give you and Mikey a better life – or just you?" Carly said and then bit her lip, wishing she had kept her mouth shut.

Jenna shrugged Carly's hand off her arm almost violently.

"I thought you were my friend," Jenna said, visibly shaken, as she grabbed her jacket and purse off the chair. "I thought you would be *happy* for me. I'm nineteen years old with a five-year-old kid. You do the math; every guy I meet does, and then I never hear from them again. I should have listened to Nick. He said you wouldn't understand. Not everyone can be as perfect as you." She headed for the living room, Carly following close behind.

"Jenna! I didn't mean what I said. I'm far from perfect – I'm scared. Please stay."

Mikey looked up from his drawing with a worried frown. "I don't want to go. I want to stay the night here. You *promised*."

"Come on," Jenna said, reaching for him, but Mikey hesitated. "I said now!"

Mikey jumped up, glancing from Jenna to Carly. His bottom lip began to tremble, and then something caught his interest behind them.

Carly whipped around to see a dark mist rolling on her wall. She gasped and stumbled back as the mist slowly changed, morphing out of the wall into a huge, powerfully built man with long black hair plaited with cornrows. He was beautiful – almost as beautiful as the men who had surrounded her at Bud Winters' place, and then again on the street with Jonah.

He smiled at her, and she was shocked by the sudden overwhelming desire in her to reach out and touch him. She took a step toward him, feeling something like the wonder she had experienced on the street in front of Bud Winters' house ... but something else ... like an almost maternal kind of warmth emanating from him. Like all he wanted to do was wrap his arms around her and love her. *Protect her* – like the mother she'd always dreamed would come back to her.

"*Let me in; INVITE ME IN,*" the deep voice coaxed.

"*DON'T.*" The word rumbled through her mind like thunder, and she stepped back just as the man reached forward to embrace her. Enraged, he lunged at her – but was stopped in midair, as if he had struck an invisible brick wall.

The man lunged a second time, and Mikey yelped and backed up so fast that he tripped over Doc. He fell hard on his butt ... and the man was gone.

"What's *wrong* with you?" Jenna yelled at her. Jenna's face was tight with apprehension and maybe a little fear as she turned back to Mikey. He was still on the floor, tears spilling down his cheeks as he stared up at Carly with a helpless look on his face.

"Mikey?" Jenna gave her a dirty look. "This is crazy! You're scaring him for nothing!" Not looking at Carly, she took Mikey's hand and helped him up. "Come on, honey, let's go home."

Home? Carly thought, horrified. Had the whole world gone crazy overnight? Surely Jenna was confused, didn't realize what she was saying. "Jenna, don't do this," Carly pleaded as she followed them. "There's something going on – like back when we were kids. I can't believe you didn't see that ... *thing*."

Jenna stopped for a moment and dug something out of her purse. "Here," she said, throwing a piece of paper at her. "You're welcome to it."

She glanced back at Carly for only a moment and then grabbed Mikey's hand and left without another word, slamming the door.

Her face ..., Carly thought as she scrambled to lock the door. *That thing was on her face – staring back at me!*

She took a deep breath and glanced down, spotting the piece of paper Jenna had thrown – and a drawing that must have fallen out of Mikey's pad. The sketch was childlike but chilling, the entire page taken up by what looked like some sort of huge creature hovering over a black car as a little boy and his mother sat inside.

The creature had large black wings ... and the eyes of a snake ...

Carly sank to the floor and hugged Doc to her tightly, shaking from the overload of adrenaline that continued to course through her body. She wasn't perfect. Far from it. If only Jenna could see her on the *inside*. There wasn't a day that went by when she wasn't hit with the overwhelming feeling that she didn't fit in. She hadn't fit in anywhere since she was twelve –

She looked up, startled.

Something's still here, she thought, freezing up. *And it's listening, waiting for ... something.* She glanced around the room again, her senses coming alive, sharper than they had been in years, but for some odd reason she wasn't afraid.

"Why is this happening to us?" she asked out loud. Doc looked up at her and then appeared to go still, like he was waiting for something too.

"Remember ..." The deep voice swirled around her as she stood. She felt the strange, shifting feeling again and saw the air change before her eyes, becoming almost liquid in appearance. A misty haze of gold light streamed around her and then began to churn as if being stirred, mixing with a blue-green color that now surrounded her.

Water, she thought, wondrously. *I remember this, it's ...*

... lake water. Carly looked around her in amazement as she swam through the murky green lake. Other bodies brushed by – bodies she knew but couldn't make out – and then she saw something else: a huge old stick of some kind weaving around them like it was stirring a pot of soup. With each turn, she saw strange markings and symbols appear in gold down the side of the stick, disbursing tiny flecks of gold through the water that clung to her skin.

She heard muffled laughter and scissored her legs, scrambling upward until she broke the surface and found herself staring back at her four old friends as they tread water around her.

"Did you see *that*?" Jenna smiled at her, and Carly was struck by how beautiful she looked. Not just because she'd lost those crazy owl glasses of hers; there was something else. She looked so happy and ... *free.*

Carly felt it too, like the best day she'd ever had in her life times *ten.* She held her arms up to see if the gold flecks were still there. *Is that what's making us feel so good?* she thought, but their connection seemed to be turned off.

"That freak of nature just disappeared when we hit the water," J said, his voice filled with awe. He looked free too; almost shiny ... and the old-man look was gone from his eyes.

"I knew you wouldn't let it get me," Jonah said, his teeth chattering as he looked at Sam. He turned to the rest of them, but his eyes fixed on Carly as a grin broke over his face, so filled with joy that it brought tears to her eyes. The tormented kid she worried over from the moment she first laid eyes on him was gone, and she saw the Jonah he was always meant to be.

"You guys really are like heroes or something – the kind that goes off to save the world ... and ..." – his teeth chattered again – "noble junk like that."

"Hey, you jumped in too, *Beav*, and I ain't ever seen anyone *that* scared in my life," Sam said with that beautiful smile of his own. "Kind of makes you the Big Kahuna of courage," he added with a small smack to Jonah's forehead.

"Did you just knight me, Wally?" Jonah grinned and rubbed his forehead gingerly. "Guess I should be glad it wasn't a *sword*."

Everyone laughed – everyone except for Jonah. Carly noticed his pale blue eyes widen as he gazed in the direction of the dock.

"Who is *that*?"

31

J onah dropped the joint he had just fired up, and it fell between
his legs to the floorboard. *What was that?* He leaned sideways in
the seat of his Bronco as he groped for the blunt. It was as if an
electric current had zapped his brain with watery images of that day
at summer camp. The fuzzy vision of a face rose before his eyes but
faded off before he could see who it was.

Another memory ... or at least part of one ...

He located the joint, sat up, and took a drag as his eyes moved
back to the front entrance of Nick Corsa's new place, over the door
of which was a sign with large, stainless steel-letters that read,
"Corsa International." The old, gray stone building with huge gargoyles posted on each corner had been used as a mortuary back in
the late 1800s, if he remembered right. The irony of it being a place
for dead people had not escaped him.

He glanced around the dark street, hoping to catch Nick or Lila
coming or going from the building.

He had promised Carly he wouldn't go near Nick — wouldn't do
anything stupid — but he couldn't help himself. She was going to be
ticked off. *Sam* would definitely be ticked off at him if he saw him
right now. But Sam was gone, his band was hacked off at him for
canceling another gig — *sorry about your bro, man, but the show
must go on!* — and he was seeing things that he was having a hard
time believing were real.

But then, what was real anymore?

He studied the paper burning between his fingers, then glanced
to the page in his journal, which lay open on the seat next to him.

*If Carly hadn't shown up like she did, I might've chalked it all up to
brain damage — done enough the past two years to pickle my freaking*

brain — but we both saw them … So who are they? Aliens? Why is it that we can see and hear them but no one else can? Why are some trying to kill us and others trying to save us?

Why us?

Why Sam? he thought and grimaced from the pain that had taken up permanent residence in his body — pain that even Old Sinsemilla couldn't put a dent in lately. He took another drag, thinking about the pills he had in his glove compartment. He wished he had something stronger … maybe something that could knock him out for a day or two …

For a moment he had the crazy feeling that Sam could see him.

"Just a little something to cut the edge off, bro," he said out loud in the empty truck and then felt like an idiot for saying it. Ozzy came alive on his ring tone, and he grabbed up his cell phone, saw Carly's name, and flipped it open.

"Yeah, I'll be there soon," Jonah said. "And no, I'm not doing anything dangerous."

"Really?" Carly said, her tone suspicious.

He caught sight of movement and turned to see two burly guys pushing an old woman in a wheelchair through the front doors of Corsa's building. A long shadow trailed along the side-walk, following right behind. Jonah narrowed his eyes, watching them closely as he tried to focus on what Carly was telling him.

"Wait a minute." He switched the phone to his left ear and grabbed his journal. "Now tell me again."

"It's *real*," Carly repeated. Jonah scribbled the words down. "There's something else: Nick told her that Sam died of an over-dose. I'll fill you in on the rest of it when you get here."

"I knew he had something to do with it!"

"I know …" Her voice sounded shaky. "There's no other way he would've known — the coroner wouldn't release that kind of information to just anyone. Promise me you won't try to take care of it yourself."

"Tell you what I promise," Jonah said, trying to keep his voice steady as he looked up to see the door close behind the little

231

group. "I'll call you back if I decide to do something, and you gotta promise me you'll stay put until I do."

He flipped the phone closed and reached for the door, determined to confront Nick — until he glanced at the page he had scribbled on:

Sam = THIS IS NOT A DREAM

Jenna = IT'S REAL

J = BUT YOU CAN'T SEE

Carly = THE TRUTH

Jonah = UNTIL YOU OPEN YOUR EYES

His mind instantly flashed to his dream of Sam, and he saw his brother standing in front of him, just as clear as if he were back in the dream again.

"This isn't a dream, Jonah — it's real," Sam said, his voice growing urgent as it rose above the wind and the rain. "But you can't see the truth ... until you open your eyes."

"You've got to be freaking kidding me," he said softly, glancing to the page again. He had written their entries down in the exact order of the words Sam had uttered in the dream. Or maybe it wasn't really a dream ... The possibility that his brother could still be alive somewhere ... He took a hit off the joint, thinking.

"You've got to be freaking *kidding* me," he said again. He exhaled, watching the cloud of smoke fill the cab of his truck, and then he frowned. There was something weird about the smoke. He leaned forward.

"*Take another drag,*" a voice whispered through his mind. "*A pill.*" The words were almost seductive, filling his head and chasing his anxiety away like a powerful opiate. Like the world's best tranquilizer, and he *wanted* it. Wanted it more than anything he had ever wanted in his *life.* All he had to do was ...

"*Listen to us; invite us in,*" the deep, calm voice answered.

"*We can heal you!*" said another voice.

Yeah, man, that sounds good, Jonah thought dreamily. *I can use all the help I can get —*

"Don't do it, Jonah," a new voice warned. "Remember your brother."

The memory of Sam's words trickled through his mind. *"You are opening a door to something you don't understand — something that wants to destroy you …"*

That's crazy. Just a crazy dream, Jonah thought. He wanted what they could give him, wanted it *bad.* And yet he hesitated.

It was the small seed Sam had planted that made him hesitate. Not the *"wants to destroy you"* part, because he was pretty sure he was already destroyed, but the *"opening a door to something you don't understand"* line. His grief was so painful, he wanted more than anything to escape from it … but what if he made it *worse?*

Jonah threw the joint out the window. A heavy silence filled his truck, and he glanced around uneasily.

He leaned forward again, squinting, just as two faces shot at him through the smoke, two grinning — *leering* — faces, striking at him like the heads of twin snakes … and then bouncing back only an inch away from him. They looked like the twins who had been following Sam through Mardi Gras — but how could that be? A memory flashed through his mind; twelve-year-old Sam turning to him with a strange look on his face. "I want you to remember this: if you're ever in bad trouble — "

The beings suddenly reared back and struck again.

"Whoa!" Jonah bleated out frantically as he jerked back, cracking his head against the back window of the cab. The beings abruptly sucked themselves back through the windshield.

Jonah's hands shook as he opened his glove box and pulled out a plastic baggie filled with weed, and another bag which held his private cache of painkillers.

He started the Bronco, stomped on the gas, and peeled out, gunning the truck down the street. He was only a mile down the expressway when he chucked his entire stash out the window.

It was only a few seconds later that he saw the red cherries of a cop car flashing in his rearview mirror.

Nick Corsa listened to the caller drone on as he swiveled his office chair and looked out the window to see one of his trucks pull around to the back of the building. *The last shipment.* Everything was proceeding just as planned.

Lila appeared in his line of vision next as she walked to her car with Mikey. A small smile played on his lips. He would have to give her a nice bonus after it was all over. She hated babysitting the kid almost as much as she'd hated playing girlfriend to Sam.

"Everything *is* under control," Nick said into his handset, gritting his teeth. He glanced to Jenna, who was passed out on the leather couch across the room. "She hasn't mentioned anything since she came back – other than she was upset and needed to lie down."

Hitting the intercom, he put down the handset and stood, feeling the need to pace a little.

"We needed that journal," a female voice snapped, her anger pulsing out into the air in the room.

"I explained that the police showed up unexpectedly. An inconvenience, yes, but it could not be prevented." He hated being humiliated in front of the Alliance members he knew were listening. "It's my understanding that the journal is in the hands of the police now."

"Perhaps you should consider your source."

She knew. Nick took a deep breath. "I am dealing with it accordingly." He hesitated and then pressed on. He had been holding on to the information, saving it for a rainy day, and now seemed the perfect time. "I am happy to report that we actually have two Watchers in our care instead of one."

"You mean, the child is a Watcher?" Soft, delighted laughter echoed over the intercom, bringing a smile to his lips again. "I heard it was a possibility. Well ... that is an interesting develop-ment. I suppose this makes my gift to you all the more timely: my friends at the police department have informed me that the brother is in custody as we speak."

Jonah Becker? Nick stopped pacing. *That is good news!*

"Tie up any loose ends that remain, Mr. Corsa. That's all for now."

The phone went dead and he punched the intercom off, then straightened up and looked around the room. A familiar feeling swirled around him.

"The old woman is here," a voice whispered through his head.

Nick hurried through the side door to the conference room and opened the door. Willa Harvey gave him a guarded look as one of his men pushed her wheelchair into the room.

"I'm so glad that we could meet like this, Ms. Harvey," Nick said, circling her wheelchair to sit on the edge of the long table. "I'm Nick, by the way." He offered his hand to her, but she just stared at him.

"I wouldn't call dragging me out of my home in the middle of the night a friendly visit, son," the old woman said in a surprisingly strong voice. "You best get on with whatever it is you have in mind."

Nick grinned. "I admire your directness," he said, nodding. "It's a shame your grandson didn't inherit that fine trait ... In fact, it's come to my attention that he's actually been playing me for a fool."

She glanced up at him, her dark eyes piercing as she studied his face. "Sounds to me like Jeremiah's finally come to his senses."

A mist of rage washed over Nick and he stood, fists clenched at his sides as he looked down at her. "You don't know who I am, do you?"

"Oh, I know who you are," Willa Harvey replied evenly. "I've seen you over and over in my life. Evil is evil no matter how many times the face changes or how you dress it up."

Nick laughed.

"Finish it," Shammah ordered, eyeing the old woman warily.

Nick motioned to his men. "These gentlemen are going to take you with them now. When the time is right, you are going to deliver a message for me."

"'Do not be afraid those who kill the body but cannot kill the soul.'" Willa replied calmly. "'Rather, be afraid of the One who can destroy both soul and body in hell.' Matthew ten, verse twenty-eight, son. You ought to look it up sometime."

"What are you waiting for?" Nick snapped at his men, startling them into action. One hurried to open the door, while the other practically shoved the wheelchair out into the hallway.

Shammah and Tola moved to the window and observed as the old woman was wheeled outside to a waiting car.

They watched as one of the men roughly grabbed up the old woman and threw her into the backseat, heard her cry of pain.

Then they exchanged smiles and disappeared into thin air.

The jail cell was cold and dark but definitely not lonely.

Jonah glanced briefly at the old drunk curled up in a ball in the corner before he resumed his pacing. The stench of vomit and sweat — and something he didn't even want to put a name to — permeated the cell, causing his stomach to do a little flip-flop as he walked. How stupid could he have been, to throw his stash out the window like that?

The fact that there just happened to be a cop waiting to snag him hadn't escaped him. He had never been into conspiracy theories, but if he were going to choose a time to start, it would be now ...

His mind went back to the cop who arrested him. A big, barrel-chested dude with a bad crew cut and protruding ears who interrogated him for over four hours, until he ran out of questions to ask and notes to scribble down. The cop, named O'Neil, grew silent after that, staring down at the table as he tapped his pen against his notepad. Tapped until Jonah thought he'd go crazy. He finally grew bored and looked up at Jonah again.

"Becker ... You wouldn't be related to Sam Becker, would you?"

Jonah nodded, waiting to see where he was taking it. He had a good hunch that the cop had known all along that he and Sam were brothers.

"Wow," O'Neil said, shaking his head. "He trained some of our guys here. Nice guy. One heck of a martial artist, from what I heard — strong as an ox. I guess it just goes to show you that it doesn't matter how strong you are; if it's your time to check out, it's your time."

He gave Jonah a creepy "get it?" kind of smile and stood and signaled for the guard.

"You're not really threatening me, are you?" Jonah asked, unable to keep his temper in check anymore as the guard started to lead him away. "Because I won't be in here forever.

I'm a first-time offender, and I'll post bail and be out by the time your shift is over!"

"Oh, I doubt that," O'Neil said, dismissing him. But Jonah noticed that the tops of his ears had turned red.

The big guard twisted the cuffs until they grated against his wrists, but Jonah refused to acknowledge the pain, staring daggers at the cop as the guard tried to drag him away.

"Wait —," O'Neil ordered the guard. A smile played on his lips as he moved closer, until he was standing only inches from Jonah's face. "Sam wasn't *really* your brother, though, was he? I mean, you were adopted, right? I heard it was a real tearjerker of a story too — the little stray that was rescued right out of a *trash* can."

Jonah started to lunge but decided against it. Instead he burst out laughing, surprising both men. "Yeah, that's right. I was adopted. So all those great things you've heard about Sam, how nice he was, how he always followed the rules, how he *hated* to fight even though he was really good at it? Well … I'm *not* Sam. You might want to remember that."

Continuing to pace, trying not to think about the smell getting worse in the cell, Jonah took a deep breath as he remembered how the cop and guard exchanged a look after his little speech.

But that wasn't the worst of it.

The worst of it was seeing their faces shift and change before his eyes.

Jonah took a few more steps, turned, and stopped.

He knew without seeing anything that something was lurking just outside his cell. He had felt them as he paced. *Two* somethings, pacing back and forth in sync with him, as if they were mocking him.

"Come on, Carly, check your voicemail," he whispered hoarsely. "I gotta get out of here."

Insane laughter echoed through the corridor. "Come on, Carly, check your voicemail!" a deep voice mimicked.

"Who is that?" Jonah demanded.

"It speaks!" the insane voice exclaimed.

"You look like you need a little something to calm you," another deep voice noted soothingly, and Jonah heard a rustle and a thump as something hit the floor and slid to a stop under the door of his cell. He glanced down, saw his stash of pills lying there, and felt something strong push at him, urging him to go for it ... to pick up the baggie and just start popping the pills like peanuts until they were all gone.

"Take the little blue pills and the story ends, right?" Jonah asked as his heart hammered against his ribs. "Everything back to normal, no more trips to jail, nobody else dies?"

"Something like that," the voice said, amused.

The image of Sam leaning through the window of his truck with that worried look on his face flashed through his mind. *"You know, sometimes the snakes are real, bro ...,"* Sam whispered from the past ... and rage took over.

Jonah kicked the baggie back into the corridor.

There was a brief silence, and then his mouth gaped open in shock as two giant beings morphed up out of the concrete floor outside the cell like they had been spewed from it.

They were massive, at least ten feet tall, and ripped better than any bodybuilder dudes he had ever seen on TV. They both wore dark jeans and long black leather coats. Their faces were chiseled, almost perfect, and exact replicas of each other. *The twins ...* He felt that if he looked at them much longer, he was going to pass out. The horrible odor grew stronger, filling his nostrils. It smelled like fear, which was strange, because he had never realized that fear even had a smell — but then, he'd never realized that evil had a smell either.

It did.

"This sudden courage of yours is ... interesting," the one with the soothing voice said. Jonah sensed that this one was the leader. The other one, with the half-shaved head, looked too whacked out.

"Let me guess; you must be ... Darryl ... and that's your other brother Darryl," Jonah deadpanned.

The leader was studying him now with a kind of curious amusement. But when Jonah finally summoned the nerve to look him in the eye, he felt all his strength leave him. *Those eyes ...* Cold, inhuman eyes that he remembered all too well. He heard the wind in his mind again, and on it the far-off sound of Jenna's cries.

Jonah started to back up, started to scream, until another voice jolted through his mind: *"Don't. Do not show any fear. They feed on it."*

The old drunk coughed. Jonah jerked around, saw the man sit up and rub his eyes. He groaned inwardly.

The old man coughed again, like he was hacking up a lung. "Don't you mind me," he said in a low gravelly voice as he struggled to stand.

Jonah whipped back around to the giants in the corridor and saw that they were now zeroed in on the old drunk.

For a brief moment the giants appeared confused. The leader snapped out of it first, narrowing his eyes as he glanced between Jonah and the old man like he was trying to figure something out.

A heavy thud echoed inside the little cell, and Jonah turned around again, half expecting to see that the old drunk had fallen. But he was crossing the cell slowly with the help of an old wood cane, each step punctuated by a strange echo as the cane struck the floor.

The old man straightened his back a little with the next step, and Jonah's eyes widened. Even in the dim light, Jonah could see he was huge – a lot bigger than he'd imagined when the dude was curled up on the floor.

"No sir, don't you mind me. Just need a little drink of water is all," the old man said as he struck the floor with his cane again, and Jonah saw the cane rise into a huge staff, gold lettering shining down its side as a blue wave of light ebbed across the floor. *That can't be the same –*

Jonah heard a harsh gasp from the corridor and spun around to see both giants taking a step back from the door of the cell.

"*Kallai,*" the crazy giant hissed.

If the old man heard him, he didn't acknowledge it.

He struck the floor again with the staff, and this time the entire floor was filled with the blue light. It radiated out and upward in waves that shot between the bars and struck the giants full in the chest, slamming them against the wall on the opposite side of the corridor. In a flash, Jonah saw their clothes melt into their bodies to form a kind of shiny black body armor. Savage-looking swords appeared in their hands.

The staff hit the floor again.

The leader let out a growl like a trapped animal, a growl that chilled Jonah to the bone, and he saw their faces change, the strong, chiseled features morphing into ugly masks of rage. The leader looked at Jonah with pure hate for a moment, a faint ripping sound pierced the silence, and both of the beings disappeared into thin air.

"Who *are* you – ?" Jonah croaked out, turning back to the old man. He was leaning over the tiny, rust-stained sink that jutted out from the wall. He filled up his dented tin cup with water and drank it down like he was dying of thirst and then leaned over to fill up the cup again.

The staff caught Jonah's eye as it slipped out from under the man's arm, the tip of it falling under the rushing water from the faucet.

"Can't you tell me what this is all about?" Jonah asked, unable to take his eyes off the staff. As the water hit it, the strange-looking symbols appeared, shining like pure gold against the wood. "I've seen one of those before," Jonah said softly. "Back when we were kids ..."

The old man turned to face him – only he wasn't old, and he definitely wasn't feeble. He was *cut*, his thick, muscular arms straining against the ragged jacket he wore. His exotic Asian features breathtaking but strong. Like the giants in the corridor had been, *but different* – a light seemed to radiate from beneath his skin, and when his eyes met Jonah's, they weren't the cold black of the others' but a warm amber color that was beautiful and ... a little fierce. *Ancient eyes,* Jonah thought, feeling again like he might pass out.

"You were there, on the street with me and Carly ... and ..." Jonah struggled.

"Remember," the old man said, his deep voice rolling through Jonah like a wave, and he wasn't in the dirty old jail cell, he was ...

... treading water in the middle of the lake, surrounded by his best buds in the whole world. He felt better than he'd ever felt before, alive and ... *protected*, which was funny because he'd never been so scared in his whole life when he dove in.

How did that snake just disappear?

His teeth started to chatter as he thought about the snake – until he looked at his friends. *They went in with me*, he thought in happy amazement. He blinked the water out of his eyes and gave Carly a grin.

"... I ain't ever seen anyone *that* scared in my life," Sam said with a smile that he'd never seen before. "Kind of makes you the Big Kahuna of courage," he added with a small but stinging smack to Jonah's forehead.

"Did you just knight me, Wally?" Jonah grinned and rubbed his forehead. "Guess I should be glad it wasn't a *sword*."

They all bust out laughing; then Jonah saw a movement above them.

"Who is *that*?"

They turned to see a huge man rising from the dock, his long black hair blowing in the wind as he pulled his pole out of the water. He was huge, taller than anyone Jonah'd ever seen in his life, and dressed in jeans and a T-shirt. A lot like the other local fishermen they'd seen around the lake – but there was something different about this guy.

Something ... not local, Jonah thought.

"That dude can't be real," J whispered, awestruck.

"Hey, mister, did you catch anything?" Jonah called out.

The man glanced sideways and smiled at them. "You might say I did," he said, his deep voice seeming to roll across the water to them.

He started to walk away, and as he did, for a brief flicker of a moment Jonah saw the clothes on his body change. The jeans and T-shirt faded off to a long cloak that parted slightly, revealing a flash of silver ... like *armor*. In place of his fishing pole was a tall wooden staff.

He was stirring that thing through the water around us!

Jonah looked around at his friends. "Are you guys seeing what I'm seeing?"

Before they could open their mouths to speak – before they could even blink – a brilliant flash of amber light encompassed them, so brilliant that they were forced to shield their eyes. The light slowly began to fade, but by the time they were able to look again, the man was gone.

Jonah fell back on the hard concrete floor with a startled grunt. *He was there when we were kids!* He shivered as he looked around the empty cell, which was now strangely devoid of all light. He hated being alone. Hated being alone in the dark, a place where he had lived the worst part of his childhood.

So, why *was he there? What did we have that made him so interested in us? What do we have now?*

He glanced around cautiously. He had no idea what to expect next anymore or *who* to expect. He felt like a pawn in an insane chess game in Wonderland, with the other pieces moving around him so fast that he couldn't figure out his next move.

He felt weak, tired, as though the whole world were collapsing on top of him.

He would have given everything he owned to be back with Sam and his friends on that sunny, magical day in August when everything in the world still seemed good and decent. When he still had hope that things could turn out all right ...

A tiny shaft of light splashed across the floor, and he looked up, noticing for the first time the postage-stamp-sized window high up on the wall. He stood with a weary sigh and crossed the room, until he was just beneath the window. Through the bars, he could see the sun slowly making its way upward in the sky, and something about the sight of it brought tears to his eyes.

The morning star, Carly's dad used to call it. *Another chance to start over again ...*

Jonah swallowed. There was a time when, like Sam, he used to believe everything Chaplain Hagan had to say. When he soaked up his stories about warriors who walked with God, and felt his heart burst with hope when the man told him that his dreams could stretch beyond just surviving his abusive childhood with Bud Winters.

Back then he had believed with all of his heart that Chaplain Hagan's God had been the one to send Sam and the others to save him — and that somehow made him his God too.

Now he didn't know what to believe ...

He watched the sun rise higher in the sky, and the cell brightened, revealing the writing on the wall — words that had been hidden to him in the dark.

A lot of writing, actually, dug into the newest layer of paint with whatever past inmates could find to scratch out their thoughts and frustrations. There was everything from the drunken ecstasy of "It was worth it! The Cardinals rock!" to the homicidal "Tin Man's going DOWN" to the justifier "Dude should've just gave me his wallet," and of course what jail cell

would be complete without the ever-popular "I was framed!"
His eyes roamed over the rest of the scribbles until he came to
a word that had been written just above the sink. It looked as if
it had been *burned* into the wall, the letters sculpted in a fancy
kind of calligraphy:

Watcher

He saw the giant being in his mind, saw the cold, inhuman
eyes again that stared at him through the bars of his cell.

His mind then flashed to the old fortune teller at Mardi Gras.
"Watcher-man," she'd rasped, clutching her ridiculous sign to
her chest and giving him that creepy smile, laughing at him as
he tried to get away. "You stumble like the blind, but *they* know
that you see."

He glanced back to the window, to the sun streaming
through the bars, trying to sort through the tangled mess of
confusion and despair that filled him, and ... he *knew.*

He somehow knew that everything he and the others had
been through so far was leading them back to that one night
that had changed them all forever —

Carly, where are you? He squeezed his eyes shut in an effort
to block out the possibility that something might have happened
to her.

Hearing the echo of heavy footsteps coming down the corridor toward his cell, he braced himself for what was to come.
Then he did something he hadn't done since he was that skinny
ten-year-old kid who hid in a dumpster.

He prayed for a miracle.

32

I feel like I've been through a war zone," Carly said, falling back on Sam's couch with a heavy sigh. Jonah still didn't understand his decision that they should stay at the warehouse, but after his night in jail, he figured there were a lot more things to fear than good memories.

Carly glanced at the room. "This *place* looks like a war zone."

"What?" Jonah swiveled on the stool he'd copped from the kitchen and looked around. Since he couldn't bear to sleep in the old bedroom he'd shared with Sam, his sleeping bag was rolled out in front of the fireplace, with his guitar sitting on top. His brother's art valises were propped against the coffee table, where his laptop sat.

In a while they would start piecing together all they had learned. For now they had declared a temporary time-out from the nightmare.

He swiveled back around to Carly. "Looks fine to me."

"You're kidding, right? Oh, wait a minute — I did see your apartment."

"Hey, it was an off day."

"Is that like a bad hair day?"

Jonah laughed, and Doc bounded into the room and jumped into Carly's lap, causing her to utter a loud *oof*. "Nutty dog," she groaned, trying to catch her breath. "He still thinks he's a puppy."

"He's a *horse*," Jonah said, reaching for his guitar. He began to strum, sneaking glances at her as he played.

She looked so good — better than anyone had a right to look after running around the city all night trying to find him. She laughed as Doc tried to lick her face, and he was struck by how normal everything felt for once. He wished with everything in him that it could stay that way.

Did they have a chance of surviving all this? A few hours ago he would have said no ... but now he wasn't so sure. A tiny seed of hope had formed when that guard appeared and told him he'd been bailed out — not by Carly but by Professor Kinney.

A miracle? He wasn't sure ... but it made him wonder.

He glanced down to his guitar and softly began to sing the song he was working on. The never-ending song, according to Kino and Bobby:

> *Darkness comes and I can't see,*
> *The face staring back at me.*
> *Memories burn in my mind,*
> *Scars and regrets from another time.*
> *Where is the road that leads me outta here?*
> *Where is the place I can lay my head?*
> *Where is the road that leads me outta here?*

"What song is that?"

"It's only half done," Jonah said with a shrug. He pretended it was no big deal, but it drove him crazy that he hadn't been able to finish the song ... like he was leaving something undone. *Like Sam's journal?* He shoved the thought away and gave her a small smile. "We use it as a short opener right now. Gets everyone's blood pumping."

"You're going to finish it," Carly said firmly, and he saw in her eyes that she understood what he wasn't able to say out loud. "And when you do finish, you're going to dedicate it to me," she added, giving him the killer smile. She hugged Doc to her, and her smile softened a little as she studied him.

First time in my life I've ever wished to be a dog, he thought wryly.

Carly grinned at him like she had read his mind, and scooted Doc off the couch as she stood. "Come on, help me get our drinks — I feel like I'm starting to fade."

He laid his guitar down and followed her into the kitchen.

"You know what's so weird," she said, glancing over her shoulder. "I've been thinking about my mom a lot lately. Wondering if she's happy, does she ever think about me ..." She shrugged a little, handed him two glasses, and opened the freezer. "Do you ever wonder about your mom?"

"To tell you the truth, I don't remember much about her," Jonah said honestly. "I remember that she cried a lot and then one morning I woke up and she was gone ..."

Carly frowned as she put ice in the glasses, handed them to him, and grabbed the Red Bulls out of the fridge. "Don't you think it's weird that three of us had mothers who deserted us when we were kids?"

"Yeah, I do," he admitted as they made their way back to the couch. "Then J's grandma gets hit by a car, and Sam's folks – *my* folks – are killed ..." He put the glasses down on the coffee table. "No wonder we're all so screwed up."

"Well, mine left because she chose to – tell me how screwed up that is."

They plopped down on the couch with a sigh.

"It's like whatever these things are have been trying to destroy us since the moment we got together," Carly said, filling their glasses. "You know, I've seen stuff like this on Syfy, and it never turns out good for the humans."

Jonah laughed; she sounded just like a female version of him.

"What?" Carly smiled hesitantly.

"Nothing ... just sounded a little like something I might say. Except I think we're way beyond anything Syfy could dream up right now."

"You know what I think? I think the good ones – at least I hope they're good – want to help us. The bad ones, they're trying to keep us confused and apart – to get us when we're alone."

"I'm not alone," Jonah said, moving closer to her. He knew they had to talk, had to face what was coming. But he wanted to kiss her too – wanted it more than anything. A small, knowing smile curved her lips, and he saw a faint blush spread across her cheeks.

"Um ... did you just use a *line* on me?"

He grimaced, embarrassed, and then looked at her with a sheepish grin. "Is it working?"

"Yeah, I think it is," Carly said quietly, her eyes reminding him of a warm summer sky as she looked up at him, and he leaned in and kissed her softly. They looked at each other, smiled, and eagerly kissed again.

Doc barked, and they jumped apart like two kids caught by a hovering parent.

"Doc, you lunatic," Carly said, laughing, as she reached for their drinks. She handed Jonah his and took a quick sip of hers.

"I think you trained him to do that."

"No ... but it's actually not a bad idea." She grinned mischievously. "Great way to get rid of the criminal element."

"Criminal element – is that how you think of me?" He gave her his best injured look. "What if I said I never inhaled?"

"That's what the cop at city jail called you." Carly laughed again. She lowered her voice. "'If you continue to associate with the criminal element of this city, Ms. Hagan, you will live to regret it.'"

"That sounds like a threat," Jonah said with a frown.

"I'm not exactly helpless, Jonah."

"Did O'Neil say anything else to you?"

"No – but he might have if Professor Kinney and his attorney weren't with me."

"That still blows me away." Jonah shook his head. "How did he even know I was in jail – and why would he go to all that trouble to help me get out?"

"I don't have a clue. It's a good thing he *did* know, since my voicemail wasn't working ..." She glanced at the valises. "Are the rest of Sam's paintings in those?"

He nodded, watching her bite her lip, thinking, and he knew they were slipping back into the place where neither one of them wanted to go. The trip to Wonderland wasn't for the faint of heart.

"Have you looked at all of them?"

He blinked at her for a moment. "Not yet – I've been kind of tied up lately."

"Well, maybe we're supposed to look at them together."

"Maybe," he admitted, then stood and walked around the coffee table before he could change his mind. Carly was right behind him, her hand resting on his back as he unzipped the first valise.

"You know, Sam's professor mentioned these paintings – he said he and Sam were supposed to hook up ..." She let her words trail away as he pulled a painting from the valise. "Oh ... man, this isn't good," she said with a groan. "That's me, isn't it?"

Jonah grimaced. There was no denying it was Carly. His eyes traveled over the image of her wrecked Jeep lying sideways in the middle of a dark intersection. A giant being in black armor, flanked by two huge, evil-looking wolves with humps on their backs, stood at the front of the Jeep in a way that suggested that *they* were what she had struck before flipping over. Smoke billowed from the hood as Carly's lifeless body lay half in, half out of the driver's side window ... as if she had tried to crawl free. A hoard of insect-like creatures with bodies of locusts and faces that were almost human swarmed over the back end of the Jeep, crawling toward the open window where she lay ...

Carly sat on the floor with a thud. "Is that what's ... going to happen to me?"

"I can't believe this is all Sam was trying to tell us ..." Jonah's hands shook as he quickly grabbed another valise, unzipping it. *Mikey. Been there, don't want to go back again — at least not yet.* He set it to the side and opened the next case.

Jenna, a dark bowl of night sky over her as she ran ... Sam had caught her in mid stride, with two big crows in close pursuit, their claws outstretched, reaching for her. An almost-transparent looking man was in front of her with his arms opened wide. A strange fire burned from his hands. Two beings in black armor stood on either side of him, whispering in his ear. But Jenna was so busy looking over her shoulder at the crows, she didn't realize that the next step she would take wasn't into the arms of the man but *through* him and off the side of a cliff.

"You think that guy could be Nick?" Jonah asked.

"I don't want to see any more, Jonah," Carly pleaded.

"Come on, Carly," he urged gently. "We can't stop now." He pulled another painting free from its case.

J was on his knees in the middle of an alley in the city, tears streaming down his face as he cradled a lifeless body in his arms. Attached to J's back was a deformed, gargoyle-like creature that appeared to be whispering in his ear. J seemed to be unaware of the creature as he stared hopelessly at the brick wall before him that rose to meet the night sky.

"Is that a kid?" Carly asked, pointing to the figure in J's arms.

"I don't think so ..." Jonah frowned and bent down to examine the image more closely. "There's a wedding band on one hand."

Carly frowned as she scanned the rest of the painting. "Wait a minute — I know that!" She pointed to the little blue zigzag line with a circle around it underneath Sam's signature. "It means add water. It's an old trick Mrs. Triefenbach taught us back in middle school." She stood and headed for the kitchen.

"Triefenbach — Sam's old art teacher?" Jonah called after her.

"*Our* old art teacher," she answered. He heard the water faucet come on a second later and then shut off. "She was really into combining mystery and art," Carly said, entering the living room again with a small glass of water and a clean rag. "She loved to tell us stories of hidden paintings she had found under other paintings." She dipped the rag into the water and gently wiped it across the painting of her. "Anyway, she taught us this cool technique — "

"Hold on — what are you doing?" Jonah asked, alarmed. "You're going to ruin the painting!"

"Trust me." She glanced up at him, and he realized she had to do it — had to try to find hope — and he no longer cared if it ruined the painting.

In the seconds it took for them to look back down at the painting, new images had already appeared on the canvas. The first thing they noticed was the detail work Sam had done around the edges. In each corner of the painting were opened doors with ancient-looking script at the top ... and spiraling out of each door were huge, shadowy beings, much like the things they had encountered on the street.

"Okay, this might have been a mistake," Carly said, her voice starting to shake. "And this is way beyond what ... I thought there might be a message ... but *simple*, like disappearing ink. I don't even know how this is possible ..."

"Wait a minute — what's that?"

They fell silent as they watched two beings appear on the canvas, wearing silver armor with the image of a lion's head etched into their chests and wielding the biggest swords Jonah had ever seen in his life. A third being was only half visible ... as if he were stepping into the picture from somewhere else.

"Okay, that's good, right?"

"Yeah, I think it is," Jonah said, unable to take his eyes off the painting. "They look a lot like the ... beings that saved us in front of Sam's place."

Carly dipped the rag into the water and wiped it over the painting of Jenna, revealing the creepy doors ... Then two more beings in silver armor appeared, their huge broadswords in a downward arc toward the crows chasing Jenna.

"Definitely better," Carly said. Jonah heard the fight back in her voice, and he smiled.

Mikey's painting was next. His revealed the same doors, with the spirit-like beings swirling out of them as well. Except to the side of each door, they saw *Jenna*, holding the doors open for the beings.

"That can't be right!" Carly exclaimed. "Jenna would never do anything to hurt Mikey."

"Maybe not on purpose ..." They watched another image appear: a giant being in silver with his eyes lifted upward as he blocked the hideous thing on the other side of the door from entering Mikey's room ...

J's painting revealed the same doors – and two beings in silver armor standing on either side of him, with huge broadswords in their hands.

"Do you think the kid could be J – like maybe it's meant to be taken symbolically instead of literally?" Carly asked, studying the painting.

"I don't know ...," Jonah said distractedly. He was looking at the two valises they had left. That meant one painting had to be his ... but who's was number six?

He took a deep breath and pulled the next canvas free.

It was a painting of the sun. A beautiful, almost iridescent sun with a narrow oak door in its center and an intricately carved lion's head that covered the entire length of the door ...

Jonah glanced at Carly, shrugged, and withdrew the final painting.

A surreal sensation washed over him as he observed himself standing in the middle of the dark jail cell. His eyes were closed, his face turned up to the tiny window ... as if he were praying. Everything had been painted, down to the most minute detail: the graffiti on the wall, the rust that covered half of the old sink ... and the two giant beings in black that stood just outside his cell, their faces drawn back into hideous masks of hate ...

Carly shivered.

"You should've been in that cell," Jonah said grimly. He handed her the painting.

She wiped the rag over the canvas and gasped as light immediately flooded the painting, streaming down from the tiny window to envelop Jonah as he stood in his cell. In his right hand was an antique-looking gold key with the same ancient script that was on the doors in the corners of the other paintings. Behind him to the right stood the giant being he remembered, his eyes flashing that amber color as he struck the floor with his staff, shooting out a wave of blue light that blanketed the bars of the cell like a shield.

"What's with the key in your hand?"

"I don't know ...," Jonah said. "That's the only part I don't get ... the doors for the cell are automatic." He looked up at Carly. "Everything else is pretty much how it happened, though."

"Do you think anyone would believe we're actually seeing this stuff?"

"Would you?"

"Probably not," she admitted. She turned back to the painting and traced her finger down the key, lost in thought. She cocked her head to one side as if she were listening to something.

" 'The prophecy cannot be fulfilled without Jonah; he holds the key ...,' " Carly said softly, almost dreamily. She looked up at him, her eyes wide with wonder – and maybe a little fear too.

"*What?*"

"It was something I heard that day at the lake – we all heard it just before we jumped into the water with you."

"And no one thought to tell me?"

"Jonah, I didn't even remember that it happened until just recently. It's like someone wiped our memories clean the moment we walked away from the lake." She hugged herself as if she were cold. "I can't remember much after that. What else did they make us forget? How are we supposed to know what's real anymore?"

Before he could answer, she crossed the living room, flipped the switch for the gas fireplace, and sat on the floor in front of it, staring into the fire. Doc got to her before Jonah did, settling his big head in her lap. He gave Jonah a wary look as he sat down next to Carly.

"There's a lot I don't remember either – and a lot I wish I didn't remember," he said. "I agree with you that whatever or whoever these things are, there are two sides: one that's trying to kill us, and the other that's trying to save us ... I think that's what Sam was trying to say through his paintings." He frowned, sensing there was more. "Maybe if we could figure out what those symbols and words mean on the paintings ..."

"Okay, but why *us*? It's not like we're geniuses or we developed the next weapon of mass destruction. It doesn't make any sense."

"Well, we know it has something to do with our memories ... Maybe we saw something we weren't supposed to see. Maybe we were at the wrong place, the wrong time ..." He brushed a hand over his face wearily.

She turned and looked at him. "You think it has to do with the night we went to see that fortune teller at Mardi Gras, don't you?"

"I –" Her eyes were boring into him, demanding the truth, and Jonah sighed. "It's got to be a big part of it. If you think about it, it was around that time when all hell seemed to break loose over our lives."

"But you don't remember anything yet?"

"Not yet, but I'm pretty sure that's where we're heading."

Carly got up, snagged his laptop off the coffee table, and sat back down.

"What are we doing now?"

"Making a list," she said, turning the laptop on. "Tell me everything you remember up to this point – and don't leave anything out."

She typed continuously for the next half hour, adding her own memories and thoughts as he shared his. Then she sat back, skimming over what she had written.

"This isn't a dream – it's real, but you can't see the truth until you open your eyes ...," she read out loud, and they both were silent. Her eyes looked tired and more than a little scared when she glanced up at him. "How much farther do our eyes have to be opened? I'm not so sure I *want* to see or remember anything else."

"That makes two of us. If it wasn't for Sam – not to mention Jenna and J – I would buy us a one-way ticket out of here."

"*J?*"

"Yeah, well, the jury is still out, but I've been wondering if maybe he was chasing that car on the street. It just doesn't make sense that he'd run us down ..."

A small smile touched her lips, and then it was gone. "I still haven't been able to get a hold of either of them." She shook her head and glanced down at the screen. "So, giant beings that are able to travel through walls, fly out of birds, morph out of floors, and pull us into other dimensions? How can we fight something like this – like *them* – by ourselves?"

"One heck of a martial artist, from what I heard – strong as an ox," O'Neil had said at the city jail. *"I guess it just goes to show you that it doesn't matter how strong you are; if it's your time to check out, it's your time."*

"I don't know," Jonah answered carefully, barely able to contain his own anger and frustration as his mind struggled to come up with an answer. "I still think it's connected to our memories – gotta be. Maybe there's something locked in those memories that they need …"

"Okay, so what happens to us after we remember and they get what they want – I mean either side?"

"I don't know," he said again. He was beginning to hate those three words. "I wish Sam was here."

"I can't believe he's gone," she said, reaching out to brush his hair back from his forehead. "Why would anyone want to hurt someone as good as him?"

Jonah looked at her for a long moment. "Did I ever tell you that he split his inheritance with me? When our folks died, they didn't have a will or anything … so Sam set it up that everything would be split down the middle – life insurance, bank accounts, all that stuff. I guess that's why he made a will up … now the warehouse is mine too."

"None of it surprises me," Carly said softly. "He loved you."

Carly fell asleep not longer after that, bundled in a blanket next to his sleeping bag like a little kid who was too scared to be alone. He watched her as she slept, trying to block out the echoes of Jenna's cries from that long-ago night while studying every inch of Carly's face by the firelight, studying it like he couldn't afford to forget …

There has to be a way, he thought desperately, turning to stare at the fire.

Those things weren't going to quit until they killed them all, and he wasn't ready to lose anybody else. *Not now,* he thought, glancing back at Carly. *Not ever.*

33

rieh crouched on the edge of the Metropolitan skyscraper's green-gabled rooftop as he watched the sun rise over the city skyline. Azaniah stood guard on the back side, long red hair blowing in the wind, Neriah and Jair flanking him on the back two corners, their faces turned skyward as a helicopter passed overhead. Kallai remained at his post at the warehouse — though his last report was that it had been suspiciously quiet all night long.

The Grigori were up to something. He could sense an ominous brewing, a building of their forces in the atmosphere and realizing they would soon be outnumbered, he considered the possible strategies. That the Grigori had once been a part of their order made his task challenging; he and Shammah were much like masters of chess guessing each other's moves. He turned his attention to the Arch and the grounds surrounding it.

"What are you thinking?" Jahdiel asked, leaning his mammoth frame against his staff.

"Have you ever heard of a gambit?"

"A chess move," Jahdiel said.

The Irinim leader nodded. "The first player takes a risk or makes a sacrifice, hoping to achieve an advantageous position." He turned his gaze to Jahdiel. "I suspect they're about to make a big move, and if it's for the reasons I think, the real battle will soon begin." He turned to his right. "Eri."

In a flash, the raven-haired Irinim fighter drew two broadswords from beneath his robes, withdrawing the invisible force field over the skyscraper's roof.

Arieh rose, his eyes briefly flickering down to the humans beginning to trickle into the city. *Race of man*, he thought, *if only you would open your hearts again and see …*

He turned and nodded to his warriors and they stepped off the building one by one, dropping effortlessly forty-two stories down through the early twilight, mammoth wings made of millions of atoms of fire rising behind them, reflecting in the glass and steel side of the building as they fell.

34

The university classroom was jammed with students—something Jonah hadn't realized until he opened the door, but by that time it was too late. He was smashed against the door as they streamed past him, heads turning to briefly check him out as they poured out into the hallway and hurried on to their next class.

He watched them go like an observer studying a world he never belonged to—a world that seemed a lot simpler, filled with finals and GPAs, text messages, and dates. They were oblivious ... and he wanted to be one of them.

He glanced away, toward the front of the auditorium, where Professor Kinney still stood at the podium, looking over his notes. The wide-screen behind him was still lit up with "History of the Supernatural: The Good, the Bad & the Ugly." Beneath it was a painting of an impressive-looking angel with his foot on the back of a creature that appeared to be half dragon, half man. Jonah stared at the sword raised above the angel's head and swallowed hard.

"So we meet again," Professor Kinney said, startling Jonah from his thoughts. Jonah approached him and set down the five valises he'd brought. The professor smiled warmly, offering Jonah his hand, and they shook.

"I really appreciate the help the other night, with ... everything," Jonah said. He dug into the pocket of his jeans and handed Professor Kinney a check. "This should cover the bail. I didn't know how much your attorney's fees were, so—"

"He did it as a favor to me." Professor Kinney held up the check. "Let's just call this even, okay?"

"Yeah, sure," Jonah said, nodding, and then he looked down at his feet, searching for what to say.

"You could start with telling me why you're really here," Professor Kinney said in a slightly amused tone. "You could've mailed the check."

Jonah looked up. "The truth? I got up this morning and it was a toss-up: you or the insane asylum downtown."

"Ah." Professor Kinney nodded. " 'Whom the gods wish to destroy, they first make mad.' "

"What's that?"

"Euripides," Professor Kinney said with a small smile. "It's fitting, don't you think?"

"The nail on the head." Their eyes met. "Do you have time to talk?"

"Let's go back to my office."

Picking up the valises, Jonah followed him through the door at the back of the classroom, glancing briefly at the odd letters and symbols carved into the doorframe. He stepped into a surprisingly spacious office with a long conference table in the middle, flanked by bookshelves that lined the walls on either side. The hippie-looking dude he had seen at Sam's funeral glanced up from a desk on the left side of the room, sandwich in mid flight toward his mouth. He put the sandwich down and stood.

"Let me introduce you to my illustrious colleague, TJ Levine," Professor Kinney said, smiling. "Brilliant theoretical physicist, engineer, and linguist" – he gazed at the pile of Subway wrappers that littered TJ's desk and shook his head – "with the metabolism of a hamster."

Jonah reached out and shook the young man's hand.

"Shalom," TJ said.

Jonah gave him a puzzled smile.

"One hundred percent USDA Jewish-Japanese," TJ explained with a grin.

Jonah grinned back; it was hard not to like the guy. "You were at Mardi Gras – at the funeral too, right?"

TJ nodded. "Sorry about your brother, man. I really dug his work."

"You've seen his paintings?" Jonah asked, looking between the two men.

258

"Not the ones you have. I spotted one of his exhibits at Tucker Hall a couple months ago," TJ said. "Hooked him up with Prof not long after that."

"Sam wasn't in my class long, Jonah," Professor Kinney explained. "Just a few weeks … It was only a couple of days before he died that he decided to tell me about the nightmares … and the paintings." Professor Kinney cleared his throat. "Were you aware that Sam had no memory of painting them?"

"He didn't remember painting them?" Putting the valises on the end of the conference table, Jonah pulled out a chair and sat. "That must have scared the heck out of him."

"May I take a look?" Professor Kinney asked.

"Sure," he said, brushing a tired hand over his face as the two men moved into action, unzipping the cases and laying Sam's paintings out on the table with great care.

"Look at the doors," TJ said excitedly. "Do you see the script above them?" He grabbed a pen and writing tablet off his desk and began to scribble as he walked past each painting.

Professor Kinney glanced up to Jonah. "Did your brother know Hebrew?"

"You're kidding, right?" He turned to TJ. "Do you know what it says?"

TJ nodded. "Okay, see the big door on the left side of each painting? The same phrase is written above each of the doors: *veshal ob*, which refers to a person who inquires of Ob the Python in order to predict the future."

Jonah felt light-headed. In his mind, he could see the huge snake rising out of the lake … and then he saw the old woman standing before him, clutching her sign … "Predict the future," he said numbly. "Like a fortune teller."

"Exactly," TJ said.

"The open door represents someone opening their body up to these spirits," Professor Kinney added. "Once the door is opened, this spirit is able to wreak havoc on that person's life."

"Spirit?"

"As in evil," TJ supplied.

"And this door?" Jonah asked weakly, pointing to his painting. He wasn't sure he liked where it was going, but he had to know.

"*Cesheph*," TJ replied. "It refers to someone who cuts up herbs and makes them into a magic brew. The Greek version of the Old Testament translates the word as *pharmaka*, meaning drug – "

Okay, I get it," Jonah said shortly. Frowning, he glanced at Carly's painting. "What about this door?"

"*Dalal*," TJ said, tracing the letters with his finger. "It means to bring low or make empty."

"And on Jenna's painting?"

"*Nasha*: to deceive and seduce with great power."

He exhaled loudly. Nick Corsa . . .

"This one represents violence, corruption – ," TJ began on J's. Jonah held his hand up. "Who are the giants in the paintings?" he asked, finally taking the plunge. "The ones that want to kill us."

TJ started to say something, but Professor Kinney silenced him with a look.

"I think he's already guessed," the professor said. He watched Jonah, waiting for his response.

"I'd like to hear your theory first," Jonah countered warily.

"Fallen angels."

"What?" Jonah half laughed as he straightened up in his chair. He looked around the room, stood up, thought about bolting, and then sat back down. "You mean like the Devil? Because I was thinking more like aliens."

Professor Kinney nodded. "A popular choice. Posing as aliens has been one of the MazziKim's finest ruses." He planted his hands on the table and leaned forward. "But the truth is that what your brother painted with such vivid detail are fallen angels."

Jonah snorted, yet deep down he *knew*. That mind-numbing evil he had felt in the jail cell . . . the wave of relief and *hope* when they were forced to leave . . . What else could cause all this? He glanced up to see both men watching him, waiting.

"And the others – "

Professor Kinney smiled. "They are the *Irinim* – God's warring angels."

"Definitely the good guys, but don't ever mistake them as weak," TJ jumped in. "One of these beings strolled into enemy camp, and when he walked out, *186,000* soldiers were dead. *One.*"

Jonah glanced up. "MazziKim – I've heard that word before."

"MazziKim, Harmers, evil spirits ... they have a lot of names." TJ shook his head and picked up his sandwich. "But all you have to remember is that they are a nasty breed, kind of like supernatural thugs that are sent in as the first line of attack."

"Okay, I'm not saying I believe all this, but if I did, why are these things so interested in us?"

"Cliff's Notes version?" TJ asked after swallowing a huge bite. Jonah nodded.

"Okay." TJ set his sandwich down. "There have always been angels that walk the earth but these fallen angels were once a part of a high order of fierce angels called Irinim that were sent to watch over the affairs of man. Two hundred of these angels – or Grigori, as they are now called – went rogue. Led by an angel called Samyaza, they bound themselves together by a curse then hit the earth, abducting women, siring giant offspring, and it all went downhill from there: Murder and mayhem, sorceries, vampirism – there are accounts of it from the book of Genesis to Enoch and other apocryphal writings ... Anyway, God sends the flood to protect what's left of the human bloodline. It wipes out the offspring's bodies – but not their spirits."

"MazziKim?" Jonah said.

TJ nodded.

"And the fallen angels?"

"Immortals can't lose their bodies, which is why the Irinim were instructed to chain them in the depths of the earth for seventy generations. At the end of that time, it's written the world will grow dark again ... and they will return. Psalm ninety, verse ten tells us a generation is seventy years – which is why our organization has been following the signs so closely." TJ leaned back in his chair. "Seventy years times seventy generations from the period of the flood ... well, it pretty much brings us to *now.*"

Jonah exhaled and looked around the room. "So ... even if this is all true, it still doesn't tell me why they're coming after us."

"Because of something planted in your DNA, you can do something that only a very small part of the world's population can do," Professor Kinney answered, rising from his chair and going to one of the bookshelves. "You can *see* them – and they know the reason for your sight."

He pulled several old leather-bound books out and returned to Jonah's side. "These are journals from people like you, Jonah," he said as he began to lay the books down one at a time. "All written during momentous times in history: the Great London Plague of 1665, the American Civil War, World War I, the Great Depression, and World War II – always during times of great human turmoil. There have been several scrolls found that prophesy about the time of the human Watchers ..." He fell silent, studying Jonah with a look that said he wanted to say more.

Jonah traced his fingers over one of the journals and was jolted by the vision of a young African American boy running down a grassy hill to what looked to be a huge battle. In the sky above the battle, huge dark figures began to appear, swooping downward. He drew his hand back from the book, as if burned and looked up at the two men. They seemed oblivious to what had just transpired.

"Hitler was obsessed with locating them," TJ spoke up.

"What? Why?" Jonah turned to TJ with an incredulous look. The fact that he had just heard the words *Hitler* and *Watcher* in the same conversation made their discussion even more surreal.

"Power, Jonah," Professor Kinney supplied. "He was convinced that he could obtain great power by having direct contact with the 'ascended masters,' as he called them, and was consumed with the idea of establishing rein with them on earth."

"We believe that Nick Corsa and his organization have the same agenda – just under a different name. And like Hitler, they plan to put Watchers on their payroll."

Jonah's head was spinning from all of the information. "Then why would they kill Sam? Wouldn't they want to use him?"

"Our theory is that the Alliance decided Sam was too old to be trained – or 'groomed,' as they call it. I suppose the final straw came when he attempted to reunite you and your friends."

"The five of you have to stick together ..." Jonah heard Sam's urgent warning ringing again in his ears. "Why is it so important for us to be together?" he asked, glancing around. There

was a shift in the air, so slight that he thought at first he might be imagining it. Then he felt it again and stood –

"Because together you have the power to fight them," Professor Kinney said as he stared down at the paintings.

"How do we get this power?" Jonah asked as his eyes searched every nook and cranny of the room. *They're here,* he thought, feeling his breath catch in his throat. *But not* in *here …*

"How do we get this power!" he demanded urgently.

"We don't know," TJ said, his voice sharp with regret.

"You don't know," Jonah whispered in disbelief as sweat broke out on his upper lip. "All these books, this brainpower, and … you don't know?"

As if from a great distance, he saw a flash of a black cloak, and then another, and he had the strangest thought that they were trying to break through. Trying to get at him. A face flashed before his eyes.

Carly …

"Jonah, are you okay, man?" TJ's voice echoed around him, filled with fear but so far away. "Do you see something?"

He bolted from the office and ran up the stairs that led out of the auditorium.

"Jonah!" Professor Kinney called after him.

But he was already out into the hallway, pounding down the steps, and through the door to the parking lot.

Carly! he thought, panic slicing through him as he ran for his Bronco. *What was I thinking! I should've never left her alone …*

Carly flipped her phone closed and glanced back at the warehouse one last time before climbing into the Jeep with Doc. She had tried to reach Jonah on his cell all afternoon – but she couldn't wait any longer. She didn't know how to explain it other than there was a horrible cold feeling that seemed to fill the rooms of the warehouse ever since Jonah left – a feeling so terrifying that it had finally driven her outside.

Outside wasn't much better. The sun hadn't gone down yet but it *felt* dark; a heavy, cloying darkness that reminded her so much of that night when they were kids, she wanted to run away. *Something's taking us back to that night again – but for what? To finally finish us off?*

She bit her lip, tried Jonah's phone again and disconnected as soon as she heard it go to voicemail. She started her Jeep and pulled out of the lot, unsure of where she was going – and unaware of the dark, spirit-like beings that clung to the back of her vehicle as she sped down the road ...

35

Jenna shivered unexpectedly as she stared out the window from the second story of Nick's home, watching the sun set over the backyard. It was beautiful, peaceful, perfectly landscaped with plants and trees that she didn't even know the names of but wanted to. So why was she shivering? Her brows furrowed together as she tried to focus her fuzzy thoughts. Carly—that was it. She had been thinking about Carly—about Jonah and J too. They were in danger … or did she just imagine seeing the words in her head? She was just so tired, it was hard to tell lately what she was really feeling and what she was imagining.

"Wait until you see my compound. I just know you will love it," Nick said, coming up behind her. He turned her around to face him. His smile was gentle. "I think a change of scenery will do you good."

"This all seems too good to be true …"

"Nothing is too good for you," he said, opening his arms to her, and she stepped into his warm embrace. He was everything she had ever dreamed a guy could be. *Almost like he's been lifted right from the pages of my own journal,* she thought, sighing into his chest as her fear evaporated. Whenever he was with her, she felt safe and … *special,* all of the things she had yearned for since she was a kid — and everything she hoped to give to Mikey …

Jenna frowned, remembering how Mikey had looked up at her with such despair when she told him they were moving, how he had refused to talk to her after that, turning his back to her as he curled up in a ball on the couch, clutching his backpack like she might take that away too. *You're just a kid,* she thought. *Everything is going to be better for us, you'll see …*

"Jenna," a deep voice called through her mind.

"I guess I better wake Mikey up from his nap," she said, pulling away.

"Don't take too long," Nick said, smiling down at her sweetly before kissing her on the tip of her nose. "I have a surprise waiting for the two of you."

"I can't wait to tell him that. He loves surprises almost as much as I do," she said as she turned and headed for the stairs. She glanced over her shoulder and gave him her best smile . . . even though her mind had begun to race with thoughts.

"What's that old saying about fools rushing in?" she heard Carly say again, then *"There's something going on — like back when we were kids!"* And finally, for just a brief moment as she hurried down the stairs, she could have sworn she heard a little girl crying . . . A little girl that sounded a lot like her . . .

Nick waited until Jenna was out of earshot before he flipped his cell phone open and quickly scrolled through his phone numbers. There was just one more little detail he had to take care of for the night.

Big J picked it up on the first ring.

"Yeah?"

"I need you at the docks tomorrow night, the usual place," Nick said, a genuine smile appearing across his face. "Let's see if you can clean this mess up better than the last one."

Silence, then, "Yeah, okay."

Nick chuckled into the phone. "Hey, you live and you learn, right?"

J walked along the street of downtown St. Louis, his eyes searching but not really seeing anything. Something wasn't right; he could sense it, like a troubling way down deep inside that he couldn't catch hold of. Now this call from Corsa . . .

Whatever it was Nick had in store for him, it was bad. He had worked for his organization just long enough to know that much. He was going to be framed for something, or he was going to die. He had seen it happen to better men than him.

Like Sam.

He paused on the sidewalk and lifted his eyes to the sky. He felt something brewing beneath the clouds, something thick and evil.

"Times that try men's souls can bring hope," his grandma always liked to say. A cold wind blew around him, and he shut his eyes against the icy blast, images of all the brutal things he had done in his life flashing through his mind.

How can I have hope, Grandma? he thought desperately. *How can I have it when I'm not so sure I have a soul left to try?*

He suddenly heard the sound of Mardi Gras beads and children's laughter. Then he heard their terrified cries again, far off, like they had been carried to him on the wind. Far off but coming closer.

Tiny gray gargoyles, with wings like grasshoppers, scurried around the Grigori's feet as he studied the human through the glass on the second floor of his home.

There was a time – *before*, when he had been sent with the others to watch over man – when for a brief moment the human species had intrigued him. But that was eons past. They no longer intrigued him; they disgusted him, believing they could rise up to *join* his kind.

He sneered, listening to Nick Corsa's voice go on and on in a ridiculous prayer to the Grigori.

He only allowed the monkey to continue to chatter for one reason – to keep the gate open. The darker their deeds, the wider the opening would become. As much as he hated following the Order, the Law was still locked in place. If using humans against each other was their only way, so be it.

Shammah waited until the last of his warriors had appeared; then he signaled, and they filed out along the balcony. He studied the faces filled with contempt for the humans inside, and he felt their growing restlessness.

Their leader Samyaza's lust for revenge was upon them all – as was his impatience.

They were all impatient for the final war to take place. He sensed the growing presence of his Grigori brothers drawing near and felt a swell of satisfaction encompass him. If all went well, this night would bring them that much closer to their reign on earth again. He jumped up to the narrow rail and smiled down at them before glancing once more through the window to the place where Nick knelt.

"What is it that our infamous leader likes to say? Stroke their pride and they will fall." He smiled as he stood to his full height and lifted his arms out to his sides.

"Time to *fly*."

Shammah arched in a backward free fall off the balcony, shooting down, waited until just the right moment, then twisted sideways and sliced his sword through the air to create an opening in it. He dove through the opening, knowing without looking back that the others were close behind.

36

I can't believe I'm doing this," Carly said under her breath as she stepped under the arched entrance of Nick's expensive, condo-like villa. She had been too creeped out to wait at the warehouse by herself, and the longer Jonah was gone, the more she worried that something bad was going to happen to Jenna if she didn't get to her in time. She glanced at the large jade dogs with gargoyle faces posted on both sides of the door and shivered. She found it hard to believe her old friend wasn't as spooked about the place as she was. It *looked* beautiful, but she sensed something bad lurking under the exterior. Really bad. She checked her cell phone one last time to see if Jonah had called, then pressed Nick's doorbell before she changed her mind.

No response.

She started to ring the bell again but hesitated, sensing that someone was watching her. She glanced over her shoulder and almost did a double take, seeing the giant of a man dressed in a long cloak standing just at the border of Nick's property. His braided silver-blond hair shone in the moonlight. A lethal-looking sword flashed at his side.

One of the good guys — she hoped.

He inclined his head to her, as if urging her on. She swallowed hard and turned and knocked on the door, waited a few seconds, and then knocked again.

The door swung open to an annoyed blonde standing in the entryway. Lila's brown eyes flicked over her, immediately dismissing her as no one of great importance. Whether she recognized Carly or not was a toss-up.

"Yeah?" she said, studying her fingernails.

"Is Jenna here?"

"She's out with Nick," Lila answered flatly. "I'm just here to watch over ... things."

"I'm Carly ..." No response. "I was a friend of Sam's?"

Carly offered her hand, but Lila just stared at it — no emotion, *nothing.* Carly almost walked away, until she caught a glimpse of the shadow that passed over Lila's face, and she felt a chill run up her spine. She had been worried about Jenna and Mikey from the moment she woke up, and she was starting to understand why; Lila wasn't the emotionless zombie she pretended to be. She was playing with her.

Who were these people?

She spotted a child hurrying down the hallway behind Lila and leaned to one side, trying to peek around her human barrier.

"I'd like to see Mikey, say hello to him, if that's okay with you," she said, and feeling unusually bold, she quickly stepped through the door before Lila could close it on her. Sam's old girlfriend gave her a cold look.

"Sure, come right in," she said, slamming the door behind them.

The great room looked like something out of *Architectural Digest*: staggering ceilings and clean lines, dark, expensive furniture ... Her eyes paused on the deck of Tarot cards that were spread across the coffee table, and she felt her entire body stiffen. She had never been particularly superstitious, but for some reason now it gave her the creeps. Something about the symbol on the card lying face-up reminded her of one of the doors in Sam's paintings. She tried to swallow, but her mouth was dry.

"Where is he?" she asked hoarsely.

"Where he is all the time — in his room," Lila said as she brushed past Carly and headed down the hallway.

Carly wasted no time following. Lila gave her one last look of annoyance before she stopped and rapped loudly on one of the bedroom doors.

"Hey, kid? There's someone here to see you."

No answer. Lila swore and raised her fist to pound on the door.

"I got it now," Carly said, stepping in front of her.

Lila eyed her for a moment, then shrugged and headed back to the living room.

"Mikey?"

"Who is it?" a timid voice asked, muffled, from the other side of the door, and she felt herself relax a little for the first time since she'd entered Nick's villa.

"Mikey, honey, it's me, Carly."

The door flew open to a relieved-looking little boy. Same dark curls and big gray eyes. Except now the eyes were shadowed by dark circles. *He's not sleeping,* she thought, her heart twisting painfully in her chest as she stepped into the room and ruffled his hair. *I need to get him out of here!*

"What are you doing all alone in your room?"

Mikey shrugged, then stepped around Carly and shut and locked the door. Without another word he crossed the room, climbed onto the bed, and hugged his backpack to his chest.

Just like Sam's painting, she thought, glancing around the room uneasily. *Exactly like his painting ...*

Carly sat next to him and was horrified to feel him shiver as she put her arm around his small shoulders.

"Mikey?"

He looked up at her. The pain in his eyes seemed too old, too horrible, for a little five-year-old boy. *Doesn't Jenna see what is happening to her own kid?*

"Can you help me and my mom get out of here?" he asked, searching her own eyes until she had to look away. What was she supposed to say to that?

The minute she walked in the door, she'd had the overwhelming feeling she should just get Mikey and run. But that had been followed by the thought that Jenna would probably never speak to her again if she did. Carly frowned. She'd never had to deal with anything like this — never been responsible for anyone but herself, and she wasn't doing such a great job of that either.

"Is Mr. Corsa mean to you?"

"There are bad things out there," Mikey answered slowly.

"Who told you that? Your mommy?"

The little boy shook his head emphatically. "No. Mom can't see right now."

"See what?"

Mikey looked up at Carly for what seemed like forever; then he leaned over and whispered, "The bad angels."

Bad angels?

Cold fear rose in her, releasing a tiny fragment of memory that disappeared before she could grasp it. She looked down at Mikey again. She had to get out of this place — had to get them both out. A tear slipped down Mikey's cheek, and he brushed it away, embarrassed. She wrapped her arms around him, slowly rocking him back and forth as she warily scanned the room that Sam had so accurately painted, her eyes finally resting on the door.

Another image from the painting flashed through her mind: a hand covered in dark scales, its long claws glinting in the light as it gripped the doorknob — like it was about to push its way in ...

She took a deep, shuddering breath, realizing she was too terrified now to leave.

"Carly?"

"Yeah, honey?"

"I think there are good ones too."

"Good what, Mikey?"

"Good angels ..."

"I ... you might be right about that," she whispered softly, hopefully, remembering the huge man outside as she kept her eyes glued to the door. When she was younger, her dad had told her countless stories about angels — God's messengers, visiting strangers, protectors of kids and runaway mothers. There were other stories too, darker tales of warriors, mighty weapons of wrath sent to wage war against fallen angels bent on wreaking havoc on humans ...

The image of those two words written in her journal a lifetime ago, or so it felt, rose before her:

THE TRUTH

Carly shivered. But even if it could possibly be true — even if her dad, if Jenna's little boy, was right — what would *any* kind of angel want with them?

Better yet, what would God want with someone like me? she wondered ... She heard the far-off sounds of Jenna's cries coming closer, rolling toward her like a wave that could no longer be prevented from hitting shore ... and she wasn't in Mikey's room anymore. She was ...

… back in Sam and Jonah's basement, leaning back in her favorite beanbag chair as she swallowed a mouthful of Doritos before taking a polite sip of Coke. Perfect end to a perfect movie. *No movie can match* The Matrix, she thought just as Jenna shot up from her spot between Sam and Jonah. She had the lightbulb-above-the-head look.

"Oh, I just got the most awesome idea!" Jenna exclaimed, confirming Carly's suspicions.

"Well, kiss my grits, Flo, let's do it!" Jonah jumped up, not bothering to ask what it is, and they all bust out laughing.

"Since Jonah put it like that, I guess I'm in too," J said, grinning.

"Me too," Carly said at the exact same time as Sam, and they yelled, "Jinx!" Carly smiled sweetly as she delivered a sound blow to Sam's arm.

"We gotta sneak out of here if you want to do it, though," Jenna said. All eyes turned on her, and she pushed her glasses back nervously. "What?"

Jonah winked at Carly, and he and Sam jumped into action. With the choreographed precision of jewel thieves, they slid the old hutch out of the way from beneath the window and replaced it with the coffee table. Jonah made a sweeping gesture to Carly. She grabbed his hand, stepped onto the table, and opened the window.

"I was with my parents at the parade when I saw her," Jenna said behind her.

Carly wiggled through the window and then turned to help Jenna through.

"Mardi Gras?" Carly heard Sam ask apprehensively as she slid to the ground with a grunt. Mardi Gras was off-limits, even though they all lived within walking distance.

She glanced back through the window. "Saw *who*?"

"I look up," Jenna continued dreamily, "and she's just kind of standing there across the street, *staring* at me."

"*Who?*" Sam echoed.

"What does she look like?" Jonah asked.

"Kind of like Halle Berry, but maybe older," Jenna said as she hit the ground outside. "Pretty."

J nodded eagerly. "Halle Berry is hot." He slipped through and sat up next to Jenna. Jonah and Sam were next.

"Anyway," Jenna said, giving J a look, "she's just staring at me, and I see a sign on the window behind her, and you know what it says? Oracle!"

"Just like in the movie," J breathed, and for some reason Carly shivered. She glanced up to see Jonah standing above her. He had that I-dare-you grin on his face as he held his hand out to her, and somehow she already knew what he was going to say ... and she didn't want him to say it. Because as soon as he uttered the words, she knew there would be no turning back.

"Do you wanna see how far that rabbit hole really goes?"

37

Jonah slammed against Sam's door as he shoved the key in the lock. The memories were coming faster now and a lot clearer. This latest one sprang into his mind so sharp and clear that he felt as if he were really there, reaching out his hand to Carly.

He unlocked the door and threw it open, hoping beyond hope that Carly would be standing there waiting for him. Her Jeep was gone from the space out back and she wasn't answering her cell phone, and the thought of something happening to her was scaring him out of his mind. He shouldn't have left her alone.

He swore under his breath, frustrated, as he glanced around the empty room.

His head filled with images once more, and he saw the five of them young again, huddled together as they walked through the crush of people that filled the streets for Mardi Gras — yelling, screaming masked faces looming at them, throwing beads. "I got a bad feeling about his," he heard Sam say breathlessly as Carly grabbed his hand. "Come on, Red," he told her, feeling a little like king of the world. "I got your back." Carly smiled at him, a hopeful, shaky kind of smile, and he felt her squeeze his hand tight ...

"The painting," a deep voice said next to him. Not in his mind but *next* to him. His breath came out in short, jerky gasps as he slowly glanced to his right. And up.

Way up.

He dwarfed everything in the room, dressed in a cloak that parted slightly to reveal silver armor underneath. Long brown hair, with two braids in the front, and ... gripping two of the biggest freaking broadaxes Jonah had ever seen in his life.

Arieh ... He recalled the name he'd heard the last time he came face-to-face with the warrior, in the middle of the street. He seemed to be their leader.

"The painting – there isn't much time," Arieh said urgently. He turned, and his fierce amber eyes swept the area, as if he expected the arrival of someone ... or *something*.

Jonah bolted down the hallway on rubbery legs and grabbed the remaining valise, which he'd returned to the hiding place in Sam's bedroom closet. He ran back to the living room, a million questions on the tip of his tongue. But before he could ask any of them, he felt himself being shoved toward the door. The warrior stepped in front of him, raising his broadaxe high above his head, his robes billowing back, melting into his armor as a harsh, cold wind – a wind Jonah remembered all too well – rushed through the room.

Another warrior appeared, the one with long black hair and exotic eyes.

Jonah held the valise to his chest, bracing himself for the onslaught, but nothing touched him. He could see the curtains flapping wildly against the window ... see the magazines fluttering open before shooting off the coffee table ... he just couldn't *feel* anything ... Like being encapsulated in an invisible shield that the wind couldn't penetrate.

A lionlike growl rent the silence as Arieh's broadaxe sliced downward, and Jonah saw the air part, revealing the fair-headed twins morphing through the brick wall of the warehouse, dressed in black body armor, swords flashing at their sides. *Grigori,* he thought, remembering TJ's words. Their eyes glittered, shifting to him briefly, before they turned their attention to the warriors who stood in their way.

"*Go – now!*" Arieh shouted as the twins advanced.

Jonah shoved the valise under his arm and dove for the door, throwing it open and flying down the steps so fast, he was sure he was going to break his neck. And then he almost did break his neck as his vision blurred just as he reached the bottom of the steps. He stumbled, rubbing his eyes with one hand, and he felt debris of some kind come loose from them. He wiped his eyes and then looked down, rubbing the strange substance between his fingers. *Soft but scaly,* he thought. *Almost like snake skin.*

He frowned, wiping his hand against his jeans as he glanced back toward the warehouse one last time.

He was there …, he thought, running for his truck. *He was that* homeless *man …* It was that night he was with his friends, and they had just …

… turned down the street to the fortune teller's place, the chaos of the Mardi Gras still ringing in their ears, when they spotted him lying over the heating grate in the street.

"Poor old dude," Jonah said as they slowly walked toward him. Even from a distance, they could see that his clothes were threadbare and way too thin for February. "He's gotta be freezing his tail off in this weather."

"Let's help him," Sam said, immediately taking his coat off.

Jonah nodded. He'd become accustomed to Sam's do-gooder ways, had even decided to emulate them. Being a recent recipient himself had made him think that Sam was onto something. "He can have my gloves and hat too."

"We can give him our socks," Carly says slowly, glancing at Jenna. "Right?"

"Right," Jenna said with a nod, and then an earnest look crossed her features. "But don't you think it'll embarrass him, giving him our *clothes?*"

"I got an idea," J said, scrounging in his pockets. He took off ahead of them, not slowing his pace until he got close to the homeless man. Jonah saw something drop from J's hand next to the guy.

"Hey, old man, looks like you dropped some money out of your pocket," J said.

Jonah and the rest of the motley crew reached J just as the homeless guy struggled to sit up. He had the longest hair Jonah had ever seen on a man. Brown with two braids, and he was big too. Kind of like an old biker.

An old biker who looks like he's been beat up pretty good, Jonah thought as he watched the man swipe the blood from his nose.

"Well now, ain't that somethin'," the old guy said. There's a note of bewilderment in his voice as he looked at the crumpled ten-dollar bill in his hand. "Wish I'd had you around a couple hours ago, big fella," he said to J. He glanced at Jonah, then at Sam and the girls. "Why, you *all* look like fighters."

"I like to fight," Jonah agreed readily, and the man smiled slightly.

"I can see that," he said. "The kind that fights to the end, aren't you?" He fell silent, glancing down the street. "But even the meanest fighters know how to pick and choose their battles, and I have to say, you kids don't look like you belong in this neighborhood."

"Oh, well, we were just taking a walk," Jenna said nervously as she pushed her glasses back.

"At this time of night?"

"Sure." Jonah shrugged. "We do it all the time."

Carly elbowed him, and he grinned at her in spite of the pain.

"We're going home soon," Sam said, trying to help him into his coat. "You're going to need this more than me."

As if to emphasize the point, a cold wind came out of nowhere, blowing litter across the street. The old man appeared more alert as he looked up and down the street. "You put that coat back on, son," he said quietly.

Jonah looked at Sam nervously. There was something different about the old guy. There was something in his tone that didn't sound ... *old* ... anymore.

"You children need to turn back now," the old guy said urgently. "Go home. It ain't safe 'round here. If you don't go now, we won't be able to protect you."

"What do you mean, we?" J asked. He barked out a nervous kind of laugh as he glanced around. "You got your gang close by or something?"

"You will be opening a door to something dangerous — something that could destroy you all before you're ready ..."

The old man glanced up, and Jonah heard J gasp as he stumbled backward, knocking into Jenna.

38

J stood at the docks, a grim feeling in his gut as the memory faded, and looked across the dark waters of the Mississippi.

Those gold eyes – and that face, turning young before our eyes! We should've just gone home after that ... should've listened to that homeless guy and never taken another step down that street ...

He glanced at his watch, then scanned the area for what seemed like the hundredth time, looking for what was no longer a horror to find but a habit. City after city, he somehow always found himself back in the same gig.

A lot of things I should've never done, he thought as he wound his way around the crates in front of the old granary. *Like agreeing to clean up Nick Corsa's mess. I should have just called the police and gotten it over with ... anything would be better than this.*

A loud rush of wind came out of nowhere, and J stumbled back as the cold force of it hit him. Soft laughter echoed around him, and he whirled, his gun ready to take out whoever Nick had sent.

But no one was there.

He frowned and turned back around ... and his eyes went right to the old penny loafer peeking out between the two wooden crates he had just been standing next to. He took a step in the direction of the shoe, and his muscles went rigid with disbelief; there was a *body* attached to it. But not just any body. He stumbled forward on wooden legs, a groan of anguish rising up in him as he looked down at his grandma's lifeless body lying on the cold ground. Her left foot was bare, as if she had lost the other shoe somewhere along the way.

"Let's see if you can clean this mess up better than the last one," Nick Corsa's words whispered through his mind, and then came the laughter. *"Hey, you live and you learn, right?"*

"Oh no," he cried out, dropping to his knees. " No!"

He scooped his grandma up into his arms, tears streaming down his face as he held her against his chest. *My fault,* he thought, rocking himself back and forth. *I killed her as sure as if I'd had the gun, as sure as I've killed everything else good in my life* ... He struggled to his feet, scanning the docks for signs of Nick's men, and then his eyes rose briefly to the night sky, searching ...

"Please not her," he choked out. "Please!"

"After all you've done – after all this time – why do you think He would listen now?" a voice inside his head whispered – not his voice but his crazy Uncle Lester's.

His head dropped, sorrow and regret burning through him as he forced himself to look at his grandma again, and somewhere in the distance of his past, he heard Jonah's grief-ravaged voice say, *"What have you done, J? WHAT HAVE YOU DONE!"*

J let out a strangled sob and took off in a dead run with her in his arms, rushing blindly down the cobblestone streets of the riverfront, past curious onlookers, and up into the heart of the city, running as hard as he could until he came to a stop in front of the emergency room entrance of the old city hospital.

Gasping for air, he watched as two EMTs helped a teenager off a stretcher and into a waiting wheelchair. They steered the kid inside, and his eyes moved back to the stretcher.

You go inside, and they'll blame you for this too. You won't ever get the chance for revenge ...

He hurried to the stretcher, scanning the area before he laid his grandmother down. "I'm so sorry, Grandma," he said, sobbing as he gently pulled the sheet up and tucked it under her chin. "I'm so sorry!" He tried to wipe his tears away with the back of his hand, but they just kept coming, grief tearing at his insides so painfully, he was unable to move.

"Hey! What are you *doing*?"

J startled at the sound of the EMT's voice and took a couple steps back from the stretcher. The man's eyes narrowed as he glanced from J to the stretcher and back again.

"What did you *do*?" the EMT demanded as J took several more steps back. The EMT hurried over and pulled the sheet back from J's grandma. As soon as he leaned over to check for her pulse, J turned and ran.

He ran as if the Devil were on his heels – and wondered in a half-crazy way if maybe he was – as the red lights of another ambulance flashed through his mind. And he was ...

... in the back of that police car again, looking through the window at Sam as he sat on the curb in front of the warehouse, head in his hands. "What did you *do*, J!" Jonah screamed, pounding on the back window of the police car, but J looked straight ahead. *"What did you do!"*

Another sob escaped from J as he turned down a dark back-street, images of that horrible night flooding his mind, and then he was ...

... in the backseat of that old beat-up Monte Carlo, listening to the two bangers talk about the place they were going to hit, as they wove through the dark streets. He felt the car come to a stop and looked up, stunned. He hadn't seen Sam or Jonah in a few years, but there was no mistaking the old converted warehouse.

"We ain't doin' this house," J said, alarmed.

"Yes we are," Gotti said, glancing over the seat at him. A shadow passed over his face – why hadn't he noticed that before? – his eyes narrowing threateningly. "You mess this up, and *granny* won't be the one in a wheelchair."

"Nobody's home?"

"That's right." The two bangers shared a look. "Nobody's home."

They left J in the car as a lookout, and he watched them break into the Beckers' home. Then he heard Mrs. Becker scream. Scrambling out of the car, he took off running toward the warehouse, running like he had never run before – and then he heard the horrible sound of two gunshots echoing in the night ...

"Just wasn't fast enough, Jonah," J gasped out miserably. "Just wasn't *fast* enough to help them ..." He glanced over his shoulder. Something or someone was still behind him – not just his past but something alive and well in the present. He could feel it like hot breath on the back of his neck as he ran.

He looked down and saw two dark shadows spill across the sidewalk on either side of him, keeping pace.

A strange shifting sensation reverberated around him, almost as if the air were splitting open. A face twisted with hate, framed by a black Mohawk and ponytail, shot out of the dark at him, and then a huge shoulder, and then ... an arm.

"Watcher!" it growled in a voice that sounded like death – not one but a hundred deaths – as it reached for him.

He darted blindly across the street, unaware of the car until the horn blared, and he turned just in time to see the impact. But the car lurched backward, the front end rising up before the tires hit the street again with the loud concussion.

J's mouth fell open as a huge being wearing silver body armor materialized out of thin air right in front of the car, long red hair whipping around him as if he were standing in the middle of a storm. His gaze was fierce, his eyes flashing that strange amber color as he looked at J. He turned his head in the direction from which J had come, and a long staff appeared in his hand. He raised it into the air and brought it down on the street, creating a tidal wave of blue light that spread out like a low, expanding mushroom cloud.

J glanced over his shoulder and saw the huge being with the Mohawk fly backward as the force of the mushroom cloud struck him.

Seeing his chance, he dove across the street and turned into an alley, running with everything he had left in him – until he looked up in horror at the brick wall that rose before him. *Dead end,* he thought dejectedly, his chest heaving as he stopped and sank down to his knees. *No way out of this.*

His life story.

Deep, gleeful laughter swirled around him, filled with malice, and a horrible weakness stole over him as he struggled to lift his head.

"I can't do this anymore," he gasped, glaring up at the night sky. "Do you hear me! Why didn't you just let me die?"

More laughter, and then … silence, as if all sound had been snuffed out, extinguished.

"Because you were meant for more," a deep voice answered.

He felt the pressure of a strong hand on his shoulder, and an electric sensation pulsed over his entire body. Feeling something in his eyes, he blinked and swiped it away.

"Remember …," the voice behind him urged.

J turned his head to look behind him, but all he could see was …

… the red neon eye on the front of the fortune teller's shop. The neon was so bright that it painted the entire street corner an eerie red. *Like blood,* J thought, feeling his anxiety ramp up a few more notches. He glanced at Jonah, whose eyes were glued to the sign.

"Looks like a snake eye, doesn't it?" Jonah said with a touch of wariness.

"Yeah …," Carly said. "I don't think …"

"Are we really doing this?" Sam asked.

"I don't think this is such a good idea anymore either," J said, finishing Carly's thought.

He saw Jenna's lips tremble. It was her idea, after all, and he'd just blown it to pieces.

"Come on, J," Jenna pleaded. "It's going to be great, you'll see!"

"You should listen to the girl," a woman's husky voice said from the shadowy doorway of the shop. She stepped forward, and the red neon bathed her face in light. Her eyes drifted over the five friends, finally resting on J, and she smiled.

She does look like Halle Berry!

He was completely awestruck.

And the first one to step through the door when she opened it wide and ushered them inside.

39

All my fault, J," Jenna said slowly, almost as if she were in a dream. "Should've just turned around and went home like he said. My fault ..."

Mikey glanced up at his mom with tears in his eyes. His heart was beating so hard, he thought it would explode at any moment. He had been so sure that Carly could save them, help them get away somehow ... and now she was gone.

"What do you mean, *she just came to talk to Mikey?*" Mr. Corsa bellowed. Mikey jumped and wrapped his arms around his mom's leg, hiding behind her even though he knew it wouldn't do any good. He wanted to go home! There was something wrong with his mom — something bad. He didn't need anyone to tell him; he just knew it, like he knew about the bad angels.

"Don't you think she would've been a little suspicious if I hadn't let her see the kid?" Lila snapped back, and then she smiled, as if his anger amused her.

The room felt cold. *Really cold,* Mikey thought, trembling.

"Scaring ... Mikey," Jenna slurred. She cleared her throat and attempted to talk again. "Carly ... just ... stupid fight."

Mikey looked up at his mom, alarmed. How did she talk so clear one moment and messed up the next? Her eyes looked weird, and she kept blinking like it would help her mouth to work right. How were they ever going to get away if his mom couldn't even stand up straight?

He glanced around the room again. *They* were here now ... somewhere.

"Ask her why," a deep voice whispered, and that's when he noticed the air around Mr. Corsa start to *change,* stretching open as two bad angels appeared, one on either side of him. Way bigger than any of the ultimate fighters. One had like a jillion dark braids in his hair; the other had really long brown hair and a bunch of tattoos all over his face and arms.

"Ask her why they were fighting," the voice urged, now attached to the bad angel with the braids.

As much as he wanted to escape – to *run* – he waited and watched for any sign that Mr. Corsa could hear the bad angel too. He didn't know why, but he knew it was important.

"Why were you two fighting, Jenna?" Mr. Corsa asked, and Mikey felt a cold kind of dread sweep over him. He *had* heard! But then, why wasn't he looking at the bad angels?

"He can't see," Mikey said and then clamped his mouth shut, realizing he had voiced the thought out loud.

Mr. Corsa glanced at him sharply.

"He's going to ruin everything if you don't take control," the bad angel with the tattoos whispered in Mr. Corsa's ear. "If he can see and hear us, he can see and hear the others too."

What others?

"Come here, Mikey," Mr. Corsa coaxed.

He sidestepped around his mom – away from Mr. Corsa.

A warm wind burst around them, and Mikey saw the bad angels disappear. Mr. Corsa glanced around the room with a confused look on his face.

Something different was happening! Mikey looked up at his mom and saw that her eyes looked clearer ... and scared, like she had been startled awake.

"Go to your room, honey," she said, voice wavering.

"Mom?"

"Go to your room and lock the door. *Now!*"

He bolted, running as fast as his little legs would carry him – fast enough to duck the arms that snaked out to grab him. He felt something else reach for him and heard a hissing sound in his ears as a breeze whispered through his hair.

"Hurry, get into your room and lock the door!" a deep voice whispered through his head urgently. *"You will be safe there!"*

Mikey made a mad dive into his room, slammed the door, and locked it. He scrambled up onto the bed and hugged his backpack to his chest as he stared at the doorknob twisting back and forth. His hands were shaking so badly, he could barely grasp the little book hidden away in the inside pocket of his backpack. He glanced up and saw the door crack open ...

Tears streamed down his face as he fumbled through the pages to the place he had marked — to the picture of his dad, or who he liked to imagine was his dad. The kind face smiled back at him. He knew it was crazy, knew Spence and Dustin would call him a sissy-baby if they saw him bawling and talking to a *picture*, but he didn't care.

"I need you to help me and my mom. *Please!*" he cried.

Something was stirring in the air. Not the cold feeling like before, but something was definitely there. Mikey glanced toward the door again and saw the air *shimmering*, like the way water moved when a soft wind blew across it.

A huge man appeared out of the shimmering air, facing slightly toward Mikey, his hand on the doorknob like he had been there all the time. A lion's roar erupted from the big man's whole body, and Mikey saw the outline of a lion's head begin to spread across the silver armor on the man's chest. Mikey scooted as far back on the bed as he could, trembling, as he watched waves of blue light roll out across the door and walls of the room.

Mikey felt his throat go dry as the man finally turned to look at him. He was so huge, his dark head almost hit the ceiling. His eyes were gold, and the power that came from them was beautiful ... and a little scary. Kind of like the bad angels that were with Mr. Corsa, but different.

Because he's good, Mikey thought with wonder. *He's really good.*

"I am Eri," the giant-man said with a grim smile. "Don't be afraid. I'm here to protect you. No matter how bad it might look or get, I won't let anyone hurt you."

Shobeck stepped back from the door, surprised. *How did the Irinim warrior get through our line without the Grigori sensing his presence?* He took another step back, dark braids swinging, as he glanced at his tattooed comrade. Tiria's face was grim as he considered their next move.

Nick rushed to the door and twisted the knob with all of his might, but it wouldn't budge. He cursed, rearing back to kick the door in, when he seemed to become aware of the presence around him.

Shobeck moved with Tiria into a back-to-back position, their swords drawn. As they began to withdraw back down the hallway, Shobeck's eyes narrowed to beady slits, the scent of yet another Irinim thick in his nostrils.

"Come ...," he commanded the human.

Nick, still convinced he was in charge, followed.

40

Jenna dropped onto her bed with a groan of pain and winced as the door to the bedroom slammed, the sound reverberating through her head. Nick was doping her — she knew it for certain now. She rubbed the tiny puncture wound on her arm and felt her anger momentarily rise above the drug. *No time for chamomile tonight, honey?* "You lowlife ... you *evil* ... PIG!" she yelled out in the empty room.

She had to do something, had to figure out how to get her and Mikey out of this mess. She was so stupid! How could she have ever doubted her friends?

The air in the room rippled around her, and she began to tremble. *Don't let me pass out,* she thought desperately, feeling like she was standing at the edge of a cliff that had no bottom. *Please don't let me pass out!*

She felt a snakelike grip dragging her arms and legs into the mattress, making it impossible for her to move as blackness began to fill the edges of her vision. What did he give her? It didn't feel the same as whatever he'd put in her tea ...

"Die, Watcher ...," a deep voice commanded.

Another voice barked out an insane laugh.

A horrible black despair swept through her, and she tried to turn her head to see where the voice came from. Something dark moved around the room. Something big and ...

Cold — how did it get so cold in here?

Her teeth began to chatter. "Please," she whispered weakly. "Please, somebody help me. My little boy ..."

"My little boy," the insane voice mocked. "He's *our* little boy now."

"You're going to fail, and you're going to drag that child through your failure ...," her father whispered from the past, and tears of self-loathing spilled down her cheeks. She had messed everything up so badly that there didn't seem to be any way out. She couldn't fight – she couldn't even get off the bed. How in the world was she going to help Mikey now? She glanced up at the ceiling, and a helpless sob rose out of her.

"Please ... God! Help me!"

A rush of warm wind entered the room, and she heard the sound of metal hitting metal. A low growl echoed in the distance, getting farther and farther away as an iridescent blue light encompassed her. Jenna blinked against the glare, her eyes filling with tears.

"Am I dying?" she whispered hoarsely.

"No."

The light faded away, and she saw a huge man looking down upon her, his African features strong but beautiful too, his amber eyes kind, and maybe a little sad. She had seen this face before.

He laid his hand on her forehead, and she felt something like a current running through her veins. *Cleaning my veins,* she thought. She didn't know how she knew, but she did.

"Who are you?" Jenna asked hesitantly. He removed his hand, and she touched the place where it had been. She was feeling stronger. Clearer. But that was impossible! How? Unless ... She glanced up at the huge man. "Are you ... *God?*"

"I am Jahdiel," he said, inclining his huge, shaved head. "His messenger."

She blinked a couple of times, confused. *His messenger?*

"There are many ways to deliver a message." He smiled slightly and then glanced around the room, turning his face up, almost as if he were sniffing the air.

Jenna studied the warrior's face through tear-blurred eyes. *He's real. An angel ...*

IT'S REAL

The words from her journal blazed into her mind as he looked down at her again, and she had the urge to hide her face. He seemed so good, so *clean* ...

"What's important right now is that you remember," he said, and she felt his voice roll through her like a wave of water.

"What if I – "

She felt something come loose in her eye, causing it to tear up like crazy. Reaching up, she touched her cheek and felt something grainy under her fingertips, like a small piece of fingernail, but softer. She looked up to find the warrior angel watching her closely. "What if I – "

She had meant to say, *"What if I don't want to remember?"*

But it was too late. She was already *there*, back in that place she had sworn she would never be in again ...

... and a breathless fear swept over her as she saw the fortune teller.

The woman was really nice at first, greeting each of them as they filed into the room. She held their hands, touched their hair. "Five little beauties!" she exclaimed. But a discomfiting look took hold in her eyes the longer she studied them. "Five," she said thoughtfully, almost to herself. And then she turned and zeroed in on Sam.

He looked up at the fortune teller with something like horror on his face. "There's a shadow ... a ... there's something moving on your face!" he blurted out.

"Just as I thought," she murmured. She hurried to the front door, shut and locked it.

When she turned back around, Jenna could see the change in her.

She looked a lot older and a lot meaner. Her eyes were cold, almost dead-looking, as she began to walk back and forth in front of them, studying them like bugs under a microscope.

A sharp sadness swept over Jenna as the woman passed her ... and somehow she knew she was really standing on the outside, looking in ... and she knew they were only steps away from losing this part of their childhood forever.

"Prophecy you want ... prophecy you have," the fortune teller said, and Jenna knew that an ancient door had swung open. She sensed that her friends all knew it too.

First it was an uneasy feeling – a thick, dark weightiness that settled over her shoulders, holding her to her spot. Then it was the smell – like wet dirt and old roots and ... maybe rotted leaves. Really bad rotted leaves.

Jenna saw the fortune teller take a deep breath – almost like she was inhaling the smell – and then she started down the line. Touching Sam's head first, she said, "A warrior who is powerless"; touched Carly's head, "The child is motherless"; touched J, "The friend who betrays"; touched Jenna, "A mother is childless"; and finally she came to Jonah.

She put a finger under his chin and lifted his face slightly so that he had to look into her eyes. "What do you *see* now, brother who is brotherless?"

It took Jenna less than a second to realize that the fortune teller wasn't a bit like the kindly Oracle in the movie, speaking a prophecy over them ...

She was speaking a curse.

41

Jonah hit the steering wheel with his hand, forcing the memory of that night back as he sped down the highway, listening to Carly's message on his cell. What was she thinking, taking off to Nick Corsa's place without him? He scanned the shoulder for police cars and then stomped on the gas. Streetlights and landscape flashed by on both sides of him, and he felt the years begin to peel back too, faster and faster, until ...

... he was back at the fortune teller's place, standing in the middle of her creepy living room as he glanced around at his friends.

Their faces looked pasty and scared, and he felt his temper begin to cook, rolling into a full boil.

Cursing us! Telling me I don't have a brother!

He glanced around the room wildly, looking for something he could show them to prove she was wrong ... and that's when he spotted the sign with the words *fortoon teler* printed across it in large black letters. It was propped up right next to the door and so idiotic, it was perfect. He grabbed it up. "Look at this! She can't even spell! Look at it! What she said to us makes about as much sense as this!"

"Should I try again?" The fortune teller swayed slyly as she stepped up in front of Sam. She raised her hand above his head and glanced back at Jonah. *That look,* he thought, feeling a hopeless kind of terror come over him as a shadow shifted over the surface of her face, like a skull but gruesome, dark, its eye sockets filled with death. *She's just like Bud Winters, but with a different face!* Rage washed over him, and before he could stop himself, the words were out:

"Don't ... you ... touch ... him ... you ... HAG!"

A hush descended upon the room as everyone stood motionless, waiting to see what was going to happen next.

The fortune teller smiled like she was pleased, like she expected an outburst but wasn't sure who was going to explode until that very moment.

"You will be the first!" she declared, placing her hand on Sam's head.

"First for what?" Jonah said, and she turned and gave him a horrible, hate-filled look.

"Why, the first to die, Watcher. And he has *you* to thank for that."

42

The first to die ..." The words echoed through Carly just as a hard gust of wind hit, and she stumbled and ran the rest of the way to her Jeep. She had been second in the line that night, second after Sam. Did that mean she was next? And what was wrong with *Jenna*?

She glanced over her shoulder and saw the dogs loping toward her, no longer jade green but black, huge ... almost spirit-like, but deadly ... They opened their jaws and let out a howl that shook her down to her soul. *Cold* – she was so cold!

Carly slammed against the door of the Jeep from a dead run and scrambled to get the keys in the lock. Her breath came out in tiny white puffs as she yanked the door open, slid inside, slammed the door, and hit the locks. Doc spun around in his seat, hair raised on the back of his neck as he snarled in the direction of the beasts. She started the Jeep and peeled out of the parking lot, glancing in her rearview mirror as she cranked the heater up as far as it would go.

It wasn't until she was back on Highway 40 that she allowed herself to breathe a little easier, to think. What did she imagine *would* happen, waiting outside Nick's place like that? That Jenna would come rushing into her open arms with Mikey, grateful that *Carly Hagan* had stepped in and fixed everything and saved the day?

She frowned. That was exactly what she had been thinking ... until that brief flash of a moment when she saw that giant man appear out of nowhere in the room, his long golden-blond hair partially concealing his face as he watched her go ...

Just as the jade dogs came to life.

Carly shivered, her teeth chattering in spite of the heat that poured from the vents in the Jeep. Those eyes ... She had no idea how long she stood there, frozen in fear, but something in the wind had broken the spell. As soon as the wind hit, the giant had faded away, like a huge rock jutting out of the sea that's masked by a wave of water … So why hadn't the dogs disappeared as well?

Her cell phone rang and she grabbed it up, relief washing over her as she saw Jonah's name.

"Oh, I'm so glad you called!" Carly said in a wavering voice, and then rushed on. "I went over to Nick's to talk to Jenna … and oh man, everything is so messed up! Lila was watching Mikey, and you could tell she didn't want to. I can't tell you how creeped out I am right now. Mikey had locked himself in his room, talking about bad angels or something; then Nick and Jenna show up, and he yells at me to get out – "

"Carly!"

"What?"

"Did you say bad *angels*?"

"Yeah," she said, her voice hitching a little in her throat. "Why?"

"Where are you right now?" Jonah asked. His voice sounded hoarse, like he had been crying.

She glanced up at the road signs. "Pretty close to my dad's place."

"I want you to go straight there, and I'll meet you, okay?"

"Okay … Hey, Jonah?"

"Yeah?"

"We're going to be okay, right?"

The phone was silent for a moment.

"Better than okay," he said finally, and she smiled.

"I better call my dad."

"Yeah, I'm going to make a call too. *Stay safe*."

She let out a huge sigh of relief and flipped her phone closed. Hearing Jonah say they were going to be okay made it seem a little more real than trying to convince herself of it. She flipped her phone open again to call her dad. She frowned as his voicemail picked up on the second ring.

"It's me. I'm on my way to the house. Jonah is too. There's some really weird stuff going on. Okay, maybe more than just weird …" She exhaled. "I hope you're there." She cleared her throat, resisting the urge to cry. "I'm so sorry for not listening to you. We *really* need your help, Dad."

She flipped the phone closed, glancing back to the road just as she came over the top of the hill – and felt all of the air rush out of her as she saw something large and dark begin to take shape in the road ahead of her. The little beaded cross that hung from her rearview mirror started to rise through the air toward her at an unnatural angle. She stomped down hard on her brakes, and ... everything went into slow motion.

She saw Doc rise in the seat, heard the low, mournful wail that came out of him just as the Jeep struck the huge man standing in the middle of the road, flanked by two horrible-looking beasts.

Just like Sam's painting, she thought dejectedly as the Jeep flipped up into the air before it came to a bone-jarring landing on its side in the middle of the road.

A hush surrounded her as she blinked, trying to get her bearings.

I'm alive! she thought with surprised wonder. Doc whined frantically in the dark, and she reached up to unhook her seat belt, groaning loudly as a blinding white pain shot up her back and into her head. *Gotta get out of here ...* She felt herself begin to go in and out of consciousness, only making it halfway out of the driver's side window before laying her cheek against the road and drifting ...

Her eyes flitted open: Doc was lying next to her, licking her face ...

Closed: She heard the distant sound of Jenna's cries coming closer ...

Open: An icy cold wind battered her as she tried to lift her head off the pavement ...

Closed: She was standing in the middle of the street in front of the fortune teller's place. Jonah had a brick or something in his hand. "She's not God!" he shouted at the top of his lungs. "She doesn't know anything about us!" He raised his arm and sailed the object right into the neon that looked like a snake's eyes. Glass shards flew as a strange wind burst out of the broken window, cold, colder than any of them had ever felt before ...

Open: They were inching toward her, those horrible, shiny gargoyle creatures with wings, like grasshoppers ... "Why don't you do us a favor and die, *Watcher*," a deep voice snarled.

Carly's eyes closed, and she wondered if they would ever open again: Jenna was crying now. Scared. They were all scared, huddled together for protection as they looked to the dark sky above them. "Don't cry, Jenna," she heard herself say. "It's just the wind." But it wasn't just the wind, was it? Because the wind ...

Doesn't feel evil.

They all glanced upward at the same time just as the dark mass began to press down over them, thick and cloying, filling the air with a bad smell, like rotten eggs. Carly felt like she was going to smother to death for sure and she was acutely aware that she couldn't hear Jenna. No puff of the inhaler, nothing ... Her heart squeezed painfully in fear. *It's so dark ... where did the streetlights go?*

"Why isn't Jenna crying anymore?" she asked breathlessly, unable to look away.

"Sam?" Jonah's voice sifted apprehensively through the dark.

"Why can't I see you guys?" J asked, terrified.

Silence. And finally a loud thrumming filled her ears, and she saw something taking shape above them.

Like a swarm, but different. It was so dark that she could just barely make out the ... wings. Huge, scaly black wings, hundreds of them, beating around their heads, some slightly tattered at the edges, some worse than tattered ... Like the picture of that flag, Old Glory, she had seen at school. Ripped and torn ... as if they had been in a major battle.

They watched together in stunned silence as the things the wings were attached to started to drop around them, and their vision cleared even more. The beings seemed to be part spirit, part real. Enormous, oblong heads, ancient faces, gray and leathery, slashed with hundreds of wrinkles and framed by white tufts of stringy hair ... and those empty, bottomless black sockets where eyes should be!

The creatures snarled, each displaying two rows of startlingly sharp teeth, before they reluctantly pulled back, forming a wide circle around the five of them.

"Something *really* bad is going to happen now," Jenna said dully, finally finding her voice.

You think? Carly fought the crazy urge to laugh and then burst into tears.

The wind picked up again, blowing harder and harder, and they huddled in a tight little group, looking around fearfully. Something like a ripping sound filled their minds, and they were surrounded by huge men ... but not men.

Not human, at least.

The giants began to stalk around their little group — one minute there, the next gone, like they'd melted into the air, only to reappear closer the next time around, each time getting nearer and nearer.

There was something odd about the way they looked. *Almost like holographic images,* Carly thought. *Like they are here ... but somewhere else too.*

"I am Shammah," the one with long pale hair announced as he tightened his circle around them. He bent down, studying each of them closely. "Five little sheep all herded together," he said, his deep voice friendly, almost amused. Then his eyes narrowed. "How convenient for *me.*"

He glanced over his shoulder. "Tola."

Another giant appeared right in front of them. A twin to the one called Shammah, except his hair was shaved on one side. *His smile is crazy,* Carly thought. *Scary crazy.*

"We *would* prefer to kill you," Shammah said conversationally. "Unfortunately, your little dip in the lake has sealed you, and that is a dilemma. *Fortunately,* we have other ways of ensuring that you will not pose a threat to our future plans ..."

"Voilà!" Tola said, startling them, and they turned to see him usher one of the winged creatures forward, its massive, leathery wings folded down into its sides. Carly saw it holding something as it drew near, but she couldn't tell what it is. She began to tremble and felt the others trembling next to her as well. *Something bad was going to happen ...*

"Open wide," the one called Tola said happily, a malevolent grin on his face. His image flickered a little again.

The creature turned its eyes on Carly.

"It will only hurt for a moment. You'll be glad afterward," Tola assured her as he looked over the creature's shoulder. Then he laughed. "Ignorance is bliss, after all ..."

As soon as the thing grabbed her, her body went cold, colder than it had ever felt before, and she sensed the others being grabbed up too, sensed their terror as they were unceremoniously slammed down on a cold, hard, slab-like thing that felt ... alive. She felt something pierce her eyes, stretching her lids wide open.

Carly screamed in pain as a harsh, gritty substance hit her eyes like wet sand, digging into them, and she heard the others scream too.

"It's really not so bad," Shammah said in an almost polite tone, his voice rising slightly above their screams. "Soon it will be just a bad memory ... and then it will be no memory at all." His voice dipped low and deadly. "It will be as if you never even knew we existed."

43

Still on his knees, J glanced up at the sky in wonder and fear, tears streaming down his face as he tried to catch his breath after running halfway across the city. He *wasn't* crazy! It had all really happened! It wasn't a dream; it was *real.*

He touched his face, feeling more of those strange, scaly pieces under his fingers again, and as he raised his hands to inspect them, something scratched at him from the back of his mind—snatches of his grandma's raspy old voice filtering back into his memory. Scales ... she had read something to him about scales. Something from the Bible. The scales fell from their eyes ... He reached deeper into the memory.

"And immediately scales fell from their eyes," her voice whispered from the past, *"and they began to see."*

BUT YOU CAN'T SEE

Wasn't that what the strange entry in his journal said?

"I can see now," J said, his voice strong and sure as he stood. "I can see now, Grandma!" he bellowed, laughing and crying as several people on the street stopped and looked at him curiously.

He couldn't have cared less.

He began to run again, and as he did, he couldn't help thinking that for the first time in his life he didn't feel like he was running away from something—he felt like he was running *to* something. He was scared out of his mind ... but he was *free.*

"What am I supposed to do now?" he whispered breathlessly ... and then his cell phone rang.

44

Jonah spotted the overturned Jeep just as he rounded the bend in the road. He let out a cry of anguish and skidded to a stop in the middle of the street. Throwing his door open, he ran to where Carly's body lay. Doc wagged his tail and went back to pacing around her, his eyes warily sweeping the area at the back of the Jeep.

"Come on, Carly," Jonah coaxed, choking out a sob as he tried to gently pull her from the Jeep. "Don't do this to me – don't you dare leave me too!"

He reached for her wrist, desperately searching for a pulse, and felt a faint throb under his fingers. Relief flooded him, and he pulled out his cell phone. Just then he heard the fortune teller's hateful voice whispering from the past, "*The first to die ... And he has you to thank for that ...*"

That meant there would be a second if he didn't do something to stop it. He flipped his phone open. Suddenly Doc growled low in his throat.

Smoke belched up from under the hood of the Jeep, and Jonah sniffed the air, detecting more than just smoke. *Gas.* Why hadn't he smelled it before? He dialed 911 and gave the operator their location, glancing around uneasily as he sensed the telltale shift in the air around him. Doc's growl rose in volume, causing the hairs on Jonah's neck to stand on end as he pocketed the phone. And then *he* was there ...

Jonah began to shake all over.

... morphing up from the road in front of the Jeep with his two hounds from hell at his side.

Jonah stood and positioned himself between Carly and what he now knew to be a fallen angel.

Shammah smiled. "A touching display of chivalry, but foolish nonetheless." He took a step toward Jonah. The beasts stepped with him, saliva dripping from their fangs.

A mist of rage filled Jonah's vision, momentarily replacing his fear. He hated them, hated all that they were and stood for, hated them for every evil moment they had wreaked havoc on five kids' lives. They *took* Sam from him—he knew it with every fiber of his being.

"You will not take one more person from me!"

"Who are you that I should be mindful of you, Watcher?" Shammah said in a soft tone. "Do you think you can stand against me alone?" He glanced around, pretending to search the street. "I don't see any backup. They are probably quite busy by now, trying to save your friends' necks ... or perhaps I should say *souls*."

"The ambulance will be here soon," Jonah said, grasping for something, *anything*. The last time he had stood up for anyone, tried to really *protect* anyone, was Sam, and ...

"... *the first to die.*" He gritted his teeth, trying to block the fortune teller's voice. "*The first to die ... And he has you to thank for that ...*"

The fallen angel laughed and took another step forward. "Let's see ... I wonder who the paramedic will be tonight? Will he be one of yours?" His voice dropped, sounding even deeper and a lot more menacing. "Or will he be one of ours?"

"It's kinda like opening a box of chocolates," Tola said, morphing up from the road with an eerie grin, his voice a perfect imitation of Forrest Gump's. "You never know what you're going to get."

Jonah took a step back and heard the dry-rattle sound again. He turned his head slowly to see those horrible creatures from Sam's painting, very much alive as they scurried in a huge wave up and over the back of Carly's Jeep.

"I'm curious—why would they leave you unguarded when you are the one who holds the key?"

Jonah turned back around, forcing himself to remain expressionless. "What key?"

"The key in the painting," Shammah snapped impatiently. "Do you think it could stay hidden from us? What does this key do, Watcher?" He took another step toward Jonah. "Tell me and I might let her live."

"I don't know," Jonah answered, stepping back. He glanced over his shoulder again, and cold lead fear filled his gut; the creatures were getting closer to Carly.

As he turned back to the fallen angel, a thought hit him, drawn from the evil being's own lips. Sam's painting. Not the one with the key ... but the one of Carly. The creatures scurrying across the side of the Jeep were almost in the exact position where Sam had painted them. And if they were there, that meant the others were —

Something shifted in his peripheral vision; the creatures were only inches away from Carly.

"No!" he yelled and made a dive at them, praying that the warrior angels were really there. He hit the ground next to the Jeep and scrambled up, coming face-to-face with the gargoyle beings. One of them raised its head and hissed at him, a high-pitched, piercing sound that drove straight into his eardrums, and then he saw what looked like a scorpion's tail rise to a striking position.

"You can't have her!" he yelled, his voice rising almost supernaturally above the sound. He felt something move under him, and just as he glanced down, a huge blue body of light rose beneath him like a wave. It crested and then came crashing down on the creatures. Their bodies rose together in the air, until a second wave struck, swallowing them whole before spitting them out into the night.

"We have unfinished business, Shammah," a deep voice announced out of nowhere.

Jonah scrambled to Carly, shielding her body with his own, and he saw two warriors appear out of thin air. The one he knew as Arieh; the other he recognized as the man in the jail cell. Both carried a staff in one hand and a huge broadsword in the other. He saw the barest hint of another warrior appearing as Arieh ran a few thunderous steps and rose into the air.

Arieh and Shammah crashed together in midair in a frenzied clash of swords as mayhem broke out below. The second warrior dove at the twin, and they collided and rolled across the road, clubbing each other with their quarterstaffs. Then the beasts lunged at the final warrior, a fierce-looking redhead who came through the opening and stepped into the middle of the road.

Jonah shrank back, watching as the redheaded warrior raised his battleaxe almost lazily and swiped it across the beasts' necks. They fell sideways in the road and crumbled into a fine green dust, from which two huge spirit beings rose and immediately climbed high into the sky.

MazziKim, Jonah thought as his eye caught the battle raging in the sky just above him. He saw Shammah drive his sword savagely downward toward Arieh, but the warrior expertly dodged the blow, twisting his body sideways and into a back flip, only to come up a second later with a hard thrust of his sword to the spot just beneath Shammah's breastplate.

The fallen angel's insides lit up with blue light that shot through the black network of veins and capillaries to his heart.

Shammah fell from the sky and hit the ground with such force that Jonah could feel the shock waves vibrating beneath him. He didn't look dead — just incapacitated. A huge, horribly deformed creature appeared next to Shammah. It looked like a Harmer gone wrong. Or a bad science experiment. It grabbed one of Shammah's arms and began to drag him away. Tola walked backward, jabbing his sword toward the warriors before he, his brother, and the creature disappeared.

And just like that it was over.

Jonah jerked back in surprise as Arieh dropped to the ground next to him and placed his hand on Carly's head.

"I don't think you should do that," Jonah said warily.

Carly groaned, stirring a little.

"Take her to her father's house," Arieh said, rising. "She will be safe there."

"She needs to see a doctor!" Jonah said, incredulous.

"She is healed."

"Is that what you said about Sam — that he was *healed?* Or did you just decide not to help him at all?" Jonah snapped, not caring if the warrior smited him ... or whatever they did to humans when they got out of line.

The thought stuck in his head: *Why hadn't they saved Sam too?*

"Sam was deceived," the second warrior said, coming up to stand next to Arieh. "Sometimes there are casualties in war, but it's not –"

"I don't want to be a part of your freaking war!"

They stared down at him, their faces grim.

"Haven't you figured it out?" Arieh said as the angels turned to walk away. His amber eyes moved to Carly and back to Jonah again. "You are our war."

"You saw, didn't you – the remaining scales? How can they remain after all he's seen – all he's remembered?"

"I don't know – but we're running out of time," the Irinim leader answered somberly. He glanced to the warrior Kallai, who stood next to him, before he turned his gaze upward, watching the dark fabric of sky roll and undulate as flashes of lightning illuminated the ever-widening tear in the center of the Arch. "We should take advantage of Shammah's injuries while we can."

He closed his eyes. *"Jair ...,"* he summoned, sending the warrior forth with his thoughts.

A crackle of electricity filled the air as Jair appeared on top of the Arch, nose raised to the air as he tracked the scent of the MazziKim. His expression turned fierce, swords immediately appearing in each hand just as a large figure shot past him in the dark.

In a flash, Jair slid down the leg of the Arch after the Harmer. Halfway down the six-hundred-foot drop, his sword found its mark, digging into the Harmer's side. The creature let out a scream – evoked by something worse than pain – as the light from the sword lit it up, eating away at the corrupted cells in rapid succession. It tumbled back through the night like a giant rag doll with wings.

"One down," Jair whispered, morphing to the center of the walkway under the Arch, swords disappearing into their sheath just as two large staffs appeared in his hands. He drove the staffs through the concrete, shooting a ring of blue light that illuminated red eyes glowering at him from the edge of the shield.

Not just one set of eyes – an entire horde.

Should have expected it, Jair thought. *Where there is one cockroach, there is usually a nest…*

"The shield will hold them off for now," the Irinim fighter reported back to Arieh in his thoughts. *"Pray we break this stronghold before their numbers grow any larger."*

45

J enna searched the room for a good twenty minutes before she
found the black duffel bag stuffed underneath the bed. She
unzipped it and grabbed the cell phone that the angel told her
she would find.

"Are you ... *God?*" Jenna heard herself ask, and then, *"I am his
messenger..."* Her hands shook as she punched in the number.

"Please answer, please –" She heard the phone pick up and
groaned as it went straight to voicemail.

"Carly? It's me, Jenna. Something really good happened to me
tonight. I just wanted to tell you. There's a lot I want to tell you ...
Oh man, you were right about Nick. He's got me locked in a room
here at his place. I've been trying to put the pieces together, and
I think he needs Mikey for something he's involved in. He's going
to be moving us to his compound outside the city. Call the police,
Carly – as soon as you get this, okay?"

Jenna exhaled, flipped the cell phone closed, and started to put it
back into the bag, when she felt something hard stuffed underneath
Nick's gym clothes. She frowned and pulled what appeared to be a
very old black book out of the bag, with the words *Die Geheime Lehre*
written in gilded script. Something about the book scared her. She
slowly opened it to the title page and saw that an inscription had
been made – in a language she didn't recognize. She was able to make
out two names: *Adolph* at the top of the page, and *Dietrich Eckart* at
the bottom. Beneath that was the faded sketch of a pentagram ...

"What –" She jumped at the sound of the bedroom door slamming.

"Did you find what you were looking for, honey?"

Jenna screamed and tried to struggle out of Nick's grasp as
she watched two of his men escort her son down the hall. Mikey
glanced over his shoulder at her, his beautiful eyes wide with fear.

She fought wildly against Nick, and he swore and pressed her to the ground, putting his knee on her back as he yelled for another one of his goons. A hulking middle-aged guy with a buzz cut hurried to them.

"What happened? She's stronger than before," Buzz Cut said with a grunt as he tried to stick the needle into her arm. It took two more tries before they were able to shoot the poison into her.

"It's only temporary – until you get yourself under control," Nick said softly against her ear, but his tone was threatening. "You keep your nose clean and you will see your son again, understand?"

She nodded and turned her head to one side to see Mikey as she waited for the drug to take effect. *Oh, Mikey, what have I done?* she thought, feeling a lone tear slip down her cheek.

Mikey must have sensed her, because he turned around at the end of the hallway and looked back. "Mom!" he yelled, legs kicking, arms reaching for her as one of Nick's men picked him up and carried him around the corner and out of sight.

"Mom!" Mikey yelled again, his voice muffled. Then she heard another familiar voice, this one deep and calm as it spoke into her mind. *Jahdiel – wasn't that what he said his name was?* She closed her eyes, allowing herself to drift as tears continued to slip down her face, and she listened.

46

"If you remember, I suggested moving to the compound awhile back," Nick said, slightly out of breath as he sat down and glanced around the conference table in the room next to his office. "It will give our reeducators time to evaluate and groom the child without any further distractions."

Heads nodded all around the table, and then he noticed some of the members glancing uneasily at the ancient-looking black woman crouched in the corner of the room. Nick cringed inwardly. At one time she had been beautiful – and very useful to their cause – but something had changed over the last few months. Her beauty had faded at an almost impossible rate. He wondered if her usefulness to them was fading as well. She had given them sound information about the child, but that could have been a fluke – like an old, broken-down vehicle starting up every once in a blue moon.

The sound of bones hitting the floor echoed in the room. The fortune teller made a strangled sound in her throat.

"What is wrong with you, old woman?" Nick said, slamming his hand on the table. If the trouble with Jenna hadn't been enough, now he had to deal with this? "Has it escaped your feeble brain that we are having a meeting here?"

"Too late," she declared ominously.

"What are you talking about?"

"Too late," she said again, and then she laughed, glancing up to give him a sly look that both unnerved and infuriated him. "Eyes you want, both great and small ... and now you have no eyes at all."

"Get her out of here," a cultured female voice snapped. "Now!"

47

Y ou found this painting with the others?" Jonah nodded
briefly to Professor Kinney, who along with TJ was standing
with him at the Hagans' kitchen table, staring down at Sam's
painting of the sun. He turned for what felt like the hundredth
time and swept the room with his eyes, every nerve ending on alert,
braced for something to appear at any moment ... for something to
happen ... and silently pleaded that it wouldn't.

"No inscription around the door," TJ murmured, sitting down in
one of the chairs. "I'm curious: why didn't you bring this one with
you to the university?"

"I don't know," Jonah said, turning back around. "I guess I didn't
think it was as important as the other ones. I mean, it's just a sun
and a door." He glanced to where Carly stood, waiting for the coffee to finish brewing. She looked fine, so fine that he would've had
a hard time believing she was in a major accident if he hadn't been
there himself.

"There's something that we're missing," Professor Kinney said
slowly as he picked the painting up. He glanced sharply at TJ. "Can
you bring the other paintings in?"

"I'm on it," TJ said, jumping up from the table.

"Did you see something we didn't see?" Jonah asked as the professor continued to study the image on the canvas.

"Possibly," Professor Kinney said. He looked up as Carly
approached them. "I hope there is caffeine in that."

"Are you kidding?" Carly gave him a grin as she set the tray down
and poured cups of coffee for everyone. "My dad thinks they should
make a law against selling decaffeinated coffee."

"I always said he was a smart man." Professor Kinney smiled as
he raised a cup to his lips.

Jonah touched Carly's arm. "You sure you feel okay?" It was probably the fiftieth time he had asked, but he couldn't seem to help himself.

"Garrett," Chaplain Hagan said, nodding to the professor as he entered the room. He grabbed a cup of coffee and glanced sideways at Jonah. "How many times are you going to ask her if she's all right, son? Maybe we should go down to the basement — a few drills might be just the ticket to calm you down."

"Step off, Mr. Miyagi," Jonah grumbled, and they all laughed.

"I'm *fine*, Jonah," Carly said, her cheeks flushing.

Jonah heard the front door open and looked up in time to see TJ rushing in, his arms loaded with Sam's valises ... and coming in closely behind him was J.

The look on J's face forced Jonah to bite back the remark that was ready to springboard off the tip of his tongue. J looked relieved and grateful ... and something else, something that Jonah sensed more than saw.

He looked like a drowning man who had just been thrown a life preserver.

Their eyes met briefly.

"Okay, let's see what we have," Professor Kinney said, spreading the paintings out across the table. He glanced at Jonah. "I didn't want to say anything until I was sure, but look: see how each of the five paintings has faint gold lines running through it — "

"Like rays from the sun," TJ murmured.

Professor Kinney smiled. "It gets better. If you look at the far right side of the paintings of Mikey, Jenna, and Jonah, and then look at the far left side of the paintings of the sun, J, and Carly, you will see an interesting pattern developing."

"It almost looks as if the edges could fit together ... like a puzzle," Carly said as she leaned against Jonah for a better look. He smiled at her and turned back to the paintings.

Professor Kinney nodded. "And when the pieces are all put together" — he arranged the paintings, frowned, and rearranged them once more before stepping back with a satisfied and somewhat awed look on his face — "you have the big picture."

The six paintings had metamorphosed into one large body of work that took their breath away. The edges of the paintings had combined to form a keyhole in the middle that connected all of the paintings together. From the sun painting on the top right, rays streamed down into each. One particularly thick beam of light traveled from the door, through the keyhole, and down into Jonah's jail cell, illuminating the gold key in his hand.

" 'The prophecy cannot be fulfilled without Jonah,' " Carly said, glancing up at him excitedly. " 'He holds the key.' "

"Come on, Carly —," Jonah said, feeling uneasy.

"I *knew* it meant something!"

Jonah noticed everyone staring at him and shifted uncomfortably.

"I remember hearing that," J said with a note of wonder in his voice. "I'm still having a hard time wrapping my mind around the fact that these things are *angels*, even though I know it's true — and the fact that Sam painted something that happened to me before ..." He swallowed, letting his words trail off as he glanced to Jonah. "Carly's right, though. We heard those words when we were at the lake that day."

"Care to fill the rest of us in?" Chaplain Hagan said, looking between them questioningly.

"What does this key do, Watcher? Tell me and I might let her live ..."

The words ran through Jonah's mind, and he stood and started pacing through the house as Carly filled them in. It wasn't just what he had witnessed back at that intersection or what the fallen angel had said that made him pace ... It was what he had felt from the moment he pulled into the Hagans' driveway: a sense of something big coming, an epiphany of such importance that it could change his life forever.

He stopped pacing and slowly turned his head to look at the molding around the front door. The same strange letters and symbols he had seen at Professor Kinney's office were carved into the wood. Why hadn't he ever noticed them before?

TJ let out a whistle. "He actually troubled the water they were swimming in."

"What?" Jonah said, reluctantly walking over to a seat. "What's that supposed to mean?"

"There are several stories I've come across about angels appearing near springs of water during certain seasons. They would stir the water — or *trouble* it, as the ancient texts would say – and as soon as anyone who was sick stepped into the water, their sickness was removed."

"But we didn't have anything wrong with us," Carly said, shaking her head.

"Maybe this angel didn't want to *take* anything from you … maybe he wanted to give you something."

"Like what?" J asked cautiously.

"Protection."

"The power to fight," Chaplain Hagan added, and they all turned to look at him.

"Sealed …," Carly said slowly. "Remember what that fallen angel said? The dip in the lake sealed us?"

Chaplain Hagan glanced to Professor Kinney, then gave TJ a slight nod.

Jonah was stunned. "Wait a minute – *you* know about all of this? You know them?"

Chaplain Hagan cleared his throat. "We've known each other for a long time," he began slowly as TJ pulled his laptop out of its case and set it on the table. "Garrett and I were in Vietnam together when we first heard about the Watchers. I wasn't a chaplain at the time. We were both placed over a special unit, a mobile guerilla force …"

"Two kids with green berets and guns," Professor Kinney said wryly.

Chaplain Hagan nodded. "There was this skinny kid on Garrett's team who we started noticing. He had always been kind of a loner, scribbling in a journal every night when the other guys were playing cards. Never talked much at all – until we received orders to head out one night."

TJ fired up his laptop as they listened.

"Then he wouldn't stop talking," Professor Kinney said, picking up the story. "He was tromping through the jungle at the front of the line – not speaking to any of us – but we could hear him talking to *someone*, asking them why there weren't any other Watchers, why it was a bad idea to move forward. Then he started saying things like, 'Too many doors are open' and 'The fallen will not be contained.'"

"Spooked the heck out of us," Chaplain Hagan said.

"He could've been stressed out of his mind," Jonah suggested, even though he knew better. He could feel his heart rate picking up speed.

"A plausible explanation." Professor Kinney nodded. "If Jeff and I hadn't dreamed that it was going to go down exactly like that the night before."

"Old men dream dreams, young men have visions," TJ murmured.

"I can take you downstairs and show you who's old," Chaplain Hagan said.

TJ grinned as he started tapping keys on his laptop.

"So what happened?" Carly asked impatiently.

"We pulled back," Chaplain Hagan replied, voiced sobered. Jonah noticed a look of regret appear as the man glanced at his daughter. "We tried our best to convince another unit, heading for the same area, to do the same, but they wouldn't listen."

"They were slaughtered," Professor Kinney said. "Only one survivor, who babbled for several hours about demon eyes that could see every move they made. They sent him home with a dishonorable discharge the next day."

Jonah felt a chill slide up his neck. *It's coming,* he thought, looking down at the painting of himself. *Whatever it is that I don't want to hear is coming ...* He glanced at Carly and J, who had changed into mannequins as they waited for the bomb to drop.

Chaplain Hagan took a deep breath. "Fast forward and I'm a chaplain on my way to the Persian Gulf. Garrett is already there, so we decide to get together at the little tent chapel they put me in charge of." He turned to the professor. "You weren't even there five minutes when that old man shuffled inside."

"Clutching what appeared to be an ancient leather scroll." Professor Kinney shook his head as if even the memory of it still mystified him. "He had to be as old as Methuselah ... He told us through his translator that a Son of Light had told him to bring the last war scrolls to *us.* He placed the scroll in my hand and walked away without another word."

Professor Kinney sighed and glanced up at them again. "When we finally got over our shock, we learned that the scroll was indeed ancient, written around the same time as the Dead

Sea Scrolls – and most likely unearthed in one of the caves where those were found. The problem for us was that it was in Aramaic."

Jonah felt his mouth go dry. *Please say TJ couldn't translate it …*

"That's when they found me," TJ said quietly as he flipped the laptop's screen around for them to read.

The Last War Scroll
I.
Remember these words well:
It is only a thin veil that hides them from our world.
As time grows near, they will increase their war upon mankind.
They will torment, attack, and cause destruction on this planet.
They will never hunger; they will never sleep.
They will walk among us unseen,
Invisible to all but those born to see.
And each generation of five that sees shall endure more than the last.
But the final generation of Watchers will not only endure, not only watch –
They will fight.

"I can't believe you didn't tell me any of this!" Carly turned and gave her dad an incredulous, injured look. "How long have you known that we might be … Watchers? What were we, guinea pigs in your little pet project? Did *Mom* know?"

"Carly –"

"Is that why she left us?"

"Carly!" Jonah said, trying to get her attention as he stared at the screen.

"What?"

"There's more," TJ said grimly.

II.

Know the time:

When the Sons of Darkness increase their number

And mankind groans under the weight of their steps,

In those days the Sons of Light will return to battle alongside the Children of Men.

They will break forth like lions from their lairs

And wake the Watchers from their slumber.

With the key, they open the door.

But they will find no rest in their hearts

Until the final battle

Of the Last War is won.

"But they will find no rest..." Jonah felt like he was standing
in one of those carnival rides and the bottom had just dropped
out from under his feet.

"It wasn't until the five of you came to summer camp that I
began to suspect that you might have the gift," Carly's dad said,
breaking the silence. "But just when I was prepared to tell you,
you were no longer friends." He sighed heavily. "I eventually
convinced myself it was my imagination ... I never mentioned
it to Garrett, until we were on our way back from Iraq with the
second scroll." His gaze shifted to Carly. "I never was in London,
honey. I'm sorry I've hidden things from you, but I was just trying to protect you."

"We weren't fully convinced it was the five of you until more
evidence came our way," said Professor Kinney.

"Unbelievable," Carly said quietly, as if she didn't have the
strength to yell. "I know it's the truth ... but ..."

"What evidence?" J asked.

TJ tapped on his keyboard, and another image appeared
before them.

"My system started detecting substantial atmospheric
changes around five states, including Missouri, just before
Mardi Gras," TJ began.

"How substantial?" Jonah asked, looking up from the screen.

"Like nothing I had ever seen before. Same night, I get a
phone call from a buddy of mine that led me to believe that a
star gate had been located in the area of the Arch. It's long been

theorized that the Grigori's return would be more like a surprise attack through one of the star gates ..." TJ glanced around the room, a look of wonder in his eyes. "Can you imagine: the Arch ... an entryway between dimensions ... for *angels*?"

"See, SyFy," Carly said, glancing at Jonah, and he smiled.

"There is actually scientific evidence now that an eleventh dimension exists within our universe." TJ paused, searching for the right words. "Think of it as living in a world within a world, and the only thing that separates us from the inhabitants of this other world is a thin membrane – or *veil*, as the Bible and other ancient texts describe it."

"You're telling us that the people who wrote the Bible figured it out way before our scientists?" Carly asked.

"Pretty much. And what I've told you is just the tip of the iceberg."

"Do *you* know how we're supposed to fight them?" Jonah asked, turning to Chaplain Hagan.

"We know that the Watchers are stronger in groups. There seems to be a joining of minds and power when they are all together. Which is why Nick and the Alliance have kept Jenna and Mikey separated from you."

"Alliance?" J shook his head. "I've never heard Nick mention anything like that."

"They're a spin-off of an occultist society started a long time ago," Professor Kinney said. "They believe they can join forces with the fallen and that together they will corrupt or destroy all inferior humans and rule the world. The scary thing is, it coincides with what theologians believe will happen as the end of time grows near."

"As it was in the days of Noah ...," Chaplain Hagan murmured.

"Who are the inferior humans?" Carly asked.

"Anyone who might come against their plan."

"Especially ..." Professor Kinney hesitated.

"The Watchers," Jonah said, finishing it for him. He stood. "I don't know about you two, but I'm thinking it might not be such a great idea for us to be here." Carly and J looked up at him curiously. "If these things are trying to take us down any way they can, don't you think they would also go after anyone who's trying to help us?"

A look of terror flashed across Carly's face as she glanced to her dad. She and J stood up at the same time. "Let's go."

The drive back to the warehouse was a little more crowded with TJ and his equipment along, but the guy wouldn't take no for an answer. And since J thought it was a good idea – *and he was the one driving* – Jonah had decided not to argue. He had enough on his mind.

"I want you to know I didn't have anything to do with your parents' deaths," J had said, taking him aside before they left. *"I tried to help, tried to get to them in time … but I messed it up, just like I did with Sam."*

He had believed him too. He might not have a week ago, definitely not a month ago. But after everything he'd seen and heard … after what he now remembered about Mardi Gras … he realized that the fallen had been playing them against each other for a long time.

He felt Carly stir next to him as she reached for his hand. "So, how are we going to do this?" she said, almost filling in his next thoughts. "I mean, we all saw how big those fallen angels are … and we're supposed to *fight* them?"

"Save the world and all that?" Jonah said casually as he rolled the window down and threw out his cigarette.

"Well, I'd like to get Jenna and Mikey first, but yeah."

"I don't know how we're going to do it, Carly. Do you have any ideas, TJ? You know more about them than we do."

"That's funny, I was just going over it all in my head, thinking about everything I've read on the subject," TJ said, glancing back at them. "There are passages in the Bible that deal with the children of Israel coming up against giants – David and Goliath, Joshua and Caleb and the huge inhabitants of Canaan … And in each of those instances, they were victorious because they knew God had their back, would give them whatever they needed to defeat them."

"But the giants weren't angels," J said as he drove.

"No, but they were children of the angels – fallen ones, that is – aka MazziKim."

"This just keeps getting more unbelievable by the minute," Jonah said. *I don't know what this key thing is, but you have picked the wrong guy,* he thought – or prayed, if you wanted to call it that. *I'm not as strong as Sam and* sure *ain't as strong as those guys TJ's talking about. Definitely sure…*

"I believe it all," J said. "But maybe that's just me; maybe it's not such a stretch to believe if you've been a guest at a loony bin."

"You always did have a way with words, J," Jonah said dryly.

"Oh my gosh, it's *Jenna!*" Carly exclaimed, putting her phone on speaker so they could hear the voicemail:

" … He's got me locked in a room here at his place. I've been trying to put the pieces together, and I think he needs Mikey for something he's involved in. He's going to be moving us to his compound outside the city. Call the police, Carly—as soon as you get this, okay?"

" 'And each generation of five …,' " J murmured. "Mikey's a Watcher too, isn't he?"

"I'm pretty sure he is," Jonah said, thinking of what Sam said in that dream, thinking of the scene at the cemetery. "And by the sound of that message, Jenna isn't exactly going along with the plan."

"If anything happens to her or her little boy …," J said, his voice like a thundercloud.

"We've got to get to them." Carly looked at Jonah. "Before something bad happens …"

She didn't have to say, *"like Sam."* He had already heard it in his mind.

48

Y ou're going to be taking a trip soon," the warrior Eri said as he studied the predawn sky outside Mikey's window. "Am I going home?" Mikey asked, feeling tired. He'd barely slept at all.

"Not yet," Eri said, turning to his charge. "They're coming to your room to take you soon. But even if you don't see me, I'm with you. Do you understand?"

Mikey nodded. He understood — and he didn't.

He didn't know exactly what was going to happen, but at least he felt safe for once. The "not yet" part gave him hope too as he lay back on his bed and stared up at the ceiling. When his mom said, "not yet," that meant it was coming soon. Like when he asked about Christmas or Thanksgiving. It didn't happen right away — but it happened.

And not yet was way better than *never* being able to go home.

He heard scuffles and yelling outside his door and bolted up to a sitting position. The warrior angel was gone —

"Hide your journal, the book! Hurry!"

He quickly stuffed his things into his tattered backpack just as one of Mr. Corsa's men slammed through his bedroom door.

"Come on, kid," the man said gruffly, yanking him off the bed. "We're taking a little ride." The bad angel with the Mohawk was standing behind him.

As the man dragged him down the hallway and out to the waiting car, Mikey looked around, hoping to catch a glimpse of the warrior. He saw his mom instead.

She looked so bad that he lost his grip on the backpack for a moment, and it tipped sideways. What happened next seemed to go in slow motion, like in the movies.

He watched helplessly as his journal and favorite book *sloooowly* slid out from their hiding place and began their horrible descent toward the spot on the driveway where Mr. Corsa stood. Then a strange blue ball of light came out of nowhere, covering his things just as they hit the pavement next to Mr. Corsa's shoe.

"Pick them up!"

Mikey stole a quick glance around, grabbed his things, and shoved them way down into his backpack. He felt shaky but good. He didn't even care that Mr. Corsa's man was giving him a mean, impatient kind of look.

"It's going to be okay, Mom," Mikey whispered as they shoved him next to her in the back of the car and slammed the door. His mom didn't answer – or couldn't – and he felt scared again.

"We will be with you – even if you don't see us all the time. Do you understand?"

He glanced out the window and immediately saw the flash of gold eyes looking back at him.

Mikey smiled a trembly smile and leaned back against the seat.

49

The News 5 helicopter was hovering in the gray, cloud-choked sky over the Mississippi, gearing up for the morning traffic report, when a brilliant burst of light flashed across the windshield, momentarily blinding the pilot.

"What in the world *was* that?" Brad Peters asked shrilly, scrambling to level the chopper. He pushed his glasses to the top of his head and looked around. "Did you see that?"

"See what?" the cameraman grumbled as he wiped the coffee off his shirt.

"That light—" Brad frowned, searching the sky. There was no light there. *No way light could get through clouds like that...*

"They're on the move again," Kallai said, morphing next to Arieh in a burst of light. "And the enemy's numbers have doubled since last night."

"Our numbers will come," Arieh said evenly. "Remember: the master plan is always in the hand of the Master." Kallai bowed in acknowledgement. The warriors looked at each other, nodded, and in a flash were standing outside the old warehouse.

Lightning cracked across the darkening sky, and Arieh felt a ripple in the air as a small dog ran past them, tail tucked between its legs. He heard the malevolent voices then, whispering deceit as they tried to draw the human out into the open.

Arieh glanced up to the window where Jonah Becker stood. "Time to take our positions, Kallai." Weapons drawn and flashing, they morphed backward into the brick warehouse, joining Azaniah, and waited for the Grigori to appear.

Thirty miles away, Shammah watched the car slowly pull to a stop in the half-moon driveway that led to the compound. Thunder rolled in the distance as his eyes zeroed in on the little boy exiting the car.

"Tiria, Shobeck, you two are to take watch over the front entrance of the property," he said, turning to the two warriors waiting for his command. "Keep watch for any signs of the Irinim. Report to me as soon as you spot them. Do you think you can handle that?"

The warriors nodded.

"Better hope for your sakes you can," Tola said, sneering.

A black mass engulfed the two warriors, depositing them at separate ends of the entrance. Shammah's eyes ran the length of the property, where the remaining Grigori had taken position, and then turned back to his brother.

"Tola, you will shadow Corsa. His ideas must be your best."

Tola grinned and was gone.

Alone again, the Grigori leader raised his head and sniffed the air.

50

Thick, dark clouds churned low in the sky as Jonah stared through the windshield like a kid sitting in the front row at a movie theater. Wild veins of lightning flashed, disappeared, and then flashed closer, imitating the hard drumbeat of his heart as he, Carly, and J sped down the road in J's Suburban, heading for Nick Corsa's compound.

How they had managed to get out of the warehouse when it was surrounded by Grigori wasn't so much a mystery as it was a shock. He hadn't expected to see three huge angels coming right out of the brick of the building and taking off into the sky after the Grigori.

"Dry thunderstorm," J murmured, peeking at the clouds as he drove. "I've heard of them but never seen them before."

Jonah looked at the sky again.

It's coming—that thing that's going to change my life forever, he thought, feeling a tremor of fear and ... *anticipation?* He glanced away from the show in the sky and noticed for the first time the odd markings around the passenger door.

"I take it these symbols are TJ's work?" He had been a busy guy, tracking down the address for Nick's compound, painting.

"Yeah," J said, keeping his eyes trained on the road he was maneuvering at mind-numbing speed. "He said it's Hebrew. Some kind of Scripture or something. He said the fallen can't cross it."

"Like a safe house ...," Jonah said. "I saw the same symbols around the door of Professor Kinney's office. Around your dad's doors too," he added, looking over the seat at Carly.

"The problem is, we can't stay inside the vehicle," Carly said as she dragged her eyes away from the sky. "We're going to have to get out to find Jenna and Mikey."

"Maybe," J said, glancing up at her in the rearview mirror. "But I can get us pretty close to the front door with this baby." He jammed his foot down on the gas, and Jonah looked forward in time to see the gates of the compound looming before them.

The shift in the air jarred through them, unlike anything they had felt before. *Almost like we're driving* into *it,* Jonah thought, grabbing the handle on the dash in front of him.

Carly gasped. "J — watch out!"

Two huge crows had appeared, one on either side of the Suburban, flapping their immense, somehow scaly wings, red eyes boring into them as they thrust their talons forward. They gripped the doors for less than a second before they were thrown back by an invisible force.

J let out a maniacal laugh.

The crows' high-pitched screeches pierced their ears, the smell of electricity and ozone filling the SUV as Jonah watched them flip backward and hit the ground, releasing the huge spirit-like beings that had inhabited them.

"That was for my grandma, you freaking bottom feeders," J said, his face set in a grim line of determination as he barreled into the gates.

Jonah felt the bone-jarring crunch of iron against steel as the doors of the gate dug into the vehicle, and he saw two of the fallen morph out of the huge stone pillars that flanked each side of the gate. J stomped on the gas again, and the vehicle lurched forward, throwing the doors of the gate off just as the fallen landed on the hood with a horrible thud. Their eyes flashed amber for only a moment before they cooled to the cold, dead black Jonah remembered from that night in his childhood.

J glanced to his left and then back to the fallen, and his eyes widened with a horrible, dawning realization. "TJ wrote over all of the *doors*, but he didn't do anything to the rest of my truck."

"Oh, *God*!" Carly said, her voice filled with dread — and maybe pleading too.

The kind of prayer you say when you don't have the breath or time left for lengthy discussion, Jonah thought as he glanced back through the windshield just as one of the beings placed his huge hand flat against the hood of the Suburban. The fallen angel looked up at Jonah and grinned.

"Time to come out and play, Watchers," a loud, menacing voice beckoned, rolling through their minds.

The locks on the doors began to fly up and down, and then the radio came on, running through the stations in a piercing electric whine, until it stopped on Lynyrd Skynyrd's "Call Me the Breeze."

"I used to sing cover on that song ... before we started playing our own stuff," Jonah murmured as the fallen angel drew closer. The song continued, the lyrics seeming to mimic their situation.

"We're dead meat," Jonah said, and then the engine went dead.

The Suburban coasted to a stop.

"I don't know about you," J said, "but I'm sick and tired of *hiding.*"

"Oh, God," Carly said again, pleading with heaven. "Jonah, stop him—"

J threw open the door, and they were hit with a force of wind—not cold but warm, rushing all around them, filling them with a burst of strength they had never felt before. They watched the fallen angel flip backward through the air.

Jonah would later wonder if it was Carly's rushed prayer or J's leap into action that brought them into the open, but at the moment, he was thinking he was never so glad in his life to see the huge warriors that encircled their vehicle.

He looked up into the lion-like eyes that flashed amber.

"Go. We can only hold them for so long," Arieh said.

They scrambled out of the vehicle and into what seemed like an immense blue force field that shimmered around them. Jonah saw four warriors posted at each corner of it, arm muscles bulging as they kept their staffs rammed into the ground. On the outside of the force field, warriors and the fallen were locked in a viscous battle in the air and on the ground, and Jonah heard muffled sounds of metal against metal as their weapons clanged and bodies clashed.

Two fallen angels tumbled to the ground with a resounding crash, and Jonah saw two of those deformed creatures lurch forward and drag them away.

Carly mumbled something incoherent.

"Go, *now!*" Arieh yelled.

They bolted, running for all they were worth across the grounds of the compound. Jonah looked back and saw Arieh morph out into the battle, leaving behind only the four warriors with staffs.

"Jenna!" J yelled, veering toward the left wing of the main building.

Jonah squinted and then spotted her too, waving frantically from a window on the second floor. She ducked inside and then appeared again. A long white rope of knotted bedsheets slipped down the side of the building. Jonah kept his eye trained on her as he ran, watching as she began to make her way down the rope. He felt a rush of pride as she neared the ground.

"She's going to make it!" Carly said, giving him a quick grin.

They turned back toward Jenna and were startled to see four muscle-bound thugs rushing out of a side door.

"No!" Carly screamed. Jonah felt her shout resonating through him, through them all, like a battle cry, and they rushed forward in a burst of speed.

"Mom!"

Mikey pressed his face against the window as he saw one of Mr. Corsa's guys skidding to a stop beneath the rope his mom was climbing down.

"Leave her alone!" he said, smacking the window as tears sprang to his eyes.

His mom dropped to the ground and spun around like an ultimate fighter and kicked the guy in the chest so hard, he *flew* backward. Really far. Like the stuff that she said only happened in movies. It was a miracle.

"Yes!" Mikey cried.

J, Jonah, and Carly appeared next to his mom, and he saw three more miracles happen before his eyes. J did a front kick to the guy's you-know-what, and the guy doubled over in time to get an uppercut to the jaw that sent him flying back. Then Jonah did this crazy spinning-kick thing that clipped another guy under the chin, and the guy flipped *backward* and did a face-plant in the dirt. Mikey glanced to where Carly stood, just in time to see the last guy standing swing on her. She blocked it, grabbed his arm, and flipped him over onto his back so hard that he bounced up before landing on the ground again.

They're like superheroes …

Mikey grinned like crazy as he blinked back his tears. Spence and Dustin would never believe it, not in a hundred million years, but he didn't care. His mom wasn't sick anymore, and no way was she scared. He felt a large hand press gently into his shoulder.

"I have to go now, but don't fear — you will not be alone."

I bet they're going to help my mom find me! he thought, ecstatic. *Almost home!*

The smile died on his lips as he saw the blue shimmery thing fade around his mom and the others, revealing a pooling mass of something dark, darker than a shadow, rapidly spreading across the ground under their feet.

"Hardest thing I ever had to do," Jenna said breathlessly as they ran. "But something told me that if I didn't convince Mikey I was doped, I wouldn't fool them." She glanced at Carly. "Can you *believe* what we just did back there?"

Carly grinned, still amazed by the power they had. "Jeet Kune Do on steroids."

"Do you know where Mikey is?"

Carly shook her head just as J let out a groan. She saw him stumble and saw Jonah, who was running next to him, reach out to help him.

"You okay?"

"Yeah," J said, sounding winded. "Just felt like a cold poker digging into my scar."

"Carly," Jonah said with a note of alarm in his voice. "You notice something missing around us?"

"See anything interesting out there, Mikey?"

Nick strolled slowly into the room, like he had all the time in the world — even though he didn't. Jenna's escape and her little friends showing up just before the Alliance's reeducators arrived was destroying all of his carefully laid plans. Now he was going to have to make amends to the Director, come up with a new plan after this little fiasco was finished. He couldn't afford to fall out of her grace.

The kid turned from the window to face him.

"You know, I regret that we were not able to work together," Nick said, "but no hard feelings, right? It's kind of like a game. You win some and you lose some. I would appreciate it if you shared that message with your mom. It would mean a lot to me."

"Is she here? What about her friends?" Mikey asked, stopping Nick as he turned to go.

"They should be here anytime to pick you up ..." Nick nodded, then left the room, shutting the door and locking it.

"... *in a body bag,*" Tola finished as he appeared next to Nick.

Nick grinned as he grabbed the cans of gasoline that sat waiting for him in the hall. He would help Jenna and her friends find Mikey. And then they would all die. It was a great idea, really. The best he'd ever had ...

Jonah glanced up as Shammah morphed out of thin air just a few feet away, blocking their way to the building. The fallen angel took a step toward him, and he felt an icy stab of terror.

"Time to die, *Watchers.*"

"Oh no," Jenna whispered, echoing Jonah's feelings. But when he turned to look at her, he noticed she wasn't looking at the Grigori leader. He frowned and followed her gaze just past Shammah to the right wing of the building, where a trail of flames was snaking across one side of the roof.

"Mikey's in there, I just know it!" she said, starting to take off toward the building. J caught up to her and held her back, wrapping her in a gentle bear hug.

"That fallen angel will kill you," J growled as she struggled against him. "We need backup."

She tried to elbow him in the midsection. "You're *crazy* if you think I'm going to leave Mikey–"

Arieh appeared, slamming into Shammah with such force that they both flew across the yard, striking the ground. The earth under the Watchers' feet rolled violently. Carly let out a startled yelp as she collided with J and Jenna, and they fell in a heap.

Jonah started toward them and then hesitated, looking back at the door of the building. Smoke was already starting to billow out from around its facing.

He felt something click inside of him then, something that felt bigger than he could ever be, like a light at the end of a tunnel growing to envelop you as you run to it.

His epiphany — that thing of great importance that he had been so scared of learning — came with such pure truth that it no longer scared him.

He turned and ran for the building.

The underground meeting room of the monastery was jam-packed with Resistance members from across the state — politicians and policemen, musicians and monks. *A lot of monks,* TJ thought ... Rabbi Leftkowitz, Father Parmely and Bishop Harper, General McClure and ... He continued to skim over the room and finally spotted Professor Kinney and Chaplain Hagan. He waved and headed over to them just as Rabbi Leftkowitz stood.

"Guide them through this battle, Almighty whose name we call Elohim," the rabbi prayed, his voice rolling through the room. "Restore to them their full birthright. Let them be a light to pierce this darkness that moves over our planet ..."

Father Parmely and Bishop Harper started to pray, and then the whole room. TJ was again struck by how so many voices and languages could blend together to form what sounded like a song ... and he joined in.

51

J onah grabbed hold of the door handles and let out a startled cry as the heated metal singed his skin. Glancing over his shoulder, he saw Carly and the others struggle up and head his way. He quickly took his jacket off, using it like an oven mitt as he grabbed the handles again and pulled. The door flew open, and he was struck in the face by a wave of intense heat. He stared in horror at the flames licking across the ceiling. It was even worse than he imagined.

He felt something swell up from deep within him and dove inside and locked the door behind him just as Carly, J, and Jenna reached the top of the steps.

"Do you see Mikey?" Jenna asked breathlessly, peering in at him through one of the small panes of decorative glass in the door. He could barely hear her. She tried to pull the handles. "Jonah, the door … I can't open it."

A second of silence followed, and he saw them looking at each other, saw what he had done begin to register in their eyes. Full impact hit and they went crazy.

J bellowed, a stricken look on his face as he tried to wrench the door open with all of his might. Jonah ducked as Jenna smashed the small glass panes, which only forced streams of black smoke to rush through them, obscuring his view. Carly screamed and pounded her fists against the door, her voice muffled by the roar of flames that swept from the ceiling and down the walls.

Then, for a brief moment, a gust of wind drove the smoke back, and he could see her clearly. He soaked in every feature on her face, etching it into his memory.

"He's just a kid. I couldn't leave him in here alone," he called out hoarsely through the smoke. "I'm sorry, Carly. There was no other way."

"There's always another way," she yelled as a sob broke loose from her. "Open the door, Jonah, and we'll do it together. I don't want you to go in there without me!"

He started to back away then, keeping his eyes on them for just a little bit longer as he remembered the day that four beautifully insane kids risked their lives to save a little boy hiding in a dumpster. He saw Carly again, standing over Bud Winters like a mini avenging warrior, the righter of all wrongs ... then J as he gently helped him out of the dumpster ... and finally Jenna, taking his grimy little hand in hers ...

The first to die ... The last to die.

"Take me," he said, barely above a whisper. "My life for theirs." He took another step back, almost fell, and then raised his hand and gave them a see-you-around wave.

Carly's eyes widened. *"No!"* she screamed, pounding on the door even harder.

The roar of the fire grew in his ears until he could only see her desperately mouthing the word over and over again, and he knew it was time to go.

Choking on the smoke and wiping the tears that streamed from his eyes, he forced a smile. "I love you guys. Don't ever forget that!" He put his jacket over his head, turned, and ran into the smoke-filled hall to search for another little boy who was praying for someone to rescue him.

Carly cried out as, all along the front of the building, windows began to shatter from the heat. She had never believed that people could really die of a broken heart, but she felt like hers was breaking, breaking away into little pieces that could never be put back together. *Jonah is going to die in there! Die!*

"Where *are* they?" she sobbed, searching the grounds for warriors who had come to their rescue so many times. "What are we supposed to do now?"

"Wait." Jahdiel's mighty hand clapped down on Neriah's shoulder in mid-morph, and the angel's body shimmered, half in, half out of the in-between.

"Arieh does not want us to intervene yet," the warrior said as Neriah materialized next to him again. Azaniah appeared next, looking frustrated as he lowered his sword. "We have another mission in the meantime..."

"All I know is that I have to get to Mikey... Oh, *Jonah*," Jenna choked out from somewhere behind Carly, and she winced, sharing Jenna's pain. "There's got to be another way in!"

Carly felt a cold, tingling sensation sweep up the back of her neck and turned just in time to see Tola appear, coming around the corner of the building. Jenna and J also turned, as though they too had sensed the evil presence. Tola spotted them and, looking as if he had been caught, disappeared from their sight in a blur of black armor.

"Let's try the other side of the building," J called out as he took off.

Carly grabbed Jenna's hand, and they followed him in a dead run.

Tola appeared next to Shammah with a smile. "Like leading lambs to slaughter."

Just need to lie down, Jonah thought, trying to catch his breath. *Just for a minute...*

He'd had a moment of hope as he delved deeper into the maze of hallways, when he realized that the fire was still confined to the front of the building, but his hope didn't last long. The blaze had grown fast, following behind him almost as if it were a living thing, stalking him as though it were determined to leave him no way out. No way out but death...

"*Death...,*" a malevolent voice whispered around him, as if it had either heard his thoughts... or planted them in his head.

Jonah pressed on, ticked off just enough to keep going. He finally reached the end of the hall, stumbled around the corner, and was hit with a breeze of fresh air. He let out a small sob of gratitude and inhaled it greedily.

Soft, *human* laughter wafted over him, and he looked up to see Nick Corsa standing there. Two gasoline cans sat on the floor at his feet.

"Well, look what the cat dragged in," Nick said, glancing over his shoulder as Jonah struggled to stand up straight. One of Nick's bodyguards stepped forward — thug one through twenty, take your pick. It was too hard to tell them apart with the cookie-cutter bald heads and bulging muscles.

"This has become a regular reunion of Watchers, don't you think?" Nick said conversationally, as if he were sitting at a bar, twirling the umbrella in his girlie drink.

Jonah remained silent, drinking in the oxygen slowly as he willed his body back to strength. He felt his eyes drawn to a picture on the wall behind Nick. It was one of those expensive, corporate kind of portraits — everyone standing together in their suits ... and dress. He froze. He would recognize that face anywhere! But what was Carly's *mom* doing standing in a portrait next to Nick?

"Too bad I can't stay," Nick said, his tone changing to reveal his hate.

Jonah cocked his head sideways, listening. He heard it again: a child crying for help!

"That would be the littlest Watcher," Nick supplied, and his bodyguard snickered.

"Over here!" J yelled. He had reached the side door of the building first and was already kicking at it savagely. Carly and Jenna joined him seconds later, and the three of them battered the steel door with all of their combined strength until it fell inward, releasing a cloud of black smoke that billowed back in their faces. J waited for the smoke to clear and then turned to his two old friends, and for the first time since they were little kids, he felt their spirits bonding together, uniting them in their mission.

"Let's go."

Arieh appeared before the huge gates in a burst of wind, his mammoth frame bowing over in petition as he dropped to his knees before the Guardians posted on each side of the gate. Standing fifteen feet in height, they bent their mighty heads to observe the warrior. With lightning-like flashes, their four faces changed with each flash; man, to lion, to oxen, to eagle. Their two sets of wings, each spanning over seven feet in length began to open, sending forth a wind that forced Arieh to use all of his strength to keep from being thrown back as the gates flew open ...

"Get out of my way," Jonah said between clenched teeth.

"And let you ruin my plans?" Nick smiled. "I don't think so."

Nick bowed to Jonah and took his fighting stance.

Jonah laughed, even though it hurt his throat. "There are three things you should know about me," he said in a conversational tone — *minus the umbrella'd girlie drink*. He tossed his jacket aside. "I don't follow the rules, I refuse to bow to any man ..." He motioned with his hand for Nick to come closer — a little Bruce Lee move that he knew Sam would get a kick out of. "Oh, and I *like* to fight."

The first palm strike was quick, and from Nick's reaction, Jonah knew it hadn't registered until Nick felt the blood pouring from his nose.

Jonah did a little dance back and waved him closer again.

Nick took the bait and with a savage growl rushed at Jonah just as he jumped into the air and delivered a blindingly fast kick to Nick's torso. The wild, raw force of it slammed Nick back into his bodyguard, and they fell and skidded across the floor.

"*That* was for Sam," Jonah growled. "That was for my brother!"

Nick struggled up, reaching for something under his jacket. He pulled the gun out and smiled as Jonah moved in closer.

"Karate this, Watcher."

Jonah did just that, with a spinning kick that broke two of Nick's fingers and sent the gun sailing across the room. He saw Nick's guy reach for his gun. Grabbing the closest thing he could find for a weapon—one of the gasoline cans—Jonah pitched it at the bodyguard just as he fired his weapon. The impact of the bullet shredded the container, dumping its contents directly on Nick.

"My eyes!" Nick screamed shrilly. "My eyes ... I can't see!"

The bodyguard scrambled to help Nick to his feet, the fear of retribution already imprinted on his features.

As soon as the bodyguard turned his back, Jonah grabbed his jacket and took off running down the hall in the direction of Mikey's voice. The boy's pitiful wails grew louder and more frantic as Jonah pounded on the doors, trying to find the room he was in.

A scared yelp came from behind the fourth door Jonah pounded on, and he kicked the door in with what felt like the last of his strength. Jenna's little boy stumbled back, a look of terror on his face until he realized who it was. A tentative smile appeared, but he was trembling.

"Are we going to die?" Mikey said with a sniff, looking up at him with those huge eyes of his. The soot that covered his face was streaked with tears as he hugged his old backpack to his chest.

"Nah, little man. We're too tough to die. We're going to live to fight another day," Jonah assured him as he took the backpack and slung it over his shoulder before reaching for Mikey's hand. He forced a smile, trying to appear confident.

"He's here even though we don't see him, right?" Mikey asked as Jonah covered him up in his jacket.

"Sure," Jonah murmured distractedly, leading Mikey by the hand over to the door. He checked the hall to make certain the coast was clear. Unable to recall which way he'd come, he guessed and went left. He moved them quickly through the smoky maze, turning down another hall, and then another, and before long he realized they were lost.

"Grigori!"

Arieh, Jahdiel, Azaniah, and Kallai immediately positioned themselves back-to-back as a large contingency of fallen angels appeared around them. Shammah materialized next. His massive, gray, battle-scarred wings folded in behind him before disappearing altogether.

"About that unfinished business …," he said, sword appearing in his hand as he moved toward Arieh.

Arieh smiled.

Jonah let out a harsh cough and stumbled forward. *Which way do I go?* He rubbed his burning eyes and looked around. In the short time he had spent getting into Mikey's room, the smoke had grown and darkened, becoming so thick that they could barely see their hands in front of their faces.

"Come on, Mikey," he said, urging the little boy down into a crawl with him. He could feel the heat of the blaze drawing closer, and he stopped and tried to decide what to do. *Is there even a way out anymore?* Getting no answer, he covered Mikey's body with his own as the heat bore down on them. Mikey murmured something under his jacket, but he was too afraid to pull the jacket back and face the little boy. He had promised him they were going to live. He had almost believed it himself.

Why did you let me find the kid if this is what is going to happen to us? he thought angrily. *Are we just pieces in a chess game that can be tossed to the side when the fun is over? Is that why you picked someone like me? Why are you freaking silent, so absent when I need you the most?*

"Die, Watcher," a rumble of voices whispered through his mind, and he turned his head slightly and saw what looked to be hundreds of malevolent, leering heads imbedded in the wall. They began to push outward, their faces stretching like taffy as they struggled to get free.

If you are real … Jonah's thought trailed off as the cold, heavy presence began to settle over him, making it even harder for him to breath. He felt separated from everything and whatever small hope he had was gone. Why try—it was useless. He felt like he was in the middle of a black hole in outer space where no one could hear him scream.

In spite of his thoughts, he felt something rising up in him, unwilling to give up. *Please,* he thought weakly. *Just don't let me die alone...*

Jonah coughed again. A strong wind swept across his back, and as he waited for the flames to hit, he felt himself begin to fade away...

He heard a little boy singing in the distance, singing that Ozzy song he used to sing, the one his mom had taught him before she disappeared. "Never Say Die" — wasn't that the name of it? He strained to hear the words, important words about the writting on the wall, about kids gathering together because ...

"We can save them ... all ..." Jonah whispered hoarsely, his voice mingling with the memory of his mother's voice the last time she whispered in his ear.

Why did you leave me alone? he wondered. *I was just a kid!*

He struggled to open his eyes and caught the familiar smell of something rotting and felt the cold fingers of dark despair; the fear, the overwhelming emptiness of being alone and he suddenly realized he's not just remembering ... he was the little kid in the dumpster again.

"*You are not alone,*" a voice swirled around him. Not human, not angel either. *God?* And in a flash of light Sam was there, smiling that smile at him as he took his shirt off and gave it to him.

Sam, he thought, brokenly.

"*Nothing of mine is ever lost,*" the same voice whispered to Jonah through the smoke and flames of the hallway. He suddenly saw an older Sam, much like he looked just before he died. He was studying some kind of ancient scroll, surrounded by warrior angels that looked over his shoulder as they stood beneath a massive tree. A tree bigger than all of the sequoias in California combined, stretching so high that its leaves seemed to be a part of the sky. *So much light,* Jonah thought, and Sam turned and looked over his shoulder at him, and he saw that there was something different about him. He seemed stronger, more sure of himself ... almost fierce. A small sob escaped from Jonah.

Sam was finally the warrior he had always dreamed of being. Jonah began to cry.

"It's not the end, Jonah. This is only the beginning," the voice promised, and somehow he knew it was true, all of it. Everything he and Sam had hoped and believed as kids. Tears streamed down his face, and as he reached up to wipe them away, he felt something hard and grainy under his fingers.

Everything suddenly looked cleaner, clearer in spite of the smoke and fire that billowed around him and a trickle of strength seeped through him. He wasn't alone – had never been alone – and it wasn't the end of him. Only the end of a lie.

"We're getting out of here, Mikey," he said, forcing himself to stand, and as he did, he felt a rush of almost superhuman strength fill him. He picked Mikey up in his arms and began to walk through the flames.

Standing guard at the base of the Arch, Jair looked up just as a mighty battalion of warrior angels burst through the star gate, their massive, fiery wings slicing through the dark, swollen sky as they turned their great bodies in the direction of the compound.

Jair yelled, a beautiful smile breaking over his face as he thrust his sword in the air.

"It's Jonah – and *Mikey*!" Jenna screamed.

"Wait!" Carly cried out, but she was already gone, running through the hall of flames. "We've got to stop her, J!"

The clash of swords was fierce, Arieh and Jahdiel against Shammah and Tola, while Azaniah, Neriah, and Kallai flanked them, fighting with all of their might.

Jahdiel glanced briefly to Arieh, then feinted to the right. Tola moved with it, and his dark eyes widened, realizing his mistake too late as Jahdiel's sword found the gap just beneath his breastplate and he drove it in to the hilt. Momentarily distracted by his twin's demise, Shammah didn't see Arieh's blow coming until it hit home. Blue veins of light shot through the Grigori twins, so powerful that they were unable to sustain their injuries, and they vanished before the Irinim's eyes ...

... and landed with a grunt in the middle of the black onyx wasteland. The force of their fall cracked the ground beneath them, and they felt a wave of heat rush up around them. Two huge black vultures appeared, swooping downward. They weakly threw their swords at the vultures but missed ... and then they braced themselves for the punishment that was to come.

"Our brothers have arrived," Arieh announced, turning his eyes to the sky, and as the Irinim warriors continued to fight, they lifted their eyes too and saw the bright flashes of amber fire breaking through the clouds.

Carly's mouth fell open. "What is she ..."

Her words trailed away as she saw the fire and smoke begin to billow out from the center of the hallway, and then she saw Jonah step through it with Mikey in his arms. A sob escaped her as that crazy crooked smile of his appeared on his face, and he passed Mikey into Jenna's waiting arms.

"'The prophecy cannot be fulfilled without Jonah; he holds the key,'" Carly said to J as tears filled her eyes. "I know what the key is now ..." She stepped into the hallway and looked over her shoulder at J. "It's faith."

J's troubled features softened, and he stepped into the hallway behind her. A fresh wind rose around them, clear and pure, pushing the smoke and flames against the walls as they made their way to Jonah.

Tears of awe filled Carly's eyes as Jenna turned back, her hair flying up around her from the fiery blast of wind. Carly laughed in amazement as she lifted her arms, noting that there wasn't even so much as a singed mark on her.

"Nothing is touching us," Carly whispered in amazement as Jonah wrapped his arms around her and kissed her on top of her head. "It's a miracle – a *real* miracle."

"Yeah ... it is," he said, drawing back finally. His gaze flickered briefly to something behind her in the hall, and for a moment he looked worried. Then he smiled and brushed a strand of hair back from her face. "So ... what do you say we get out of here, go on a real date?"

Carly laughed as she gazed up into his pale blue eyes. "You are crazy."

"I'm serious!" Jonah grinned. "A *normal* date. Like maybe dinner and a movie ..."

A roar of victory erupted around Jonah and his friends out on the grounds of the compound as warriors appeared on every side of them, and Jonah felt a joy well up in him that in all of his years of running, he never knew he had, never believed he *could* have.

He reached out for Carly and pulled her next to him, draping his arms over her shoulder as they walked. Carly glanced up at him and smiled, her face smudged with soot and streaked by tears and he thought he'd never seen anyone more beautiful in his life. He smiled down at her, wondering if he would ever have the courage to tell her about the portrait of her mom that he had seen on Nick Corsa's wall.

I'd rather walk through fire again than be the one to break her heart, he thought grimly, watching two fire trucks barrel through the gate of the compound.

"I knew you would get us out," Mikey said, a little of his old swagger returning as he caught up with them.

"Oh, yeah? How did you know?"

Mikey gave him a nonchalant shrug. "Someone was with us," he said, looking up at Jonah. "I couldn't see him, but I felt him with us the whole time ..."

Jenna smiled, and J fell into step next to him, looking like he had died a thousand deaths; relieved, and maybe even a little teary-eyed.

"I knew if anyone could bring him out alive, it would be your crazy butt," J said. He glanced to the cigarette in his hand, then snapped it in two. "Guess we better get rid of the sticks if we're going to do this right."

"As much as I hate to admit it," Jonah said, pulling his pack out of his jacket and tossing it, "you're right. But just so you know, I'm not into drinking raw eggs or punching sides of frozen beef. I gotta draw the line somewhere."

Epilogue

I wish I could say my story ends here, tucked away with the happily-ever-after endings of TV Land, but that's just not the way life rolls.

A bitter pill to swallow, coming from an ex-fantasy-land junkie like me, but I'm willing to choke it down, knowing what I know now. Nick is regrouping even as I write this. Being blind has not slowed him down – if anything, it has added fuel to the fire. A fire that the fallen love to fan.

They are never far.

One found me tonight just as I was opening the door of my truck.

"Do you think this is over, Watcher?" he hissed behind me. "Just like your brother, your time will come and you will die."

"Maybe," I shot back. "But I've been doing a little reading, and I found out that you don't have all the time in the world either. One day there's going to be a big flush, and you will be sent back to the cesspool where you belong."

I guess I wasn't thinking, because I pushed him out of my way and he went flying backward across the street.

Pretty cool ... but I got a feeling it doesn't happen all the time.

Which is probably why Carly's dad has stepped up the training lately. The fighting seems to come natural to us, but he still pushes running, lifting ... pretty much all the stuff I hate. TJ and the professor are just as bad, cramming our heads with as much information as we can take. Mikey led a revolt a week ago, and we played hooky, holed up in the warehouse, trashing it with junk food and a constant run of comedies on Carly's DVD player. Laughter can cure just about anything.

So can hope. Another miracle played out before our eyes with the news that Willa Harvey wasn't dead at all but in a coma – and first thing out of her mouth when she woke up was directed at me and J: "I see you two lunkheads have mended fences," she said, pursing her lips and everyone laughed, and then they cried – even J's friend Tiny who kind of looks like a poster boy for America's Most Wanted.

Believe it or not, I still have hope for this crazy world...

But I'm scared for us too.

All I have to do is turn on the news to see the prophecy unfolding, to feel it pounding through my veins like a distant drumbeat that's getting closer and closer.

For every evil act, another door is opened to them.

It's then that I am reminded that our fight is far from over.

That I realize this war has only just begun ...

Discussion Questions

1. In the opening of the book, we learn that dark forces are brewing around Jonah and his friends. Have you ever sensed something mysterious happening in your life that was out of your control? How did you deal with it?

2. As the friends make their way to St. Louis, they encounter some frightening obstacles. Would you have continued on or turned around and gone back home? What do you think kept them going?

3. Sam's paintings suggest that the Watchers were attacked because of their involvement in things they didn't understand. Do you believe there are doors that can be opened by drugs, violence, or the occult? Would you experiment in these areas? Why or why not?

4. Why was it so important for the five friends to remember their past?

5. Sam, Jonah, Carly, Jenna, and J all face temptation in *The Prophecy* and must learn how to resist their personal demons—literally. Yet we learn they have been chosen to fight alongside an elite order of angels. Do you think other teens should have been chosen? Why or why not?

6. Inside the burning building, after raging at God, Jonah's memory of his abusive childhood ends up freeing him and the other Watchers as well. Has anything from the past changed your life forever? Could that experience help others?

7. Do you think Jonah should have told Carly about her mother? How would you have handled the situation?

8. TJ explains to the Watchers that the Grigori and the rest of the fallen will attempt to separate mankind from the protection of God before the final showdown. Do you feel this is possible?

9. Would you live your life differently if you knew there was an invisible world that existed around you and that there was more to life than you ever imagined?

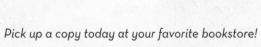

Forbidden Doors

A Four-Volume Series from Bestselling Author Bill Myers!

Some doors are better left unopened.

Join teenager Rebecca "Becka" Williams, her brother Scott, and her friend Ryan Riordan as they head for mind-bending clashes between the forces of darkness and the kingdom of God.

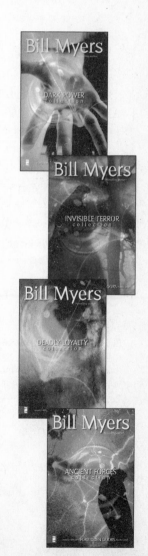

Dark Power Collection
Volume One

Softcover • ISBN: 978-0-310-71534-4

Contains books 1–3: *The Society, The Deceived,* and *The Spell*

Invisible Terror Collection
Volume Two

Softcover • ISBN: 978-0-310-71535-1

Contains books 4–6: *The Haunting, The Guardian,* and *The Encounter*

Deadly Loyalty Collection
Volume Three

Softcover • ISBN: 978-0-310-71536-8

Contains books 7–9: *The Curse, The Undead,* and *The Scream*

Ancient Forces Collection
Volume Four

Softcover • ISBN: 978-0-310-71537-5

Contains books 10–12: *The Ancients, The Wiccan,* and *The Cards*

Teen Study Bible

As an on-the-go teen, you're moving fast. God is moving faster! Totally revised, this bestselling Bible will help you discover the eternal truths of God's Word and apply them to the issues you face today.

Features include:

- We Believe — Unpacks the Apostles' Creed to reveal the biblical foundation of faith
- Panorama — Keeps the big picture of each book of the Bible in view
- Tip-in Pages — Explain ancient ruins, foreign languages, music, and more
- Key Indexes — Help with in-depth Bible study
- To the Point — Reveals what the Bible says about pressing issues
- Dear Jordan — Offers biblical advice for teens
- Instant Access — Tells what God says to you personally
- Q&A — Tests your knowledge of Bible trivia
- Bible Promises — Highlight Bible verses worth remembering
- Book Introductions — Provide an overview for each book of the Bible
- Complete NIV Text — The most read, most trusted Bible translation

Italian Duo-Tone™, Melon Green: 978-0-310-71681-5
Italian Duo-Tone™, Silver: 978-0-310-93519-3
Italian Duo-Tone™, Compact, Jasper/Leaf Green: 978-0-310-94062-3
Italian Duo-Tone™, Compact, Mist Blue/Kiwi: 978-0-310-94061-6
Italian Duo-Tone™, Compact, Mud Splat Moss: 978-0-310-71682-2
Hardcover, Jacketed Printed: 978-0-310-71642-6
Softcover: 978-0-310-71680-8

Pick up a copy today at your favorite bookstore!

Visit www.zondervan.com/teen

Share Your Thoughts

With the Author: Your comments will be forwarded to the author when you send them to *zauthor@zondervan.com*.

With Zondervan: Submit your review of this book by writing to *zreview@zondervan.com*.

Free Online Resources at
www.zondervan.com

Zondervan AuthorTracker: Be notified whenever your favorite authors publish new books, go on tour, or post an update about what's happening in their lives.

Daily Bible Verses and Devotions: Enrich your life with daily Bible verses or devotions that help you start every morning focused on God.

Free Email Publications: Sign up for newsletters on fiction, Christian living, church ministry, parenting, and more.

Zondervan Bible Search: Find and compare Bible passages in a variety of translations at www.zondervanbiblesearch.com.

Other Benefits: Register yourself to receive online benefits like coupons and special offers, or to participate in research.